Withdrawn

The Investigators

G·K
Hall
&Co.

Also by W.E.B. Griffin
in Large Print:

Behind the Lines
Blood and Honor

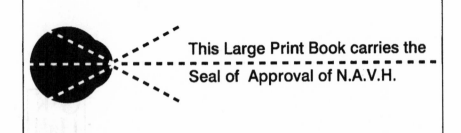

This Large Print Book carries the
Seal of Approval of N.A.V.H.

The Investigators

A *Badge of Honor* Novel

W.E.B. Griffin

G.K. Hall & Co. • Thorndike, Maine

Copyright © 1997 by W.E.B. Griffin

All rights reserved.

Published in 1998 by arrangement with G.P. Putnam's Sons, a member of Penquin Putnam Inc.

G.K. Hall Large Print Core Series.

The text of this Large Print edition is unabridged.
Other aspects of the book may vary from the original edition.

Set in 16 pt. Plantin.

Printed in the United States on permanent paper.

Library of Congress Cataloging in Publication Data

Griffin, W.E.B.
    The investigators / W.E.B. Griffin.
      p. cm.
    "A badge of honor novel."
    ISBN 0-7838-0139-4 (lg. print : hc : alk. paper)
    ISBN 0-7838-0140-8 (lg. print : sc : alk. paper)
    1. Police — Pennsylvania — Philadelphia — Fiction.
    2. Philadelphia (Pa.) — Fiction. 3. Large type books. I. Title.
    [PS3557.R489137I58   1998]
    813'.54—dc21   98-14315

For Sergeant Zebulon V. Casey
Internal Affairs Division
Police Department, Retired,
the City of Philadelphia
He knows why.

One

A nearly new, but quite dirty, antenna-festooned Buick pulled into the employee parking lot of the *Philadelphia Bulletin* and into a parking space bearing a sign reading "RESERVED Mr. O'Hara."

Mr. Michael J. O'Hara, a wiry, curly-haired man in his late thirties, wearing gray flannel trousers, loafers, a white shirt with the collar unbuttoned and the tie pulled down and a plaid sports coat that only with great kindness could be called "a little loud," got quickly out of the car, slammed the door, and entered the building.

He took the elevator to the third floor, where it deposited him in the city room. He walked quickly across the room crowded with desks holding computer terminals, filing cabinets, and the other impedimenta of the journalist's profession to a glass-walled office, the door of which also bore his name. He went inside, opened a small refrigerator, and took out a bottle of Coca-Cola.

Then he sat down at his desk, punched the computer keys that would inform him of messages received in his absence, found nothing that could not wait, and took a swallow of his Coke.

An assistant city editor — Seymour Schwartz, a skinny, bespectacled forty-year-old whom Mickey regarded as about second among equals of the assistant city editors — appeared at his door.

"You got anything for me, Mickey?" Sy asked.

"Genius cannot be rushed," Mickey said. "I thought I already told you that."

"We go to bed in about fifteen minutes."

"Hold me a large chunk of page one," Mickey said. "Journalistic history will be made in the next five minutes. Presuming, of course, that you leave me alone."

Sy Schwartz threw up both hands in a gesture of surrender and walked away.

He both liked and admired Mickey O'Hara, who had not only won the Pulitzer Prize for his crime reporting, but was regarded — by his peers, including Sy Schwartz, not only by the sometimes politically motivated Pulitzer Prize committee — as just about the best police reporter between Boston and Washington. But as long as he had known O'Hara and worked with him, as many elbows as they had rubbed together, he never knew when Mickey was being serious or pulling his chain.

He did know him well enough, however, to know that when Mickey said he wanted to be left alone, the thing to do was leave him alone. He went back to his desk to wait for whatever Mickey was about to send him.

O'Hara looked at the blank computer screen, wiggled his fingers, reached for the Coke bottle, and took another swallow. Then he locked his fingers together, wiggled them, and, without looking, reached into a desk drawer and came out with a long thin cigar. He bit the end off, spit the

8

end out, and then very thoughtfully and carefully lit it.

He put it in one corner of his mouth, flexed his fingers a final time, and began to tap the keys. Very rapidly. And once he had begun to write, he did not stop. The words appeared on the computer screen.

Slug: (O'Hara) "Really Ugly" Woman Robs Bucks County Bank
by Michael J. O'Hara
Bulletin Staff Writer

Riegelsville, Bucks County — A bandit described as "a really ugly white woman with hairy legs" robbed the Riegelsville branch of Philadelphia's Girard Savings Bank of more than $25,000 shortly after the bank opened this morning.

FBI agents and State Police swarmed over this small village on the banks of the Delaware to assist Riegelsville's one-man police force — part-time Constable Karl Werner — in solving the crime.

According to P. Stanley Dailey, 28, of Riegelsville, assistant manager of the bank and the only witness, the bandit, wielding a sawed-off double-barreled shotgun, took him by surprise as he was entering the bank by the rear entrance shortly after 8 A.M.

"She waited until I had unlocked the door, and had turned off the alarm, and then put her shotgun in my ear," Dailey, still visibly shaken hours after the robbery, told this reporter.

The bandit then took him, Dailey said, into the rear of the bank, where she ordered him to lie on his stomach on the floor of the employees' rest room, and then bound and gagged him with air-conditioning duct tape.

It was while he was being bound, Dailey reported, that he noticed that beneath her black patterned stockings, the robber's legs were unshaven. She was dressed, he said, in a blue and white polka-dot dress, over which she wore a tan raincoat. Her hair was covered with a scarf, and she was wearing heart-shaped glasses, decorated with sequins.

The robber then proceeded to the public area of the small bank, Dailey believes, and waited for the automatic timing device of the bank's vault, set to open at 8:15, to function.

She then helped herself to "the loose cash" — that is, currency involved in the previous day's business, which had been placed in the vault in cash drawers at the close of the previous day. She apparently made no attempt to force her way into any of the vault's locked interior compartments.

The robber then left the bank building by the rear door, locking it after herself. Mr. Dailey's keys were later found by the FBI in the parking lot.

At 8:25 A.M. the branch bank's manager, Mrs. Jean-Ellen Dowd, 42, of Upper Black Eddy, arrived at the bank.

"I knew something was wrong the minute

I found the door locked," Mrs. Dowd told authorities and this reporter, "because Stanley [Mr. Dailey] is as reliable as a Swiss watch. But I thought he had a flat tire or something. I never dreamed it was something like this."

She entered the building and found Mr. Dailey in the rest room. Once she had taken the duct tape from his mouth, and he told her what had happened, she activated the alarm. The sound of the alarm was heard by Constable Werner at his full-time place of employment, the Riegelsville plant of the Corrugated Paper Corporation of Pennsylvania, where he is a pulper technician.

He rushed from the plant in his personal vehicle, a pickup truck, which is equipped with a siren and a red flashing light. En route to the scene of the crime, he collided with a Ford sedan driven by Mr. James J. Penter, manager of the Corrugated Paper Corporation's Riegelsville facility, who was on his way to work.

Neither Constable Werner nor Mr. Penter was injured in the collision, but Constable Werner's pickup truck was rendered *hors de combat.* Mr. Penter then drove Constable Werner to the scene of the crime, where, after questioning Mr. Dailey, he notified the State Police, who in turn notified the FBI.

State Trooper Daniel M. Tobias of the Bethlehem Barracks was first to arrive at the scene. After obtaining from Mr. Dailey a more complete description of the robber as a female approximately five feet eight inches tall, approximately thirty years of age, with large, dangling earrings and an unusually thick application of lipstick and cheek rouge, Trooper Tobias put out a radio bulletin calling for the apprehension of anyone meeting that description and then secured the crime scene pending the arrival of other law enforcement officials.

The Philadelphia office of the FBI dispatched a team of four special agents under the command of Assistant Special Agent in Charge (Criminal Affairs) Frank F. Young.

After questioning Mr. Dailey and Constable Werner, Mr. Young spoke with the press regarding the crime.

"The FBI regards bank robberies as a very serious matter," Young said, "and can point with pride to its record of bringing the perpetrators to justice. I have no doubt that when the FBI has had time to fully apply its assets, this crime will be solved."

Mr. Young, when asked by this reporter if a shotgun-wielding female with unshaven legs, dangling earrings, and an unusually thick application of lipstick and cheek rouge had been involved in other bank robberies, declined to answer.

He also declined to offer an opinion about when an arrest could be expected, and when asked by a reporter from the Easton *Express* to identify the FBI agents with him, stated that it was FBI policy not to do so.

The FBI agents with Mr. Young were

known to this reporter as John D. Matthews, Lamar F. Greene, and Paul C. Lomar.
  END

He stopped typing, pushed the Page Up key, and read what he had written. He tapped his fingertips together for a moment, then pushed the Send key on his keyboard. This caused as much of the slug of the story as would fit — it came out as (O'Hara) "Really Ugly" Woman Robs B — to appear on the computer monitor on Mr. Schwartz's desk.

Schwartz immediately called the whole story up on his monitor screen.

He read it, chuckling several times, and then pushed a key that caused a printed version of the story to emerge from a printer on a credenza behind him. He snatched it from the printer and walked across the city room to O'Hara's office.

"Very funny," he said. "A bank robber dressed up like a woman."

"It was a Chinese fire drill, from start to finish," Mickey said. "I was going up Route 611 when the FBI, two cars, goes around me, lights flashing, sirens screaming, as if I was standing still. Then they got lost, I guess, because I got to the bank ten minutes before they did."

Schwartz smiled.

"The first thing Young did, when he finally showed up, was to order one of his underlings to throw me out of the bank," O'Hara went on.

"I noticed you had your knife out for him,"

Schwartz said. "This is what is known as Time For Second Thoughts."

"Fuck him," Mickey said. "Let it run."

"Your call."

"Sy, that constable was really something," O'Hara said, laughing at the memory. "He told me the reason he ran into his boss's car was because he had just remembered he had left his gun home, and was wondering if he should go get it before going to the bank."

"You really want to say his truck was 'rendered *hors de combat*'?"

"Why not? I love that phrase. It calls up pictures of horny naked women in foxholes."

Schwartz laughed.

"Who do you think did it?"

"That state cop was pretty clever. I had a chance to talk to him before Young showed up and threw me out of the bank. The state cop thinks it was probably some guy from the coal regions, out of work for a long time, maybe in deep to some loan shark. You know, really desperate. If he is an amateur, and gets smart and quits now, he's probably home free. Despite what that pompous asshole from the FBI declared, they catch damned few bank robbers."

"Maybe this one will be easy to find. Hairy legs. Too much lipstick."

"I think that description — the 'really ugly' part, too — may not be all that reliable."

"Tell me?" Schwartz asked, smiling.

"I had the feeling after talking to Dailey that he was more than a little disappointed that once the broad had him all tied up she didn't do all sorts of wicked sexual things to him. Hell hath no fury, et cetera."

"Jesus, Mickey!"

"There's probably going to be surveillance-camera pictures of him — or, for all we really know, her — you can judge for yourself."

"There's pictures? When do we get them?"

"So far as Young is concerned, after I told him off, I'll get them the day after hell freezes over," O'Hara said. "But the state cop said he'd send me a copy when he gets his."

"We can lean on the FBI, if you think we should."

"I don't think it would be worth the effort. They're generally pretty lousy pictures, even if the camera was working, and I wouldn't bet on that. I asked the state cop for a copy just to satisfy my curiosity."

"Okay, Mickey. Nice little yarn. Would you be heartbroken if I ran it on the first page of the second section?"

"I'm surprised that you're going to run it at all," O'Hara said. "It's not much of a story."

"I like it," Schwartz said, meaning it. "A little droll humor to brighten people's dull days."

Without taking her eyes from the inch-thick, bound-together-with-metal-fastener sheaf of papers lying open on her cluttered desk, Susan Reynolds reached for the ringing telephone and put it to her ear.

"Appeals, Reynolds," she announced.

"Miss Susan Reynolds?" an operator's voice asked.

15

"Right," Susan said.

"Deposit fifty-five cents, please," the operator ordered.

Susan could hear the melodic bonging of two quarters and a nickel.

She felt sure she knew who was calling. She seldom got long-distance calls made from a pay phone in the office.

Confirmation came immediately.

"Susie?" Jennie asked.

Jennie was Jennifer Ollwood.

"Hi," Susan said.

"Could you call me back?" Jennie asked. "I'm in a phone booth and I don't have any change."

"Give me the number," Susan said, reaching for a pencil, then adding, "It'll be a minute or two. They don't let me make personal toll calls."

Jennie gave her the number. Susan repeated it back to her.

"I have to go down to the lobby," Susan said. "There's no pay phone on this floor."

"Thank you," Jennie said in her soft voice.

Susan hung up and then stood.

Susan Reynolds was listed on the manning chart of the Department of Social Services of the Commonwealth of Pennsylvania as an "Appeals Officer, Grade III." She was single, twenty-six years old, naturally blond, blue-eyed, with a fair complexion, and, at five feet five and 130 pounds, was five pounds heavier than she wanted to be.

She occupied a third-floor office in the Department of Social Services Building in Harrisburg. Through its one window, she had a view of the golden dome of the statehouse. Her office was just barely large enough to hold her desk and chair, her bookcase, her three filing cabinets, and the three straight-backed chairs intended for use by visitors.

On half of one shelf of her bookcase, Susan kept a small vase, sometimes holding a fresh flower; a photograph of her parents, and a photograph of herself standing in the snow with half a dozen other young women taken while they were all students at Bennington College in Vermont.

The other five shelves of the ceiling-high bookcase were filled with books, notebooks, binders, and manila folders all containing laws, regulations, interpretations, and court decisions having to do with providing social services to those entitled to it.

Just who was entitled to what social services under what conditions was frequently a subject of bitter disagreement between those who believed in their entitlement to one social service or another, and those employees of one governmental agency or another who didn't think so.

It was often difficult, for example, for someone who had been a recipient of a monthly check from Harrisburg intended for the support of his or her minor children to understand why, simply because one of the children had turned nineteen, the amount of the check had been reduced.

The laws — and there were several hundred of them — generally provided that support — and there were forty or fifty different types of support — for dependent children terminated when the child reached his or her nineteenth birthday. Or was no longer resident in the home. Or had been incarcerated or become resident in a mental institution. Or joined the Army.

Ordinarily, the situation could be explained to the recipient at the local Social Services office. But not always. If he or she wanted to appeal, the initial appeal was handled locally. If the local social services functionary upheld the decision of the social worker, the recipient could appeal yet again.

At that point, the case moved to Harrisburg, where it was adjudicated by one of twelve appeals officers, one of whom was Miss Susan Reynolds.

When she had first come on the job three years before, Miss Reynolds had been deeply moved by the poverty and hopeless situations of those whose appeals reached her desk.

Emotionally, she had wanted to grant every one of them, feeling that there was simply no justification in wealthy America to deny anyone whose needs were so evident. And, in fact, for the first three weeks on the job she had granted relief to ninety percent of the appellants.

But her decisions were subject to review by her superiors, and more than ninety percent of her decisions granting relief had been overturned.

She had then been called before a review board that had the authority to terminate her probationary appointment as an Appeals Officer, Grade I.

It had been pointed out to her, politely but firmly, that she had been employed by the Department of Social Services to adjudicate appeals fairly, and not to effect a redistribution of the wealth of the Commonwealth without regard to

18

the applicable laws and regulations.

She had seriously considered resigning her appointment — an act she knew would please her parents, who were mystified by her choice of employment — but in the end had not, for several reasons.

First, she knew that many, perhaps even most, of the decisions she had made had not been fair, but rather based on her emotional reaction to the pitiful lives of the people who had made the appeals. And second, she decided that she could make adjudications in the future that, while paying attention to the letter of the law, could be tempered with compassion.

Most important in her decision not to resign was her belief that if she stayed on the job, she would be able to make some input into the system that would make it better. It was such a god-awful mess the way it was now, she had thought, that improvement had to be possible.

She hadn't been able to make any improvements to the system in her three years on the job — she now realized that thinking she could have had been really naive — and she had been forced to accept that a substantial number of the appeals she was called upon to adjudicate had been made by people who believed there was nothing morally wrong in trying to swindle the state out of anything they could get away with.

But on the other hand, she thought, she had been able to overturn the adverse decisions of a large number of social workers that would really have hurt people with a legitimate entitlement to the small amounts of money provided by the state.

And she had been promoted twice, ultimately to "Appeals Officer, Grade III." And both times she had wondered if she had been promoted because she was doing a good job, or whether someone higher up had examined her record and found it satisfactory using the percentage of appeals rejected as the criterion.

Susan looked at the photograph of the Bennington girls on her shelf — Jennifer Ollwood was standing next to her in the picture — then shifted the frame slightly.

She picked up her purse and left her office, stopping at the adjacent office, of Appeals Officer, Grade IV, Veronica Haynes, a black woman who, Susan had decided, believed that the only people who should receive aid from the state were the aged in the last few weeks of their terminal illness.

"If anybody asks, Veronica, I'll be back in a couple of minutes."

Veronica smiled at her. "Couple, as in two? Or several, as if you're going out for coffee?"

"Several, wiseass," Susan said, smiling, and walked to the elevators.

On the way down, she looked in her coin purse and found that it held two nickels and a dime.

Somewhat reluctantly, the proprietress of the lobby newsstand, an obese harridan with orange hair, changed two dollars into silver for her. Susan found an empty telephone booth and went in.

Jennifer answered on the second ring. Her voice seemed hesitant.

"Hello?"

"It's me."

"That didn't take long."

"I hurried. What's up?"

"Are you planning to come this way anytime soon?"

"I hadn't planned on it," Susan said.

But I could. Daffy asked me please, please come to her husband's birthday party.

"I'd really like to see you," Jennie said.

"And I'd like to see the baby," Susan said.

"Bryan has something he wants you to keep for him. For us," Jennie said.

So that's what this is all about. Damn him!

Bryan was Bryan Chenowith.

If I had a file on him, he would be categorized as "Father of (illegitimate) child, residing with mother. Employable, but not employed."

"How's the baby?" Susan asked.

"Wonderful!" Jennie said, her voice reflecting the pride of the new mother.

"I can't wait to see him," Susan said.

"Then you can come?"

"Daffy's having a birthday party for Chad," Susan said. "On Saturday. She's called me twice, begging me to come. You know what I think of him."

"Is it too late to change your mind?" Jennie asked, a hint of desperation in her voice. "Philadelphia's not far from here."

"I could call her," Susan said.

"In for a penny. In for a pound," as they say.

"That's a 'yes'?"

"I want to see the baby," Susan said, as much to herself as to Jennie.

"Will you stay with Daffy?"

"No," Susan said. "Probably the Bellvue."

"You'll drive down Saturday morning?"

"Right."

"I'll call the hotel and tell you when and where to meet me," Jennie said.

"You don't want to tell me now?"

"I'd better come up with a plan," Jennie said, giggling.

"Okay. I'll be at the hotel after twelve, I guess. Why don't you call me about one?"

"I will."

"Is there anything I can bring you?"

"No. Thank you, but no. We're doing fine."

Said the noble bride from the deck of the sinking ship.

"Well, then, I'll see you over the weekend," Susan said.

"I really love you, you know that," Jennie said, and the phone went dead.

Susan made two more telephone calls before going back to her office. The first was to Daphne Elizabeth Browne Nesbitt, who was also in the photograph of the Bennington girls on Susan's bookshelf. She told Daffy that her plans had changed and that she now could come to Chad's party, if that would be all right.

Daffy said she would have the crème de la crème of Philadelphia's bachelors lined up for her selection.

I was afraid of that. It was another reason I didn't

22

want to come to your asshole of a husband's birthday party.

"I would rather snag my men on my own hook, Daffy. Thank you just the same."

"Don't be silly," Daffy said. "Advertising pays. Ask Chad about that. And besides, we have to stick together, don't we? Help each other out?"

Oh, do we ever!

"Right," Susan said. "See you Saturday."

Then Susan called her mother and told her that she had changed her mind about going to Chad Nesbitt's birthday party in Philadelphia over the weekend.

"Well, baby, I'm very glad to hear that," Susan's mother replied.

"Mother, would you call the Bellvue and see about a room? It's so close to the weekend that I'm afraid —"

"No, I won't," her mother replied. "But I will call Mrs. Samuelson. She's very good at that sort of thing."

Mrs. Dorothy Samuelson was her father's executive assistant, and she was, indeed, very good at things like that. It was what Susan had hoped her mother would do, pass the buck to Mrs. Samuelson.

Now that she had committed herself to Jennie, she would need to have a room in the Bellvue-Stratford Hotel.

Two

From where Officer Herbert Prasko of the Five
Squad of the Narcotics Unit of the Philadelphia
Police Department had stationed himself on the
second-floor balcony of the Howard Johnson
motel on Roosevelt Boulevard, he had an extraordinarily good view of the vehicle he was
surveilling.

The new four-door Chevrolet sedan was
parked, nose out, in front of a row of rooms in
the rear of the motel. It was a Hertz rental, picked
up at the Philadelphia International Airport four
hours before by Ronald R. Ketcham, white
male, twenty-five, five-ten, brown hair, 165
pounds, no previous arrests, who resided in a
luxury apartment on Overbrook Avenue not far
from the Episcopal Academy, of which he was
a graduate.

Mr. Ketcham, who was not quite as smart as
he believed himself to be, was laboring under the
misimpression that the use of a rental automobile
rather than his Buick coupe was one more clever
thing he had done to conceal both his illegal
activity and identity from both the police and
other criminals.

Officer Prasko didn't know if the other criminals involved knew Mr. Ketcham's identity — the
scumbags probably couldn't care less — but his
identity had been known to Five Squad for five

24

weeks, from the time they had first followed Amos J. Williams, black male, thirty-two, six-three, 180 pounds, twenty-eight previous arrests, and four of his goons to a delivery rendezvous with Mr. Ketcham, who seemed to be one of his better customers.

For a number of reasons, it had been decided not to make an arrest at that time, but it had not been hard at all to trace the customer's rental car back through the Hertz main office to their airport rental operation, and from the rental agreement to identify Mr. Ketcham in some detail.

Hertz had been very cooperative. They had promised to notify Five Squad the next time Mr. Ketcham rented a car, and had done so today. Officer Prasko thought that was pretty dumb on Mr. Ketcham's part, to go back to Hertz; he should have changed to Avis, or somebody else. And it was also dumb for him to go back to the Howard Johnson motel. There were a lot of other motels. If he had set up this meet someplace else, he would not be about to find his ass in a very deep crack.

Five Squad had come up with a plan after the first time they had followed Mr. Williams to his rendezvous with Mr. Ketcham. On being notified by Hertz that Mr. Ketcham had again rented an automobile, a Five Squad plainclothes officer — who turned out to be Officer Prasko — would proceed to the Howard Johnson motel, and there await the possible arrival of Mr. Ketcham.

Herb Prasko, en route to the motel in an undercover car — a two-year-old Mercury, formerly the property of another drug dealer scumbag —

25

had thought the odds were that he would be pissing in the wind. But you never could really tell. Sometimes people were really stupid, as Mr. Ketcham had turned out to be by returning to the same Howard Johnson motel instead of going someplace else to do his business.

But he had waited, parked just inside the motel, slumped down on the front seat of the Mercury, watching the entrance to the motel, for nearly three hours, before Ketcham had shown up.

He had a dame with him, white female, early twenties, 120 pounds, blonde, nice figure, who sat in the car while Mr. Ketcham went in the motel office for the key. Officer Prasko slipped down all the way on the seat of the Mercury as they drove past him, and then watched where they were going in the rearview mirror.

Then, when the Chevy had gone around the first row of rooms to the back, he got out of the car, trotted quickly after them, and got to the corner of the building in time to see Mr. Ketcham enter 138, a ground-floor room in about the middle of the back row of rooms.

He then went to the pay phone outside the motel office and called Sergeant Patrick J. Dolan at Narcotics and told him what he had. Dolan — who could be a prick — made him repeat everything he said, and then told him not to let the door to 138 out of his sight, as if he thought Prasko had come on the job last Tuesday and had to be told shit like that.

Five Squad would be there as soon as they could get there, Dolan said, and said to meet them on the H Band. That was the special radio frequency assigned for the use of detectives, but available for other purposes as well.

Officer Prasko then took a pair of binoculars and a walkie-talkie from the floor of the backseat of the Mercury and went up the stairs to the second-floor balcony of the first building. He stationed himself between a Coke machine and an ice machine in an alcove, from where he could see the rental Chevy and the door to 138.

He had a good view of both the door and the car, especially the car and the girl in it.

She was a looker. And she was nervous. She lit a cigarette and took only a couple of puffs before putting it out and turning to look at the door, which made her breasts stretch the thin material of her blouse. Then she lit another cigarette.

A little after that, she put her hand in her blouse and adjusted her bra, which Prasko found exciting.

What the hell was Ketcham thinking, bringing a girl like that along on a meet like this? Amos Williams was a mean son of a bitch, and the first thing he was likely to do if something went wrong was grab the girl. By the time Ketcham fixed whatever Williams didn't like, Christ only knew what Williams and his goons would do with a white girl like that, a real looker.

"Six?" the radio went off. Too loud.

He recognized the voice. It was that of Officer Joe Grider. More important, it wasn't Dolan's, which was a good thing, meaning they could put Plan B into operation.

Officer Prasko adjusted the volume and the squelch before putting the microphone to his lips.

27

"Six," he said.

"He still there?"

"Yeah."

"Where's the room?"

"Around in the back. Middle. Ground floor."

"Any sign of his friends?"

"No."

"We're about there. I'm going to park up the street and see who shows up."

"What are you in?"

"The van."

The van was not standard, but a 1971 Dodge panel truck, also formerly the property of someone who had been apprehended while illegally trafficking in controlled substances. After the forfeited vehicle had been turned over to Five Squad for undercover work, they had chipped in and had it painted in the color scheme used by — and with the logotype of — Philadelphia Gas Works.

"Who's the super?"

"I am. Plan B," Officer Grider replied.

"Just the van?"

"One car."

"One of you block the Chevy."

"You got it."

Officer Prasko picked up his binoculars again. The curtains were drawn across the picture window of 138 — *Why the fuck do you suppose they put in picture windows? Nobody ever looks out of a motel room, and if you did, all you would see is the other part of the motel* — and there was no sign of activity. The blonde in the front seat of the Hertz Chevy was lighting a fresh cigarette from the butt of the old one.

Three minutes later, the radio went off again. He couldn't hear what was being said.

"Repeat," he ordered.

"Turn the goddamn volume up!"

"I just did."

"Bingo, here comes our friends. Light blue new Olds 98. Tell me when he gets inside, and we'll come in halfway."

Officer Prasko scurried across the balcony, keeping low so that he wouldn't be seen.

He saw the Blue Olds 98 — well enough to recognize Amos Williams sitting beside the driver — enter the motel area and drive toward the rear. And stop.

"He stopped halfway to the back," Prasko reported.

"Being careful," Officer Grider replied.

Mr. Williams was careful for three minutes, which seemed like much longer, and then the driver's-side rear door of the Olds 98 opened and Marcus C. aka "Baby" Brownlee, black male, thirty-six, six-one, 240 pounds, thirty-two previous arrests, got out, looked around, and walked very quickly toward room 138.

"Baby Brownlee going to the room," Officer Prasko reported.

He dropped his binoculars to the Chevy. The blonde was not in sight.

Probably dropped onto the seat. I would if I was a good-looking piece like that and saw that mean-looking dinge walking my way.

"Knocking on the door," Officer Prasko reported, and added a moment later, "He's in."

"Wait," Officer Grider replied.

29

Baby Brownlee was in room 138 for two minutes forty seconds, which seemed like much longer.

"Door opening," Officer Prasko reported. "Baby's coming out. Moving toward car."

"Five?"

"Ready."

Five was Officer Timothy J. Calhoun, and he was apparently driving the unmarked police car.

"At the car," Officer Prasko reported. "Getting in."

Baby Brownlee was in the Olds 98 for fifty seconds, which seemed like much longer.

The blonde's head appeared in the Chevy. She took a look around and then dropped from sight again.

Christ, I'd like to jump the bones of something like that.

"Car's moving," Officer Prasko reported.

"Five?"

"Car's turning around," Officer Prasko reported.

"Just say when," Officer Calhoun replied.

"Car's stopped. Now facing toward exit," Officer Prasko reported.

"What are they doing?" Officer Grider inquired.

"Getting out of the car. Baby's out. Amos is out. Opening trunk."

"And? And?"

"Baby's got a beach bag."

"Go! Go! Go!" Officer Grider ordered.

Officer Prasko stood up and walked as far as he could toward the stairs without losing sight of the Olds 98, the Hertz Chevy, and the door to room 138.

The van came in first, tires squealing, the rear door already open and stopped in front of the Olds 98. Half a dozen plainclothes police officers, weapons — four pistols, two pump-action 12-gauge shotguns — at the ready, jumped out.

Officer Calhoun's unmarked car skidded to a stop in a position blocking the Hertz Chevy. Calhoun and another plainclothes officer, revolvers drawn, jumped out of the car.

Prasko descended the stairs as rapidly as he could, considering the fucking binoculars were banging on his chest, and he had to be careful holding the walkie-talkie, otherwise he'd drop the son of a bitch and have to pay for the fucker.

As he reached the ground floor, Prasko stooped and drew his snub-nosed .38 Special–caliber revolver from its ankle holster.

This act coincided with the appearance, at a full run, of an individual black male, twenty-five to thirty, five-ten, 150 pounds, noticeable scar tissue left cheek, who had not obeyed the orders of the other police officers to subject himself to arrest.

Just in fucking time!

"Freeze, motherfucker!" Prasko ordered.

The individual almost visibly debated his chances to evade Prasko and then apparently decided attempting to do so would not be in his best interests.

He stopped running and raised his hands above his head.

"Up against the wall!" Prasko ordered, spinning the man around, then pushing him toward the wall.

"Oh, shit, man!" the individual responded.

"Spread your legs!" Prasko ordered, as Calhoun appeared around the corner.

"I got the bastard, Timmy," Prasko said.

"Put your left hand behind your back," Prasko ordered, then looked at Calhoun.

"You want to cuff him, please, Timmy?"

Calhoun placed handcuffs on the man's left wrist, then grabbed the other wrist, which caused the man's face to fall against the wall.

"Shit!" he exclaimed.

Calhoun finished cuffing him, then performed a perfunctory search of his person to determine if he was armed.

"Clean," Calhoun informed Prasko.

"Do him," Prasko requested.

Calhoun emptied the man's pockets onto the ground beside him, but no controlled substances or any other illegal matter were discovered.

"Nothing," Calhoun reported.

"I'll bring him. You want to take my walkie-talkie?"

Calhoun took Prasko's walkie-talkie, and then, at a half-trot, ran back around the building.

Prasko dropped to his knees beside the pile of items and picked up the man's wallet. It contained his driver's license and other documents, a color photograph of a white female performing fellatio on a black male (not the individual), and seven hundred and sixty-three dollars in currency, five hundred of it in one-hundred-dollar bills.

Officer Prasko became aware that his heart was beating rapidly, and that he had to take a piss.

Prasko put two of the one-hundred-dollar bills in his pocket, replaced the rest of the currency into the wallet, and then placed the wallet and other material back into the man's pockets.

"Turn around," he ordered.

The man turned around with some difficulty, being cuffed, and looked at Prasko with what Prasko believed was mingled loathing and contempt. Prasko believed he understood why. It had to do with the criminal justice system and their relative compensation. The guy was almost certainly aware that since he had been apprehended without being found in possession of controlled substances, or a firearm or other deadly weapon, he could reasonably expect to be released from custody on bail within a matter of hours.

He was also aware that he made more money in a day than a policeman made in a week. Or ten days. Or two weeks. Or maybe even a month, depending on how valuable he was to Amos Williams.

Prasko gestured for him to start walking back the way he had come. When they got there, they found Amos Williams, Baby Brownlee, and two other men under arrest, their arms handcuffed behind them.

"Wagon's on the way," Officer Grider said. "And the tow truck."

"You," Prasko ordered the individual, "with them."

He placed his hand on the man's cuffed hands and guided him to the end of the line of handcuffed figures. Then he walked to Officer Grider.

"What did we get?" Prasko asked.

"Baby had in his possession two packages, approximately one kilo in weight, of a white crystalline substance which appears to be cocaine," Grider said.

"Plan B?" Prasko asked.

Grider nodded.

"I want you to stay here with Calhoun until the tow truck removes the Olds," he said.

"Right," Prasko said.

Two minutes or so later, a police van assigned to the 7th District rolled into the motel in response to Grider's radio request for prisoner transport.

One by one, the individuals arrested were hauled to their feet and placed in the van. Then the van started to leave. It had to stop and back up when, warning lights flashing, a police tow truck came into the motel area.

Officer Grider and the other members of Five Squad got into the Dodge panel truck with the PGW color scheme and logotype and pulled up behind the 7th District van.

Calhoun directed the tow truck toward the Olds 98. When the passage was clear, the van and the PGW Dodge drove out of the parking lot.

"Timmy, take my Mercury," Prasko called to Calhoun. "Keys in that?" he asked, pointing to the unmarked police car that blocked the Hertz Chevy.

Calhoun threw Prasko the keys to the unmarked car. Prasko caught them in midair and dropped them into his pocket, then walked toward room 138.

The blonde was not in sight, but after a moment, looking through the Chevy's window, he saw her on the floor of the front seat. She was on her side, and he was sure that she hadn't seen him. She had had to wiggle around to find room for herself on the floor, and in the process her skirt had been pushed up so that he could see her underpants.

Nice legs, too!

Officer Prasko felt sure that she wasn't going to try to leave the car until either Mr. Ketcham came for her or a long time had passed.

He looked at the tow truck. It already had the wheels of the Olds 98 off the ground. Calhoun started walking toward where Prasko had parked his Mercury, so that he would be able to follow the tow truck and testify in court that the vehicle had not been out of his sight from the place of arrest until it had been taken to the Narcotics Unit at 22nd and Hunting Park Avenue where it would be searched.

Prasko waited until the tow truck had disappeared around the corner of the front row of rooms, and then he walked to the door of room 138. There he took his pistol and knocked three times on the door with the butt.

It took Mr. Ketcham a long time to respond.

Come on, Ketcham. I know you're in there, and I know you can't get out.

"Who is it?" Ketcham finally inquired.

"Police, open up," Prasko called.

The door opened.

"Is something wrong, Officer?" Ketcham asked.

"You know fucking well what's wrong, Ketcham," Prasko said, somewhat nastily.

He spun Ketcham around, then twisted his left hand and arm around his back and upward and propelled him into the room, where he pushed him facedown on the bed and quickly handcuffed him.

"May I say something?" Ketcham inquired.

"Don't open your mouth. Don't turn over, don't even move," Prasko said, and holstered his pistol.

Then he searched the room methodically until he found what he was looking for under the cushion in the room's one armchair: two business-size envelopes held closed with rubber bands. Each was stuffed with ten rubber-band-bound sheafs of one-hundred-dollar bills, ten bills to a sheaf, for a total of $20,000.

Prasko put the envelopes on the table beside the armchair, then went to the bed and rolled Ketcham over.

"You got something to say?" he asked.

"I really have no idea what all this is —"

Prasko interrupted Ketcham by striking him with the back of his open hand.

"Bullshit time is over," Prasko said.

"Am I under arrest?" Ketcham asked after a moment.

"Not yet."

"Why don't you take that money and leave?" Ketcham asked, reasonably.

Prasko considered the suggestion.

"Your father would be very embarrassed if you had to call him and tell him you had been arrested for dealing in drugs," Prasko said. "It would probably cause him trouble at the bank."

"Oh, Jesus!" Ketcham said.

"Who's the girl?" Prasko asked.

"What girl?"

Prasko struck him again with the back of his hand.

"I already told you, bullshit time is over."

"My girlfriend," Ketcham said. "She doesn't know anything about this. You could let her go."

"What did you do," Prasko inquired sarcastically, "tell her that tonight you were going to do something new? You were going to rent a motel room and go in, and she was going to sit outside in the car?"

"Take the money. Who'd ever know?" Ketcham said.

Prasko considered that again, then reached down and unlocked one of the handcuffs. He then motioned Ketcham to get to his feet.

"This is really the mature way to deal with this situation," Ketcham said, extending the wrist that still had a handcuff attached, obviously expecting Prasko to free him of that cuff, too.

Instead, Prasko firmly took Ketcham's arm and led him into the bathroom, where he ordered him to sit on the floor beside the toilet. Then he attached the free end of his handcuff to the pipes running to the flushing mechanism of the toilet.

"What are you doing?" Ketcham asked.

Prasko ignored him, went out of room 138 to

37

the car, and tried the passenger-side door. It was locked.

"Come out of there, honey," he ordered.

He saw the blonde looking up from the floor with horror in her eyes.

"Open up," Prasko ordered.

The blonde tried to move away as far as she could.

Prasko unholstered his revolver and used the butt as a hammer to shatter the window. Then he reached inside and unlocked the door.

"You can come out," he said, "or I can drag you out."

She scurried across the floor to the open door, which caused her skirt to rise even higher.

Peggene had legs like that when I first met her. Now her legs look like shit.

He took the girl's arm and led her into room 138 and closed and locked the door without letting go of her arm.

When she saw Ketcham handcuffed to the crapper, she sucked in her breath.

"What you are, honey," Prasko said, "is an accessory to a felony, possession of controlled substances with the intent to distribute."

"Ronny?" the girl asked, looking into the bathroom.

"We're working something out, Cynthia," Ketcham said. "Just take it easy."

The girl looked at Prasko defiantly.

Prasko walked to the bathroom door and closed it.

"He had some money," he said to the girl. "I may let him go. What have you got to trade?"

38

"I've got a little money," she said.

"He had twenty thousand. You got that much?"

"No!"

"Then I guess you're both going to jail."

"I could probably get you some money," the girl said.

"Twenty thousand? That kind of money?"

She shook her head, no.

"How about five minutes of your time?" Prasko asked.

"Five minutes of my time? I don't understand."

"Yeah, you understand," Prasko said.

"Oh, my God!"

"That's probably what your mother'll say when you call her from Central Lockup and tell her you need bailing out, and for what."

The girl started to whimper.

"You gonna start taking your clothes off, or not?" Prasko said. "I don't have all night."

Sobbing now, the girl unbuttoned her blouse and shrugged out of it, then unfastened her skirt and let it fall to the floor.

"All of it, all of it," Prasko said.

The girl unfastened her brassiere and then, now moving quickly, pushed her white underpants down off her hips. Then she backed up to the bed and lay down on it, her legs spread, her face to one side, so she didn't have to look at Prasko.

Officer Prasko dropped his trousers and then his shorts and moved to the bed.

When he was done, he went into the bathroom and struck Ketcham in the face with his revolver, hard enough to draw blood and daze him. Then he unlocked the handcuffs.

"Stay where you are for five minutes or I'll come back and blow your fucking brains out," Prasko said.

Then he went into the bedroom, glanced quickly at the naked, whimpering girl on the bed, took the twenty thousand dollars from the table, and left room 138.

As soon as Ketcham heard the sound of the car starting, and then driving away, he got off the bathroom floor and went into the bedroom and tried to put his arms around the girl.

She pushed him away and shrieked.

"Cynthia," he said, trying to sound comforting, and again tried to put his arms around her.

Cynthia shrieked again.

Three

The District Attorney of Philadelphia, the Hon. Thomas J. "Tony" Callis — a large, silver-haired, ruddy-faced, well-tailored man in his early fifties — looked up from his desk, and saw Harrison J. Hormel, Esq. — a somewhat rumpled-looking forty-six-year-old — standing in the door, waiting to be noticed.

Harry Hormel was arguably the most competent of all the assistant district attorneys Callis supervised. And he had another characteristic Callis liked. Hormel was apolitical. He had no political ambitions of his own, and owed no allegiance to any politician, except the current incumbent of the Office of the District Attorney.

"Come in, Harry," Mr. Callis called.

Hormel slipped into one of the two comfortable green leather armchairs facing Callis's desk.

"What do you want to happen to James Howard Leslie?" Hormel asked, without any preliminaries.

"Boiling in oil would be nice," Tony Callis said. "Or perhaps drawing and quartering."

Mr. James Howard Leslie, by profession a burglar, had been recently indicted for murder in the first degree. It was alleged that one Jerome H. Kellog, on returning to his home at 300 West Luray Street in Northwest Philadelphia, had

41

come across Mr. Leslie in his kitchen. It was further alleged that Leslie had thereupon brandished a blue .38 Special five-inch-barrel Smith & Wesson revolver; had then ordered Kellog to raise his hands and turn around; and when Kellog had done so, had shot Kellog in the back of the head, causing his death. It was further alleged that after Kellog had fallen to the floor of his kitchen, Leslie had then shot him again in the head, for the purpose of making sure he was dead.

When Leslie had discussed the incident with Sergeant Jason Washington of the Special Operations Division of the Philadelphia Police Department, Leslie had explained that he had felt it necessary to take Kellog's life because Kellog had seen his face, and as a policeman, would probably be able to find him and arrest him for burglary.

The question Hormel was really asking, Callis understood, was whether the City of Philadelphia wanted to go through the expense of a trial, seeking a sentence that would incarcerate Leslie for the rest of his natural life, or whether Leslie should be permitted to cop a plea, which would see him removed from society for, say, twenty years, which was, in practical terms, about as long behind bars as a life sentence would mean.

Ordinarily, there would be no question of that. The full wrath and fury of the law would suddenly descend on the shoulders of anyone who had in cold blood taken the life of a police officer. Or even someone who had shot a cop by mistake, while in the act of doing anything illegal.

Ordinarily, Callis himself would have personally prosecuted Leslie. For one thing, he really believed that letting a scumbag get away with shooting a cop really would undermine the very foundations of civilized society. For another, press reports of the vigorous prosecution of such a villain by the district attorney himself would be remembered at election time.

It was not much of a secret that District Attorney Callis would be willing to serve the people of Philadelphia as their mayor if called upon to do so. And neither was it lost upon him that one of the reasons the incumbent mayor of Philadelphia, the Hon. Jerome H. "Jerry" Carlucci, had been elected and reelected with such comfortable margins was his reputation of being personally tough on criminals.

But the case of Leslie was not like, for example, that of some scumbag shooting a cop during a bank robbery. For one thing, Officer Kellog had not been on duty at the time of his tragic demise. Perhaps more important, Leslie was going to be represented at his trial by the Office of the Public Defender, specifically by a lawyer whom Callis most commonly thought of — not for publication, of course — as "The Goddamned Nun."

Ms. Imogene McCarthy — who had been known as Sister Luke during her ten years as a cloistered nun — had two characteristics that annoyed Callis, sometimes greatly. She devoutly believed that there were always extenuating circumstances — poverty, lack of education, parental abuse, drug addiction — which caused people like James Howard Leslie to do what they did, and which tragic circumstances should trigger not punishment but compassion and mercy on the part of society; and she was a very skillful attorney, both in the courtroom and in the appeals processes.

Tony Callis was determined that The Goddamned Nun, as good as she was, was not going to get her client off on this one. Indeed, in her heart of hearts, she probably didn't want to see him walk. What she didn't want was for the Commonwealth of Pennsylvania to put James Howard Leslie into handcuffs and march him off to Rockview Prison in State College for what the judge had just told him would be incarceration for the rest of his natural life, thereby destroying all of his hopes to be educated, rehabilitated, and returned to society as a productive, law-abiding member thereof.

What, Callis believed, McCarthy saw from her perspective as a reasonable solution to the case of James Howard Leslie was that he be allowed to plead guilty to Murder Three (voluntary manslaughter), a lesser offense that, she would be prepared to argue, would not only punish him and remove him from society for a very long period — say, seven to ten years — so that he could cause others no harm, but save both the Office of the District Attorney and the Office of the Public Defender the considerable cost in time and money of a trial and the following appeals processes.

There was a certain logic to her position. If Kellog had not been a police officer, Callis might have entertained her plea-bargain offer. But Kellog had been a cop, and Leslie had killed him in cold blood, and deserved to be locked up permanently. Strapping the murdering son of a bitch into the electric chair was unfortunately — thanks to bleeding hearts and the Supreme Court — no longer possible. The only way to get him locked up for life was to bring him to trial.

After some thought — it would do his political ambitions little good, he had reasoned, if he personally prosecuted Leslie only to have The Goddamned Nun get him off with something like seven to ten — Callis had decided to delegate the responsibility for prosecuting Leslie to Assistant District Attorney Hormel.

"Phebus wants to prosecute," Harry Hormel said. "He asked me."

Anton C. Phebus, Esq., was another of the assistant district attorneys under Callis's supervision.

Callis was not surprised that Tony Phebus wanted to prosecute Leslie, or even that Phebus had asked Hormel for the job. Phebus was an ex-cop, and thus felt a personal interest in seeing to it that Leslie, after a fair trial, would be locked up permanently. And Harry Hormel was de facto if not de jure, like one of Mr. Orwell's pigs, the most equal of all the assistant district attorneys.

"You don't want to prosecute?" Callis asked.

"I will," Hormel said. "But if Phebus does, it will give him the experience."

Phebus was a relative newcomer both to the practice of law and the District Attorney's Office. He had served twelve years as a police officer, rising to sergeant, and attending law school at Temple University whenever he could fit the hours into a policeman's always changing schedule. He had joined the Office of the District Attorney fourteen months before, shortly after being admitted to the bar.

Callis suddenly remembered — he had a very good memory, which had served him well — that Phebus had been a sergeant in the Narcotics Unit of the Philadelphia Police Department when he had been a cop, and that Jerome H. Kellog had also been assigned to the Narcotics Unit.

"He and Kellog were buddies in Narcotics?" Callis asked. "Partners?"

It would be unwise to have a man with a really personal interest in sending the accused away for life serve as his prosecutor.

"No. I checked that out. They never worked together, and they weren't friends," Hormel said.

Callis was not surprised that Hormel had checked out that possible problem area before coming to see him.

"What are you suggesting, Harry? That maybe Phebus couldn't get around McCarthy?"

"We have everything we need to get a conviction," Hormel said. "A statement, everything. Phebus stands as good a chance of getting a conviction as I do. Miss McCarthy'll give him her best shot, which would be a good learning experience for him both at the trial and during the appeals."

Obviously, Callis thought, *Phebus has got himself a rabbi. Harry wants him to try this case. Probably because he figures Phebus will not resign to go into private practice anytime soon.*

Only a few assistant district attorneys make a career of it. Most leave to enter private practice after a few years on the job. Harry's obviously interested in keeping Phebus. Nothing wrong in that. And Phebus is the kind of guy — he's no mental giant, and he has a civil service mentality — who will want to stay on here.

So what's the downside?

The Goddamned Nun makes a fool of him, and Leslie walks. Unlikely, but possible. But — even if it's that bad — the public perception will be that I made an understandable mistake in assigning an ex-cop to prosecute a cop-killer. That's better than McCarthy making a fool of me or Harry.

More likely — we've got a strong case — Phebus will be able to get a conviction. The District Attorney's Office will get the credit for the conviction, and I may even get a little credit for assigning an ex-cop to prosecute a cop-killer. The cops, at least, will appreciate that.

The Goddamned Nun will appeal, of course, all the way to the Supreme Court, to get that scumbag out of jail. She may even be able to get away with it. Fighting the appeals will be both a pain in the ass and time-consuming. Right now, Phebus's time isn't all that valuable, and like Harry says, it will be a good learning experience for him.

"Let Phebus prosecute, Harry," Callis ordered. "But keep an eye on him. If there are problems, let me know."

Thirty-five-year-old Peter Frederick Wohl looked like — and was often mistaken for — an up-and-coming young stockbroker, or an attorney. He was fair-skinned, with even features, and carried 165 pounds on a lithe body just under six feet tall. He wore his light brown hair clipped short, and favored well-tailored, conservatively styled clothing, almost always worn with a crisply starched white button-down-collar shirt, regimentally striped neckties, and well-shined loafers. He drove a perfectly restored, immaculately maintained Jaguar XK-120 roadster, in the back of which could usually be found his golf clubs or his tennis racquet, or both.

He was in fact a police officer, specifically the youngest inspector — and in the Philadelphia Police Department inspector is the second senior rank, after chief inspector. On those very rare occasions when he wore his uniform, it carried a silver oak leaf, like those worn by lieutenant colonels in the Army or Marines.

Wohl was the commanding officer of the Special Operations Division, which was housed in a building at Frankford and Castor avenues that had been built in 1892 as the Frankford Grammar School. Wohl's small, ground-floor office had been the office of the principal.

He glanced up from a thick stack of paper demanding his administrative attention at the clock on the wall and saw that it was quarter past four. He shook his head in resignation and shoved all the paperwork in the side drawer of his desk, locking it.

He took the jacket to a light brown glen plaid suit from a hanger on a clothes rack by the door and walked out of his office.

Officer Paul Thomas "Tommy" O'Mara, a tall, fair-skinned, twenty-six-year-old in a suit Wohl suspected he had bought from the Final Clear-

48

ance Rack at Sears Roebuck, got to his feet. Tommy O'Mara was Wohl's administrative assistant, and Wohl liked him despite the fact that his assignment had more to do with the fact that his father was Captain Aloysius O'Mara, commanding officer of the 17th District and an old friend of Peter's father — Chief Inspector Augustus Wohl, Retired — than any administrative talent.

"I'll be with Chief Lowenstein in the Roundhouse, Tommy," Wohl said.

Chief Inspector Matthew Lowenstein was Chief of the Philadelphia Police Department Detective Division, and maintained his office in the Police Administration Building — universally called the Roundhouse because of its curved walls — at 8th and Race streets.

"Yes, sir."

"If he calls, I left five minutes ago," Wohl said.

"Yes, sir."

Tommy reminded Wohl of a friendly puppy. He tried very hard to please. He had five years on the job, all of it in Traffic, and had failed the examination for detective twice. Chief Wohl had asked his son to give him a job — working for Wohl meant an eight-to-five shift, five days a week — where he would have time to study for a third shot at the detectives' exam.

Wohl's previous administrative assistant had been a graduate, summa cum laude, of the University of Pennsylvania, who had ranked second on the list the first time he had taken the detectives' examination.

Wohl thought of him now, as he started out of the building. He glanced at his watch, shrugged, and started up the stairs to the second floor of the building, taking them two at a time. At the top of the stairs, he walked down a corridor until he came to what had been a classroom but was now identified by a sign hanging over the door as the "Investigations Section."

He pulled the door outward without knocking and went inside.

A very large (six feet three, 225 pounds) man sitting behind a desk quickly rose to his feet with a look of almost alarm on his very black face, holding his right hand out, signaling stop, and putting the index finger of his left hand to his lips, signaling silence.

Wohl stopped, smiling, his eyebrow raised quizzically.

The black man, who was Sergeant Jason Washington, chief of the Investigations Section, and Inspector Wohl were old friends, going back to the time Detective Washington, even then regarded as the best homicide investigator in the Philadelphia Police Department, had taken rookie homicide detective Wohl under his wing.

If Sergeant Washington had had his way, he would still be, as he put it, a simple homicide detective. And he would have cheerfully and with some eloquence explained why: A good homicide detective — and there was no question in anyone's mind, including his own, that Jason Washington had been the best of that elite breed — earned, because of overtime, as much money as a chief inspector. And for another, he had liked being the best homicide detective. It was intellectually challenging, stimulating work. He had routinely been given the most difficult cases.

Washington's friendship with Peter Wohl had been seriously strained when Wohl had had him transferred to the newly formed Special Operations Division eighteen months before. There had been no harsh words — Jason Washington was not only genuinely fond of Wohl, but regarded him as the second-smartest man in the Philadelphia Police Department — and by rationalizing that if he intended to retire from the department as at least an Inspector, now was the time to start taking the promotion exams, Washington had accepted his new duties.

Washington pointed to a full-length mirror mounted on the wall. In it was reflected the image of a good-looking young man with earphones on his head, seated before a typewriter. His face was contorted with deep frustration and resignation. His eyebrows rose in disbelief. He shook his head, then typed very quickly and very briefly.

It was comical. Wohl was tempted to laugh. And did.

"The tapes," Sergeant Washington said.

"Ah, the tapes," Wohl said.

The young man, whose name was Matthew M. Payne, and who had been Wohl's administrative assistant before his promotion to detective, sensed that he was the subject of their attention, and tore the earphones from his head.

"It is not kind to mock a young detective doing his best," he said.

"Chagrin overwhelms me," Sergeant Washington said.

Wohl walked to Payne's desk.

"How's it going?" he asked.

Payne pointed at the sheet of paper in the typewriter.

"Slowly and painfully," he said.

"Get anything?" Wohl asked.

"They speaketh in tongues," Payne said. "I have learned that they have a 'Plan B' and a 'Plan C,' but I have no idea what the hell that means."

"It's a dirty job," Wohl said, gently mocking, "but someone has to do it."

"Why me, dear Lord, why me?"

"Because you can type," Wohl said. "Where did you get that?" he asked, pointing to the dictating apparatus Payne was using.

"There's a place on Market Street, across from Reading Terminal," Payne said.

"You bought it?"

"It was either buy it or suffer terminal index finger using that thing," Payne said, pointing to a tape recorder, and miming — jabbing his index finger — as he added, "ahead three seconds, rewind three seconds, ahead three seconds. I was wearing out my finger."

"What did it cost?"

"Don't ask."

Wohl chuckled.

"How's it coming?"

"There are thirteen tapes. I am on number three."

"We still on for tomorrow?"

"Yes, indeed, sir. I wish to play for ten dollars a stroke, plus side bets. It would please me greatly to have you pay for this electronic marvel."

"Merion at twelve? Right?"

"Bring your checkbook."

The relationship between Inspector Wohl and Detective Payne was unusual. Generally, it was believed that Wohl had elected to become Payne's rabbi, which was to say he had seen in the younger man the intelligence and character traits that would, down the pike, make him a fine senior police officer, and had chosen to be his mentor. That was true, but the best explanation of their relationship Peter had ever heard had come from his mother, who had said Matt was the little brother he had never had.

Wohl turned and walked out of the room, pausing before Washington's desk.

"If he shows any signs of slowing up — much less trying to leave — use your whip," he said.

"Yes, sir," Washington said.

Detective Payne replaced the headset, then held his hand, middle finger extended, in a very disrespectful gesture, over his head.

Wohl went down the corridor, got into his official unmarked car, and headed downtown for his meeting with Chief Inspector Lowenstein.

Five minutes later, the telephone in the Investigations Section rang. Sergeant Washington answered it, called out "Matt!" and when there was no answer, got up and walked to Payne's desk, tapped him on the shoulder, and then pointed to the telephone.

Payne took his earphones off, punched an illuminated button on the telephone on the desk, and picked it up.

"Payne," he said.

"Would you hold please for Mr. Nesbitt?" a

53

female voice said.

"No," Payne said.

"Excuse me?"

"You tell Mr. Nesbitt when he finally learns how to dial a telephone himself, I'll be glad to talk to him," Payne said, and hung up.

He looked over at Washington.

"That pisses me off," he announced.

"What, specifically, causes you to have an uncontrollable impulse to pass water?" Washington asked.

"Would you hold please for Mr. More Important Than You Are?" Matt said in a high soprano.

Washington chuckled.

Less than a minute later, the telephone rang again.

Washington let it ring until it penetrated Matt's concentration and he reached for it.

"Detective Payne," he said.

"What the hell is the matter with you?" Chadwick Thomas Nesbitt IV demanded.

"If you want to talk to me, Chad, you call me."

"That's what secretaries are for," Nesbitt said.

"Now that you have me, what's on your mind?"

"Tonight."

"As a matter of fact, I was just about to call you, myself, about tonight."

"You *are* coming?"

"That's what I was going to call about. I will not be coming."

"Why the hell not?"

"I seem to have come down with a virus."

"What kind of a virus?"

"Some kind of Asiatic flu. Not to worry, it will

only last twenty-four hours. They call it, 'The Don't Go To Chad's Birthday Party Virus.' "

"You want to tell me why not?"

"You really want to know?"

"I really want to know."

"Okay. Daffy will try to fix me up with one of her airheaded friends."

"I promise that won't happen."

"Reason number two: At least one of our friends will ask me to fix a little ticket he got for running through a red light into a busload of nuns while under the influence."

"If that happens, tell him to go fuck himself. You're very good at that."

"Reason three: Daffy, carried away with her notions of having become a wife, mother, and homemaker, will probably try to cook."

"It's being catered, of course. So you will be there, right?"

"Chad, I don't want to."

"Do it for me, buddy. We've been going to each other's birthday parties since we were in diapers. And hell, we never see each other anymore. Penelope Alice *is* your goddaughter."

That was all true. Chad Nesbitt had been Matt Payne's best friend since they had worn short pants. And they rarely got together anymore. And Penelope Alice Nesbitt, Chad and Daffy's first-born, named after the late Penelope Alice Detweiler, with whom, before she inserted too much — or bad — heroin into her veins, Matt had fancied himself in love, was indeed his goddaughter.

He sighed.

"I'll be there," Matt said. "Against my better judgment."

He hung up before Chad could reply and went back to work.

The festivities that would commemorate the birth twenty-five years before of Chadwick Thomas Nesbitt IV were, in the opinions of his mother and his mother-in-law (Mrs. Soames T. Browne), far more important than a simple birthday party.

It would, so to speak, if not introduce, then *reintroduce* the young couple to Philadelphia society. There had been a number of problems. For one thing, Chad had gone off into the Marines three days after graduating from the University of Pennsylvania.

A suitable wedding, given that, would have been difficult under any circumstances, but it had been further complicated by the unfortunate business of Daffy's best friend — Penny Detweiler, who was to have been her maid of honor — getting herself involved with drugs and gangsters.

Their hearts went out, of course, to Grace and Dick Detweiler, who were old and dear friends, but that didn't change the fact that Penny not being Daphne's maid of honor because she was in Hahnemann Hospital recuperating from being shot did cast a pall upon a wedding.

And then the Marines had sent Chad off to Okinawa, without Daffy, for more than two years. She had waited for him in her parents' home in Merion — married woman or not, her taking an apartment alone didn't make any sense — and then Chad had come home, and the second thing he'd done after taking off his hat was to get her in the family way.

And while she was pregnant, Chad had gone to work for Nesfoods, starting at the bottom, of course, as a retail salesman. His father — now chairman of the Executive Committee of Nesfoods International — had started out that way. And, for that matter, so had his grandfather. And Dick Detweiler, Nesfood's chief executive officer. And *his* father.

But you can't really have much of a social life when you're working as a retail salesman at the bottom of the corporate ladder, and with a pregnant wife.

Things were a good deal better now. Chad had proved his worth, and shortly before the baby was born, had been promoted. He was now an assistant vice president, Sales.

And the baby was healthy and adorable. Chad and Daffy had named her Penelope Alice, after Penny Detweiler, who had broken *everyone's* heart, not just her parents', by taking one illegal drug too many and killing herself.

Both Grandmother Nesbitt and Grandmother Soames believed that naming the baby after poor Penny wasn't the wise thing to do, but there's no talking to young people.

Look to the good, look to the future.

At least they had their own place now. Number 9 Stockton Place, in Society Hill. Large enough, and nice enough, to have their first real party.

Society Hill — around Independence Hall and

the Liberty Bell in central Philadelphia — was where the social elite of pre-Revolutionary Philadelphia made their homes. It was said, with some accuracy, that Society Hill had gone downhill from the moment the loyal subjects of His Majesty King George III, alarmed at the presence in nearby Valley Forge of a rebel named George Washington and his ragtag revolutionary army, had begun to leave town.

Society Hill had continued its slow but steady decline to a slum for the next century and a half. Then a real estate developer had decided there was probably a good deal of money to be made by gutting the old houses and converting them into upscale accommodations for the affluent.

In the process of gaining clear title to the blocks of property involved, it was discovered that an alley called Stockton Place had never been deeded to the City of Philadelphia. That being the case, it was the prerogative of the owner to declare it private property and keep the riffraff out. Exclusiveness sells, as they say in the real estate trade.

At considerable expense, a sufficient quantity of cobblestones had been acquired, and Stockton Place was repaved with them. As soon as that was done, one end of the alley was permanently closed with a brick wall, and at the other end, a Colonial-style guard shack was erected. A striped pole, controlled by a Wachenhut Corporation rent-a-cop, ensured that no one but the residents or their authorized guests was permitted to tread, or drive upon, the newly laid cobblestones.

Number 9 Stockton Place, which had been

purchased by NB Properties, Inc., was arguably the most desirable of all the residences. It was a triplex constructed behind the facades of four of the twelve pre-Revolutionary brownstone buildings on that block of Stockton Place. The entrance was at Number 9. Cleverly concealed behind the facade of Number 11 was the entrance to the underground garage, with space for three vehicles.

The property was leased by NB Properties, Inc., to Mr. and Mrs. Nesbitt IV at a rate a good deal lower than it would have brought on the open market. At the time they had moved in, young Chad was being paid no more and no less than any other retail salesman employed by Nesfoods International, and it seemed the least his father — who was the sole stockholder of NB Properties, Inc. — could do for him. Chadwick Thomas Nesbitt III well remembered when he had been starting out with the company, on the bottom rung of the ladder.

There would be more than two hundred guests. A buffet, of course. Chad and Daffy's apartment was large, but not large enough to have that many people seated for dinner. Mrs. Nesbitt III had toyed with the idea of giving the party at the Merion County Club, and Mrs. Browne had offered the Brownes' home — a forty-two-room copy of an English manor house, circa 1600, in Merion — for the occasion, but in the end she decided the thing to do was have Daffy give the party at her own home — with, of course, the help of her mother and her mother-in-law.

Daffy didn't really have the experience to do it, and she was busy with Penelope — both grandmothers were determined that the child never be called "Penny" — and it just had to be *right*.

The guest list had been difficult. Chad and Daffy's friends had to be invited, of course, but after Daffy had presented her list, that criterion was changed to "Chad and Daffy's oldest and dearest friends," which cut it down to less than a hundred, and left about that number of spaces for people who were important to the young couple, socially and business-wise. All six vice presidents of Nesfoods International and their wives were invited, of course, and some other businessmen connected to the company. And the Episcopal bishop of Philadelphia, of course, and the cardinal archbishop of Philadelphia. And the mayor. And the senator. And then the friends, most of whom had known Daffy and Chad all their lives.

Bailey, Banks & Biddle did the invitations, and the Rittenhouse Club was engaged to cater the affair.

There was a reception line, the birthday couple (a privileged few would be taken upstairs, later, to view Penelope Alice) and both sets of grandparents.

Matthew M. Payne entered the line at seven-fifty, a moment after Mrs. Nesbitt III had given Mrs. Browne a significant look, indicating that she believed they should abandon the line to mingle with the children's guests.

"Hello, Matt," Mr. Chadwick Thomas Nesbitt III said.

"Good evening, sir," Matt said.

"You look so nice in black tie, Matt," Mrs. Chadwick Thomas Nesbitt III said.

"Please tell my mother," Matt said.

"Your mother and dad are here," Mr. Soames Brown said.

"Daphne was afraid you wouldn't be coming, Matt," Mrs. Soames Brown said.

"That was when I thought Daffy was going to do the cooking."

"Matt, must I ask you yet again not to call her that?" Mrs. Soames Brown said.

Matt snapped his fingers in mock chagrin, indicating he had forgotten.

"Well, the birthday boy himself," he said, extending his hand to Mr. Nesbitt IV. "Congratulations!"

"Thank you for coming, buddy."

"And the mother of my goddaughter! About to spill out of her dress!"

"Oh, fuck you, Matt," Mrs. Nesbitt IV said.

The grandparents pretended not to hear.

Mrs. Soames Browne remembered again, as she usually did on such occasions, that at age five Matt Payne had talked Daphne into playing doctor and that she had concluded at that time that there was something wrong with him.

Over the years, he had done nothing to disabuse her of that notion.

There is a screw loose in him somewhere, she thought. *The policeman business was another proof of that. The very idea of someone with a background like his being an ordinary cop is absurd.*

61

If the truth were known, he probably had more to do with Penny getting on dope than anyone knows. When you roll around in the mud with pigs, you're going to get dirty.

Four

Matt Payne took a look at the buffet laid out in the game room, then at the line waiting to get at the food, and walked to the bar.

"A glass of your very best ginger ale, if you please, my good man," he said, but then changed his mind. "Oh, to hell with it, give me a scotch, no ice, and soda."

The barman smiled at him.

"My mother's here. What I was going to do, was wait for the question, phrased accusingly, 'What are you drinking?' to which I would have truthfully responded, 'Ginger ale.' Just to get her reaction."

"What changed your mind?" the barman asked as he made the drink.

Matt gestured around the crowded room.

"I need a little liquid courage to face all these merrymakers."

The barman chuckled.

And then Matt spotted a familiar face.

"I'll be damned," he said. "There is someone human here, after all."

He crossed the room to a small, wiry, blond-headed man standing beside a somewhat taller female. There was a thick rope of pearls around the woman's neck, reaching down to the valley between her breasts, and on the third finger of her left hand was an engagement ring with a four-carat emerald-cut stone in it.

"Hello, Matt," the woman said, smiling at him. "How are you?"

"Feeling sorry for myself," Matt said.

"How's that?" she asked.

"My superiors are cruel to me. You wouldn't believe what they've had me doing all day. And all day yesterday."

The man smiled.

"The tapes?"

"The obscenity-deleted tapes," Matt agreed.

"Getting anything?" the man asked.

"Stop right there, the two of you," the woman ordered firmly. "No shop talk! Really, precious!"

Precious was also known as Captain David R. Pekach. He was commanding officer of the Highway Patrol, and one of the two captains in Special Operations. The lady was his fiancée, Miss Martha Peebles.

In the obituary of Alexander F. Peebles in the *Wall Street Journal*, it was reported that he had died possessed of approximately 11.5 percent of the known anthracite coal reserves of the United States. Six months later, the same newspaper reported that Miss Martha Peebles's lawyers had successfully resisted efforts by her brother to break her father's will, in which he had bequeathed to his beloved daughter all of his worldly goods of whatever kind and wherever located.

One night six months before, Captain Pekach had twice gone, at the "suggestion" of Mayor Carlucci, to 606 Glengarry Lane in Chestnut Hill

64

to personally assure the citizen resident therein that the Philadelphia Police Department generally and the Highway Patrol in particular was going to do everything possible to apprehend the thief, or thieves, who had been burglarizing the twenty-eight-room turn-of-the-century mansion set on fourteen acres.

On his first visit that night, Captain Pekach had assured Miss Peebles that he would take a personal interest in her problem, to include driving past her home himself that very night when he was relieved as Special Operations duty officer at midnight. Miss Peebles inquired if his work schedule, quitting at midnight, wasn't hard on his wife. Captain Pekach informed her he was not, and never had been, married.

"In that case, captain, if you can find the time to pass by, why don't you come in for a cup of coffee? I rarely go to bed before two."

During Captain Pekach's second visit to 606 Glengarry Lane that night, Miss Peebles had gone to bed earlier than was her custom, and for the first time in her thirty-five years not alone. Their engagement to be married had been announced three weeks before by her attorney, and her father's lifelong friend, Brewster Cortland Payne, Esq., of Mawson, Payne, Stockton, McAdoo & Lester, at a dinner party at 606 Glengarry Lane.

"There's something there, captain," Detective Payne answered, ignoring her.

"Matt, please!" Miss Peebles said.

"Matt, I worked Narcotics for four years," Captain Pekach said. "If there was something, I would know!"

"Matt, go away," Miss Peebles said.

"Well, I hope you're right," Matt said. "But . . ."

"Precious!" Miss Peebles said firmly.

"Nice to see you, Matt," Captain Pekach said.

"If you'll excuse me," Matt said, smiling, "I think I'll mingle."

"Why don't you?" Miss Peebles said, smiling.

Matt looked around the room for his parents, and when he didn't find them, climbed the stairs from the game room to the dining room on the floor above. There he saw them, at the far end of the room. Talking with Penny's parents.

Christ, I can't handle that!

Penny's mother pities me, and her father thinks I'm responsible.

He turned so that they wouldn't see him.

And found himself looking at the rear end of a good-looking blonde and then the reflection of her face in the huge sheet of plate glass that offered a view of the Delaware River and the Camden works of Nesfoods International.

He walked to her.

She looked at him, and then away.

"Hi!" he said.

"Hello," she said.

"You may safely talk to me," he said.

"How's that?"

"I'm the godfather of the new rug rat," Matt said.

That got a smile.

"Have you got a name, godfather?"

"Matt Payne."

She gave him her hand.

66

"Susan Reynolds," she said. "I was Daffy's big sister at Bennington."

"That must have been a job."

That got him another smile.

"Can I get you a drink?" Matt asked.

"Why not?" Susan Reynolds said.

"What?"

"They have Chablis."

"Don't go away."

"We'll see."

He went to the upstairs bar and ordered a Chablis and a scotch and soda, no ice, for himself, and returned to Susan Reynolds.

"Thank you," she said.

"You're not from here, are you?" Matt said.

"Now you sound like Chad."

"How's that?"

"A pillar of Philadelphia society, surprised at meeting a barbarian within the gates."

"I didn't mean it that way. But I've never seen you around before. I would have noticed."

"Harrisburg," she said. "Outside Camp Hill."

"Hello," a female voice said behind him.

"Miss Reynolds, may I introduce my mother and father?" Matt said. "Mother, Dad, this is Susan Reynolds."

Matt's mother did not look her forty-five years. She had a smooth, tanned, unwrinkled complexion and a trim body. It was often said that she looked at least fifteen years younger than her husband, a tall, well-built, dignified, silver-haired man in his early fifties.

"How do you do?" Patricia Moffitt Payne said. "Daffy's told me about you."

67

"You're not supposed to call her Daffy," Matt said.

"I've known her since she was in diapers," Patricia Payne said. "I'll call her whatever I please."

"And it does fit, doesn't it?" Susan Reynolds said.

"I didn't say that," Patricia Payne said.

"I think you're a friend of Mr. Emmons, aren't you, Mr. Payne?" Susan Reynolds asked.

"Charles Emmons?" Brewster Payne asked.

She nodded. "He's a good friend of my father."

"Does that make you Thomas Reynolds's daughter, by chance?"

"Guilty."

"Charley and I went to law school together," Brewster C. Payne said. "I don't know your father. But Charley often mentions him."

"Matt," Patricia Payne said. "You're going to have to say hello to the Detweilers. They know you're here."

"Oh, God!"

"Matt!"

"Yes, ma'am," Matt said.

"Now would be a good time," Patricia Payne said.

"Will you excuse me, please?" Matt said to Susan Reynolds. "I will return."

Making his manners with Penny's parents was as painful as he thought it would be. And it took five minutes, which seemed like much longer.

When he returned to Susan Reynolds, his parents were gone, replaced by two young men who had also discovered the good-looking blonde without visible escort.

"What do you say, Payne?" one of them said. His name was T. Winslow Hayes, and they had been classmates at Episcopal Academy. Matt hadn't liked him then, and didn't like him now. The other one was vaguely familiar, but Matt couldn't put a name to him.

"What do I say about what?"

"Can I get you another drink, Susan?" the other one asked.

"Thank you, but I have appointed Matt booze-bearer for the evening," Susan said, and, raising her glass, added, "And I already have one."

Am I getting lucky?

T. Winslow Hayes and the other left shortly thereafter.

Their hostess appeared.

"I feel duty-bound to warn you about him, Susan," Daffy said.

"Daffy has never forgiven me for refusing to marry her," Matt said. "Don't pay any attention to her."

"You shit!" Daffy said.

Susan Reynolds chuckled.

"He doesn't look very threatening to me," Susan said.

"There are some very nice boys here I could introduce you to," Daffy said.

"Thank you, but no thank you."

I am getting lucky.

"Well, don't say I didn't warn you," Daffy said, and left them.

"Oddly enough, I think Daffy likes you," Susan said.

"In her own perverted way, perhaps," Matt said.

"Are you a lawyer, like your father?" Susan asked.

"No."

"You look like a lawyer."

"How does a lawyer look?"

"Like you."

"Sorry."

"What do you do?"

"Would you believe policeman?"

"No."

"Cross my heart and hope to die. Boy Scout's honor."

"How interesting. Really?"

"Detective Matthew Payne at your service, ma'am."

He saw that she now believed him — and in her eyes that he was no longer going to be lucky.

Let's cut to the chase.

"Do you like jazz, Susan?"

"What kind of jazz?"

"Dixieland."

She nodded.

"There's a club, in Center City, where there's a real live, imported-directly-from-Bourbon-Street-in-New-Orleans-Louisiana Dixieland band," Matt made his pitch. "Could I interest you in leaving these sordid surroundings and all these charming people to go there? They serve gen-u-ine southern barbecue ribs and oysters and beer."

Susan Reynolds met his eyes.

"Sorry," she said. "Try somebody else."

70

"Daffy scared you off?"

"Look, I'm sure you're a very nice fellow, but I'm just not interested. Okay?"

"Ye shall know the truth and the truth shall make you free," Matt said. "May I get you another drink before I leave?"

She held up her glass.

"I have one. Thank you just the same."

"Have a nice night, Susan."

"You, too," Susan Reynolds said.

Although she had hoped to be able to get away from the party without being seen, Susan Reynolds ran into her hostess as she was going down the stairway to the first floor.

"You're not leaving so soon?" Daffy asked, pro forma.

"Thank you for having me, Daffy," Susan said. "I had a lovely time."

"Even if you're leaving alone?" Daffy challenged. "You didn't find anyone interesting?"

"I don't recall saying I didn't find *anybody* interesting," Susan said, "just that I was leaving *here* alone. A policeman offered to take me someplace where the jazz is supposed to be good."

She winked at Daffy, who smiled with pleasure.

"Have a good time," Daffy said.

"I will try," Susan said, and kissed Daffy on the cheek.

"He's really not as bad as I said," Daffy said.

"Now you tell me?" Susan said. "After I get my hopes up?"

Daffy laughed appreciatively.

Susan walked to the end of Stockton Place and

handed the claim check to her car to the man in charge of the valet parking. It was delivered much sooner than she expected, but with what she had come to regard as the ritual expression of admiration.

"Nice wheels," the valet parking driver said.

Susan had come into a trust fund established for her by her paternal grandfather when she had turned twenty-five. The Porsche 911 had been her present to herself on that occasion.

"Nice engine, too," Susan said, and slipped him two dollar bills.

He looked like a nice kid, and he smiled warmly at her.

"Thanks a lot," he said.

Susan got behind the wheel, smiled up at the kid, and drove away.

She drove to City Hall, then turned left onto North Broad Street. There was probably a better way to get out of town — there was a superhighway close to the Delaware River — but she was reluctant to try something new, and wind up in New Jersey.

Near Temple University, she spotted the first sign identifying the road as Pennsylvania Route 611, and that made her feel more comfortable. Now she was sure she knew where she was.

She thought of the cop.

The truth of the matter is, I really would rather be sitting in some smoke-filled dive listening to Dixieland with him than coming up here.

As a matter of fact, there are probably two hundred things I would rather be doing than coming up here.

But at least I will get to see Jennifer and the baby.

Not, of course, the father of the baby. If I never saw that son of a bitch again, it would be too soon.

The Chinese had it wrong. Boy babies should be drowned at birth, not girl babies. Just keep enough of them for purposes of impregnation, and get rid of the surplus before they grow up and start doing terrible things.

Girl babies don't grow up to do the awful things that grown-up boy babies do — is there such a thing? I have seen very little proof that boy babies ever really grow up, even after they have beards — and if grown-up girl babies were running things, the world would be a better place.

No wars, for one thing.

They are such bastards, really. That cop was barely out of sight before his pals started telling me what a mixed-up screwball he was. That he had become a cop to prove his manhood in the first place, and that he wasn't really a cop, just playing at being one.

Was that a put-down of him, per se? Or were they putting him down to increase their chances — their nonexistent chances; I would really have to be desperate to let either of them close to me — of getting into my pants?

What about the cop?

Under other circumstances, would I have . . .

There are no other circumstances, and I know it, largely because of the male bastard I'm going to see tonight.

When they cause trouble, they don't cause trouble just for themselves, but for everybody around them. In this case, Sweet Jennie and now a baby. And, of course, me.

And they just don't care!

*Maybe I would be better off if I were a lesbian.
But I'm not.*

Is that a good thing or a bad thing?

It's a good thing. The truth is that I would kill . . .

*That's a lousy choice of words. There's enough
killing.*

*The truth is that I would give a good deal to be in
Daffy Nesbitt's position. To have a husband, and a
baby, and not to have to worry about anything more
important than changing diapers.*

*Not to have to worry about — try to deal with —
other people's problems. Most of which, I have
learned, they bring on themselves.*

I would really like that.

What does that make me, a selfish bitch?

*And since I do worry about the problems other
people have caused for themselves, what does that
make me, St. Susan the Martyr?*

*Stop feeling sorry for yourself. You got yourself in
this, and now you're going to have to pay the price,
whatever the hell that price ultimately turns out to
be.*

*And anyway, the Dixieland band would probably
have been terrible, and the worst possible man for me
to get involved with would be a cop. And despite how
his good buddies tried to put him down, I think
whatsisname — Payne, Matt — is probably a pretty
good cop. His eyes — I noticed that about him —
were intelligent. I don't think much gets by him.*

She drove through the suburbs of Jenkintown
and Abington and Willow Grove, and shortly
after 10:30 reached the outskirts of Doylestown.
She drove through town, past the courthouse with
the Civil War cannon on the lawn, and spotted

74

the Crossroads Diner just where Jennie had told her it would be.

The parking lot was jammed, also as Jennie had told her, when she had called the Bellvue, it would be. The diner, Jennie had said, was more than a diner. It had started out as a diner, but had grown into both a truck stop and a restaurant with a bar and a motel.

Jennie said that I should drive around to the rear of the diner, to the part of the parking lot between the restaurant and the motel. That there would be the best place to leave the car.

Susan glanced at her watch. It was twenty minutes to eleven.

I'm ten minutes late. Or twenty minutes early. Jennie said between half ten and eleven, and that if she didn't show up by eleven, that would mean something had come up and that we would have to try it again later.

By something coming up she meant that Bryan, or whatever he's calling himself this week, got drunk, again, or wrecked the car. Again. Or is off robbing a bank somewhere.

I'll have to watch myself to make sure that Jennie doesn't see how much I loathe and detest that son of a bitch. She has enough on her back without my adding to her burden.

As she drove behind the lines of parked cars between the restaurant and the motel, looking for a place to park, the lights came on in one of them — she couldn't see which one, but there was no question that someone, almost certainly Jennie, was signaling to her.

Or maybe it's just another admirer of Porsche 911s.

She found a spot to park between two large cars, an Oldsmobile and a Buick, and backed in.

Both were large enough so that the Porsche was hardly visible, which was nice.

With a little luck, too, the drivers of both are the little old ladies of fame and legend, who will open their doors carefully and not put large dings in mine.

Susan found her purse where it had slipped off the seat into the passenger-side footwell, then got out of the car, carefully locking it.

Then she started to walk back between the rows of parked vehicles, the way she had driven in.

Halfway, she heard the sound of a door opening, and her name being softly called: "Susie!"

It was Jennie's voice.

The vehicle was a four- or five-year-old Ford station wagon, a different car than the last time, but equally nondescript.

As she walked to the station wagon, the passenger door opened, but there was no light from the inside.

"Jennie?"

"Hi, Susie!"

Susan got in.

The car stank, a musty smell, as if it had been left out in the rain with the windows down, but there was an aroma, too, of baby powder.

Jennie was wearing a white blouse and blue jeans. She leaned across the seat to kiss Susan, and then immediately started the engine, turned on the headlights, and started off.

"You're not running from anybody, are you?" Susan asked.

God, why did I let that get away?

"No. Of course not," Jennie said.

"You took off like a shot," Susan said.

Jennie didn't reply, which made Susan uncomfortable.

"How's the baby?" Susan asked.

"Take a look for yourself," Jennie said, and pressed something into Susan's hand. After a moment, Susan realized it was a flashlight.

"There's something wrong with the switch," Jennie said. "Switches. The one that turns on the inside light, and the one in the door."

And I'll just bet Bryan's been fixing them, hasn't he?

"Try not to shine it in his eyes," Jennie said. "That wakes him."

Susan understood from that that the baby was in the back. She turned and leaned over the seat. She could make out blankets, and the smell of baby powder was stronger.

I'd really like to have a look, but if I shine the light, he'll wake up for sure.

She turned around.

"I'll wait 'til we get where we're going," she said. "And have a good look at him."

Jennie grunted.

"Where *are* we going?" Susan asked.

"Not far. Just the other side of New Hope," Jennie said. "Bryan found a house on a hill. You can see the Delaware."

"Where is he?"

"Working," Jennie said. "He plays from nine to one."

"Plays?"

"The piano. In a bar outside New Hope."

77

"How long has he been doing that?"

"Couple of weeks. He used to go there at night and play for the fun of it. So the owner asked him if he would play for money. Off the books."

"He doesn't need money," Susan said. It was a question.

"I think he likes to get out of the house," Jennie said. "The baby makes him nervous."

And I wouldn't be a bit surprised if there were single women around this place where he plays the piano.

Matt Payne was lying on his back, sound asleep, his arms and legs spread, his mouth open, and wearing only a T-shirt, when the telephone rang. He was snoring quietly.

The second ring of the telephone brought him from sound asleep to fully awake, but except to open his eyes and tilt his head so that he could see the telephone half-hidden behind his snub-nosed revolver in its ankle holster on his bedside table, he did not move at all.

The telephone rang twice more, and then there was a click as the answering machine switched on, and then his prerecorded voice filled the tiny bedroom.

"If this is an attempt to sell me something, your telephone will explode in your ear in three seconds. Otherwise you may wait for the beep, and leave your name and number, and I will return your call."

There was a beep.

And then a rather pleasant, if somewhat exasperated in tone, male voice came over the small loudspeaker.

"Cute, very cute! Pick up the damned telephone, Matt."

Matt Payne recognized Peter Wohl's voice. His arm shot out and grabbed the telephone.

"Good morning," he said.

"Is it too much to hope that I'm interrupting something lewd, immoral and probably illegal?"

"Unfortunately, you have found me lying here in a state of involuntary celibacy."

"Mighty Matthew has struck out? How did that happen?"

"I strongly suspect the lady doesn't like policemen. I was doing pretty well, I thought, before what I do for a living came up."

"Sometimes that happens." Wohl chuckled.

"What's up, boss?"

"Golf is off, Matt. Sorry."

"Okay," Matt said. "I'm sorry, too."

"Carlucci called my father last night and 'suggested' everybody get together for a little pasta at my father's house this afternoon, and then 'suggested' who else should be there. You weren't on the list. I wish I wasn't."

The mayor's habit of issuing orders in the form of suggestions was almost infamous. Chief Inspector Augustus Wohl, Retired, had been Carlucci's rabbi as Carlucci had worked his way up through the police ranks. Carlucci had once, emotionally, blurted to Peter that Chief Wohl was the only man in the world he completely trusted.

"What's it about?"

"Lowenstein and Coughlin will be there. And Mike Weisbach. And Sabara. You're a detective. You figure it out."

It wasn't hard to make a good guess. Matthew Lowenstein and Dennis V. Coughlin were generally regarded as the most influential of all the chief inspectors of the Philadelphia Police Department. Michael Weisbach was a staff inspector, generally regarded as one of the best of that group of senior investigators. Captain Michael J. Sabara was deputy commander of Special Operations.

"Not Captain Pekach?" Matt asked,

"Not Captain Pekach. I think the mayor heard him say 'if there was anything dirty in Narcotics, I would know about it' once too often."

"That makes it official? We're going to get stuck with that Five Squad business?" Matt asked.

"This makes it, I'd guess, a sure thing. Official will probably come down on Monday."

"Damn!"

"Sorry about golf, Matt. I was really looking forward to it."

"Yeah, me, too."

"I'll call you when I know how bad it is," Wohl said.

"Damn," Matt repeated.

The phone went dead in his ear.

He held it a moment in his hand, as his mind ran through all the ramifications — none of them pleasant — of the mayor "suggesting" to Police Commissioner Taddeus Czernich that Special Operations — not Internal Affairs — conduct an investigation of alleged corruption in the Five Squad of the Narcotics Unit.

He looked up at the ceiling, where a clock on

the bedside table projected the time of day. It was 9:15 A.M. He had gone to bed after two. He had planned to sleep until noon, by which time he presumed he would be rested, clear-eyed, and capable of parting Peter Wohl — who was a pretty good golfer — from, say, a hundred dollars at Merion.

Now he was awake, and once awake, he stayed awake. What was he going to do now? And, for that matter, for the rest of the day?

A call of nature answered that question for the immediate future. Matt put the telephone in its cradle, got out of bed, and went into his tiny bathroom. He was subjecting a rather nasty-looking bug who had fallen into the water closet to a strafing attack when the telephone rang again.

He cocked his head toward the open door so that he could hear what Caller Number Two had on his or her mind.

The prerecorded message played, and there came the beep.

"Matt, damn you, I *know* she's there, and I *absolutely* have to talk to her this *instant!* Pick up the telephone!"

The voice was that of Mrs. Chadwick Thomas Nesbitt IV.

Without taking his eyes from the bug he had under relentless aerial attack, Matt raised his left hand, center finger extended, the others bent, over his head and in the general direction of the loudspeaker on the telephone answering device.

Dear Daffy, Matt reasoned, *is almost certainly referring to good ol' blue-eyed, blond-haired, splendidly-knockered, Whatsername — Susan Reynolds*

81

— with whom I struck out last night.

Daffy thinks she came here with me.

Can it be that the Sweet Susan — Daffy knows her well — has been known to do with others what she would not do last night with me?

Damn!

He flushed the toilet by depressing the lever with his foot, pulled his T-shirt over his head, and stepped into his tiny shower stall. He had just finished what he thought of as Phase One (rinse) of his shower and reached for the soap to commence Phase Two (soap) when the telephone rang again.

He slid the shower door open to listen.

This time it was Mr. Chadwick Thomas Nesbitt IV himself.

"Matt, if you're there, for Christ's sake, answer the phone! Daffy's climbing the walls!"

Matt walked naked and dripping to the telephone and picked it up.

"She's not here, whoever she is," he said.

"Then where the hell is she?" Chad Nesbitt challenged.

"Since I'm not even sure who you're talking about, pal —"

"Susan Reynolds, of course," Chad said shortly.

"Not here. The last time I saw the lady, she was in your dining room."

"She's not with you?" Chad asked, obviously surprised, and went on before Matt could reply. "But she was, right?"

"Listen carefully. She is not here. She has never been here. Let your imagination soar," Matt said.

"Consider the possibility that she left your place with someone else."

"You were putting the make on her, Matt," Chad challenged.

"Indeed I was. But the lady proved to be monumentally uninterested."

"She didn't call home," Chad said.

"Thank you for sharing that with me."

"She always calls her mother before she goes to sleep," Chad said.

"How touching!"

Daffy Browne Nesbitt came on the line. "Don't be such a sarcastic son of a bitch, Matt. Honestly, you're a real shit!"

"I would appreciate it if you would attempt to control your foul tongue when under the same roof as my goddaughter," Matt said solemnly.

"She didn't call her mother last night," Chad said. "So her mother called her. At the Bellvue. And then she called here."

"Why did she call there?"

"I just told you," Chad said, somewhat impatiently. "There was no answer at the Bellvue. Then she called here, at half past two. Daffy told her that she had gone with you to listen to jazz."

"Daffy told her what? Why?"

"I certainly didn't want to tell her mother that she was in your apartment," Daffy said.

"Have you been eavesdropping all along, Daffy, or did you just come on the line? The reason I ask is because I have already told Chad that your pal is not now, and never has been, in my apartment."

"Then where is she?" Daffy challenged indignantly.

"This is where I came in. I haven't the foggiest idea where she might be, Daffy, and" — he shifted into a Clark Gable accent — "frankly, my dear, I don't give a damn."

Chad chuckled.

"The both of you are shits," Daffy said, and hung up.

"You might try washing her mouth out with soap," Matt said.

"She's upset. She lied to Susan's mother, and now she's been caught at it."

"I'm the one who should be pissed about that, old buddy. She told Mommy that the family virgin was out with me."

"You're close," Chad said. "Be a good chap, won't you, and go by the Bellvue?"

"You're as close as I am, Chad," Matt protested.

The Bellvue-Stratford Hotel, on South Broad Street, was nowhere near equidistant between Matt Payne's apartment — which consisted of a bedroom, a bath not large enough for a bathtub, a kitchen separated from the dining area by a no longer functioning sliding partition, and a living room from which one could, if one stood on one's toes, catch a glimpse of a small area of Rittenhouse Square, four floors below, through one of two eighteen-inch wide dormer windows — and the Nesbitt triplex on Stockton Place.

"No, it's not," Chad replied. "And you know it. Besides, I can't leave Daffy and the baby alone!"

"Perish the thought! That nanny you just imported is to impress the neighbors, right? You certainly couldn't trust her to watch the kid, could you?"

"Daffy's right. Sometimes you are a sarcastic ass," Chad said.

"What am I supposed to do at the Bellvue?"

"See what you can find out. See if her car's there, for example. And call me."

"What kind of a car?"

"Daffy, what kind of a car does Susan drive?" Matt heard Chad call, and then he came back on the line. "Oddly enough, one like yours. Only red."

"A 911? A red 911?"

"That's what Daffy says."

"That's why I asked."

"Thanks, pal," Chad said, and the line went dead.

Matt put the phone back in its cradle, but didn't take his hand from it.

"Matthew, my boy," he said aloud. "You have just been had. Again."

Then he dialed a number from memory.

On the second ring, the phone was picked up.

"Hello," his mother said.

"This is the son who never seems to find time to even drop by for a cup of coffee," Matt said.

"Is it really?"

"Do you think you could throw in a doughnut?"

"If I thought the offer was genuine, I would be willing to go so far as a couple of scrambled eggs and a slice of Taylor ham. Whatever it takes. Sometime this year, I would dare to hope?"

"How about in an hour?"

"I will believe my extraordinary good fortune only when you physically appear. But I will light a candle and leave it in the window."

"Good-bye, Mother."

Matt returned and finished his shower and toilette, shaving while under the shower.

He dressed quickly, in a single-breasted tweed jacket; gray flannel trousers; a white, button-down-collar shirt and slipped his feet into tasseled loafers. Just before he left his bedroom, he took his Smith & Wesson Undercover Model .38 Special–caliber revolver from the bedside table, pulled up his left trouser leg, and strapped it on his ankle.

He started down the steep, narrow flight of stairs that led to the third-floor landing, then stopped and went back into his living room. He pulled open a drawer in a cabinet, took from it a key, and slipped it into his pocket.

"Be prepared," he said aloud, quoting the motto of the Boy Scouts of America. An almost astonishing number of things he had learned as a Boy Scout had been of real use to him as a police officer. The key, so far as he knew, would open the lock of every guest room in the Bellvue-Stratford Hotel. That might come in handy.

By the time he had gone quickly down the stairs to the third-floor landing and pushed the button to summon the elevator, however, he had had second thoughts about the passkey.

For one thing, the very fact that he had it constituted at least two violations of the law. For one thing, it was stolen. For another, it could be construed to be a "burglar's tool." To actually use it would constitute breaking and entering.

He had come into possession of the key while he had been — for four very long weeks — a member of an around-the-clock surveillance detail in the Bellvue-Stratford Hotel. The Investigation Section of the Special Operations Division of the Philadelphia Police Department had been engaged in developing evidence that a Central Division captain and a Vice Squad lieutenant were accepting cash payments from the proprietress of a call girl ring in exchange for permitting her to conduct her business.

During the surveillance, his good friend, Detective Charles Thomas "Charley" McFadden, had arrived to relieve him, not only an hour and five minutes late but wearing a proud and happy smile.

"We won't have to ask that asshole to let us in anywhere anymore," Charley had announced, and handed him a freshly cut key. "We now have passkeys of our very own."

The asshole to whom Detective McFadden referred was the assistant manager assigned by the Bellvue-Stratford management to deal with the police during their investigation, and who had made it clear that he would rather be dealing with lepers.

"Where did you get them?" Matt had asked.

"I lifted one off the maintenance guy's key rings while he was taking a crap," Charley announced triumphantly. "I had four copies made —"

"I thought it was illegal to duplicate a passkey," Matt had interrupted.

"— and dropped the key just where the guy thought he must have dropped it," Charley had gone on, his face suggesting that Matt's concern for the legality of the situation was amusing but not worthy of a response. "One for me, one for you, one for Jesus, and one for Tony Harris."

Matt had decided at that time that what Jesus thought of the purloined passkey was wholly irrelevant. He and Detective Jesus Martinez were not mutual admirers. Detective Martinez often made it clear that he regarded Detective Payne as a Main Line rich kid who was playing at being a cop, and whose promotion to detective, and assignment to Special Operations, had been political and not based on merit.

On his part, Detective Payne thought olive-skinned Detective Martinez — who was barely above departmental minimums for height and weight and had a penchant for gold jewelry and sharply tailored suits from Krass Brothers — was a mean little man who suffered from a monumental Napoleonic complex.

What Tony Harris thought of Charley's boosting a passkey from a hotel maintenance man — and more important, how he reacted — would, Matt had realized, instantly decide the matter once and for all.

Tony Harris, de jure, just one of the four detectives assigned to the Investigations Section, was de facto far more than just the detective in charge of the surveillance by virtue of his eighteen years' seniority. He had spent thirteen of those eighteen years as a homicide detective, and earned a department-wide reputation as being among the best of them.

He was consequently regarded with something approaching awe by Detectives Payne, McFadden, and Martinez, who had less than a year's service as detectives.

Tony's response when handed the key had surprised Detective Payne.

"Maybe you're not as dumb as you look, McFadden," he had said, dropping the key in his pocket.

And they had used the keys during the rest of the surveillance.

The difference, it occurred to Matt as he waited for the elevator, was that they had done so under cover of law. Believing in probable cause, a judge had issued a search warrant authorizing search and electronic surveillance of "appropriate areas within the Bellvue-Stratford Hotel."

The search warrant had obviously expired when those being surveilled had been arrested and arraigned.

Matt was about to unlock his door, and leave the key inside his door, when the elevator appeared. He shrugged and got on, and it began its slow descent to the basement garage.

The turn-of-the-century brownstone mansion had been gutted several years before by Rittenhouse Properties, Inc., and converted into office space, now wholly occupied by the Delaware Valley Cancer Society. The idea of turning the garret into an apartment had been a last-minute idea of the principal stockholder of Rittenhouse Properties, Inc. He thought there might be, providing a suitable tenant — a widow living on a small pen-

89

sion, for example — could be found, a small additional amount of revenue from the apartment, and failing finding a suitable resident, that it would be useful — as much for parking space in the basement as for the apartment itself — to himself and his family.

At the time, it had never entered the mind of the principal stockholder of Rittenhouse Properties, Inc., Brewster Cortland Payne II, that his son would move into the apartment to comply with the requirement of the City of Philadelphia that its police officers live within the city limits.

There were two cars in the parking spots closest to the elevator in the basement of the building set aside for the occupant of the garret apartment. A new Plymouth four-door sedan sat in one, and a silver Porsche 911 in the other. The Plymouth was an unmarked police car assigned to Detective Matthew M. Payne. The Porsche had been a present from his father and mother, on the occasion of his graduation — *summa cum laude* — from the University of Pennsylvania.

After a moment's indecision, Matt unlocked the door of the Porsche and got behind the wheel. He was off-duty. He was going to the Bellvue-Stratford to see about Daffy's missing friend — and afterward to have breakfast with his father — as a private citizen. The taxpayers should not be asked to pay for his gas and wear and tear on the car when he was off-duty. And besides, he liked to drive the Porsche.

Five minutes later, after inching through early-morning inner-city traffic, he pulled to the curb on South Broad Street in an area marked "Tow

Away Zone." He took from under the seat a cardboard sign on which was stamped the gold seal of the City of Philadelphia and the words "POLICE DEPARTMENT — Official Business" and placed it on the dash of the Porsche.

He entered the hotel, went directly to the house phones, and asked the operator to connect him with Miss Susan Reynolds.

There was no answer.

He put the telephone down and started to leave, then picked it up again.

"Operator," he said. "I've been trying to get Miss Susan Reynolds in 802. I'm sure she's there, but there's no —"

"Miss Reynolds is in *706*, sir," the operator said after a moment, and more than a little scornfully. "I'll ring."

Matt felt just a little pleased with himself. He was now possessed of good ol' Susan's room number. He knew if he had asked for it — unless he had identified himself as a cop, which he didn't want to do, running down one of Daffy's friends not being legitimate police business — the hotel would not have provided it to him, as a security measure.

He had learned a good deal about the security measures practiced by the Bellvue-Stratford Hotel while on the surveillance detail.

He paused thoughtfully for a moment by the house phones, then decided that one possibility was that Susan might have been willing to show the etchings in her hotel room to another of the young gentlemen who had been at Daffy and Chad's.

91

And conceivably, at this very moment, Saint Susan might be doing with someone else — even that horse's ass T. Winslow Hayes was a possibility — what she had been unwilling to do with him, and, if this was true, be absolutely uninterested in talking to her mother or Daffy or anyone else while so engaged.

If she was so engaged, her car would be in the hotel garage. If that was so, he could call Daffy and tell her so. It would be a confession of failure on his part to seduce the lady, but on the other hand it would get Daffy off his back.

He went out the side door of the hotel and walked the half block to the public parking garage that also provided parking services for guests of the Bellvue-Stratford.

En route, without really thinking about it, he made the choice among his options. He could ask the attendant if there was a red Porsche 911 in the garage, which the attendant might not know; if at that point he tried to have a look for himself, that might require that he produce his badge, which he didn't want to do. Or he could just march purposefully past the attendant — the garage was self-park — as if he were going to reclaim his car and have a look.

He chose the latter option. The attendant in his little cubicle didn't even raise his head from the *Philadelphia Daily News* when he walked past him.

There was no Porsche on the ground, or first and second floors, but there were two, both 911s on the third. Neither was red, but he thought Daffy might be wrong about the color.

The blue Porsche 911 had Maryland tags, so that obviously wasn't it. The second, black, Porsche had Pennsylvania plates. Half a bingo. There weren't that many Porsche 911s around, so the odds were that a black Porsche 911 with Pennsylvania plates belonged to Saint Susan. But on the other hand, one should not jump to premature conclusions.

He peered through the rear window for some kind of connection with Saint Susan, and found none. Quite the opposite. He didn't think Saint Susan would have left a battered briefcase and a somewhat raunchy male golf hat on the seat of her car.

"Can I help you, buddy?" a male voice demanded.

He looked up and found himself being regarded with more than a little suspicion by a Wachenhut Security Service rent-a-cop.

Matt immediately understood that it was less an offer of assistance than a pointed inquiry.

"No, thanks," he said with a smile.

"What are you doing?" the rent-a-cop demanded.

Matt produced his detective's identification, a badge and a photo identification card in a leather folder.

"Police business," he said.

"Lemme see that," the rent-a-cop said, holding his hand out for the folder.

Matt was not surprised. He was aware that he looked like a nice young well-dressed man from the suburbs — someone just starting to climb the corporate ladder at the First Philadelphia Bank

& Trust, for example — and had grown used to people being surprised to learn that he was a detective.

The rent-a-cop carefully compared Matt's photograph with his face, then changed his attitude as he handed the ID back.

"Anything I can help you with?"

"I was looking for a Porsche 911 like this," Matt said. "But red. This isn't the one."

"I don't think we got one," the rent-a-cop said, searching his memory, and then added, "We had one yesterday. With a really good-looking blonde in it. She went out about half past five, just as I was going off duty."

"That's probably what I was looking for," Matt said. "Thanks for the help."

"Anytime," the rent-a-cop said.

Matt left the garage and walked back toward Broad Street.

There's a pay phone just inside the lobby of the Bellvue. I'll call Chad from there, and tell him that wherever Susan is doing whatever she is doing, she's not doing it at the Bellvue.

He got as far as the bank of pay phones before he had second thoughts about that. He realized he had a growing feeling — cop's intuition — that something was not entirely kosher here.

It wouldn't hurt to have a look at her room.

He walked across the lobby and got on one of the elevators.

He stopped before room 706 and knocked at the door. When there was no answer, he called, "Susan, it's Matt Payne. If you're in there, please open the door."

94

When there was still no answer, he took the passkey from his pocket and unlocked the door and walked in.

There was no one in the room.

The bed had not been slept in. The cover had not been pulled down, and it was not mussed, as if Susan had not lain down on it.

A matching brassiere and scanty underpants, a slip, and a sweater and skirt were on the bed.

The bathroom was a mess. Tidiness was apparently not among Susan's many virtues. She had apparently showered before going to Daffy and Chad's. Discarded towels were on the floor. And she had shaved her legs and/or armpits. Her lady's-model razor was in the sink.

And it was apparently that time of the month, for there was an open carton of Tampax on the shelf, beside a bottle of perfume, a stick of deodorant, and other feminine beauty supplies and tools.

He first decided that when Susan had left her room, she had had absolutely no intention of bringing anyone male with her when she returned, otherwise she wouldn't have left all the junk out in the open, and then he had the somewhat ungallant and immodest thought that the reason she had put him down so firmly was that, under the circumstances, there was no way they could have done anything about it.

And then he was suddenly very uncomfortable, to the point of shame, with the sense of being an intruder on her very personal life.

I've got absolutely no right to be in here. What the hell was I thinking about? Jesus Christ, what would

95

I have done if she suddenly had walked in here?

He walked quickly out of the bathroom, and through the bedroom to the corridor, carefully closing the door behind him. As he turned toward the elevator, he saw two women of the housekeeping staff examining him carefully.

Shit!

He rode down to the lobby, walked quickly through the lobby and out onto South Broad, and got into his car.

On the way to Wallingford, he pulled into a gas station and called Chad from a pay phone. He didn't want his parents to overhear him, as they probably would if he called from what he thought of as home.

He told Chad what he knew, that when he called from the lobby of the Bellvue-Stratford, she didn't answer her telephone, and that the rent-a-cop at the parking garage told him he remembered seeing a blonde in a red Porsche 911 leaving early the previous evening.

He did not mention to Chad that she had apparently not spent the night in her room — the unmade bed suggested that — because that would have meant letting Chad know he'd gone into her room.

He now recognized that going into her room was another item on his long list of Dumb Things I Have Done Without Thinking First.

The whole incident should be finished and done with, but once again he had that feeling that something wasn't kosher and that the incident was *not* closed.

Five

Patricia Payne found her husband on the flag-stone patio outside the kitchen, comfortably sprawled on a cast-aluminum lounge, and, surprising her not at all, with a thick legal brief in his hands.

"Guess who's coming to breakfast?" she asked.

Mr. and Mrs. Brewster Cortland Payne lived in a large, rambling house on four acres on Providence Road, in Wallingford, on Pennsylvania Route 252. It was a museum, Payne often thought gratefully, that Patricia had turned, with love, into a home.

What was now the kitchen and the sewing room had been the whole house when it had been built of fieldstone before the Revolution. Additions and modifications over two centuries had turned it into a large rambling structure that fit no specific architectural category, although a real estate saleswoman had once remarked in the hearing of Patricia that "the Payne place just *looked* like old, old money."

The house was comfortable, even luxurious, but not ostentatious. There was neither swimming pool nor tennis court, but there was, in what a century before had been a stable, a four-car garage. The Payne family swam, as well as rode, at the Rose Tree Hunt Club. They had a summer house in Cape May, New Jersey, which did have a tennis court, as well as a berth for their boat, a thirty-eight-foot Hatteras, called *Final Tort IV.*

The only thing wrong with it, Brewster Payne now thought, was that the children were now gone.

"Not Amy," he said. "I just talked to her."

Amelia Alice Payne, M.D., was the eldest of the Payne children.

"Matt."

"I'll be damned."

"He called here," she said. "And he said he would be here in an hour."

"I wonder what the probability factor of that actually happening is?"

"Maybe he's got something on his mind," Patricia said. "He seemed a little strange last night."

"He didn't seem strange to me," he said.

The telephone, sitting on the fieldstone wall that bordered the patio, rang.

Patricia answered it, then handed it to her husband.

"Brewster Payne," he said.

"Charley Emmons, Brew. How the hell are you?"

Charles M. Emmons, Esq., was a law-school classmate and a frequent golf partner of Brewster Payne, and the senior member of a Wall Street law firm that specialized in corporate mergers.

"Charley, my boy! How the hell are *you?*"

"At the moment, a little embarrassed, frankly."

"I can't believe you want to borrow money, but I will listen with compassion."

"I don't have to borrow money from you; I can

98

take all I need from you on the links."

"Do I detect a challenge?"

"Unfortunately, no. I wish it was something like that."

"What's up, Charley? What can I do for you?"

"You don't know Tom Reynolds, do you?"

Thomas J. Reynolds, if that's who he's talking about, Brewster Payne recalled, *is chairman of the board, president, and chief executive officer of — what the hell is the name? — a Fortune 500 company that has been gobbling up independent food manufacturers at what looks like a rate of one a week.*

"Only by reputation. But if we're talking about the same fellow, Pat and I met his daughter last night."

"Susan?"

"Yes."

"Tom knows we're friends," Charley Emmons said.

"And how might Mawson, Payne, Stockton, McAdoo and Lester be of service to — what's the name of his company?"

"Tomar, Inc.," Charley furnished.

"Yes, of course, Tomar, Incorporated. You know our motto, Charley: 'No case too small, no cause so apparently harebrained, so long as there is an adequate retainer up front.' "

Charley Emmons laughed dutifully.

"The thing is, Brew — the firm is in pretty deep with Tomar; otherwise, believe me, I wouldn't be making this call — about Tom's daughter."

"Oh?"

"You were at young Nesbitt's last night?"

99

"Yes, we were. I rather thought we'd see you there."

"The story as I get it, Brew, is that Susan left the party with Matt and hasn't been seen since."

There was a perceptible pause before Payne replied.

"Charley, Matt is no longer a child. And neither is that young woman. Matt, you know, has an apartment in the city . . ."

"I understand, I understand," Charley said. "But the thing is, the girl always telephones her mother when she's out of town, just before she goes to bed, and she didn't call last night."

"How old is the girl? Twenty-two, twenty-three, something like that?"

"Actually, a little older. Twenty-six or twenty-seven."

"So when it comes to defending my son, I won't have to worry about statutory rape, will I?"

"Now, take it easy, Brew. No one is suggesting . . ."

"What exactly are you suggesting, Charley?"

"I'm suggesting that I have a very important client — and a friend, too — who is worried about his daughter. You can understand that."

"All right. What is it you want me to do?"

"Find Matt, and have him have the girl call home. Do you have any idea where he is?"

"What makes Mr. Reynolds so sure his daughter is with Matt?" Payne asked.

"When her mother, in the wee hours, called her hotel — the Bellvue — and there was no answer, she called young Nesbitt's wife — the

100

girls were at Bennington together — and she told her Matt had taken the girl somewhere to listen to jazz."

"Charley, I'm more than a little reluctant to intrude in Matt's personal life."

"I understand that, Brew. But under the circumstances . . ."

"Does the phrase 'consenting adults' ever come up in your practice, Charley?"

"Brew, the girl's an only child. A Presbyterian Jewish Princess, if you like."

"That doesn't sound like Matt's type," Payne said, thinking aloud. "As a matter of fact, Charley, Matt's on his way out here. I will, with great discretion, ask him if he is acquainted with this young woman, and if there is any way he can suggest to her that she should telephone her mother."

"And you'll call me, right?"

There was a perceptible pause before Brewster Cortland Payne II replied.

"All right, Charley, I'll call you."

He replaced the telephone in its cradle.

"The phrase 'consenting adults' caught my attention, darling," Patricia said.

"You remember the girl we met last night? Talking to Matt?"

"What about her?"

"No one seems to know where she is," Payne said. "When last seen, she was in the company of one Matthew Payne, headed for some jazz place."

"No," Patricia said.

"No?"

"I went looking for Matt last night. I couldn't find him, but that girl was still there."

"Maybe he was there and you couldn't find him."

"No. I asked Martha Peebles if she had seen Matt, and she said she had seen him leaving. And that was before I saw the girl. Her name is Susan Reynolds, by the way."

"Apparently, no one knows where *Susan Reynolds* is. She apparently calls home when she's away. She didn't do that last night, and she didn't answer the telephone at the Bellvue."

"But someone thinks Matt knows? Is there a problem of some sort?"

"I don't think so," Payne said. "Do you think it would be too much to hope that Matt has the whole day free? That he might have time for nine holes?"

"What you could do is ask him," Patricia said.

Peter Wohl had more than once told his mother, who kept raising the question, that the reason he had not married was that with the Jaguar to support, he obviously could not also afford to support a wife. His mother was not entirely sure that he was pulling her leg.

The Jaguar, on which he had spent a good deal of time and a great deal of money restoring, was an XK-120 Drop Head Coupe. It was now in better mechanical and cosmetic condition than when it had left the Jaguar factory in Coventry, England.

While he had never entered the Jaguar in any of the Concours d'Elegance competitions frequently held in Philadelphia and its suburbs, he attended many of them whenever he could find the time. He had disqualified his car from competition — very reluctantly — by adding to it what classic-car buffs call somewhat scornfully "an after-market accessory."

The accessory was not noticed by most people, even those pausing to take long and admiring looks at the pristine, always gleaming roadster, but the antenna, approximately ten inches in height, mounted precisely in the center of the trunk lid, would not for long have escaped the eagle eyes of Concours d'Elegance judges. And once they had noticed that desecration of form and style, it wouldn't take them long to start snooping around the passenger compartment, where they would have found, carefully concealed beneath the dash, the police-band shortwave transceiver to which the antenna was connected.

When Peter Wohl carefully turned the Jaguar into Jeanes Street in Northwest Philadelphia, the gleaming black Cadillac limousine provided by the City of Philadelphia to transport its mayor, the Hon. Jerome H. "Jerry" Carlucci, was parked before the comfortable row house in which Wohl had grown up.

Two police officers in plainclothes were in the process of removing insulated food containers from the trunk of the mayoral limousine and carrying them into the house. He recognized the police officers. One was Sergeant Charles Monahan, who was the mayor's chauffeur, and the other was Lieutenant Jack Fellows, a tall, muscular black man who was officially the mayor's bodyguard. It was also said of Jack Fellows that he was the police officer closest to the mayor, except, of course for Chief Inspector Augustus Wohl, Retired.

When Lieutenant Fellows saw the Jaguar, he smiled and mimed staggering under the weight of the insulated food container. Peter Wohl waved and smiled, and then, when he had pulled up behind the limousine, reached under the dashboard of the Jaguar and came up with a microphone.

"William One," he said into it.

Regulations of the Philadelphia Police Department required, among thousands of other things, that senior police supervisors — such as the inspector who was the commanding officer of the Special Operations Division — be in contact with the police department twenty-four hours a day, seven days a week, year round.

Inasmuch as senior police supervisors required to be in constant contact are also furnished around-the-clock, radio-equipped police cars, most often unmarked, so that they may quickly respond to any call of duty, this usually poses no problems for the individuals concerned. Peter Wohl, however, was quite fond of his Jaguar, and determined to drive it when he thought of himself as off-duty.

So, with some pain, he found himself purchasing with his own funds the very expensive police radio, and with even greater pain, drilling a hole in the center of the Jaguar's trunk lid to mount its antenna.

He justified the expense to himself by rationalizing that he had just been promoted to Inspector, and didn't have a wife and children to support, and he tried hard not to think about the hole he had had to drill in the trunk lid.

"William One," a female voice responded to his call.

"Until further notice, at Chief Wohl's home," Wohl said. "You have the number."

"You and everybody else," the female voice responded, with a chuckle.

The reference was not only to the mayor's limousine (radio call sign "Mary One") but also to the four other identical — except for color — new Plymouth sedans parked along Jeanes Street, the occupants of which were also required to make their whereabouts known around-the-clock to either Police Radio or Special Operations Radio and had done so.

Two of the cars were assigned to Chief Inspector of Detectives Matt Lowenstein and Chief Inspector Dennis V. Coughlin, who were widely acknowledged to be the most influential of the eight chief inspectors of the Philadelphia Police Department. The other two were assigned to Staff Inspector Mike Weisbach and Captain Michael Sabara.

Staff inspectors — the rank between captain and inspector — and captains are not normally provided with new automobiles. There is a sort of hand-me-down system in vehicle assignment. Deputy commissioners and chief inspectors get new unmarked vehicles every six months to a year. Their "used" vehicles are passed down to inspectors, who in turn pass their used cars down the line to staff inspectors and captains, who in turn pass their cars down to lieutenants and detectives. At this point, the cars have reached the end of their useful lives, and are disposed of.

Mayor Carlucci, who was a political power far beyond Philadelphia, had managed to obtain substantial grants of money from the federal government for the ACT Program.

ACT was the acronym for Anti-Crime Teams. It was a test, more or less, to see what effect saturating a high-crime area with extra police, the latest technology, and special assistance from the district attorney in the form of having assistant district attorneys with nothing to do but push ACT-arrested criminals through the criminal justice system would have, short and long term, on crime statistics.

Mayor Carlucci was believed to be — and believed himself to be — the best-qualified mayor of all the mayors of major American cities to determine how the federal government's money could be most effectively spent to provide "new and innovative means of law enforcement."

On Jerry Carlucci's part, this belief was based on the fact that before he ran for public office, he had held every rank — except policewoman — in the Philadelphia Police Department from patrolman to commissioner of police. The federal officials charged with dispensing the taxpayers' largesse in the ACT Program, moreover, became aware that both of Pennsylvania's U.S. senators and a substantial majority of Pennsylvania's congressional delegation shared the mayor's opinion, and not only because most of them owed their jobs to him.

As soon as the money started flowing, Police Commissioner Taddeus Czernich — at Mayor Carlucci's suggestion — announced the formation of the Special Operations Division. The new unit to test new and innovative crime fighting ideas took under its wing the existing Highway Patrol, which had evolved from a highway-patrolling — often on motorcycles — police unit into an elite unit, two police officers per radio patrol car, with citywide authority, and a number of other police officers were transferred to it as ACT personnel.

Staff Inspector Peter Wohl had been appointed commanding officer of Special Operations. There was some grumbling about this, both within police ranks and in the press, especially in the Philadelphia *Ledger*, which usually found something wrong with whatever the police department did.

The charges made in this case said Wohl's appointment was another example of cronyism within the department. The *Ledger*'s readers were told that Peter Wohl was the son of retired Chief Inspector Augustus Wohl, who was generally acknowledged to be Mayor Carlucci's best friend.

On the other hand, there was approval of Peter Wohl's appointment by many members of the police department, especially from those who knew him and were regarded as straight arrows. They pointed out that he had been the youngest-ever sergeant in Highway Patrol, the youngest-ever captain, and the youngest-ever staff inspector. In the latter capacity, from which he had been promoted to command of Special Operations, he had conducted the investigation that had sent — following a lengthy and well-publicized trial — Judge Moses Finderman off to pass an extended period behind bars.

Mayor Carlucci had been as deaf to the grumbling about the appointment of Peter Wohl to command Special Operations as he was to the grumbling within the department and howls of indignation from the federal government about how he elected to spend the ACT grants.

Since mobility of forces was essential to the idea of quickly saturating high-crime areas with police, one of the first expenditures of the federal funds available made by Commissioner Czernich — at Mayor Carlucci's suggestion — was to purchase for Special Operations a fleet of new cars, some unmarked and all equipped with the very latest and most expensive shortwave radio equipment.

Commissioner Czernich also went along with Mayor Carlucci's suggestion that a large part of the federal grant be expended to make "emergency" repairs to Special Operations' new headquarters, which had begun life in 1892 as the Frankford Grammar School and had been abandoned three years before by the Board of Education as uninhabitable and beyond repair.

In cases that drew a good deal of attention from the press, Peter Wohl's Special Operations Division had quickly proved its worth, and was thus also to prove Wohl to be the extraordinary cop that Mayor Carlucci and his friends knew him to be.

The commissioner, at Mayor Carlucci's suggestion — it was said that the commissioner rarely did anything more innovative than blowing his nose without a friendly suggestion from the mayor — gave to the newly formed Special Operations Division the responsibility for running to earth a gentleman referred to by the press as the "Northwest Serial Rapist."

This gentleman had been shot to death by Wohl's administrative assistant after trying to run over the law officer with his van. At the time, he had neatly trussed up in the back of his van another naked young woman whom he had been regaling with specific details of what he planned to do to her just as soon as they reached some quiet spot in the country.

A massive Special Operations operation had run to earth another gentleman — a bank employee without any previous brushes with the law — who believed that God had told him to blow up the Vice President of the United States and was found at the time of his arrest to be in possession of the Vice President's Philadelphia visit itinerary as well as several hundred pounds of the latest high explosive, together with state-of-the-art detonating devices.

A Special Operations/ACT Task Force had, in a precisely timed operation, simultaneously arrested a dozen armed and dangerous individuals scattered all over Philadelphia on warrants charging them with murder in connection with the robbery of a South Philadelphia furniture store. With one exception, the arrests had been made without the firing of a shot. In the one exception, the individual had tried to gun down a Special

Operations officer, who, although wounded, had saved the Commonwealth of Pennsylvania the cost of a lengthy trial with a well-placed fatal pistol shot.

More recently, Special Operations investigators had uncovered an operation smuggling heroin through Philadelphia's International Airport. The operation had escaped the attention of the Narcotics Unit, and also — a police officer had been involved — that of the Internal Affairs Division, which had the responsibility for uncovering dishonest cops.

On the heels of that, Special Operations investigators had uncovered a call girl ring operating in Center City Philadelphia with the blessing of both the Mafia and the district commander — what are called "precincts" in most large cities are called "districts" in Philadelphia — and a lieutenant of the Vice Squad, who were being paid a percentage of the profits.

Commissioner Czernich's response to that — at, of course, Mayor Carlucci's suggestion — was to form another organization, to work very closely with, and be supported by, Special Operations. It was called the Ethical Affairs Unit (EAU). Staff Inspector Michael Weisbach, whose reputation — smart as a whip, straight as an arrow — was much like Peter Wohl's, was named to head EAU and charged with making sure that never again was the Philadelphia Police Department — and thus Mayor Jerry Carlucci — going to be embarrassed by a senior police official getting caught selling his badge.

Mike Weisbach had barely had time to find a

desk in the Schoolhouse and turn in his battered unmarked Ford for one of Special Operations' brand-new Plymouths when another case caught Mayor Jerry Carlucci's personal attention.

Officer Jerome H. Kellog, who worked as a plainclothes officer in the Narcotics Unit, had been found brutally murdered in his own kitchen. Among the initial suspects in the homicide had been Officer Kellog's estranged wife, Helene, and Mrs. Kellog's close friend, Mr. Wallace J. Milham, into whose apartment she had moved when she left Officer Kellog's bed and board. Mr. Milham fell under suspicion not only because of possible motive, but also because it was known that Mr. Milham habitually carried on his person a pistol of the type and caliber that had killed Mr. Kellog.

Mr. Milham was a detective in the homicide division of the Philadelphia Police Department.

Shortly after her husband's death, Officer Kellog's widow had appeared at the apartment of Sergeant Jason Washington of Special Operations. Mrs. Kellog told him that she had come to him because he was the only cop besides Wally Milham of whose honesty she was sure. She then went on to say that if they really wanted to catch whoever had shot her late husband, they need look no further than the Five Squad of the Narcotics Unit, all of whom, she stated flatly, were dirty.

Jerry, she suggested, had been killed because he knew too much, or was about to blow the whistle on the others, or, probably, both.

Sergeant Washington had of course considered

111

it possible that Mrs. Kellog was making these accusations to divert attention from herself and Detective Milham, but he didn't think so. He believed himself to be — and in fact was — an usually skilled judge of humankind, especially in the areas of veracity and obfuscation.

Washington reported to Inspector Wohl his encounter with Mrs. Kellog and his belief that she, at least, believed what she was saying. Wohl, knowing that Mayor Carlucci would want to know immediately of even a hint that a police officer had been murdered by other policemen, had passed what he knew on to the mayor.

At that point, the murder of Officer Kellog had been solved by a longtime ordinary uniformed beat patrolman, Woodrow Wilson Bailey, Sr., of the 39th District. Bailey, who had been keeping a more or less routine eye on one James Howard Leslie, whom he knew to be a burglar, had found in Leslie's burned trash pile a wedding photograph of Officer and Mrs. Jerome H. Kellog.

Correctly suspecting that Mr. Leslie had not been a close enough friend of Officer Kellog to have been given a wedding photograph, Officer Bailey investigated further, and sought assistance from other police officers. Soon after that, Mr. Leslie explained to Sergeant Washington why he had felt it necessary to shoot Officer Kellog.

That cleared Officer Kellog's widow and Detective Milham of any suspicion in the matter, of course. But it did not address the Widow Kellog's allegations that the entire Five Squad of the Narcotics Unit was dirty, and at least in her opinion, capable of murdering one of their own to ensure his silence.

Three months before, investigation of such allegations would have been routinely handled by the Internal Affairs Division, which was charged with uncovering police corruption. But three months before, Internal Affairs hadn't dropped the ball on that dirty cop passing heroin through the airport, or on the dirty Center City captain and Vice Squad lieutenant taking money from a call girl madam.

Three months before, Mayor Carlucci hadn't felt it necessary to suggest the formation of the Ethical Affairs Unit.

Inspector Peter Wohl, as he walked up to the front door of his childhood home, knew that while there would be lots of beer and whiskey and wine, and lots of tasty Jewish, Italian, German, and southern barbecue food served in the basement recreation room of his father's house this afternoon, as well as lots of laughs, and almost certainly a long trip down memory lane, that was not the reason Jerry Carlucci had suggested that everybody get together.

When the mayor decided the time had come, what they were going to do in good ol' Augie Wohl's recreation room this afternoon was decide how they were going to clean up the Narcotics Unit, and how to do it right, so that nobody dirty would get to walk because some goddamned defense lawyer caught them with an *i* they hadn't dotted, or a *t* they'd forgotten to cross.

He went in without knocking, and walked to the kitchen to kiss his mother.

There were six wives in the kitchen, dealing with the food: Chief Lowenstein's comfortably plump wife, Sarah; Angeline "Angie" Carlucci, the slight, almost delicate woman who was said to be the only human being of whom Mayor Carlucci lived in fear; Mike Weisbach's Natalie, a younger version of Sarah Lowenstein; Mike Sabara's Helen, a striking woman with luxuriant red hair; Jack Fellows's Beverly, a tall, slim woman who was an operating-room nurse at Temple Hospital; and Peter's mother.

Peter wondered tangentially how Martha Peebles — once she became Mrs. Captain David Pekach — was going to fit in with her fellow officer's wives. She would try, of course — she was absolutely bananas about her "Precious" — but her experience with feeding people was limited to telling her butler how many people would be coming to dinner, when, and what she would like to have them fed.

For that matter, he absolutely could not imagine Amy Payne in a kitchen, stirring spaghetti sauce, either.

Mrs. Carlucci and Mrs. Lowenstein insisted on their right, as women who had known him since he wore diapers, to kiss him.

"Your father and everybody's downstairs," his mother said.

"Really?" Peter replied, as if that was surprising.

"He's always been a smarty-pants," his mother said.

"Yes, he has," Sarah Lowenstein agreed. "But his time is coming."

"How's that?" Peter asked.

"There's a young lady out there — you just haven't bumped into each other yet — who will change you."

"And any change would be an improvement, right?"

"You took the words out of my mouth."

Peter smiled at her and went down the narrow steps into the basement.

He made his manners first with Mayor Carlucci, a tall, large-boned, heavyset fifty-three-year-old with dark intelligent eyes and a full head of brown hair brushed close to his scalp.

"Mr. Mayor," he said.

"I like your suit, Peter," Carlucci said, and tried to crush Peter's hand with his.

He failed.

"You're stronger than you look," the mayor said.

"Thank you, sir."

"Smarter, too," Peter's father said, draping an arm around his shoulders.

Peter shook hands with the others, then made himself a drink.

The trip down memory lane started. Peter didn't pay much attention. He had heard all the stories at least twice before. He sensed that both Mikes, Weisbach and Sabara, were slightly ill at ease.

Sabara's uncomfortable, probably, Peter thought, because he's here and Dave Pekach isn't. And Weisbach is legitimately worried about how much of this Five Squad investigation is going to be placed on his shoulders.

The conference vis-à-vis the investigation of allegations of corruption within the Narcotics Unit began when everyone declined another piece of cake, whereupon Mrs. Wohl announced that she would put another pot of coffee on and leave them alone.

"Peter, you help carry the heavy things upstairs," she ordered.

In three minutes, the Ping-Pong table pressed into service as a buffet table and all the folding tables were cleared and put away.

"I always like a second cup of coffee to settle my stomach," Mayor Carlucci announced.

Lieutenant Fellows quickly served him one.

"Don't mind me," the mayor said. "If anyone wants something harder than coffee, help yourselves."

Chiefs Coughlin and Lowenstein went to the refrigerator and helped themselves to bottles of Neuweiler's ale. The others poured coffee. The pot ran dry.

Lieutenant Fellows went upstairs to see how the fresh pot was coming.

"I talked to Jason Washington about this," the mayor began. "Maybe I should have asked Augie to have him here for this. Anyway, Washington told me he believes Officer Kellog's widow believes what she told him about the whole Five Squad being dirty. No disrespect to Captain Pekach intended — he's a fine officer — but despite what he says about if there was something dirty going in Narcotics he would have known about it, I don't think we can ignore what the widow said. Now, what else have we got?"

"The threatening telephone call," Peter Wohl said. "I believe that Mrs. Milham —"

"Mrs. *Milham?*" Mayor Carlucci interrupted.

"She and Wally Milham went to Maryland and got married, Mr. Mayor," Peter said. "I thought you knew."

"Now that you mention it . . . go ahead, Peter."

"I believe there was such a call," Peter said. "And so does Wally Milham."

"He would have to believe it, wouldn't you say, Peter? I mean, after all, he was slipping the salami to her before her husband was murdered."

"Wally Milham is a good cop, Mr. Mayor," Peter said.

The mayor looked at him for a long moment without expression.

"Tell me about the tapes," the mayor said finally.

"They're in the process of being transcribed," Peter said.

"Still? Christ, you've had them for a week."

"The tapes were damaged by fire, Mr. Mayor," Peter said. "They're very hard to transcribe."

"Get somebody good to do it. Somebody smart and fast."

"Detective Payne is transcribing them," Wohl said.

"And working hard at it, sir. Like last night at midnight," Mike Sabara interjected. "I listened to a little of them . . ."

"Did you?" the mayor asked, not pleasantly.

"I was surprised he's able to get anything off them at all," Sabara said.

"So they're useless?" the mayor said.

"No, sir," Peter Wohl said. "Both Payne and Sergeant Washington, who has read what Payne has transcribed so far, believe there will be something useful in them when we're finished. "

"The point I'm trying to make, Peter, and I'm not just trying to give you a hard time, is that we really don't have anything, except accusations made by a Five Squad wife who wasn't sleeping with her own husband," Carlucci said. "Against which, we have the opinion of a damned good cop who used to work Narcotics and says if there was anything wrong, he would have known about it."

No one replied.

The mayor looked at Chief Inspector Dennis V. Coughlin.

"You think we'd be spinning our wheels on this one, Denny?"

"It may turn out that way, but I think we have to do it," Chief Coughlin said.

"Matt?" the mayor asked, turning his head to Chief Inspector Matthew Lowenstein.

"I agree with Denny," Lowenstein said, looking at the butt of his cigar.

"You think we should go ahead, in other words?"

"Yeah, Jerry, I do."

"You don't seem very happy about it."

"No, I'm not. For one thing, if we find dirty cops in Five Squad, the whole department looks bad. Internally, so does Internal Affairs because we dug it out, not them. Let's say you give this to Peter —"

"I'm thinking of suggesting to the commissioner that it be given to Ethical Affairs."

"Same thing. Nothing personal, Mike," Lowenstein said, looking at Staff Inspector Weisbach, "but you can't do it without Peter's help, which, the way I see it, puts Peter in charge."

"And since Peter — nothing personal, Peter —" the mayor said, "can't do it without the help of the chief inspector of detectives, the way you see it, does that put you in charge?"

"Come on, Jerry."

"Or without the help of Chief Coughlin, does that put Denny in charge?"

"What are you driving at, Jerry?" Coughlin asked "That you want me, or Matt, to take this?"

"Nobody pays attention to what I say is what I'm driving at. I'll try again. I'm going to suggest to Commissioner Czernich that an investigation of certain allegations concerning the Narcotics Unit is in order, and that it should be conducted by the Ethical Affairs Unit. Therefore, Mike Weisbach will be in charge. I am also going to suggest to the Commissioner that he direct Peter, Denny, and you, Matt, to provide Mike with whatever he thinks he needs to get the job done. Now, is that clear in everybody's mind?"

There was a chorus of "Yes, sir."

"And since everybody involved is an experienced police officer, it will not be necessary for me to tell you that the best way to blow this investigation is to let those scumbags even suspect somebody's taking a close look at them, right? Do I make that point? I want them. I want them bad. If there's anything worse than a drug dealer, it's a police officer either hiding drug dealers behind his badge, or, God forbid, dealing drugs himself."

He looked around at all of them.

"Peter, since you'll be working closer with Mike than anybody else, once a day, either Fellows or myself will telephone you and you'll tell us what's happened in the past twenty-four hours. You'll also keep Matt and Denny up to speed. As little as possible in writing. Papers have a way of turning up in the wrong hands."

"Yes, sir," Peter Wohl said.

Six

When Matt Payne glanced into the lobby as he drove past the Delaware Valley Cancer Society Building, he saw two men in business suits sitting on the leather-and-chrome seats facing the receptionist's desk.

Except for the Wachenhut rent-a-cop the Cancer Society installed behind the receptionist's desk, they closed down tight at night and on weekends. It was therefore possible — even likely — that anyone in the lobby was waiting for him, not for someone connected with the Cancer Society.

He slowed and took a closer look. He recognized neither man. He shrugged and drove around the block, to the rear of the building, where he had to get out of the Porsche and use a difficult key to open the steel door lowered on weekends over the entrance to the basement garage. He entered the garage, then got out of the Porsche again to reclose the door.

He rode to the fourth-floor landing on the elevator, unlocked his door, and climbed the narrow stairway to his apartment.

Which seemed to be in even a greater mess than he remembered. An unpleasant sweetish odor told him that he had again forgotten to get rid of the goddamned garbage under the sink. He would, he realized, have to deal with both problems tonight.

Just as soon as he dealt with his answering machine, the red light of which was blinking.

"Matt," the recorded voice said. "Mike Weisbach. Sorry to bother you on your day off. If you get in before, say, half past ten, give me a ring at home, will you? 774–4923."

He slumped onto the couch and reached for the telephone.

A woman answered.

"Inspector Weisbach, please. Detective Payne returning his call."

"Hi, Matt. This is Natalie. I'll get him."

"Thank you."

Why the hell can't I remember her name?

"Hey, Matt. Glad I caught you."

"What's up, Inspector?"

"Peter Wohl asked me to call you. We'll be working together on the Five Squad mess."

"Yes, sir. I spoke with the inspector earlier. He said he thought we'd get stuck with that."

"I'm going to get together with everybody in the morning, nine o'clock, your office. But what I'm calling about now is the tapes."

"Yes, sir."

"It seems to me the first thing we need is the tapes. How are they coming?"

"Slowly and painfully."

Weisbach chuckled.

"Captain Sabara said you were working on them late last night."

"Yes, sir."

"How would you like some more overtime, Detective Payne?"

"I'm very much afraid the inspector means to-night," Matt said.

"Other plans, Matt? Unbreakable?"

"No, sir. I can go out there. But, Inspector, I can't finish them tonight."

"Maybe we can come up with something to-morrow. Get you some help. But the more I could have before the meeting tomorrow, the better."

"Yes, sir. I'll go out there and do what I can."

"I appreciate it, Matt. Maybe I can make it up to you."

"I'll do what I can, sir."

"Thank you, Matt. See you in the morning."

"Yes, sir."

Matt put the telephone back in its cradle.

"Shit!" he said.

His doorbell sounded.

"Now what?"

He had an intercom, but it was less trouble to go down the stairs and open the door than to use it, and he did so.

The two men he had seen in the lobby were standing there.

"Matthew Payne?" the taller one said.

Matt nodded.

"I'm Special Agent Jernigan of the FBI, and this is Special Agent Leibowitz." He showed Matt his identification, then went on: "We'd like to talk to you. May we come in?"

"Talk to me about what?"

"May we come in?"

"Talk to me about what?" Matt repeated.

"If you don't mind, Mr. Payne, we'll ask the questions," Special Agent Jernigan said.

"What is this, some sort of a joke?" Matt asked, aware that his temper was simmering just below the surface.

"I assure you, this is not a joke."

"Ask your questions," Matt said.

"Is Miss Susan Reynolds in your apartment?"

"I don't see how that's any of your business, but no, she's not."

"We'll decide what's our business, if you don't mind."

"And I will decide whether or not I'll answer your questions, if you don't mind."

"You understand, of course, Mr. Payne, that interfering with a federal investigation is a crime?"

"I heard that somewhere. But I also heard that declining to answer questions is not considered interfering with an investigation. I think they call that the Fifth Amendment."

"We understand, Mr. Payne," Agent Leibowitz said, "that you were with Miss Reynolds last night?"

Matt understood when Leibowitz spoke that Leibowitz was the senior agent of the two, and that Leibowitz had opened his mouth only because he understood that Agent Jernigan and the interviewee had developed a personality conflict that would interfere with the interview.

"Yes, I was," Matt said.

"Would you mind telling us where you went with her when you left the Nesbitt residence together?"

"I did not leave the Nesbitt residence with anyone," Matt said.

Christ, have these guys been talking to Daffy?

What the hell is this all about?

"We believe you did," Agent Leibowitz said.

"Frankly, I don't care if you believe in the Easter Bunny," Matt said. "I'm telling you I left the Nesbitt residence alone, and that's absolutely the last thing I'm going to tell you until you tell me what this is all about."

"I don't understand your hostility, frankly, Mr. Payne," Leibowitz said. "You have something against the FBI?"

"Some of my best friends are FBI agents, but I don't think I would want my sister to marry one," Matt said.

Matt saw that Agent Jernigan's face had grown red. And that pleased him.

"Where are you employed, Mr. Payne?" Jernigan asked, somewhat menacingly.

"I don't think you're supposed to be asking any more questions, are you? Didn't Agent Leibowitz take over the interview?"

"Thank you for your time, Mr. Payne," Agent Leibowitz said, and walked toward the elevator.

" 'Bye, now," Matt said. "Have a nice night!"

He started back up the stairs to his apartment.

I wonder what the hell that was all about?

Jesus! Kidnapping?

Did somebody kidnap Susan Reynolds? That would involve the FBI.

And they must have talked to Daffy.

And she told them Susan had left with me, because that's what she told Susan's parents.

Goddamn her!

Wait a minute. Don't leap to conclusions.

Daffy told Susan's mother *that Susan was off*

125

somewhere with me.

Susan's mother, or father, told Dad's pal, Lawyer Emmons, that Susan had gone off with me.

One of them, probably Lawyer Emmons, went to the FBI, and told the FBI the same thing.

The FBI is investigating the kidnapping, or at least the disappearance and possible kidnapping of Susan Reynolds.

So soon? She only turned up missing at two A.M. this morning.

The victim is the daughter of Mr. and Mrs. Thomas Reynolds. Reynolds, a multimillionaire, is president of Tomar, Inc.

And important enough to get the FBI working on a weekend.

Goddamn Daffy!

I am, if not a suspect, then the last person known to have seen the victim.

Those FBI clowns were just doing their job. I probably shouldn't have given them such a hard time. But they are such an arrogant bunch of bastards! "I am Special Agent Jernigan of the FBI, Mr. Payne. We'd like to talk to you. May we come in?" and then that "Where are you employed, Mr. Payne?" bullshit. Translation: "We're going to get you in trouble with your boss, wise guy."

Fuck them! All they had to do was tell me they were looking for Susan Reynolds, that they thought she might have been kidnapped. Even if I was the kidnapper, that wouldn't have hurt their investigation. And I would have told them everything I know . . . except, of course, that I don't think she spent the night in her room, because I went into her room and the bed hadn't been slept in.

Goddamn it, going into her room was really stupid!

He reached the top of the stairs, crossed to his couch, slumped into it, and put the telephone in his lap.

"Hello?"

"Daffy, curiosity overwhelms me. Where did your pal Susan finally turn up?"

"Matt," Daphne Browne Nesbitt said solemnly, "I am so sorry."

"So sorry about what?"

"Can you keep your mouth shut?"

"Of course."

"She was there all the time," Daffy said.

"She was where all the time?"

"In her room. She didn't want to answer the telephone."

"How do you know that?"

"Because she told me."

"When was this?"

"About an hour ago. She called just before she checked out of the hotel."

"You're sure it was her?"

"Of course I'm sure."

"Did she tell you why she didn't want to answer the telephone?"

"No, but I can guess, can't you?"

"You're suggesting she was in the sack with some guy all the time?"

"I suggested nothing of the kind. Susan isn't that kind of girl."

"Where is she now?"

"Probably, about now, about halfway to Harrisburg. Matt, I feel like such a shit for getting you involved."

127

"Involved in what?"

"I know about her father's lawyer calling your father."

"No major problem, Daffy."

"You want to come to supper? There's all kinds of leftovers."

"I'll take a rain check."

"You want Susan's telephone number? If at first you don't succeed, et cetera, et cetera . . ."

He stopped himself just in time from saying "no." He wrote the number down, then said good-bye to Daphne.

Do I want to take another shot at that dame? No, I do not. Then why did I take down her phone number?

He crumpled the sheet of notepaper up and threw it at an overflowing wastebasket. He missed.

He spent the next thirty minutes in an only partially successful attempt to clean up the apartment, then started carrying bags of garbage down the stairs to the elevator. On his third trip, emptying the wastebasket in brown kraft paper bags from Acme Supermarkets, he saw the crumpled ball of paper with Susan Reynolds's telephone number on it. He picked it up and after a moment's hesitation stuffed it into his pocket.

Then he went down in the elevator with the half-dozen bags of garbage, set them where they would be collected in the morning, and walked back to the Porsche. He debated a moment about taking the unmarked car, then decided not to. He was going on duty, sure, extra duty, and therefore the taxpayers of Philadelphia should be happy to pay for his transportation.

But on the other hand, driving the Porsche was fun. And there was probably going to be little chance to drive it during the next week or ten days. With His Honor the mayor paying personal attention to the investigation of dirty cops in Narcotics, there was almost certainly going to be a lot of overtime.

He drove out of the garage, closed it after him, and then started for Special Operations, via Broad Street. As he passed Hahnemann Hospital, he glanced in the rearview mirror to change lanes and saw Special Agent Leibowitz of the FBI at the wheel of a green Chevrolet, with Special Agent Jernigan sitting beside him.

I'll be goddamned! Those clowns are surveilling me!

They were still behind him after twenty minutes and a lengthy trip up and down the back alleys off Frankford Avenue when he pulled into the Special Operations Division parking lot and into the parking spot reserved for the unmarked car he had left in the Cancer Society Building garage.

First of all, he thought, not without a certain pleasure, *they'll be wondering what I'm doing here. After a while — a long while, it is to be hoped — they may actually interrupt their dedicated surveillance of the kidnap suspect long enough to enter the building, identify themselves to the sergeant or the duty officer, and inquire of him if they happen to know what the occupant of the silver Porsche is doing in here.*

At that point, they may actually get in touch with their supervisor, who will tell them that there is no kidnapping after all, and they will be denied the great pleasure of hauling the uncooperative wiseass off in handcuffs.

He went up the stairs to the Investigation Section, turned on the lights, worked the combination lock on "his" filing cabinet, took the tapes from the cabinet, seated himself at his desk, and turned on the dictating machine.

Staff Inspector Michael Weisbach looked around the Investigations Section office at the people he had summoned — in the case of Sergeant Jason Washington, politely asked — to participate.

Among them was the only man in uniform, Sergeant Elliot Sandow, a slight, sickly-looking former Traffic officer who had been struck on the job by a Strawbridge & Clothier delivery truck, spent four months in the hospital, and personally petitioned Mayor Carlucci to stay on the job rather than go out on disability.

He had proved to be an unusually skilled administrator, whom Weisbach had found working in Personnel and arranged to have transferred first to the Staff Inspection Unit, and then, when he had been named to command the Ethical Affairs Unit, to EAU. At the moment, Weisbach and Sandow were the EAU.

Also present were Detectives Anthony C. Harris, Jesus Martinez, Charles McFadden, Matthew M. Payne, and Officer Foster H. Lewis, Jr., a very black twenty-four-year-old who stood six feet three inches tall, weighed 230 pounds, and was known, perhaps inevitably, as "Tiny."

Foster H. Lewis, Sr., a lieutenant in the 9th District, was very unhappy that his son was a police officer at all, and working plainclothes in the Investigations Section of Special Operations in particular. As a parent, he would have much preferred that his son had remained a medical student rather than join the police department. As a policeman, he would have much preferred that his son learn the police profession as he had, working his way up from walking a beat, rather than going almost directly from the Academy to a plainclothes Special Operations assignment that carried with it so much overtime that he was bringing home almost as much money as his father and was usually provided with an unmarked car.

Lieutenant Foster was truly ambivalent about his son having recently taken — just as soon as he was eligible — the examination for promotion to detective. If he passed it and was promoted, Lieutenant Foster knew that he would really be proud of his son — despite his genuine belief that his son hadn't been on the job long enough to be a good beat patrolman, much less a detective.

"I'm sure," Staff Inspector Weisbach began, "that everyone was as thrilled as I was to learn that this morning Commissioner Czernich, by classified communication, charged the Ethical Affairs Unit with investigating certain allegations of misbehavior in the Five Squad of the Narcotics Unit, and further directed Inspector Wohl to make available to EAU whatever Special Operations resources are needed, which includes the services of everybody in this room."

"Shit," Detective Harris said, but smiled.

"Thank you, Detective Harris," Weisbach said, "for so succinctly summing up the feelings of so many of us."

There were general chuckles.

"But we're cops, gentlemen, all of us. And we do what we're ordered to do, so let's get on with it," Weisbach said. "My first order — I don't give many orders, so pay attention when I do — is that this is one job that nobody talks about. Not to your wives, not at the FOP bar, not to your buddies. Not to anyone. If there's something dirty going on in Narcotics Five Squad, and they even suspect we're looking close at them, they'll just shut down whatever they're doing and wait until the storm blows over. Which obviously means our job would be much harder. Everybody got that clear in their minds?"

He looked at Matt Payne so long that Matt nodded. And then he kept looking. Finally, Matt understood what was expected of him. He stood up and said, "Yes, sir."

Weisbach looked at everybody but Sergeants Washington and Sandow in turn, and waited until each of them stood up and said, "Yes, sir."

"For all practical purposes, Sergeants Washington and Sandow will not be taking a very active role in this," Weisbach said. "Sergeant Sandow for the obvious reasons, he'll be handling the paperwork, and Sergeant Washington because he really is a legend in his own time, and the first time he started asking questions, looking around Five Squad, they would wonder why. To only a slightly lesser degree — he is not nearly as visible as Sergeant Washington — this also applies to Detective Harris.

"This does not mean," Weisbach went on, to be interrupted by a chorus of chuckles, and then went on, "that Sergeant Washington and Harris will not be involved in this — quite the opposite — just that they won't be out ringing doorbells. The flow of reports will be through Washington to me, and I expect Washington to bring Harris in on everything. Okay?"

There was a chorus of "Yes, sirs," and Washington nodded his understanding.

"Is there anybody here who doesn't know how and where the interest in Five Squad began?" Weisbach asked. "I mean the accusations made to Sergeant Washington by Officer Kellog's wife at the time of the murder? Hands, please."

No hands went up.

"I'm not surprised. My wife says cops gossip more than women," Weisbach went on. "Okay, let me bring everybody up-to-date on what's happened since. If you've heard this before, bear with me."

"When these allegations first came up, I spoke with Captain Pekach. He was surprised to hear them. He felt, I suppose still feels, that if anything was going on in Narcotics, he would have heard about it, or at least had suspicions. Now, since Captain Pekach is both not naive, and an experienced police supervisor, what that means is — let's go on the presumption that there are dirty cops in the Five Squad — that they're smart and doing what they're doing skillfully enough to keep a smart supervisor like Captain Pekach from even

133

suspecting that something's going on."

He looked at Detective Jesus Martinez.

"Jesus, when you worked Narcotics, did you hear anything about the Five Squad? Suspect anything?"

Martinez shook his head, "no."

"Charley?" Weisbach asked, looking at Detective McFadden.

"No, sir," McFadden said. "Five Squad were the hotshots. They hung together. They didn't even talk to the peasants."

Weisbach nodded.

"More proof that they know how to keep their mouths shut," Weisbach said. "I asked Captain Pekach to let his imagination run free, and come up with how Five Squad could illegally profit from the performance, or nonperformance, of their official duties.

"Captain Pekach said he doesn't think Five Squad is taking payments from drug dealers or others to ignore their criminal activities. He made the point that the statistics — the number of 'good' arrests resulting in court convictions made by Five Squad — are extraordinary.

"That, he said — and I think he's right — left one possibility: if there is something dirty going on, it's taking place *during* raids and arrests. I looked into this idea, and found out that the number of times Five Squad conducted raids and arrests *without* support from other police units, the districts, Highway Patrol, and ACT teams is unusual.

"In other words, with no one present during a raid or arrest but fellow members of the Narcotics

Five Squad, it's possible that Five Squad is illegally diverting to their own use part of the cash and other valuables that would be subject to seizure before it was entered upon a property receipt."

"Yeah," Detective McFadden thought out loud.

"McFadden?" Weisbach asked.

"They run a bust. The bad guy has, say, ten thousand in cash. They turn in say, eight or nine thousand. What's the bad guy going to do? 'Hey, I got ripped off of a thousand'? Who's going to believe him?"

"I think it will probably turn out to be something like that," Weisbach said.

"Or controlled substances," Jesus Martinez said. "They bust the guy, he's got fifty bags of crap. They turn in forty. Same story."

"If Martinez is right about that — and I'm afraid he might be — that would mean that Five Squad is putting drugs back onto the street," Weisbach said.

"Are we talking out of school here?" McFadden asked.

"Yes, we are."

"I done a little of that myself," McFadden said. "Took a couple of bags here and there to feed my snitches."

"You never *sold* any, Charley," Jesus said.

"What I'm saying is that's how it could have started," McFadden said. "You need to make a car payment or something, you got five, ten bags you took away from some scumbag to feed your snitches. Fuck your snitches, sell the shit, make

135

your car payment."

Staff Inspector Weisbach had spoken to Captain Pekach about Detectives Martinez and McFadden, who had worked for him when he'd been a lieutenant in Narcotics.

They both had been assigned to Narcotics right out of the Academy, solely because Narcotics needed a steady stream of undercover officers whose faces were not known on the street. Until they were "burned" — that is, became known — rookie cops were very valuable in making buys, and thus causing arrests. Many rookies were psychologically unable to work undercover, and many other rookies, because of inexperience or just plain bad luck, were quickly burned. Once burned, rookie cops working undercover Narcotics then resumed a rookie's normal police career. Most of them wound up in districts, walking a beat, until such time as their superiors felt they could be trusted working district wagons.

McFadden and Martinez had been the exception to the general rule. They liked what they were doing, and had been extraordinarily good at it. They had come to be known as "Mutt and Jeff," after the comic book characters, because of their sizes. They made a large number of good arrests, and they had been on the job over a year before they had been burned.

And the way they were burned had set them aside from their peers, too.

The commanding officer of Highway Patrol, Captain "Dutch" Moffitt, a very colorful and popular officer, had been shot to death when, off-duty and in civilian clothing, he had tried to stop an armed robbery of a diner on Roosevelt Boulevard.

The identity of the shooter, a drug addict, was known, and the entire Philadelphia Police Department was looking for him. Mutt and Jeff had run him down on their own time, at the Bridge Street elevated train station. McFadden had literally run the shooter down, chasing him down the elevated train tracks at considerable risk to his own life, until a train had come along, and the shooter had fallen under its wheels.

The two had received their commendations from Mayor Carlucci himself, which had caused their photographs to be plastered all over the front pages of all the newspapers in Philadelphia except the *Ledger*, and thus effectively burning them from further duty as undercover narcs.

It wouldn't have been fair, under those circumstances, to send the two of them out to a district to turn off fire hydrants in the summer, transport prisoners, and do the other things that other rookies with an out-of-the-Academy undercover narcotics assignment usually did after they were burned.

Chief Inspector Dennis V. Coughlin had arranged for their assignment to Highway Patrol, considered the elite of the uniformed force. Normally, police officers couldn't even apply for transfer to Highway unless they had at least five very good years on the job elsewhere.

They'd taken the examination for detective as soon as they were eligible. Martinez had placed two spots below Matt Payne, and McFadden two spots above the cutoff point at the bottom on the rankings.

They had to be considered outstanding young police officers, Staff Inspector Weisbach thought. And while there was no question in his mind that they were both straight arrows, there was something very disturbing to him in their matter-of-fact acceptance that it was perfectly acceptable — if admittedly illegal — police procedure to take drugs from evidence with the intention of using them to pay informers. That the end, so to speak, justified the means.

He was not morally outraged — he had been a policeman too long for that — but it bothered him.

"You think something like that happened, McFadden?" he asked.

"I don't think anybody, any dirty cop, starts out by saying, 'Fuck it, today I start being dirty.' They have to have some reason, something that makes it all right. Tell themselves, for example, 'Just this one time, when I make this car payment, that'll be the end of it. I'll never do it again.' "

"If you're right, and I think you may be, that doesn't explain how the whole Five Squad went bad," Weisbach said.

"Are we sure they're all dirty?" Martinez asked.

"If they're not all actually involved," Washington said, "I find it difficult to accept that anyone on Five Squad is not fully aware of what the others are doing."

"Cops don't snitch on other cops?" McFadden replied.

Washington nodded.

"Not unless their option is, their own innocence aside, going down with the others," Tony Harris said. "Maybe the way to get into this is to find the one guy — if there is one — who is not dirty."

"How do we find him, Tony?" Weisbach asked.

"Easy. He's the one who doesn't have money he shouldn't have," Harris said.

"Well, that's where we're going to begin. With money," Weisbach said. "We're going to see if anybody on the Five Squad has been spending — or saving — more money than seems reasonable on what the department is paying him. Frankly, I would be surprised if we can quickly, or easily, come up with something. If, on the first go-around, we can find anything suspicious at all."

"I don't understand, Inspector," Matt Payne said.

"I think one of the things we all have to keep in mind, Payne, is that although Internal Affairs hasn't been given this job specifically, that doesn't mean they're incompetent, or stupid. They're always looking for signs of unusual affluence, and I would suspect they look closest at cops in jobs where taking bribes, or doing something else illegal, would be more likely. I'm sure they routinely check Narcotics people, is what I'm saying. And they didn't find anything suspicious, or else they would have started their own investigation. Chief Coughlin tells me Internal Affairs was not conducting any kind of a specific investigation of anybody in Narcotics before we got this job.

"What I think that could mean is — presuming

some members of Five Squad are dirty — that they are also too smart to go out and buy a new Buick in their own name, or a condo at the shore, or put money in their own bank account. You still with me?"

"Yes, sir."

"Well, we — and by 'we' I mean McFadden and Jesus and Tiny — are going to go through the motions of looking for unexplained amounts of money. I expect a thorough job. I would be delighted if they don't find unexplainable money and prove me wrong. Call that the first go-around. And while they're doing that, Payne, you're going to come up with a data base of names of people in whose names Buicks and condos, et cetera, could be bought. Still with me?"

"No, sir. Sorry."

"Relatives. Friends. A brother-in-law. You want to buy a condo at the shore and you don't want to attract Internal Affairs attention, so you give your brother-in-law or your uncle Charley the money, and he buys the condo at the shore. Or you put the money in his bank account. Got it?"

"Where do I start?"

"Start with personnel records. Sergeant Sandow can set that up for you. At night, Elliot. I don't want it to get out that somebody from Special Operations or Ethical Affairs is checking personnel records."

"Yes, sir," Sergeant Sandow said.

"That'll give us some names to start with," Weisbach went on. "I don't want to start ringing doorbells until we have to. We can't afford to have somebody say, 'Hey, Charley, there was a cop here asking questions about you.' "

"Yes, sir," Payne said.

"Your first job, though, Payne, is the tapes. We need them transcribed, the sooner the better. Sandow will see that everybody gets a copy. Then I want everybody, individually, to try to make sense of them. Then we'll get together and brainstorm them. I want a brainstorm session every day or so. We all have to know what everybody else is doing, and maybe somebody will be able to make sense out of something the other guy doesn't understand."

He looked around the room.

"Any questions?"

No one had any questions.

Seven

When, accompanied by a discreet ping, one of the buttons on his telephone lit up, a look of mingled annoyance and resignation flickered on and off the face of Brewster Cortland Payne II.

The telephone would not have, as he thought of it, pinged, had not Mrs. Irene Craig, his silver-haired, stylish, fiftyish secretary, been quite sure he would want to take the call. Irene had been his secretary — and confidante and friend — from the moment he had joined his father's law firm fresh from law school. She had been the first employee of B. C. Payne, Lawyer, when he had started out on his own, and their law offices had been two small and dark rooms in a run-down building on South Tenth Street.

The law offices of Mawson, Payne, Stockton, McAdoo & Lester now occupied all of the eleventh floor and most of the twelfth floor of the Philadelphia Savings Fund Society Building on Market Street, east of Broad, and as befitted the executive secretary to the managing partner of what had arguably become Philadelphia's most prestigious law firm, Mrs. Craig's annual compensation exceeded that of seventy percent of the lawyers in Philadelphia.

She had other duties, of course, but she — quite correctly — regarded her primary function as the management of her employer's time, which included putting only those telephone calls through to him that she believed he not only would want to, but should, deal with himself.

A half hour before, she had been asked to bring him a pot of coffee and then to see that he wasn't disturbed. Under that circumstance, Mr. Payne knew Mrs. Craig would normally put through only a call from the President of the United States offering to nominate him for the position of chief justice of the United States Supreme Court, or from his wife. Everybody else would be asked if he could return their call.

He picked up the telephone.

"Brewster Payne," he said.

"Sorry to bother you," Mrs. Craig said, "but Armando C. Giacomo, Esquire, is on the line, begging for a brief moment of your time."

"The Colonel's not here?"

"I tried that. Manny wants to speak with you."

The Colonel was J. Dunlop Mawson, Esq., the other founding partner of Mawson, Payne, Stockton, McAdoo & Lester, who had served as a lieutenant colonel, Judge Advocate General's Corps, U.S. Army, and loved the sound of that rank.

It was arguable whether the Colonel or Manny Giacomo was the most successful criminal lawyer in Philadelphia. Giacomo & Giacomo — the second Giacomo was his son, Armando C. Giacomo III — was a thirty-plus-attorney law firm with its own building on South 9th Street that did little else but criminal law.

The elder Giacomo — a slight, lithe, dapper, fifty-year-old who wore what little was left of his

hair plastered to the sides of his tanned skull —
was very good, and consequently, very expensive.
Like Colonel J. Dunlop Mawson, he had a well-
earned reputation for defending, most often successfully and invariably with great skill, people
charged with violation of the whole gamut of
criminal offenses. His clients in criminal proceed-
ings were seldom ordinary criminals, however, for
the very good reason that ordinary criminals seldom had any money.

The difference between them was that from the
beginning it had been understood between the
Colonel and Brewster Payne that their firm would
not represent the mob — as often called the Mafia
— under any circumstances, and Giacomo often
did.

Giacomo, himself the son of a lawyer and
whose family had been in Philadelphia from the
time of the Revolution, was a graduate of the
University of Pennsylvania and the Yale School
of Law. He had flown Corsairs as a naval aviator
in the Korean War. He could have had a law
practice much like that of Mawson, Payne, Stockton, McAdoo & Lester's, which drew most of its
clientele from the upper echelons of industry,
banks, insurance companies, and from familial
connections.

Manny Giacomo had elected, instead, to become a criminal lawyer, and had become known
(unfairly, Payne thought, since mobsters were
only a small fraction of his clients) as the mob's
lawyer. Payne had come to believe — he knew
Giacomo's personal ethics were impeccable —
that Giacomo represented the mob primarily be-

cause they had the financial resources to pay him, but also because he really believed that an accused was entitled to the best legal representation he could get.

Giacomo was also held in high regard by most police officers, primarily because he represented, *pro bono publico,* police officers charged with police brutality and other infractions of the law.

Payne reached for one of the telephones on his desk and pushed a flashing button, aware that he was doing so for the same reason Mrs. Craig had put the call through: curiosity why Manny Giacomo wanted to speak to him, rather than the Colonel.

"Armando, how are you?" Payne said.

"Thank you for taking my call, Brewster."

"Don't I always take your calls?"

"No, I don't think you do. Sometimes, frankly, when Mrs. Craig tells me you just stepped out of the office, I suspect that you're at your desk and just don't want to talk to me."

"You don't really believe that, do you, Armando? Isn't that the tactic of putting someone on the defensive?"

Giacomo laughed. "Did it work?"

"To a degree. But it also heightened my instincts of self-preservation. What are you about to try to talk me into, Armando, that you already know I would rather not do?"

"I need a personal favor, Brewster."

"Personal? Or professional?"

"Truth to tell, a little of each."

"My curiosity is piqued. Go on."

"I represent a gentleman named Vincenzo Savarese."

"A 'gentleman' named Vincenzo Savarese? If that's the case, your Mr. Savarese is not the same chap who immediately came to my mind."

Silver-haired, sixty-four-year-old Vincenzo Savarese was the head of the Philadelphia mob.

"Mr. Savarese, *my* Mr. Savarese," Giacomo said, "has never been convicted, in any court, of any offense against the peace and dignity of the Commonwealth of Pennsylvania or any of the other United States of America."

"Possibly he has a very good lawyer."

"I've heard that suggested," Giacomo said.

Payne chuckled.

"What do you want, Armando?"

"Mr. Savarese would be very grateful if you could spare him a few minutes, no more than five, of your time."

"He wants to talk to me?" Payne asked, incredulously. "What about?"

"What Mr. Savarese hopes is that you will give him five minutes of your time, in person."

"He wants to come here?"

"He would be grateful if you would permit him to do so."

"What does he want?"

"He would prefer to discuss that with you in person."

"What the hell is going on, Armando?"

"Mr. Savarese would like to ask a personal favor of you."

"What kind of a personal favor?" Payne asked, just a little sharply.

146

There was a perceptible pause before Giacomo replied.

"It has to do with your daughter," Giacomo said.

"My daughter?" Payne asked, genuinely surprised, and then, without giving Giacomo time to reply, asked another question. "Is he there with you?"

"Yes, as a matter of fact, he is."

"I presume your client is aware that I do not accept criminal cases?"

There was another pause before Giacomo replied.

"Mr. Savarese has asked me to say that this is a personal matter and has nothing to do with the law."

"But it has something to do with my daughter?" Payne asked, rhetorically. "And when would he like to come see me?"

"Right now, if that would be convenient," Giacomo replied immediately. "For no more than five minutes."

Now there was a pause before Payne replied.

"I'm giving you the benefit of the doubt, Armando, based on our past dealings."

"But you will see Mr. Savarese?" Giacomo asked.

"You want to come right now? You are coming with him, Armando?"

"Yes. And yes."

"Come ahead," Payne said.

Payne replaced the telephone in its cradle, shrugged, and then pushed the button that would cause Mrs. Craig's telephone to tinkle.

147

She didn't answer.

She put her head in the door.

"You want me to find the Colonel?"

"I don't care what he's doing, I want him in here with me."

"Very curious," she said.

"She said, in massive understatement," Payne said.

When Mrs. Irene Craig pushed open the door to Brewster Cortland Payne's office to admit Armando C. Giacomo, Esq., and Mr. Vincenzo Savarese, Mr. Payne, who was behind his desk, stood up. So did Colonel J. Dunlop Mawson, a slim, dignified fifty-six-year-old, who had been seated in a green leather armchair to one side of a carved English (circa 1790) coffee table.

"Good morning, Counselor," Giacomo said, walking to Payne with his hand extended. "Thank you for receiving us on such short notice."

"Hello, Armando," Payne said, and took the hand.

Giacomo crossed to Mawson. He did not seem surprised to find him in Payne's office.

"It's always a pleasure to see you, Colonel," he said. "How nice to bump into you, so to speak, like this."

"It's always a pleasure to see you, Armando," Mawson said.

"Gentlemen, may I introduce Mr. Vincenzo Savarese?" Giacomo said.

Savarese was slight, and had very pale, almost translucent skin. His eyes were prominent and intelligent, and he was dressed in a conservative, nearly black single-breasted, vested suit.

This man is a thug, Payne thought, *and if the stories are true, a murderer by his own hand when he was younger — and in many other ways a criminal. I don't want to forget that.*

Savarese crossed first to Payne.

"I am in your debt, Mr. Payne, for receiving me under these circumstances."

He put out his hand. Payne took it and was surprised at how fragile and soft it was.

Didn't I hear someplace that he is an accomplished violinist?

"Colonel Mawson and I were having a cup of coffee," Payne said, gesturing toward the coffee table and the green leather furniture. "May I offer you a cup?"

"Thank you, no," Savarese said. "I don't want to take any more of your and Colonel Mawson's time than I have to."

"How may I be of service, Mr. Savarese?" Payne asked after Savarese had lowered himself gingerly onto the couch.

"I hope you will believe me that I would not have troubled you if it was not absolutely necessary," Savarese said. "May I get directly to the point?"

"Please do," Payne said.

"I come to you as a father and grandfather who needs help he cannot get elsewhere for his daughter and granddaughter."

"Go on," Payne said.

"My daughter is grown, a married woman, married to . . . Her husband is Randolph Longwood, of Bala Cynwyd. Perhaps you are famil-

149

iar with the name?"

"The builder?" Colonel Mawson asked.

"Yes, the builder. I think I should say that I have no business relationship of any kind with my son-in-law."

"You know Randy Longwood, Brew," Mawson said. "He belongs to Rose Tree Hunt."

"Of course," Payne said, a little uncomfortably, and more than a little surprised that the identity of Longwood's father-in-law had escaped the Rose Tree Hunt Club Membership Committee. He had had trouble getting Colonel J. Dunlop Mawson past it, as they had had questions about the suitability for membership of a lawyer practicing criminal law.

"My daughter has a daughter," Savarese went on, "who has recently suffered some sort of emotional shock."

Payne looked at him but said nothing.

"The nature of which we really don't know," Savarese continued. "Except that, whatever it was, it was quite severe. She is currently hospitalized at University Hospital. Her family physician had her admitted, and arranged for her to be attended by Dr. Aaron Stein."

"Stein is a fine . . ." — Payne stopped himself just in time from saying 'psychiatrist' — "physician."

"So I understand," Savarese said. "He has recommended that my granddaughter be seen by Dr. Payne."

"Stein and my daughter are friends," Payne offered. "That's how I came to meet him."

They are friends, Payne thought. *But that's now.*

150

It used to be Humble Student sitting at the feet of the Master.

Stein was as old as he was. Amy had originally gone to University Hospital thrilled at the chance to work with him, to learn from him. They had — surprising the psychiatric fraternity; Stein had a reputation for holding most fellow psychiatrists as fools — become friends and ultimately colleagues, and Payne knew that Stein had even proposed a joint private practice to Amy, which she had declined, for reasons Payne had not understood.

"So he told my daughter," Savarese said. "But apparently, that friendship hasn't been enough to convince Dr. Payne to see my granddaughter."

Stein sends Amy a patient and she turns her — which means Dr. Stein, her guru — down? That sounds a bit odd.

"I don't really see, Mr. Savarese, what this has to do with me," Payne said.

I know damned well what it has to do with me. He wants me to go to Amy, who certainly had her reasons to refuse to see the granddaughter, and ask her to reconsider.

It's absolutely none of my business. Amy would first be amazed, and then, justifiably, more than a little annoyed that I was putting my nose into her practice. Particularly in a case like this.

Or is it my fault? Amelia Payne, M.D., Fellow of the American College of Psychiatry, is also Amy Payne, loving daughter of Brewster C. Payne, and has heard, time and time again, his opinions of organized crime and its practitioners. It is unlikely, but not impossible, that Amy turned down this girl either

151

because of me, or because she doesn't want to get involved with anyone involved with the mob.

"My granddaughter is very ill, Mr. Payne," Savarese said. "Otherwise, I would not involve myself in this. Neither Dr. Seaburg, her family physician, nor Dr. Stein, is aware of our relationship. But I love her, and my daughter, and so, as one father to another, I am willing to beg for help for her."

"You want me to speak to my daughter, is that it?"

"I am begging you to do so," Savarese said simply.

Where are we? Amy has declined to see this girl for reasons that have nothing to do with me — he let me off the hook on that, when he said neither the family physician nor Dr. Stein knows he's the girl's grandfather — or with Savarese.

And the girl, obviously, should not be punished for the sins of the grandfather in any event. And in this case, he is the grandfather, not the Mafia don.

"Will you excuse me for a moment, please?" Payne said, and walked out of his office, past Mrs. Craig's desk, across the corridor and into Colonel J. Dunlop Mawson's office.

"I need the Colonel's office a moment, Janet," he said to Mawson's secretary.

He went into Mawson's office, sat on his red leather couch, and pulled the telephone to him.

It took him nearly five minutes to get Amy on the line, and when she came on the line, there was worry and concern in her voice.

"Daddy? They said it was important?"

"Indulge me for a moment, Amy," he said.

"I'm always afraid you're calling to tell me Matt got himself shot again," she said, her relief evident in her voice.

"As far as I know, the only danger Matt faces at the moment is from the understandably irate father of the girl he took from Chad Nesbitt's birthday party and who has not called home since," Payne said.

There was a short chuckle, and then — now with a tone of impatience in her voice — she asked: "What's important, then, Daddy? I'm really up to my ass in work."

"Did Dr. Stein send you a patient, a young woman, by the name of Longwood?"

"Aaron sends me a lot of patients, or tries to, but that name doesn't ring a bell. Why do you ask?"

"Aaron"? It wasn't that long ago when she reverentially called him "Doctor Stein."

And: We are no longer Daddy Dear and Daughter Darling. That was The Doctor putting A Nosy Lawyer in his place.

"Her grandfather is in my office," Payne said.

"Wait a minute," Amy said. "Now I remember the name. Cynthia Longwood. A Bala Cynwyd maiden who had a traumatic experience with her boyfriend. I told Aaron, sorry, no, I have a lapful of really sick people. How did you get involved in this? Is her grandfather a client?"

"No. He's not. Her grandfather is Vincenzo Savarese."

"The gangster?"

"That has been alleged."

"Is this important to you, Daddy?"

153

"I don't really know how to answer that. He came here — Armando Giacomo brought him — which must have been difficult for both of them, and appealed to me as a father. I thought the decent thing to do was call you."

"Where is she?"

"University Hospital."

"Okay, I'll see her," Amy said simply.

"Thank you."

"It would be dishonest of me to say 'you're welcome,' " Amy said. "What this is is pure curiosity. I wonder why Aaron didn't tell me who she was?"

"I don't think Dr. Stein knows who her grandfather is."

"Got to run, Daddy," Amy said, and the line went dead.

Payne returned to his office.

"I've just spoken to my daughter, Mr. Savarese," he said. "She will see your granddaughter."

Vincenzo Savarese rose slowly from the couch and walked to Payne. He put out his hand, and when Payne put out his, held it with both hands.

There are tears in his eyes!

"I am very much in your debt, Mr. Payne," Savarese said.

"Not at all."

"I am very much in your debt, Mr. Payne," Savarese repeated. "And now I will not take any more of your valuable time."

Savarese walked to Colonel J. Dunlop Mawson, politely shook his hand, and then walked out of the office.

154

"I owe you a big one, Brewster," Armando C. Giacomo said softly, winked at Payne, and followed Savarese out.

Walter Davis, a tall, well-built, nearly handsome man in his middle forties, had, while taking luncheon at the Rittenhouse Club, what he considered to be a splendid idea. Actually, it was the second time he had the same idea, and now he wondered why he hadn't followed up on it before.

Davis, who was the Special Agent in Charge of the Philadelphia Office of the Federal Bureau of Investigation, was not a voting member of the Rittenhouse Club. By virtue of his office, however, he enjoyed all the privileges of membership. Similar *ex officio* memberships were made available to certain other public servants — the mayor; the admiral commanding the Philadelphia Navy Yard; the police commissioner; the president of the University of Pennsylvania, et cetera — highly successful practitioners of their professions whom the membership felt would, had they been in the private sector, not only have been put up for membership but would have been able to afford it.

It was said that full membership in the Rittenhouse Club was something like Commodore Vanderbilt's yacht: if you had to ask how much it cost, you couldn't afford it.

Davis did not often use the Rittenhouse Club's facilities, which included an Olympic-size swimming pool, a fully equipped gymnasium in addition to its bar, lounge, and dining facilities. For one thing, it was expensive. For another, Davis was a shade uneasy about taking anything for nothing.

He tried to limit his visits to those that, at least, had a connection with the FBI. A monthly luncheon with Police Commissioner Taddeus Czernich, for example, was usually on his schedule. There were exceptions, of course. When Mrs. Davis was climbing the walls about something, dinner in the elegance of the Rittenhouse Dining Room — the only room in the building where the gentle sex was welcome — did wonders to calm her down.

And today was another exception. Andrew C. Tellman, Esq. — known in their days at the University of Michigan Law School as "Randy Andy" — was in town from Detroit and had called suggesting they get together.

Randy Andy was now a senior partner — he had sent Davis the engraved announcement — of the enormous Detroit law firm he had joined right out of law school, when Davis had gone to Quantico to the FBI Academy.

The stiff price of taking Randy Andy to lunch at the Rittenhouse seemed justified, as sort of a statement that he hadn't done so badly himself, and the proof of that seemed to have come immediately.

"Oh, you belong to the Rittenhouse, do you?" Randy Andy had asked when Davis had suggested "one-ish at the Rittenhouse."

Davis had taken this further, arriving at the club on Rittenhouse Square a few minutes after 12:30. He wanted Randy Andy to have to ask the porter — a master of snobbery — to ask for him, and then be led into the oak-paneled lounge where he would be sitting at one of the small tables.

"I'm expecting a guest," he said to the porter, a dignified black man in his sixties.

"Yes, sir. And who are you, sir?"

"Walter Davis."

"Ah, yes, Mr. Davis. And your guest's name, Mr. Davis?"

"Tellman. Andrew C. Tellman."

"You'll be in the lounge, Mr. Davis?"

"Yes."

"I'll take care of it, sir," the porter said.

He then went to a large board behind his porter's stand. On it were listed, alphabetically, the names of the three-hundred-odd members of the Rittenhouse Club. Beside each name was an inch-long piece of brass, which could be slid back and forth in a track. When the marker was next to the member's name, this indicated he was on the premises; when away from it, that he was not.

He moved the piece of brass to indicate that Davis, W. was now on the premises.

Davis examined the board. The names listed represented the power structure of Philadelphia. And their children. Both Nesbitt, C. III and Nesbitt, C. IV had small brass plates. As did Payne, B. and Payne, M.

Davis knew Payne, B. only by reputation, that of a founding partner of the most prestigious law firm in Philadelphia, Mawson, Payne, Stockton, McAdoo & Lester.

Payne, M. he had met. Payne, M. was a policeman. Davis had once taken Inspector Peter Wohl to lunch. They had gone in Wohl's car, which had been driven by a Philadelphia police officer — Payne — in plainclothes. Officer Payne had played straight man to Wohl, while Wohl vented his annoyance at being kept waiting for Davis with "witty" remarks, and by taking him to a closet-size Italian greasy spoon in South Philadelphia for lunch, instead of to the elegant Ristorante Alfredo in Center City.

Davis had subsequently learned, from Isaiah J. Towne, his ASAC (Assistant Special Agent in Charge) for counterintelligence, just who Payne was. Not only that he was Brewster Cortland Payne's son, or that he was the policeman who had, in Towne's somewhat admiring description, "blown the brains of the Northeast Serial Rapist all over the inside of his van with his service revolver," but why he had become a policeman instead of following in his father's prestigious footsteps in the practice of law.

Towne, a tall, hawk-featured, thirty-nine-year-old balding Mormon, who took his religion seriously and who had once told Davis, dead serious, that he regarded the Communists as the Antichrist, was in charge of what were called, somewhat confusingly, FBIs. The acronym stood for Full Background Investigation. FBIs were run before the issuance of federal security clearances, and before young men were commissioned into one of the Armed Forces.

An FBI had been run on Matthew Mark Payne during his last year at the University of Pennsylvania. He had then been enrolled in the USMC Platoon Leaders' Program, which would see him commissioned a second lieutenant on his graduation.

At the last minute, young Payne had failed the precommissioning physical, and had not gone into the Marine Corps.

Towne's FBI on him, however, had already been run, and it had provided some very interesting details about Payne, Matthew Mark. For one thing, he was a very wealthy young man, largely because of an investment program established for him at age three and administered — and generously contributed to — by his father thereafter.

It also revealed that he was not Brewster Cortland Payne II's biological son. He was the biological son of Sergeant John Francis Xavier Moffitt, of the Philadelphia Police Department, who had been shot to death answering a silent burglar alarm call months before his only child was born.

The Widow Moffitt had gone to secretarial school and found employment with Lowerie, Tant, Foster, Pedigill and Payne, a top Philadelphia legal firm, as a typist.

Shortly thereafter, she had met the just-widowered Brewster Cortland Payne II, the son of the founding partner — and heir apparent to the Payne real estate fortune. Mrs. Brewster Cortland Payne II had been killed in an automobile accident returning from their summer home in the Pocono Mountains, leaving her husband and two infant children.

Brewster Cortland Payne II's reaction to his father's description of Patricia Moffitt as a gold-digging Irish trollop and his absence from their

159

wedding had been to resign from Lowerie, Tant, Foster, Pedigill and Payne and strike out on his own.

Shortly after the birth of their first child — which coincided with the death of Chadwick Thomas Nesbitt, Jr., the chairman of the board of Nesfoods International; the assumption by Chadwick Thomas Nesbitt III, Brewster Payne's best friend, to that position; and the retention of what was then Payne & Mawson as Nesfood International's Counsel — Brewster Cortland Payne went to his wife and announced that since he loved Matt as well as his other children, it seemed only logical that he adopt him, and requested her permission to do so.

Matthew Mark Payne's rejection by the Marine Corps had been shortly followed by the death of his uncle, his biological father's brother, another policeman, Captain Richard C. "Dutch" Moffitt. Moffitt, a colorful character, who had been the commanding officer of the Highway Patrol, had, off-duty, walked in on a holdup of the Waikiki Diner on Roosevelt Boulevard, and been shot to death trying to talk the robber, a drug addict, into handing over his .22-caliber pistol.

When Matthew Mark Payne had applied for appointment as a Philadelphia police officer immediately thereafter — the only graduate, *summa cum laude,* of the University of Pennsylvania to do so in anyone's memory — it was generally agreed both that it was understandable — Matt's masculinity, challenged by rejection by the Marines, would be restored by his becoming a policeman; and he probably had some childish idea

160

about getting revenge for both his biological father and his uncle — and that his police career would end just as soon as he came to his senses.

When he surprised everyone by lasting through the rigors of the Police Academy, Chief Inspector Dennis V. Coughlin, who had graduated from the Police Academy with his best friend, John Francis Xavier Moffitt — who had knocked at Patty Moffitt's door to tell her, "Honey, Jack just had some real bad luck," and who had no intention of knocking on her door again to tell her Jack's boy had been shot — arranged to have him assigned as administrative assistant to Inspector Peter Wohl.

He had been on that job less than six months when, off-duty, he spotted the van used by the Northwest Serial Rapist, attempted to question the driver, nearly lost his life when the driver attempted to run him down with the van, and then shot him in the head.

Not quite a year after that, the Philadelphia Police Department planned and executed a massive operation intended to cause the arrest without firing a shot of a gang of a dozen armed robbers on warrants charging them with murder in connection with the robbery of Goldblatt's Department Store in South Philadelphia.

Officer Payne's role in this meticulously planned, theoretically foolproof operation was to "escort" — keep him (and incidentally himself) out of any possible danger — Michael J. "Mickey" O'Hara, the Pulitzer prize–winning *Philadelphia Bulletin* police reporter. They were to wait in an alley a safe distance from the building in which the robbers were known to be until the arrests had been successfully accomplished.

One of the robbers, wielding a .45 Colt automatic pistol, appeared where he wasn't supposed to be, in the "safe alley," and let off a volley of shots. One of them ricocheted, grazing Payne in the forehead. He was able to draw his revolver and return fire.

That evening's *Philadelphia Bulletin* carried an "Exclusive Photo By Michael J. O'Hara" that showed Officer Payne, blood streaming down his face — from a wound that looked a great deal worse than it was — standing, pistol in hand, over the felon he had fatally wounded in a shoot-out.

Ninety percent of police officers reach retirement without once having been forced to use their pistols. A cop who, in less than two years on the job, finds himself involved in *two* good shootings is obviously something out of the ordinary.

No one was surprised when Officer Payne passed the examination for Detective on the first attempt. He was, of course, a *summa cum laude* university graduate who had little trouble with the examination. He ranked second when the examination results were posted, and was promoted shortly thereafter.

It was said, however, that Mayor Carlucci would have had him promoted if it had been necessary to send two chief inspectors into the examination room with him to show him which end of the pencil to use, and otherwise be helpful.

Neither were many people in the Philadelphia Police Department surprised to hear that Mayor Carlucci had "suggested" that Detective Payne be reassigned to Special Operations after a very short assignment to one of the detective divisions.

Mayor Carlucci was aware of the value of good public relations.

What Walter Davis thought when he saw Payne, M. on the membership board of the Rittenhouse Club was first that Payne was almost certainly a regular rather than nonvoting, *ex officio* member, and second that the FBI was always looking for outstanding young men to join its ranks.

He had, he realized, had that thought before.

Why didn't I follow through with it then?

His lunch with Randy Andy Tellman (turtle soup, London broil, and asparagus) went well until he called for the check to sign. Tellman snatched it from his hand and scrawled his initials on it.

"I didn't know you belonged," Davis blurted.

"Out-of-town member," Randy Andy told him. "The firm picks it up."

As soon as he returned to his office, Davis told his secretary to ask ASAC Towne if he could spare him a minute.

Towne answered the summons immediately.

"Correct me when I'm wrong, Isaiah," Davis told him. "The subject is Detective Matthew Payne of the Philadelphia Police Department."

"Yes, sir?"

"To the best of your recollection, nothing came up in your FBI that would disqualify him for the Bureau?"

"No, sir."

"Including his physical condition? What caused

the Marines to reject him?"

"It was some minor eye problem, as I recall, sir. I don't think the Bureau even looks at that sort of thing."

"And I think we have an agent to whom it was suggested that getting close to Detective Payne might be a good thing to do?"

"Yes, sir. Special Agent Jack — John D. — Matthews."

"Refresh me. How did Matthews come to meet Detective Payne?"

"I believe it was in connection with the vice presidential threat," Towne said. "We sent Matthews over to liaise with the Secret Service. The Special Operations Division of the Philadelphia Police Department was providing the Secret Service with bodies to help find that lunatic. I believe they became friendly while that was going on."

"And, if memory serves, despite Agent Matthews's best efforts, we have learned virtually nothing, via Detective Payne, of interesting things going on within the Philadelphia Police Department that we would not have learned of through other channels?"

"I'm afraid that's true, sir."

"That speaks well for Detective Payne, wouldn't you say, Isaiah?"

"From the viewpoint of the Philadelphia Police Department, yes, sir, I would say it does."

"It has occurred to me, Isaiah, that Detective Payne might very well have the makings of an outstanding FBI agent. How does that strike you?"

"Absolutely," Isaiah Towne said. "He would bring to the Bureau a level of practical experience —"

Davis cut him off.

"See if Matthews is in the office, please," he said. "If he is, why don't you and I have a little chat with him about recruiting Detective Payne?"

Towne picked up one of the telephones on Davis's desk, pushed the button marked "Duty Officer," learned that Special Agent Matthews was in the office, and told the duty officer to send him to the office of the SAC.

Eight

Detective Matt Payne's concentration was finally broken by the ringing telephone. He muttered a routine obscenity; pulled the dictating machine's headset out of his ears; turned from the typewriter; looked around the office and saw that it was deserted and that it was dark outside; muttered another routine obscenity; glanced at his wristwatch, saw that it was half past seven; muttered a third routine obscenity; and picked up the telephone.

It had been a long, tiring, and not very productive day.

He had been working without interruption on the obscenity-deleted tapes since Weisbach's meeting in the morning.

All he had had to eat all day was a hamburger and a small fries. Jason Washington, who had felt sorry for him, had brought that to him in the middle of the afternoon.

He was nowhere near finished, and at half past four, Sergeant Sandow had informed him he was expected in Personnel in the Roundhouse anytime after half past nine, to go through the records of the men on Five Squad.

"Special Investigation, Detective Payne," Matt said, as courteously as he could manage.

"As an act of Christian charity, your friendly local FBI agent is prepared to spring for supper," his caller said.

"Jack, I'm really up to my ass in work."

"You have to eat," Special Agent Jack Matthews said, reasonably.

"Where are you?"

"At the FOP."

The Fraternal Order of Police Building was on Spring Garden Street, just off North Broad Street. The well-patronized bar was in the basement. Matt could hear bar sounds; Matthews was using the phone on the bar.

"This is social, then, rather than official?"

"A little of each, actually," Matthews said, surprised at the question. "Why did you ask?"

"You're going to deliver a friendly lecture on the criminal penalties provided for interfering with FBI agents, right?"

"What the hell are you talking about?"

"You're right. I have to eat. You said you're paying?"

"Right."

"In that case, since I really deserve it, something expensive. A lobster comes immediately to mind. Does Bookbinder's, the Old Original, on Second Street, make you want to regret your kind offer?"

"Not at all. This feast goes on the expense account."

"So those assholes did report me? I thought they'd be too embarrassed."

"I have no idea what you're talking about."

"Of course you don't. You want to meet me there? Or should I pick you up?"

"I'll meet you there. When can you leave?"

"As soon as I can turn out the lights. I'm starved."

He hung up, looked out the window and saw that it was not only dark but raining, and went to what had been the classroom's cloakroom for his trench coat. When he picked it up, there was something heavy in the pocket. He fished it out. It was the small tape recorder that had come with the dictation system he had bought to transcribe the Kellog tapes, still in its box with compartments for the device, batteries, and three tape cassettes.

He started to put it on his desk, but changed his mind when he thought it might be useful to transcribe information at the Roundhouse. He put it back in the trench coat's pocket, turned off the lights, and left.

"If you had a decent paying job, you wouldn't have to put in so much overtime," Special Agent Matthews, a tall, muscular, fair-skinned man in his late twenties, said to Detective Payne when Matt slid onto a stool beside him in the bar.

"Why do I suspect there is something significant in that remark?" Matt said. "What are you drinking?"

"Johnny Walker Black," Matthews said. "Would you like one?"

"You're paying?"

"The Bureau is paying."

"In that case, yes, thank you, I will," Matt said. He caught the bartender's eye and signaled for the same thing. "I will ask why the Bureau is paying later. I would have thought they would be just a little annoyed with me."

"Whatever for? The purpose of this little rendezvous is to point out to you all the nice things that would happen if you joined us."

"You're kidding."

"Not at all. Davis called me into his office and ordered me to wine and dine you with that noble purpose in mind."

Matt chuckled.

"You can tell Mr. Davis what I told the two assholes. One of my best friends is an FBI agent, but I wouldn't want my sister to marry one of them."

"Which two assholes would that be?"

"The two I led on a wild-goose chase up and down the alleys of North Philadelphia."

"FBI agents?" Matthews asked. Matt nodded. "Did they have names?"

Matt called the names from his memory.

"Jernigan and Leibowitz," he said. "Leibowitz seemed to be the brighter of the two."

"Never heard of them," Jack Matthews said. "Why did you lead them on a wild-goose chase?"

"They annoyed me," Matt said.

"Why did they annoy you?"

"They thought I had kidnapped an innocent maiden."

"You don't know any innocent maidens. There may not be an innocent maiden over the age of eleven in Philadelphia. Kidnapped? What the hell are you talking about, Matt? Try starting at the beginning."

"This is really the first time you're hearing this?" Matt asked.

Matthews held up his hands in a gesture of innocence.

"Somewhat reluctantly, I will take you at your word," Matt said, and told him of his encounter with Special Agents Leibowitz and Jernigan.

"We don't have any agents by those names in our office, Matt," Matthews said when Matt had finished. "Are you sure they were FBI agents? Not Treasury, or Secret Ser—"

"They had FBI credentials," Matt shut him off. "Which they shoved close enough under my nose for me to take a good look."

"I don't understand this at all," Matthews said. "And your lady friend was not kidnapped at all?"

"How do you get 'kidnapped at all'? Wouldn't that be like being a little pregnant?"

Matthews chuckled.

"Have you told anyone else about this?" he asked. "Wohl, for example?"

"Not a soul. And especially not Wohl. That would have triggered his 'we must be kind to the FBI' speech."

"I have no idea —"

"Let's get a table and eat," Matt said. "I'm starved. And when I'm finished, I have another couple of hours' work at the Roundhouse, which means I better not have another drink, even if the FBI is paying for it."

"What are you doing?"

"Is that you or the FBI asking?"

"Me."

"Checking some personnel records. It doesn't make me feel like Sherlock Holmes, but it's a dirty job that someone has to do."

Matthews chuckled.

"May I tell Mr. Davis that you have taken his kind offer of employment under consideration?"

"I don't give a damn what you tell him," Matt said. "Let's eat."

Cynthia Longwood took a long time to wake up, and when she did, she had no idea at all where she was. The room was dark.

She became aware first that she was wearing one of those awful hospital gowns that tie down the back and let your fanny hang out. And then, quickly, she realized that she was in a narrow hospital bed with chrome rails to keep you from falling out; and put that together to understand that she was in a hospital room.

She sat up — her muscles seemed stiff and she didn't seem to have much strength — and saw the glow of a cigarette. Someone was in the room with her.

Who? A nurse?

Cynthia let herself fall back on the bed.

The last thing she remembered clearly was being in her own room in Bala Cynwyd. Dr. Seaburg had been there.

Mother called him when I couldn't stop crying.

And he gave me something, a pill. A pill. A pill and then a shot. And told me it would let me sleep.

And then I was in a car, and going downtown. . . .

They must have brought me here.

Dr. Seaburg was here, too. He had some other doctor with him. A nice old man.

My God, what did he give me? I can't seem to

think, and I feel like I just swam across the Atlantic Ocean!

"Are you supposed to be doing that?" Cynthia challenged.

"Doing what?" a female voice near the cigarette glow asked.

"Smoking in here?"

"I didn't think anyone would notice. I'll put it out."

"No!" Cynthia said. "I don't mind. I could use one myself."

A body appeared at the bedside. A female body. Extending a lit cigarette.

"Will you settle for a puff on this?" she asked. "I don't want you falling asleep again with a lit cigarette."

Cynthia had trouble finding the hand holding the cigarette. But finally she got the cigarette to her lips and took a puff.

"You're right," the woman said. "I shouldn't be smoking in here. But it's been a long day, and I'm a nice girl, and I figured, what the hell?"

Cynthia chuckled and took another puff on the cigarette, and in its glow saw that the woman was young, and wore a simple cotton blouse and a skirt, with a sweater over her shoulders.

"Would you like something to drink?" the young woman asked. "There's water and 7-Up."

"Oh, yes, please, 7-Up," Cynthia said.

"Would it bother you if I put the lights on?" the young woman said. "I don't want to spill 7-Up all over you."

"Go ahead," Cynthia said. "Who are you?"

"My name is Amy Payne."

"You're a nurse?"

"No."

"I was wondering where your uniform was," Cynthia said.

The lights came on, painfully bright. It took what seemed to be a long time for her eyes to adjust to them.

When she finally had everything in focus, she saw that Amy — attractive, but no real beauty — was extending a paper cup to her.

Cynthia quickly drank it all, and held out the cup for a refill.

"If you promise not to gulp it down the way you did that one," Amy Payne said. "I don't want you to toss your cookies."

Cynthia chuckled. She liked this woman.

"Funny, that sounded like a nurse talking," she said. "But okay. I promise."

"Not to gulp? Girl Scout's honor?"

"I said I promised," Cynthia said, and added: "Actually, I was a Girl Scout."

"So was I. I hated it."

"Me, too," Cynthia said.

Amy gave her another glass of 7-Up. Cynthia took a sip.

"If you're not a nurse, what are you doing in here?" she asked.

"Actually, I'm a doctor."

"You're putting me on."

"Girl Scout's honor," Amy said.

"I'll be damned."

"Your doctor, if you'd like. Both Dr. Seaburg and Dr. Stein think that might be a good idea."

"Dr. Stein?"

"Little fat fellow. Looks like Santa Claus with a shave. Talks funny."

Cynthia giggled when the description called up the mental image of the doctor who had been with Dr. Seaburg.

"Why do Drs. Seaburg and Stein think it would be a good idea if you were my doctor?"

"I don't know about you, but I always have trouble talking about some things — the female reproductive apparatus, for example, or sex, generally — with a man. With another woman, provided she's not old enough to be my grandmother, it's much easier."

"What makes you think I would want to talk to you? About sex or anything else?"

"I don't know if you would want to or not," Amy said.

"You're a shrink, right?"

"Right. A pretty good one, as a matter of fact."

"You don't look like a shrink."

"Dr. Stein looks like what most people think of when they hear the word 'shrink,' " Amy said. "Wise and kind, et cetera. Would you rather talk to him?"

"I don't really want to talk to anybody."

"You're going to have to talk to somebody, and I think you know that," Amy said. "Maybe I could help. Your call."

"I really don't want to talk to Dr. Seaburg, or the other one."

"Can I take that as a 'yes'? Do you want to give it a shot, see if I can help?"

"God, I don't know. I'm so damned confused."

"When you're damned confused is usually a

174

pretty good time to talk to a shrink," Amy said.

"Let me think about it," Cynthia said.

"Counteroffer," Amy said. "Give me a temporary appointment as your physician until, say, half past eight in the morning."

"Why?"

"Under those circumstances, I can prescribe medicine and offer advice."

"If you were my physician, what medicine would you prescribe?"

"None. No more sedatives. I don't like the side effects — what they gave you really makes you feel like a medicine ball at the end of a long game — and I don't think it's indicated."

"You just have been appointed my temporary physician," Cynthia said. "What's the advice?"

"Two things. First, when they come in here in the morning and ask you how you want your eggs, say 'poached' or 'soft-boiled.' What they do to fried and scrambled eggs around here is obscene."

Cynthia giggled.

"And second?"

"Try to trust me. Whatever's wrong, whatever happened, we can deal with it."

"Oh, shit," Cynthia said. "I really don't . . ."

"That bad, huh?" Amy said.

"Yeah, that bad."

"Okay, we'll talk about it. Now, after a word with the nurse, I'm going home."

"What kind of a word with the nurse?"

"Orders. One, no more sedatives. Two, you have my medical permission to smoke. Not now, in the morning, after that sedative wears off."

"You'll be back in the morning?"

"After you've had your breakfast."

"Okay," Cynthia said, and then said, "What do I call you, 'Doctor'?"

"If you can remember that I'm your doctor, you can call me 'Amy.' I'd like that."

"I don't think I understand that," Cynthia said.

"I don't know about you, Cynthia, but every time I've told one of my friends something I really didn't want anybody else to know, it was all over town by the next day. What you tell me as your doctor goes no further."

"Not even to another doctor? Or my parents?"

"What you tell me goes no further, period."

"I may not tell you anything."

"That's up to you, what you tell me or don't. Okay?"

"Okay," Cynthia said.

Dr. Payne touched Cynthia Longwood's shoulder and walked to the door. She turned off the lights, smiled at Cynthia, and walked out of the room.

When Matt went into Personnel Records at the Roundhouse a few minutes before ten, Sergeant Sandow's contact, a heavy-set civilian, led him into a closet-size office where he had laid out the personnel jackets of the Narcotics Unit's Five Squad.

"I'll stick around until you're finished," the civilian told him, "in case somebody wonders what the lights are doing on in here. But make it quick, will you?"

"Right now, that is the guiding principle of my

176

life," Matt said, and took off his trench coat. He fished the pocket recorder out again, looked at it, shrugged, put batteries and a tape in it, and tested it.

It worked. The question was whether or not it would be quicker to use the machine and the transcribing device, or whether he should just use pencil and a notebook.

He decided in favor of modern technology, sat down at the desk, and started to work his way through the foot-high stack of records in front of him.

It took him more than two hours. Dictating names and addresses into the recorder proved, he thought, much quicker than writing them down would have been; the question remained how long it would take him to transcribe them in the morning.

None of the names and addresses of relatives and references rang any bells, except tangentially. Officer Timothy J. Calhoun of the Five Squad had uncles and aunts and cousins in both Harrisburg and Camp Hill, and was a graduate of Camp Hill High.

It was unlikely that they knew each other, but Miss Susan Reynolds, who had not been kidnapped at all, was from Camp Hill.

What was that bullshit she told Daffy all about, that she was in her room all the time? Her bed had not been slept in. Period. Wherever she was when everybody was looking for her, she wasn't in the Bellvue-Stratford. At least not in her room.

When he left the tiny office, Sandow's civilian was asleep in his chair, and when wakened, not in what could be called a charming frame of mind.

Matt rode the curved elevator down to the lobby and left the building. As he walked up to his car, a scruffy-looking character got out of a beat-up car, took a good look, without smiling, at Matt, then walked toward the Roundhouse.

I know that face, Matt thought. *From where?*

He unlocked the unmarked car and got in.

I've seen that face somewhere, recently.

Like an hour ago!

Officer Timothy J. Calhoun's photograph in his records was a mug shot of a freshly scrubbed, cleanly shaven, crew-cutted inmate of the Police Academy.

He looks like a bum, because undercover guys in Narcotics have to look like bums. When Captain Pekach was a lieutenant in Narcotics, he wore his hair in a pigtail.

I wonder what Calhoun's doing at the Roundhouse at midnight?

Matt pulled the key from the ignition switch and got out of the car in time to see Officer Calhoun enter the Roundhouse.

He walked quickly after him, and had his identification folder in his hand when he entered the building.

He showed it to the corporal on duty.

"The guy who just came in here?" Matt asked.

The corporal jerked his thumb to Matt's right, to the door leading to Central Lockup.

Matt went through the door. It led into sort of a corridor. To his left, on the other side of a glass wall, was the magistrate's court. Here, after being transported to Central Lockup and being booked, prisoners were brought before the magistrate to determine if they could be freed on their own recognizance, on bail, or at all. To his right were several rows of chairs where the prisoner's family, friends, or, for that matter, the general public could watch the magistrate in action.

At the end of the corridor was a locked door with a glass panel leading to the Central Lockup and the booking sergeant's desk.

Matt went and looked through the panel.

A uniform came to the window and indicated with a jerked thumb that he would prefer that Matt go away. Matt showed him his detective's identification, which visibly surprised the uniform, who then moved to open the door.

Matt shook his head, "no."

The uniform shrugged and walked away.

Matt looked into the booking area. Officer Timothy J. Calhoun of the Narcotics Five Squad, now in the company of another scruffy-looking character, whom Matt recognized from the photograph on his records but could not put a name to, was watching the process by which two district uniforms were relieved of responsibility for four prisoners.

Two of the latter were black, and dressed in flashy clothing. The other two were white, and dressed in a manner that suggested to Matt that they had white-collar jobs of some sort; had been out on the town; had decided that acquiring and ingesting one controlled substance or another would add a little excitement to the evening; had been in the process of acquiring same from the black gentlemen, whereupon all four had been busted by members of the Five Squad.

There was nothing else to see.

Matt turned and walked back out of the corridor, then changed direction. He motioned for the corporal behind the plate glass to open the door to the lobby of the Roundhouse. Once inside, he availed himself of the facilities of the gentlemen's rest room, and then finally left the building.

He got back in the unmarked car and backed it out of its parking slot.

As he drove out of the parking lot, Officer Timothy J. Calhoun and the other male Caucasian suspected of also being a police officer attached to the Five Squad of the Narcotics Unit, walked toward him.

He didn't have the headlights on, so there was no blinding light to interfere with Officer Calhoun's view of the driver of the unmarked car. Confirmation that Officer Calhoun recognized him as the man who had been in the parking lot a few minutes earlier seemed to come when Matt glanced in his rearview mirror and saw that Officer Calhoun had stopped en route to his car, turned, and was looking curiously at Matt's car.

On what is that curiosity based? Simply that he remembered seeing me before, and a policeman's mind picks up on things like that? Or because his sensitivity to things like that has been increased because he's a dirty cop?

He almost certainly made this thing as an unmarked car. So what is a young guy doing driving a new unmarked car? Is he going to put that together and decide it's a Special Operations unmarked car? And come up with a suspicion that

Special Operations is watching him?

That would be illogical. There are a hundred other reasons why somebody from Special Operations would be at the Roundhouse at this hour having nothing to do with the Five Squad.

But if I were a dirty cop, I would be a little paranoid.

Did I do something stupid, following him into the Roundhouse? Did he see me looking through the window?

Well, to hell with it. It's done.

Matt turned the headlights on as he left the parking lot, and headed for Rittenhouse Square.

"Who was that in the unmarked car?" Officer Tom Coogan inquired of Officer Timothy Calhoun as soon as they were inside the well-worn Buick Special.

"I just made him," Calhoun said. "Remember the guy that popped the sicko, the serial rapist? Blew his brains out?"

"John Wayne, something like that?"

"Payne. His name is Payne."

"That was him?"

"That was him, I'm sure. That fucking new unmarked car makes me sure. He's one of them hotshots in Special Operations. Every one of them fuckers gets a new car, did you know that?"

"I heard it," Coogan said. "I ran into Charley McFadden — remember him? — at the FOP."

"I remember him, sure. He made detective, didn't he?"

"Him and the spic. Martinez. Mutt and Jeff both made detective, and both of them are in

Special Operations, and both run around in brand-new unmarked cars."

"There's a moral in there, Coogan. Shoot a bad guy, and get yourself promoted."

"Mutt and Jeff didn't *shoot* a bad guy, they tossed him under an elevated train," Coogan replied.

Calhoun laughed.

"What the fuck do they do out there in Special Operations?" he asked.

"Who the fuck knows? They're Carlucci's fair-haired boys. They caught that loony tune who wanted to blow up the Vice President. Shit like that."

"How do you get in Special Operations?"

"Shoot a bad guy, I told you. Get your picture on TV."

"If we shoot one of our bad guys, we'd wind up on charges for violating the fucker's civil rights," Calhoun said.

"Speaking of our bad guys, what did we get?"

"Nothing. Zip," Calhoun said.

"Nothing?"

"The two johns had eighty-five bucks between them," Calhoun explained. "The dinges had a half-dozen bags and three hundred bucks and change. I figured it wasn't worth the risk to take any of it."

"Three hundred bucks is three hundred bucks. A little bit here, a little bit there . . ." Coogan made a little joke.

It went over Calhoun's head.

"Somebody might have thought it strange that the dinges had only a hundred or so," he replied seriously. "And we don't take it all, remember? Don't be so fucking greedy, Coogan."

"Up yours, Calhoun!"

They drove to the Narcotics Unit's office at 22nd Street and Hunting Park Avenue, decided finishing the paperwork could wait until they had a beer, and walked across the street to the Allgood Bar.

It was late, and not shift-change time, and there was hardly anybody in the place. Except, sitting at a table in the rear, a stocky, swarthy man in his late thirties, who raised his bottle of Ortlieb's beer in greeting when he saw them.

Coogan and Calhoun stopped at the bar only long enough to get beers of their own and then walked to his table carrying them.

"What did you do to your face, Calhoun?" Assistant District Attorney Anton C. Phebus asked.

Calhoun touched his face gingerly. Under three days' growth of beard on his right cheek was an angry red bruise.

"There was this guy, six feet six, one of them Zulus," Calhoun said. "Skinny as a rail. I don't think he weighed 130 pounds," Officer Calhoun explained. "I started to put cuffs on him, got one on him, and then he decided he didn't want to be arrested . . ."

He mimed the action, spilling a little beer in the process, of someone suddenly spreading his arms to avoid being handcuffed.

". . . and the loose cuff got me," he finished.

"And what did you do to him?" Phebus asked, chuckling.

"He's gonna sing soprano for a while. You wouldn't believe how strong that skinny fucker was!"

"Maybe he was on something," Phebus suggested.

"Maybe," Calhoun said, considering this. "But I don't think so. He was just strong, is all. And he took me by surprise."

"Aside from that," Phebus chuckled, "how was the arrest?"

"Zip," Coogan offered.

"Zip?" Phebus asked, surprised, and then looked at Calhoun. "Zip, like in zero?"

"You told me to think, I thought," Calhoun said. "What they had wasn't worth the risk."

"Good boy," Phebus said. "There's always another day."

"So you keep saying," Calhoun said.

Phebus looked as if he intended to reply, but changed his mind.

"Two things," he said. "They're going to let me prosecute Leslie, which means I can get —"

"Who's Leslie?" Coogan interrupted.

"The junkie shit who popped Kellog," Calhoun furnished, contemptuously.

"Sorry," Coogan said, flushing, aware he had just said something stupid.

"Which means," Phebus went on, "that I can finally get to listen to what's on Kellog's fucking tapes."

"There's probably nothing on them," Calhoun said. "Kellog wasn't stupid."

"He was covering his ass," Phebus said. "Which means he was scared. People who are scared do stupid things."

"Where are the tapes now?" Coogan asked.

"We have them," Phebus said. "But I just couldn't go to the evidence room and ask for them. Before. Now that I'm prosecuting Leslie, I'll be expected to look at them, listen to them."

Coogan nodded, then said, "You said 'two things.' "

Phebus did not reply directly. He looked at Calhoun and asked, "Calhoun, you planning to go to Harrisburg anytime soon?"

"Should I?"

"Get the wife and kid out of the city, why don't you? Get them a little fresh air out in the country. See your wife's family."

"Right."

"What's going to happen to Leslie?" Coogan asked.

"Probably, I can get him convicted of first-degree murder. He's going away for a while."

"Christ, we ought to give him a medal. He done us a favor," Coogan said.

"Like what?" Phebus asked sarcastically. "Calling all the attention he did to the Five Squad? Letting people listen to those tapes?"

"Kellog won't be making any more tapes," Coogan said. "Will he?"

"Who else is going to listen to those tapes?" Calhoun asked.

"Nobody now, I don't think. Special Operations made copies of them when they were looking for Kellog's shooter."

"You don't think they got anything off them, do you?" Calhoun asked.

"Good question. I don't know."

"We just saw one of those hotshots," Calhoun said. "At the Roundhouse. The one that shot the serial rapist."

"Payne?"

"Yeah."

"What was he doing?"

"Beats the shit out of me. He was in the Roundhouse parking lot. I seen him twice, once when I went into Central Lockup and when I come out."

"He's Inspector Wohl's errand boy," Phebus said. "There's no telling what he could have been doing."

"Maybe he's listening to Kellog's tapes. Maybe he's already listened to Kellog's tapes. Maybe that son of a bitch Kellog said my name on those tapes. Maybe he was watching me," Calhoun said.

"Jesus Christ, just when I think you're getting some smarts," Phebus said, "you start bouncing off the walls. If Special Operations was taking a close look at Five Squad, the word would be out."

"And what if we do hear some word like that?"

"Then we shut down. As simple as that. If we don't do something stupid here, or something stupid in Harrisburg, there's nothing for Special Operations, Internal Affairs, this new thing — what the fuck do they call it? 'Ethical Affairs' — or anybody else to find."

Calhoun didn't reply.

"If Prasko hadn't made that stupid telephone call to Kellog's widow, Calhoun," Phebus went on, "Special Operations wouldn't have been in on this at all. That beat cop would have caught Leslie the way he did, and that would have been the end of it. Nobody would have given a shit what might be on those tapes. Frankly, you and Prasko worry me more than Kellog ever did."

"It's a shame they wasn't both at home when that asshole picked the wrong house to rob," Calhoun said. "Then Prasko wouldn't have had to call to protect all our asses."

"What Prasko did was threaten her life," Phebus said coldly. "He didn't —"

"He told her to keep her mouth shut about what she knew, or thought she knew, about us. What's so wrong about that?"

"Prasko knew Kellog's wife was shacked up with a homicide detective. And he should have known the minute he made a threatening call, she was going to tell her boyfriend, the homicide detective, about it. That was fucking stupid!"

Calhoun looked at him a moment and then shrugged, granting the point.

"Let me worry about protecting our asses," Phebus said. "You stay off the fucking telephone!"

"Watch it," Calhoun said, nodding his head toward the door.

Sergeant Patrick J. Dolan of the Narcotics Unit had entered Allgood's Bar.

He walked directly to their table.

"What do you know good, Tony?" he said to Phebus. "What are you doing in here? Homesick for Narcotics?"

"How are you, Pat?" Phebus said, offering him his hand.

187

"Say hello to Gladys for me," Dolan said.

"I'll do that."

Dolan turned to Coogan and Calhoun.

"You two are supposed to do the paper *before* you start bending your elbows," Dolan said.

"Give us a break, Sergeant," Calhoun said.

"Break, my ass. Finish your beer and come across the street."

"Right," Calhoun said.

"See you around, Tony," Calhoun said as he got to his feet.

Sergeant Dolan walked to the door, waited there until Coogan had finished his beer, then led Coogan and Calhoun across Hunting Park Avenue and into the Narcotics Unit.

Nine

Special Agent Jack Matthews, who had been sitting in one of the two armchairs in the outer office of SAC Walter Davis, got to his feet when Davis walked in, in the process of taking off his topcoat.

Davis believed that an important key to leadership was to have one's subordinates believe that you were concerned about them, and that a splendid way to do this was, under certain circumstances, to address them by their Christian and/or nicknames.

Yesterday, he could not have told you this nice young man's first name if his life depended on it. He remembered it now, most likely because of his late-afternoon conversation with him vis-à-vis the recruitment of Detective Payne of the Philadelphia Police Department.

"Good morning, Jack," Davis said with a smile.

"Good morning, sir."

"You're waiting to see me, Jack?" Davis asked, now just a shade annoyed. He had told Matthews to let him know what happened, but he hadn't really requested a first-thing-in-the-morning report, before he'd even had a chance to have a cup of coffee.

"If you can spare me a few minutes, sir."

"A *few*, Jack," Davis said, waving at him to indicate he had his permission to follow him into his office.

189

Davis went behind his desk, took a quick glance at his In basket to see if anything interesting had come in overnight, then glanced up at Matthews.

"Have a seat, Jack," he said. "Tell me, how did it go?"

"Well, sir, Payne doesn't seem to be very interested in joining the Bureau. But . . ."

"If at first you don't succeed, et cetera. What exactly did he say?"

Matthews smiled uneasily.

"I don't think you want to know, sir," he said.

"Of course I want to know. What exactly did he say, Jack?"

"He said that some of his best friends are FBI agents, but he wouldn't want his sister to marry one."

My God, what an insulting, outrageous thing to say! With obvious racial overtones!

"That remark, Matthews, was in particularly poor taste, wouldn't you say?"

"Sir, the way he said it . . . sort of took the bite out of it. But . . ."

"Well, perhaps it's a good thing this attitude of his came out so soon. There is no room in the Bureau for racial prejudice, Matthews, no room for a racist."

"Sir, Payne isn't a racist. I know that."

"How do you know that?"

"Well, I know him, sir. And he's very close to a sergeant named Jason Washington. . . ."

"I know Washington. Unless I'm wrong, he's Payne's supervisor."

"Yes, sir, he is. But Payne is also very close to Officer Lewis, who is also black."

"I believe the preferred term is 'African American,' Matthews," Davis said. "And I am personally acquainted with an African American lieutenant named Lewis, who told me his son is also a policeman. Would that, do you think, be the Officer Lewis with whom Payne is so friendly?"

"Yes, sir. Lewis's father is a lieutenant."

"Well, there, under those circumstances, I don't think we can be assured that Detective Payne is color-blind, can we?" Davis said.

Matt, you really pissed the old fart off with that crack.

"Sir, with respect, I cannot agree that Payne is any way a bigot," Matthews said.

Davis glowered at him for a moment.

"Did he offer any explanation for his contempt for the FBI?"

"I don't think he holds us in contempt, sir —"

"That's what it sounds like to me!"

"Sir, that's really why I came to see you first thing."

"What is?"

"Sir, Payne told me he had an unpleasant encounter with two special agents. Two days ago."

"An 'unpleasant encounter'? What sort of an 'unpleasant encounter'? Who were the agents?"

"Payne told me their names were Leibowitz and Jernigan."

"I don't have anybody with those names."

"Yes, sir, I know."

"Payne must be mistaken. We don't have agents by those names, and if any of our people

191

were going to be dealing with a Philadelphia police department officer, I would know about it. That's standard operating procedure."

"Yes, sir."

"Possibly, your friend Payne had this 'unpleasant encounter' with some other federal officer. A postal inspector, a Secret Service agent."

"Sir, Payne insists he saw FBI credentials."

"What was the nature of this 'unpleasant encounter'? Did he say?"

"Yes, sir. He said the agents were investigating a kidnapping that didn't happen."

"A kidnapping?"

"Yes, sir. Payne said that there was no kidnapping."

"Was there or wasn't there?"

"Payne said the FBI agents believed there was a kidnapping; he knew for sure there was not."

"Do you think your friend Payne was pulling your leg, Matthews? He has a strange sense of humor."

"No, sir. I feel sure he wasn't."

"But there are no agents with those names."

"Not here, sir. I was going to ask for permission to check with the Bureau —"

"Do that right now," Davis ordered, pointing to one of his telephones. "Call the Bureau, tell them you're calling for me, and see if there are agents with those names."

"Yes, sir," Matthews said, and picked up the handset.

"There are several possibilities," Davis went on. "One, that your friend is pulling your leg. Two, that someone is in possession of fraudulent credentials, which is a felony, you know. Three, that these people are legitimate FBI agents of another jurisdiction, operating in our area of responsibility —"

"Sir," Matthews interrupted him. "I checked that with ASAC Williamson. Neither of those names is familiar to him."

Glenn Williamson, a well-dressed man of forty-two, who took especial pains with his full head of silver-gray hair, was the Philadelphia FBI office's assistant special agent in charge for administration. As such, he would be aware not only of the names of every FBI agent assigned to Philadelphia, but of the names of FBI agents assigned to other offices who might be working temporarily in Philadelphia's area.

"— without checking in with Williamson. I won't have that, Matthews. That's a clear violation of standard operating procedure, having other people's agents running around like loose cannons in your area of responsibility."

"Yes, sir."

Two minutes later, Special Agent Matthews was informed that the FBI agents he was asking about were more than likely Howard C. Jernigan and Raymond Leibowitz.

"They're with the Anti-Terrorist Group, working out of the Bureau. But they go all over, of course," he was told.

"Thank you very much," Matthews said. "We may have to get back to you."

"Well?" Davis asked.

"According to the Bureau, sir, there are agents named Jernigan and Leibowitz. They're assigned to the Anti-Terrorist Group working out of head-quarters."

"What?" Davis exclaimed, but before Matthews could repeat what he had told him, he picked up his telephone and issued an order to his secretary: "Helen, would you please ask Mr. Towne, Mr. Williamson, and Mr. Young to come in here immediately?"

He put the telephone back in its cradle and looked at Matthews.

"There is very probably a very reasonable explanation for all of this, Matthews," he said. "Which we shall probably soon have."

"Yes, sir."

"When this meeting is over, I want an official report of your meeting with Detective Payne. If what I suspect has happened is what has happened, I'm going to the assistant director with this, and I want everything in writing."

"Yes, sir."

"Good morning," Amelia Payne, M.D., said as she entered Cynthia Longwood's room.

"What's good about it?" Cynthia replied, tempering it with a smile.

"I've been wondering the same thing. It's still raining and I didn't get enough sleep. When I was in medical school, and an intern, they told us when we entered practice, we could expect to get some sleep. They lied."

"When were you an intern? Last year?"

"I will take that as a compliment. I don't look old enough to have been a doctor very long?"

"Not even in your doctor suit," Cynthia said,

making reference to the stethoscope hanging around Amy's neck and her crisp white smock, onto which was pinned a plastic badge reading, "A. A. Payne, M.D."

"When I finish here, I'm going to make what they call rounds. We take medical students with us. I wear my doctor suit so that the visiting firemen don't mistake me for one of them."

"Visiting firemen?"

"Visiting distinguished practitioners of the healing arts," Amy said. "Who, when I offer an opinion, take one look at me and decide I couldn't possibly be an adjunct professor of psychiatry, and therefore are dealing with an uppity young female who doesn't know her place."

Cynthia giggled.

"You don't look old enough to be a doctor, much less a professor."

"I'm getting perilously close to thirty," Amy said. "I got my M.D. at twenty-two."

"*Twenty-two?*" Cynthia asked incredulously. "I thought it took six years *after* you got out of college to be a doctor."

"When I got my M.D., I already had a Ph.D.," Amy said. "I was what you could call precocious."

"You're a genius?"

"So they tell me."

"I'm impressed," Cynthia said.

"On one hand, that's good," Amy said. "I'm smart and I am a good doctor. Statement of fact. Keep that in mind when you get annoyed with me."

"Am I going to be annoyed with you?"

"If you extend my temporary appointment as your physician, if you want me to try to help you, we can count on that happening sooner or later."

"Why's that?"

"Because what we're going to have to do is get your problem out in the open, and you're not going to like that."

Cynthia considered that.

"No, I wouldn't."

"It's your call, Cynthia. First, you're going to have to face the fact that something happened in your life that's made you ill. Next, that you can't deal with it yourself and need help. And finally, whether or not you really believe that Amy Payne — *Dr.* Amy Payne — can help you."

"When do I have to decide?"

"First answer that will annoy you: right now. Putting off decisions is something you can't do. That sort of thing feeds on itself."

Cynthia considered that for fifteen seconds.

"Okay," she said. "Okay."

"Okay," Amy said. "Your mother and father are outside."

"Oh, God!"

"I called her last night and asked her to bring you some clothes, your makeup, et cetera. You're going to have to deal with them. You don't have to tell them anything that makes you uncomfortable — tell them I said that, if you like — but I think it would help them, and you, if you told them you think I can help."

"You must have been pretty sure I'd . . . make you my doctor last night," Cynthia challenged.

"No, I wasn't. Last night, when I called your

196

mother, that was one young female taking care of another. I hate those damned hospital gowns myself."

"Thank you."

"I'm going to keep you in here for at least a couple of days," Amy said. "But that doesn't mean in bed. If you'd like, put some clothes on, and we can have lunch in the cafeteria. The food isn't any better, but it's not on a tray."

"Thank you," Cynthia said.

Amy smiled at her and walked out of the room.

When Inspector Peter Wohl walked into the Investigations Section of Special Operations, he found just about the entire staff, plus Staff Inspector Mike Weisbach and Captain Dave Pekach, in the former classroom. Pekach, in the unique uniform — breeches and boots — of the Highway Patrol, was the only one in uniform.

"Am I interrupting anything important?" Wohl asked.

"A suitable description of our present labors," Sergeant Jason Washington announced in his deep, sonorous voice, "would be 'spinning our wheels.'"

"What are you doing?" Wohl asked.

"Trying to make sense of Matt's transcriptions of the Kellog tapes," Pekach explained. "And getting nowhere."

"They're useless?"

"They've made me change my mind about nothing dirty going on in Five Squad," Pekach said. "But what, nobody seems to be able to figure out, at least from the tapes. And as far as using them as evidence —"

"Is Payne essential?" Wohl asked.

Matt picked up on Wohl calling him by his last name; he suspected it might suggest he was in disfavor.

What did I do?

Shit, those FBI clowns did report me!

"I fear that all those hours our Matthew put in transcribing the tapes were a waste of time and effort," Washington said.

"Not a waste, Jason," Weisbach said. "Finding nothing we can use, so to speak, has taught us they are (a) up to something and (b) rather clever about whatever it is."

"I stand corrected, sir," Jason said.

"I can have Payne?" Wohl asked.

"He's all yours," Weisbach said. "See me later, Matt."

"Yes, sir," Matt said.

Matt stood up and followed Wohl out of the room. Wohl walked quickly, and Matt almost had to trot to catch up with him.

"What's up?" Matt asked.

Wohl ignored him.

They went down the stairs and then up the corridor to Wohl's office. Matt followed him inside.

Chief Inspector Dennis V. Coughlin — a tall, heavyset, large-boned, ruddy-faced man with good teeth and curly silver hair — was sitting on the couch before Wohl's coffee table in the act of dunking a doughnut in a coffee mug.

For all of Matt's life, Coughlin had been "Uncle Denny" to him. He had been his father's best friend, and Matt had come to suspect that Denny Coughlin, who had never married, had been in love — secretly, of course — with Patricia Stevens Moffitt Payne, Matt's mother, for a very long time.

He also suspected that this was not an occasion on which Chief Inspector Coughlin should be addressed as "Uncle Denny."

"Good morning, Chief," he said.

Coughlin looked at him for a long moment, expressionless, before he replied.

"Matty, what's with you and the FBI?"

"Is that what this is about?"

"I asked you a question," Coughlin said evenly.

"I suppose I shouldn't have taken them on the wild-goose chase like that, but they're —"

"Start at the beginning," Wohl shut him off. "And right now, neither the Chief or I are interested in what you think of the FBI."

Matt related, in detail, his entire encounter with Special Agents Jernigan and Leibowitz. When he came to the part of leading them up and down the narrow alleys of North Philadelphia before finally parking in the Special Operations parking lot, Chief Inspector Coughlin had a very difficult time keeping a straight face.

"Okay," he said finally. "Now let me tell you what's happened this morning. I had a telephone call from Walter Davis. You know who he is?"

"Yes, sir."

"Davis said that he would consider it a personal favor if I would set up a meeting, as soon as possible, between himself, the two agents you got into it with, Peter, and me. And that he would be grateful if I kept the meeting, until after we'd talked, under my hat. Do you have any idea what that's all about, Matty?"

"No, sir."

"Somehow, I think there's more to this than you being a wiseass with his agents," Coughlin said. "I think if that's all there was to this, the Polack would have gotten a formal letter complaining about the uncooperative behavior of one of his detectives."

The Polack was Police Commissioner Taddeus Czernich.

"Yeah," Inspector Wohl said thoughtfully.

"And he wants me to keep this under my hat until after we have a meeting," Coughlin went on. "Which makes me think of something else. Did either of the FBI guys do anything they shouldn't have done, Matty?"

"Well, they should have been sure there *was* a kidnapping before they started asking a lot of questions," Matt said.

"That's not what I mean. Did they violate any of your civil rights? Push you around? Brandish a pistol? Anything like that?"

"No, sir."

"Maybe Matt's onto it with what he said," Wohl said. "Maybe Davis is embarrassed that he had people running around investigating a nonkidnapping. And doesn't want Matt to tell the story to an appreciative audience at the FOP Bar. The FBI is very image conscious."

Detective Payne was enormously relieved that he had become "Matt" again.

"Could be," Chief Coughlin said. "But I have

a gut feeling there's more to this than that. I have been wrong before."

Coughlin heaved himself off the couch with a grunt, walked to Wohl's desk, consulted a slip of paper he took from his pocket, and dialed a number.

"Chief Inspector Coughlin for Mr. Davis, please," he said to whoever answered, and then, a moment later: "Dennis Coughlin, Walter. Sorry it took so long to get back to you. I've had a chance to speak with Peter Wohl. The best I have been able to set up is half past four at the Rittenhouse Club. Would that be convenient?"

Davis's reply could not be heard.

"Look forward to seeing you, too, Walter," Coughlin said, and hung up. He looked at Wohl and Payne. "Pay attention, you two," he said, smiling. "Write this down. When dealing with the enemy, never meet him on his own turf — Davis wanted us to come to the FBI office — and, if possible, keep him waiting."

Walter Davis, trailed by Special Agents Howard C. Jernigan and Raymond Leibowitz, walked up to the porter's desk in the Rittenhouse Club at 4:15 and announced, "I'm Mr. Davis. I'm expecting a gentleman named Coughlin."

The porter turned and examined the membership board.

I'll be damned. Coughlin is a member. Of course. He would have to be. He suggested this place to meet. Why didn't I think of that?

"Chief Coughlin is in the bar, sir," the porter

said, his tone suggesting that life would be much easier if stupid members took a look at the membership board themselves.

Coughlin, Peter Wohl, and Matt Payne were sitting at a large table — with room for six chairs — and had been there, Davis saw, at least long enough to get bar service.

The three of them stood up as Davis approached.

"You're looking well, Walter," Coughlin said, offering his large hand.

"As you do, Dennis," Davis said, and offered his hand first to Wohl — "Thank you for making time for me, Peter" — and then to Matt. "How are you, Payne?"

"Very well, thank you, sir," Payne said.

"You've met these fellows," Davis said. "But let me introduce them to Peter and Dennis. Raymond Leibowitz and Howard Jernigan."

The men shook hands.

A waiter appeared. Davis ordered a Jack Daniel's on the rocks, Leibowitz the same, and Jernigan ginger ale.

"I'd really like to be somewhere where we won't be overheard," Davis said. "Is there somewhere . . ."

"Matty's father told me they spent a lot of money designing this room," Coughlin said, gesturing at the high, paneled ceiling, "as someplace where people could have discreet conversations. But if you're uncomfortable, Walter, there are private rooms."

"No. I'm sure this will be fine," Davis said.

"You're the commanding officer of Special Operations, I understand, Inspector," Jernigan said, oozing charm.

"Yes, I am," Peter said, and added mischievously, "I understand you've seen our headquarters."

Jernigan colored.

Coughlin laughed, and after a second, somewhat artificially, Davis joined in.

"Let's clear the air," Coughlin said. "Detective Payne should have told your people he was a police officer, and he should not have taken them on — what should we call it? — a *tour* of the scenic attractions of North Philadelphia, and he is prepared to apologize, isn't that so, Matty?"

"Yes, sir. We just got off on the wrong foot. I'm sorry."

The waiter appeared with the drinks.

"I propose a toast to peace, friendship, and cooperation between the Philadelphia Police Department and the Federal Bureau of Investigation," Coughlin said, and raised his glass.

"A very appropriate toast, one I quickly agree to, under the circumstances," Davis said.

"What circumstances would those be, Walter?" Coughlin asked.

"I think I'll let Raymond get into that," Davis said. "But first let me tell you that Raymond and Howard aren't in my office. They operate out of FBI Headquarters in Washington; they're members of the Anti-Terrorism Group."

"Anti-Terrorism?" Matt blurted.

Coughlin and Wohl frowned at him.

"Before we came to see you, Detective Payne," Leibowitz said. "There just wasn't time to check

203

in with the Philadelphia office. If there was, we would have known who you were. Are."

"I thought you were investigating the kidnapping of Susan Reynolds," Matt said. "Actually, the nonkidnapping."

" 'Kidnapping'?" Leibowitz said, visibly surprised. "Where'd you get that?"

"Well, then, what the hell were you investigating? She's rich; rich people get kidnapped; she was missing — the FBI knew she was missing. Her father is a very important man; I figured that was why the FBI was working on a weekend."

"Jesus Christ!" Leibowitz said. "You really thought we were investigating her *kidnapping?*"

"I had the feeling you thought I had done it," Matt said. "Understandably, I was a little annoyed."

"Well, I'll tell you what we were investigating, what we are investigating," Leibowitz said. "But it can't go any further than this room."

"I'm sure, Leibowitz," Davis said pointedly, "that we can trust the discretion of Chief Coughlin, Inspector Wohl, and Detective Payne."

Special Agent Leibowitz's face showed that he was more than a little uncomfortable trusting the discretion of Detective Payne.

"Does the name Bryan C. Chenowith mean anything to you, Detective Payne?"

Matt searched his memory, then shook his head, "no."

"Eloise Anne Fitzgerald?"

Matt shook his head again.

"Jennifer Ollwood?"

Matt shook his head.

"Edgar L. Cole?"

Matt held up both hands in a gesture of helplessness.

"Never heard of any of them," he said.

"They're all wanted by both the federal government and the Commonwealth of Pennsylvania on a number of charges —"

"University of Pittsburgh?" Chief Coughlin interrupted.

"Right," Leibowitz said.

Matt looked at Coughlin curiously

"So far as we're concerned," Leibowitz went on, "we want them, and some others, on — among other federal charges — unlawful flight to avoid prosecution."

"Prosecution for what?" Wohl asked.

"Murder."

"Correct me if I'm wrong," Coughlin said. "They're the people who blew up the Biological Sciences building at the University of Pittsburgh?"

"Thereby causing the unlawful deaths of eleven persons, according to the indictments handed down by the grand jury in Allegheny County — Pittsburgh."

"As a gesture of their displeasure with the use of monkeys in medical research, right?" Coughlin said, now bitterly. "Eleven innocent people were blown up!"

"Yes, sir," Leibowitz said.

"What's this got to do with Susan Reynolds?" Matt asked, unable to easily accept the accusation that Daffy's friend had been involved in blowing anything up.

"We have reason to believe Miss Reynolds has in the past, and is now, aiding and abetting these fugitives in their unlawful flight," Leibowitz said. "Sufficient reason for us to have obtained permission in federal court for a wiretap on her parents' residence and, for that matter, wherever she happens to be."

"I'm more than a little confused," Wohl said. "How did you guys get to Matt?"

"Well, we'd like to have enough people to surveille her around the clock, but we don't," Leibowitz said. "But we listen to her phone calls, and when something interesting comes up — her mother getting excited that Susan didn't make the usual 'Good night, Mommy dear' phone call and calling Mrs. Nesbitt to find out where Susan was, for example — we act on it."

"She disappeared in the company of a guy named Matt Payne," Jernigan amplified. "Was she really off somewhere passing money, or whatever, to Bryan Chenowith, and his murderous band of animal activists? And who is Matt Payne? Is he part of the animal-activist underground railroad? Just as soon as we got the word from the wiretappers — and checked the phone book and found only one Payne, Matthew M. in Philadelphia — we drove up from Washington to find out."

"She told Daffy — Mrs. Nesbitt," Matt said, "that she was in her room at the Bellvue-Stratford all night, and just hadn't answered the telephone. She wasn't in her room all night."

"How do you know that?" Jernigan asked.

"I know."

"She was with you, you mean?" Jernigan pursued.

"No. The last time I saw her — I told you guys this — she was in the Nesbitts' house in Society Hill. I don't know where she was, but she did not sleep in her hotel room that night."

"How do you know that?" Jernigan demanded.

"Forget I said it."

"How do you *know* that she wasn't in her room?"

"She didn't use the bed. She strikes me as the kind of a girl who would not sleep on the floor."

"I keep asking you how you know all this."

"I decline to answer the question on the grounds that my answer might tend to incriminate me," Matt said.

"What the hell is that supposed to mean, Matty?" Chief Coughlin asked angrily.

"Chief," Matt said after a perceptible pause, "if, hypothetically, someone gained access to premises under conditions that might be considered breaking and entering, wouldn't he be foolish to admit that to the FBI?"

"Jesus, Matty, what the hell were you doing?" Coughlin said.

"Why would this hypothetical person we're talking about, Payne," Davis asked, "break into this hypothetical other person's hotel room?"

"We're out of school, Davis, right?" Denny Coughlin came to Matt's defense.

"Absolutely. You have my word," Davis said.

"Watch yourself, Matt," Wohl said, which earned him a look of gratitude from Chief Coughlin and looks of annoyance from Davis,

207

Jernigan, and Leibowitz.

"The morning after the party, I got a call from Chad Nesbitt, who, like his wife, was under the impression that Susan Reynolds had left the party with me. They thought she had spent the night with me. I told them she hadn't —"

"Who is this guy Nesbitt?" Jernigan asked. "This is the first time that name came up."

"He's in the grocery business," Matt said.

"Matty!" Coughlin warned, and then turned to Jernigan and explained: "Nesbitt's father is chairman of the board of Nesfoods International."

"We have noticed that a number of these people who like to blow things up in the name of love for animals come from the, quote, better families, unquote," Jernigan said. "Is there any chance Mr. Nesbitt might be connected with Chenowith and Company?"

"I think that's very unlikely," Matt said, coldly angry.

"Why?"

"Well, he's an ex-Marine, for one thing."

"So am I," Leibowitz said. "But on the other hand, so was Lee Harvey Oswald."

"I think we can safely proceed on the assumption that Mr. Nesbitt — or his wife — is not in sympathy with these people you're looking for," Wohl said. "Payne was telling us about his telephone call."

"Right. So Nesbitt asked me, since I live only a couple of blocks away from the Bellvue, to go there and see what I could find out."

"As a police officer, you mean?" Leibowitz asked. "Your friend was now concerned with the welfare of the Reynolds woman? Because she was missing?"

"He was concerned because his wife was on his back about her friend," Matt said. "And I went to the Bellvue as a civilian. Not as a police officer."

"And while you were there, you somehow found yourself in her hotel room?" Leibowitz asked.

"I didn't say that," Matt said.

"Payne, we're all on the same side here," Davis said.

"Hypothetically, Matt, how could someone gain access to her hotel room?" Wohl asked.

"Hypothetically, with a master key."

"Apropos of nothing whatever," Wohl said, "Detective Payne recently participated in a surveillance operation at the Hotel Bellvue-Stratford."

Leibowitz and Jernigan exchanged glances suggesting they fully understood the usefulness to a surveillance crew of a master key that might not have been acquired under innocent circumstances.

"The Reynolds girl's bed had not been slept in?" Leibowitz asked.

Matt shook his head, "no."

"You find out anything else that might be useful?"

"The rent-a-cop in the hotel garage said he remembered a red Porsche with a good-looking blonde in it leaving the garage about half past five the previous afternoon. Where — presuming this was in fact, Susan Reynolds; there really aren't that many good-looking blondes in red Porsches — she was from five-thirty until she went to the Nesbitts' at half past seven or so is anyone's guess. I don't *know*, but I'll bet she did not put the car into the hotel garage again until a couple of hours after I was there."

"Why did Mrs. Nesbitt tell the suspect's mother the suspect had left with you?" Jernigan asked.

"I think she thought at the time that she had."

"You were friendly with her at the party?"

"I tried to be. She was not interested."

"Pity," Jernigan said.

"Do you think you could change that situation?" Davis asked.

"What do you mean by that?" Matt asked.

"I mean get close to her," Davis said.

"What's the opposite of her being 'overwhelmed' by my charms?" Matt asked.

"What are you driving at, Walter?" Chief Coughlin asked.

"Off the top of my head," Davis said. "And I'm hearing a lot of this for the first time myself, which sometimes cuts through the fog. What I'm hearing is that the Reynolds girl is not all that close to the Nesbitts. But she goes to the Nesbitts' party. And disappears overnight. That suggests she may have had a rendezvous with the fugitives. That suggests they may be here, or near here. Since it worked this time, they may try it again. If Detective Payne could get close . . ."

"You're suggesting that he work with you on this?" Coughlin asked.

"You would have problems with that?"

"Frankly, Walter, I have a lot of problems with it," Coughlin said. "For one thing, he's up to his neck right now in an important investigation."

"These people have been indicted by the Allegheny County Grand Jury for murder, Chief Coughlin," Leibowitz said. "They're fugitives from a Pennsylvania jurisdiction. They're not just a federal problem."

"Still," Coughlin said, somewhat lamely.

"I see a lot of practical problems," Wohl said, coming to Coughlin's aid. "Presuming Chief Coughlin would go along with this. For one thing, Payne says the Reynolds girl was not . . . at all receptive to his charms. Even if she was, this is a long way from Harrisburg. Does she know you're a cop, Matt?"

"Yes, sir. Her eyes just sort of glazed over when she heard that."

"You didn't think that was a little odd?" Jernigan asked.

"Unfortunately, it happens to me all the time," Matt said.

"On the other hand," Davis said. "She might decide what better cover could she have when making frequent trips to Philadelphia than a cop boyfriend?"

Wohl thought: *He's right. Why am I surprised? You don't get to be the FBI Philadelphia SAC if you're stupid.*

Then he saw something on Matt's face.

"What, Matt?" he asked.

"You know why I went to the Roundhouse last night?" Matt asked.

Wohl had to think a moment before recalling

that Matt had been sent to Personnel by Staff Inspector Weisbach.

"There was some sort of a Harrisburg connection?" Wohl asked.

Coughlin's face indicated that he was having a hard time holding his questions about that until later.

Matt nodded.

"Something that would justify you being in Harrisburg on police business?" Davis asked.

"What Matt is working on is sensitive," Coughlin said. "There are people we don't want to know he'll be going to Harrisburg."

Walter Davis confirmed Wohl's realization that stupid people do not get to be senior FBI officers:

"An internal matter, eh?" Davis said. "Well, I can probably help you there a little, if you like. The chief of police there is not only an old friend, but he owes me a couple of favors. You tell me what sort of a cover story you'd like for Payne to have, and I'll see that it's leaked from the chief's office."

"That could be very useful," Wohl said, thinking out loud.

"There is something else," Davis said. "Payne can move easily in the same social circles as the Reynolds woman; that could be very useful, I would suspect."

"I'd have to clear Matt working with you on this with the commissioner," Coughlin said. It was his last line of defense.

"I don't think that will pose a problem, Denny," Davis said. "The last time I had lunch with the mayor — here, as a matter of fact — he gave me quite a speech about these people who blow up medical-research facilities because they use animals. He called them something I wouldn't repeat in mixed company. He said they were more dangerous to the country than most people realized. I have the feeling that if he knew about this, he would 'suggest' to Commissioner Czernich that it was a splendid idea."

You may be an ass, Walter Davis, Peter Wohl thought, *but you are not a stupid ass.*

Ten

When the telephone rang in the elegantly furnished study of his South Philadelphia residence, Mr. Vincenzo Savarese, his jacket removed, his stiffly starched cuffs turned up, his eyes closed, was playing along from memory with a tape recording of the Philharmonica Slavonica's recording of Max Bruch's Violin Concerto in G Minor, Opus 26, on a circa 1790 G. Strenelli violin for which he had paid nearly fifty thousand dollars.

Mr. Pietro Cassandro, a very large, well-tailored forty-year-old who faithfully paid federal and state taxes on his income as vice president of Classic Livery, Inc., where his duties were primarily driving the Lincolns and Cadillacs in which Mr. Savarese moved about town, frowned when the telephone rang. Mr. S. did not like to be disturbed when he was playing the violin.

Cassandro looked at Mr. Savarese to see his reaction to the ringing telephone. Only a very few people had the number of Mr. Savarese's study.

Mr. S. stopped playing and looked at Cassandro. Then he pointed with the bow at the telephone.

Cassandro picked it up. "Yeah?" he said, listened a moment, then spoke to Mr. S.: "It's the lawyer."

"Mr. Giacomo?" Cassandro nodded. "Tell him I will be with him directly."

Mr. Savarese walked to the reel-to-reel tape recorder and turned it off, and then to a Steinway grand piano on which he had placed the Strenelli violin's case, carefully placed the violin, and the bow, in the case, and then closed it. He then pulled a crisp white handkerchief from his shirt collar and laid that upon the violin case.

Then he walked to Cassandro and took the telephone from him.

"Thank you for returning my call, Mr. Giacomo," Savarese said.

"I'm sorry it took me so long," Armando Giacomo said. "I was in court."

"So your secretary said."

"How may I be of service?"

"I thought you might be interested in hearing that I have had a report from my daughter about my granddaughter."

"Yes, I would."

"Dr. Payne has seen her three times so far," Savarese said. "Late last night. The first thing this morning, and at lunch. My granddaughter is apparently very taken with her."

"I'm glad to hear that."

"I am grateful to you, Mr. Giacomo, for arranging for me to meet with Mr. Payne."

"I was happy to have been of service."

"And, of course, I am very grateful to Mr. Payne for speaking to his daughter on behalf of Cynthia. That is one of the reasons I asked you to call."

"Brewster Payne was sympathetic to your problem. He is a very nice man."

"What I wanted to do was ask your advice

about making some small gesture of my appreciation to Mr. Payne," Savarese said.

"I don't think that's necessary, Mr. Savarese."

"I have several bottles of some really fine cognac I thought would be appropriate."

"May I speak freely, Mr. Savarese?"

"Of course."

"You went to Mr. Payne as a father and grandfather asking help from another father. He understood your problem and did what he could to help, one father helping another, so to speak. Under those circumstances, I don't really think that a gift is in order."

Savarese didn't reply for a long moment.

"You think it would be inappropriate? Is that what you're saying?"

"Yes, both unnecessary and inappropriate."

"You're suggesting he would be offended?"

"Let me put it this way, Mr. Savarese," Giacomo said. "If I had gone to Brewster Payne as you did, and he had responded as he did, I would not send him a gift. I would think that in his mind he had done only what a decent human should have done, and therefore, no attempt to repay —"

"I take your meaning, Mr. Giacomo," Savarese interrupted him. "And I respect your wisdom and trust your judgment in matters of this nature."

"Thank you," Giacomo said.

He hoped that his relief at being able to talk Savarese out of sending Brewster Payne a couple — he said "several bottles," so maybe six, maybe a dozen — $500 bottles of French booze was not evident in his voice. There would be no telling how Payne would react. Payne regarded Vincenzo Savarese — loving grandfather or not — as a murdering gangster, and he didn't want — worse, almost certainly would not accept — a present from him. Payne was entirely capable of sending the booze back, which would insult Savarese, and there's no telling what trouble that would cause.

"I would be grateful, Mr. Giacomo, if Mr. Payne could somehow be made aware that I consider myself deeply in his debt."

"I don't think that's necessary, Mr. Savarese. As I said before, Mr. Payne believes, in his mind, that he only did what a decent man was obligated to do."

"When the opportunity presents itself, Mr. Giacomo, as I'm sure it soon will, I would consider it a personal favor for you to tell Mr. Payne that I consider myself deeply in his debt. Would you do that for me, Mr. Giacomo?"

"Of course."

You need anybody shot, Brewster? Somebody stiffing you on a fee, needs to have his legs broken? Just say the word. Vincenzo Savarese told me to tell you he owes you a big one.

"Thank you. And there is one other thing about which I would be grateful for your advice, Mr. Giacomo."

"I'm at your service."

"Could you recommend a good, and by good I mean both highly competent and very discreet, private investigator?"

A private investigator? Now what?

"I don't think I quite understand," Giacomo said.

"I need someone to make some discreet inquiries for me."

"Well, there's a lot of people in that business, Mr. Savarese. I use half a dozen different ones myself. Good people. It depends, of course, on the nature of the information you want."

There was a perceptible pause, long enough for Armando C. Giacomo to decide Savarese was carefully deciding how much, if anything, he was going to tell him.

"What I had in mind, Mr. Giacomo, was to look around my granddaughter's environment, so to speak, and see if I couldn't come up with some hint about what has so greatly disturbed her."

"I don't think I would do anything like that until I'd spoken with Dr. Payne," Giacomo said quickly.

"All this information would be for Dr. Payne, of course."

Unless it turns out that the girl was raped or something — which might damned well be the case — in which case the cops would have an unlawful death by castration to deal with.

"I just don't see where any of the people who work for me would be any good at that sort of investigation. I could ask —"

"That won't be necessary, thank you just the same, Mr. Giacomo. And thank you for returning my call. I'm grateful to you."

"I'm glad things seem to be working out for your granddaughter," Giacomo said.

"Thank you. I very much appreciate your interest," Vincenzo Savarese said, and hung up.

He looked at Pietro Cassandro.

218

"Mr. Giacomo does not seem to feel that any of the investigators with whom he has experience would be useful," he said.

Cassandro did not know how to interpret the remark. He responded as he usually did in similar circumstances. He held up both hands, palms upward, and shrugged.

When Vincenzo Savarese's daughter had told him how kind Dr. Payne was, even calling to tell her to bring Cynthia's makeup and decent night clothes to her in the hospital, she also said that Cynthia had told her that Dr. Payne had told her she was not to tell her mother, or her father, for that matter, anything that made her uncomfortable to relate.

Savarese hadn't said anything to his daughter, but he'd thought that while that might be — and probably was — good medical practice, it also suggested that there was something that Cynthia would be uncomfortable telling her mother about. He was naturally curious about what that might be.

There was something else Savarese thought odd. The young man Cynthia had been seeing a lot of — his name was Ronald Ketcham, and all Savarese knew about him was that he was neither Italian nor Catholic, and Cynthia's mother hoped their relationship wasn't getting too serious — had not been around since Cynthia had started having her emotional trouble.

"Tell Paulo to put the retired cop to work," Mr. Savarese ordered.

Paulo Cassandro, Pietro's older and even larger brother, was president of Classic Livery, Inc., in which Mr. Savarese had the controlling — if off the books — interest.

"Right, Mr. S.," Pietro Cassandro said. "What do you want me to do with the cognac?"

"Send it back to the restaurant," Mr. Savarese said, making reference to Ristorante Alfredo, one of Philadelphia's most elegant establishments, and in which he also had the controlling — if off the books — interest.

"Right, Mr. S. I'll do that on my way home."

Mr. Savarese changed his mind.

"Keep out two bottles," he said. "No. Three bottles. Drop them off at Giacomo's office."

"Got it, Mr. S."

Mr. Savarese looked as if he was searching his mind for something else that had to be done, and then, that he had found nothing.

He walked to the Steinway grand piano, took the handkerchief from the top of the violin case, and tucked it into his collar. Then he opened the violin case, took out the bow, tested the horsehair for proper tension, took out the Strenelli, and, holding it by the neck, walked to the reel-to-reel tape recorder and turned it back on.

Then he tucked the Strenelli under his chin, raised the bow to its strings, and began to play along with the Philharmonica Slavonica's rendition of Max Bruch's Violin Concerto in G Minor, Opus 26.

During the briefings given to Detective Matt Payne by the Philadelphia Police Department and the Federal Bureau of Investigation to prepare him for his role in the apprehension of the fugitives Bryan C. Chenowith, Jennifer Ollwood, Edgar L. Cole, and Eloise Anne Fitzgerald (known to the FBI as "The Chenowith Group"), Matt had a number of thoughts he was aware would annoy or confound (probably both) both the FBI and his fellow officers of the Philadelphia Police Department.

The first of these was his realization that Sir Walter Scott had been right on the money when he proclaimed, "Oh, what a tangled web we weave, When first we practise to deceive!"

Chief Inspector Coughlin, Inspector Wohl, Staff Inspector Weisbach, and Sergeant Jason Washington were responsible for bringing this conclusion to Payne's mind.

They had spent the better part of hour, starting at 8:15 A.M. in Denny Coughlin's Roundhouse office, conducting a discussion of the cover story Matt would use in Harrisburg. Detective Payne had been present, but it had been made immediately clear to him that his participation had not been solicited and was not desired.

The three senior police supervisors decided that so far as the members of the Special Operations Division Investigation Section were concerned, they would be told that Matt would be in Harrisburg attempting to uncover suspicious financial activity on the part of any member of the Narcotics Unit Five Squad, with special attention being paid to Officer Timothy J. Calhoun, who had relatives in Harrisburg and Camp Hill.

Only those with the need to know were to be made privy to the fact that Matt would also be "cooperating" with the FBI in their investigation of the Chenowith Group while he was in Harrisburg. Weisbach decided those with a need to know were those present, plus Sergeant Sandow.

The Intelligence Division of the Philadelphia Police Department was to be made privy to Matt's role vis-à-vis the FBI, but *not* to the fact that he would be in Harrisburg investigating the Narcotics Five Squad. The Intelligence Division, to prevent any possible leaks that might come to the attention of the Five Squad, was to be told a second cover story. This one had Matt looking into possible connections between vice operations in Philadelphia and Harrisburg.

Chief Coughlin felt this second cover story would have a certain credibility, inasmuch as Lieutenant Seymour Meyer, who had commanded the Central District's Vice Squad, had been relieved of his command and his badge and was presently awaiting trial on charges that he had sold his protection to the madam of a call girl ring.

His replacement — and the new commanding officer of the Central District (Inspector Gregory F. Sawyer, Jr., the former commander, had been relieved of his command at the time of Meyer's arrest) — would be told that the Special Operations investigation of Center City prostitution had not been completed, and that Detective Payne, specifically, was in Harrisburg working on it.

Chief Coughlin also felt, and Inspectors Wohl and Weisbach agreed, that because of the close working relationship between the Central District generally, and the Central District's Vice Squad and the Narcotics Unit, the word would quickly reach the Five Squad that Special Operations had sent Detective Payne to Harrisburg hoping that he would there find the final nails to drive in Lieutenant Meyer's coffin.

This second cover story was the one Mr. Walter Davis would be asked to have the chief of police in Harrisburg — who he said was both an old friend and owed him several favors — spread around the Harrisburg Police Department. The chief of police would be told in confidence that Detective Payne's investigations involved the Chenowith Group, but *not* that he was looking into the financial affairs of certain members of the Five Squad.

This meant, Matt understood, that Chief Coughlin would prefer that neither the FBI nor the Harrisburg Police Department be aware what specific rotten apples Matt was looking for in the Philadelphia Police Department's barrel.

The FBI Briefing on the Chenowith Group began at 9:45 in the Conference Room of the FBI's Philadelphia office. Present were Chief Coughlin, Inspector Wohl, and Detectives Payne and Wilfred G. "Wee Willy" Malone, a six-foot-four-inch giant of a man who was assigned to the Philadelphia Police Department's Intelligence Unit. The FBI was represented by SAC Walter Davis; ASAC (Administration) Glenn Williamson; ASAC (Criminal Affairs) Frank F. Young; and FBI Special Agents Raymond Leibowitz and Howard C. Jernigan of the Anti-Terrorist Group, and Special Agent John D. Matthews of the FBI's Philadelphia office.

Everyone was seated in comfortable upholstered chairs around a long, glistening conference table. Before each participant had been laid out a lined pad, four sharpened pencils, a coffee mug, a water glass, and an ashtray. Two water thermos bottles, two coffee thermos bottles, and cream and sugar accessories were in the center of the table. On a shelf mounted on the wall were both a slide projector and a 16-millimeter motion picture projector. At the opposite end of the room was a lectern, complete to microphone, and, Matt supposed, controls to operate the lights and the slide and motion picture projectors. A roll-down beaded projection screen was mounted on the wall behind the lectern.

This caused Matt to think, first, *This is a hell of a lot fancier than Czernich's conference room in the Roundhouse,* and next, *Well, what the hell, they're spending federal tax dollars, which no bureaucrat considers real money, so why not?*

SAC Walter Davis stepped to the lectern, thanked everyone for coming, and turned the meeting over to ASAC Frank Young, a red-headed, pale-faced man in his forties on the edge between muscular and plump.

Young went to the lectern, thanked everyone for coming, and asked if everybody knew everybody else. Everyone did, except for Wee Willy Malone and Jack Matthews, and Detective Payne and ASAC Williamson, who leaned across the table to shake hands.

"SAC Davis has assigned Special Agent Matthews to liaise with Detective Payne while we're doing this," Young announced. "Presuming that meets with your approval, Chief Coughlin?"

"Certainly," Coughlin said.

What the hell does "liaise with" mean? Detective Payne wondered.

"I thought that the best way to get this show on the road," Young said, "was to run a film we put together showing why we're all looking for the Chenowith Group."

The room lights dimmed and the film projector started.

The seal of the United States Department of Justice appeared on the screen, then the seal of the Federal Bureau of Investigation, then a notice announcing the film was classified "Official Use Only" and was not to be shown to unauthorized persons.

"The Biological Sciences building of the Medical School of the University of Pittsburgh," a voice announced.

The screen now showed still photographs, obviously taken during different seasons of the year, of a three-story brick building of vaguely Colonial design.

"At 5:25 P.M., 1 April," the voice intoned without emotion, "an explosion occurred, causing extensive damage to the building and the deaths of eleven individuals. More than fifty other individuals were injured, some of them seriously. The death count of eleven reflects both immediate deaths and deaths which occurred later."

The screen now showed the building immediately after the explosion.

Looks like they got this from TV news film, Matt thought.

Fire hoses were still playing their streams on

225

the shattered and smoking building, and firemen and police were shown entering and leaving the building. Ambulance crews were treating and transporting injured people, some of them badly injured.

Jesus, they didn't show something like that on the six-thirty news! Matt thought.

The film — now not of "broadcast quality," and including some still photographs and thus probably shot by the police — showed some of the victims who had been killed immediately, where their bodies had been found.

"Holy Mother of God!" someone said, and after a moment Matt recognized Denny Coughlin's voice.

The exclamation was understandable. Legless bodies and heads smashed by tons of steel and concrete are not pretty sights.

"Investigation by the FBI and local agencies," the narrator went on dispassionately, as the screen showed the interior of the building sometime later — the bodies were gone — "indicates that the explosives used were Composition C-4 and Primacord. Composition C-4 is not available on the civilian market, and chemical analysis indicated the composition of the Primacord used to be identical to that procured for the military services.

"This makes it probable that the explosives used were stolen from U.S. military stocks, most probably from the explosives depository of the 173rd Light Engineer Company, Pennsylvania Army National Guard, located on the Indiantown Gap Military Reservation near Harrisburg, Pennsylvania.

"This depository was robbed, at gunpoint, on 13 February. Three hundred pounds of Composition C-4; fifty pounds of Primacord; forty-eight electrical and twenty-five fire-actuated detonating devices; six U.S. carbines, caliber .30 M2 — the M2 is the fully automatic version of the carbine — six .45-caliber pistols, model 1911A1; and a substantial quantity of ammunition of these calibers was stolen.

"The perpetrators were two white males and at least one white female who drove a Ford panel truck, later determined to be stolen. The perpetrators wore ski masks over their faces, but during the robbery the civilian guard, who was bound, gagged, and blindfolded, was nevertheless able to obtain sufficient vision around his blindfold to make a positive identification of one of the robbers, who had pulled his ski mask off his face. Bryan C. Chenowith, twenty-six, white male, five feet eight, 160 pounds, light brown hair, hazel eyes, no distinguishing markings or features."

A mug shot of Bryan C. Chenowith appeared on the screen.

"At the time of the Indiantown Gap robbery, Mr. Chenowith was a fugitive from justice on charges of unlawful flight to avoid prosecution in connection with the hijacking at gunpoint of a truck engaged in interstate commerce. The truck contained orangutans being transported from Kennedy International Airport, New York, to the Medical School of the University of Pittsburgh. The animals were freed from their cages near Allentown, Pennsylvania.

"Mr. Chenowith at the time was a student at the University of Pittsburgh School of Medicine. While at the University of Pittsburgh, Mr. Chenowith was active in the Fair Play for Animals and Stop the Slaughter programs."

Another still photograph of Chenowith appeared on the screen. It showed him carrying a sign showing an oranguntan tied, Christ-like, to a cross.

"Mr. Chenowith and two of his known associates, Jennifer Downs Ollwood, white female, twenty-five years of age, five feet four inches, 130 pounds, black hair, brown eyes, no distinguishing marks and/or features, and Edgar Leonard Cole, white male, twenty-five years old, five feet ten inches, 170 pounds, dark blond hair, four-inch scar left calf, have been positively identified as having been in and around the Biological Sciences building the day before and the day of the explosion."

Several still photographs first of Jennifer Ollwood and then of Edgar Cole appeared on the screen, as the narrator furnished details of their backgrounds.

Jennifer Ollwood was a rather pretty young woman who wore her black hair in bangs. In one photograph she was wearing a fringed leather jacket. In another, she was pictured holding a sign reading, "Stop the Torture!" and in a third, a sign reading "Save the Animals!"

"Miss Ollwood," the narrator announced, "was an undergraduate student at the University of Pittsburgh at the time of the bombing. She had previously been a student at Bennington College,

228

from which she had been expelled as a result of her participation in antivivisectionist activities, and her arrest for having assaulted a campus police officer. She was active in the animal-activist movement at the University of Pittsburgh.

Edgar Cole had acne so bad that it was visible beneath his scraggly beard.

"Mr. Cole is also a former University of Pittsburgh student, where he was also active in animal-activist activities. At the time of the Indiantown Gap robbery, he was also being sought on unlawful-flight-to-avoid-prosecution warrants in connection with the truck hijacking, and by the Bethlehem, Pennsylvania, police department to answer charges of being in possession of more than one pound of marijuana with intentions of distributing same."

"A trio of outstanding American youth," Wohl offered. "Your lady friend, Matt, has some interesting friends."

"On 3 April," the narrator interrupted, "Pittsburgh police conducted a raid on premises known to have been occupied by Mr. Chenowith and Miss Ollwood and Miss Eloise Anne Fitzgerald, white female, twenty-four years of age, five feet two, 110 pounds, light red hair, pale complexion, green eyes, no distinguishing marks or features, at 1101 West Hendricks Street in Pittsburgh."

A picture of Eloise Anne Fitzgerald appeared on the screen. It showed a demure-looking, short-haired redhead, wearing glasses, and looking about as menacing, Matt thought, as a librarian's assistant.

"This photo of Miss Fitzgerald," the narrator

went on, "was acquired from the publisher of the Bennington College yearbook, and portrays Miss Fitzgerald as a sophomore. She was expelled from Bennington at the same time Miss Ollwood was expelled, and for approximately the same reasons, although there is no record of her arrest on any charges anywhere. She subsequently enrolled at the University of Pittsburgh, seeking a degree in social work. She was active there in the animal-activist movement."

The screen next showed first a photograph of the exterior of the house, a large, run-down, Victorian-era building, and then of two rooms inside the house.

"The occupants had recently vacated the premises, apparently in some haste, and leaving behind five pounds of Composition C-4, one point five pounds of Primacord, three electrical detonators, and two M2 carbines and several bandoliers of carbine ammunition.

"It was quickly determined, by their serial numbers, that the recovered firearms were among those stolen from Indiantown Gap. Labeling of the C-4 uncovered at the West Hendricks location indicates it is from the same manufacturing lot as the C-4 stolen from Indiantown Gap; laboratory analysis of the Primacord indicates that it is from the same manufacturing lot as the Primacord stolen from Indiantown Gap; and other tests indicate the detonators are of the same type and age as those taken from the National Guard depository."

The screen now went back to shots of the sparsely furnished apartment in the old house on

West Hendricks Street.

"In addition to statements made by other residents of the building at 1101 West Hendricks that Mr. Cole was a frequent visitor to the premises, physical evidence, including fingerprints and personal property, indicates this is the case."

"On 16 April, the Grand Jury of Allegheny County returned indictments against Mr. Chenowith, Mr. Cole, Miss Ollwood, and Miss Fitzgerald, charging them with causing the unlawful deaths by explosive device of eleven individuals."

The screen now showed — in most cases snapshots, in one case a standard high-school graduation portrait, and in two others police photographs taken in an autopsy room — photographs of the eleven individuals who had lost their lives as a result of the explosives detonated by the Chenowith Group on the University of Pittsburgh campus.

"Mr. Chenowith's and Mr. Cole's difficulties brought them under FBI attention, and after Miss Fitzgerald and Miss Ollwood were positively identified as having been at Bennington College, Vermont, subsequent to their indictment in Pennsylvania, federal indictments were sought and obtained charging both females with unlawful flight to avoid prosecution.

"Because of the nature of the offenses alleged, FBI supervision of the cases involved, collectively referred to as 'the Chenowith Group,' has been assigned to the Anti-Terrorist Group at FBI Headquarters.

"The fugitives sought are known to be armed,

and should be considered highly dangerous."

Abruptly the screen went white, and the room lights brightened.

"Nice friends you have, Payne," Wee Willy Malone said.

"I think that we should keep that in mind, Detective Malone," SAC Davis said.

"Excuse me?" Malone asked.

"If I had to offer one reason that the FBI has so far been unable to apprehend these fugitives, the so-called Chenowith Group, it would be that they are 'nice.' They all come from upper-middle-class backgrounds — in the case of the Ollwood woman, an upper-class background. Not only are they highly intelligent, but they can move, with relative ease, from one socioeconomic environment to another. We don't really know where to look for them at any given time."

"Okay," Wee Willy said after considering that.

"Should we go on, sir?" Williamson asked.

"Please do," Davis said.

Special Agent Leibowitz got up from the table and took Williamson's place at the lectern.

The lights dimmed again and the slide projector began, with a thunk, to show a color slide of what Matt recognized as the Bennington College campus in the spring.

"We wondered why Ollwood and Fitzgerald went to Bennington, which is way to hell and gone from Pittsburgh in Vermont," Leibowitz began. "I mean, they both got the boot from the college, and there was still a local warrant outstanding against Ollwood for socking the campus cop, so why go back? Unless, of course, they had a good reason. We found it. There's a little white box around a blonde's face in the next couple of slides. Take a good look at her."

The slide machine thunked, and a black-and-white slide of a group of young women sitting on the wide steps of a large brick house appeared on the screen. There were circles around the faces of Misses Ollwood and Fitzgerald and a white box around the face of Susan Reynolds. And he recognized two other faces in the photo.

"I know a couple of other faces in that picture," Matt said. "Is that important?"

The slide was replaced by another snapshot.

"It could be," Davis said. "Who?"

Leibowitz, with some difficulty, managed to get the group shot back on the screen.

"The blonde, second from the left in the second row, is the former Daphne Elizabeth Browne," Matt said. "Now Mrs. Chadwick Thomas Nesbitt the Fourth."

"Interesting," Davis said. "The hostess of the party, right? We should have picked up on that."

"I don't think Daffy is the type to blow things up, and/or help fugitives," Matt said.

"Take my word for it, Detective," Jernigan said. "Assuming that 'nice' people can't be involved in some pretty nasty business isn't smart."

"Which is rather what I had in mind when I mentioned to Detective Malone that 'nice' is something we should all keep in mind."

Matt didn't reply.

"You said you knew a couple of faces?" Davis went on.

"Sitting beside Daffy is a female named

Penelope Alice Detweiler," Matt said, "who I *know* is not aiding and abetting our fugitives."

"How do you know that?" Jernigan challenged.

"She's dead," Matt said.

"Penny Detweiler died of a narcotics overdose," Chief Coughlin said.

"I see. Well, that would seem to buttress my observation about the meaning of the word 'nice,' wouldn't it?" Davis said.

The group shot disappeared from the screen and was replaced by a series of other snapshots of Bennington girls, each showing Susan Reynolds with a square box around her face and a circle around the face of either (or both) Eloise Anne Fitzgerald or Jennifer Ollwood — in some shots, of both.

"The blonde is Miss Susan Reynolds, of Camp Hill, Pennsylvania, white female now twenty-six years of age, five feet five, 130 pounds, blond hair, pale complexion, blue eyes, who has puncture wounds, entrance and exit, on her inside upper thigh caused by her having taken an arrow during archery practice at summer camp when she was sixteen."

There were chuckles around the table.

Somebody — Matt could not tell for sure, but it sounded like Jack Matthews — asked incredulously, "*Archery* practice? Some girl didn't know the bow was loaded?"

There were more chuckles.

Another photo of Susan appeared, a more recent photograph. In it she was wearing a dress.

"This was taken three months or so ago, outside the Department of Social Services Building in Harrisburg, where Miss Reynolds is employed as an appeals officer," Leibowitz said. "She resides with her parents in Camp Hill and drives a red Porsche 911 — which she obviously didn't buy with what they pay her at Social Services — and in which she frequently drove to her family's summer home in the Pocono Mountains on weekends.

"When this came to our attention," Leibowitz continued, "we sought and received assistance from the local authorities."

"What 'local authorities'?" Chief Coughlin asked.

"The county sheriff, Chief," Leibowitz said. "We gave him a camera with a tripod and a telephoto lens —"

"You *gave* him a camera?" Peter Wohl asked.

"I asked about that myself, Peter," Walter Davis said. "It was cost-effective, Agent Leibowitz told me. I suppose a good camera like that is worth five hundred dollars. . . ."

"I think that particular camera outfit cost us $412.50," Leibowitz said.

"How do I get on your gift list?" Wohl asked.

"Anytime you're willing to place a premises such as the Reynolds summer home under at least part-time surveillance and save the FBI the man-hours of keeping it under surveillance ourselves."

"Clever," Wohl said appreciatively.

"And it has a certain public-relations aspect, too, Peter," Davis said. "Getting a camera from the FBI makes the local authorities look on us as their friends. As hard as you may find this to believe, not all police officers look on us fondly."

"But on the other hand, Walter," Wohl said, "some of my officers like FBI agents so much that they take them on sight-seeing tours, absolutely free of charge."

"Actually, now that my temper has had time to cool down," Leibowitz said, "I have to admit that was sort of funny. But let me show you what our $412.50 bought."

A somewhat grainy photograph of a Ford sedan came on the screen.

"We ran the plate. The *plate* was stolen. There were no recent reports of a Ford like that having been stolen in a four-state area."

"They switched plates," Denny Coughlin thought out loud.

"We think that's probable. And there are just too many two-year-old Fords like that to make it cost-efficient to run every one of them down."

"Yeah," Wohl agreed.

"This is, in case anyone can't guess, the Reynolds summer house," Leibowitz said. "And this gentleman is Mr. Bryan C. Chenowith," he said, as a picture of a young man in sports clothing and wearing horn-rimmed glasses getting out of the Ford appeared on the screen.

"Bingo!" Chief Coughlin said.

"On this occasion," Leibowitz said, "Mr. Chenowith was accompanied by Miss Ollwood."

The screen now showed Jennifer Ollwood, wearing a tweed skirt and a sweater, standing on the porch of the Reynolds cabin. She was being embraced by Susan Reynolds.

Jesus Christ! Matt thought. *There's no question about it now. Susan is in with these lunatics up to her cute little ass.*

"Obviously," Chief Coughlin said, "you didn't get this in time to do anything about it, and the sheriff's deputy?"

"We asked the local authorities to locate and identify, not apprehend," Leibowitz said. "We want the Chenowith Group alive, taken into custody without the firing of a shot. The last thing we want to do is kill one of them and make a martyr out of him," Leibowitz said, "or, especially, one of the females."

"But aren't these photographs enough to pick up the Reynolds girl?" Denny Coughlin asked. "Charge her with aiding and abetting? Accessory after the fact? Lean on her hard?"

"*After* we get the Chenowith Group, Chief," Leibowitz said, "I'm sure the U.S. Attorney will go after her. But the priority is the apprehension of the Chenowith Group."

"I understand," Coughlin said.

"Once we had these pictures, and identified Chenowith and Ollwood, we put the premises under surveillance, of course," Leibowitz said. "And the to-be-expected result of that, of course, was that they never went back to the Poconos."

"They spotted the surveillance?" Peter Wohl asked.

"That's possible, of course," Leibowitz replied. "But we think it's equally possible that they simply suspected they had been using that rendezvous point too often. Whatever the reason, they never went back to the Reynolds summer house."

"What's the purpose of the rendezvous?" Matt asked.

"I was about to get to that," Leibowitz said. "First of all, we think it has to do with money. We believe that since we have been looking for them, the Chenowith Group has been involved in as many as four bank robberies. We have surveillance-camera proof that Chenowith and Ollwood have been involved in two bank robberies. A total of $140,000, in round figures, has been taken. One of them was a very recent case."

The lights went out and several surveillance-camera images of a female with a kerchief on her head wearing a raincoat and large dangling earrings appeared on the screen.

"That's Ollwood?" Detective Wee Willie Malone asked doubtfully.

Leibowitz chuckled. "That's Mr. Chenowith," he said.

"My God, the very ugly white woman with hairy legs," Wohl said, laughing. "The Girard Bank job in — where was it?"

"Bucks County. Riegelsville," Leibowitz furnished.

"I'm missing the point of the humor here," Chief Coughlin said.

"Mickey O'Hara wrote a hilarious story about it," Matt said. "The guy in the bank described the bandit as a very ugly white woman with hairy legs."

"That woman is Chenowith?" Coughlin asked.

"The lab did some interesting stuff, comparing the nose, hands, ears, and so on, of the 'woman' with Chenowith's features. That's him, Chief."

The news did not seem to please Coughlin.

"So they're wanted on bank-robbery charges, too?" he asked.

"In a sense, Chief," Leibowitz said. "We have not charged any of them with bank robbery. We don't want them to know we know they're involved. Our thinking here — the thinking of the attorney general — is that once we apprehend them, we can quickly bring them to trial in Federal Court and get a conviction, using the surveillance-camera footage as proof. There is very little sympathy for bank robbers, and the evidence for the two bank jobs where we have surveillance-camera footage is *not* circumstantial. Their defense cannot bring up the morality of using animals in medical research, et cetera. And once they are convicted, then we can try them on the University of Pittsburgh bombing charges."

"Public relations, huh?" Coughlin said in disgust.

"Unfortunately, that has to be considered," Davis said.

"Now, our thinking is that *they* are thinking that since we are not searching for them on the bank-robbery charges we may not know about the bank robberies. Consequently, if we should get lucky and get them into custody, they don't want to be found in possession of a large sum of money that even the none-too-bright FBI might decide came from unsolved bank robberies."

"You mean you think Reynolds is holding the bank loot for them?" Matt asked.

"Yeah," Leibowitz said. "And dispensing it as needed to pay their expenses. Being a fugitive is expensive."

"I thought she might be getting money to them," Matt said. "Not the other way around."

"In a sense, she is, Payne," Davis said. "But I see what you mean."

"And even if you could get a search warrant," Wohl said, "the question would be where would you search?"

"Precisely, Inspector," Leibowitz said. "If we'd tumbled onto the Reynolds woman's connection to the Chenowith Group earlier, maybe we could have done something. And, of course, the minute we would serve a search warrant on her, that would be the end of any meetings with any of them."

"Yeah," Wohl said thoughtfully.

"So what we have to do is find out where the Reynolds woman is going to meet with the Chenowith Group, or Chenowith individually, in sufficient time to set up an arrest that can't possibly go sour. We don't, to repeat, want to have to shoot any of these individuals and turn them into martyrs."

"If we winged one of them in the arm," Jernigan said. "Their defense counsel would wheel them into the courtroom in a wheelchair, in a body cast, with intravenous tubes feeding him blood, an innocent college student showing his — even worse, her — grievous injuries suffered at the hands of the American Gestapo."

"That bad?" Coughlin asked.

"We think that's exactly what would happen. We want to take these people without giving them a bruise," Davis said. "So that, Payne, is where you come in. Get close to the Reynolds woman;

make that happen."

"When I call 'the Reynolds woman,' " Matt said, "she's liable to tell me the same thing she told me when I tried to get her out of the Nesbitt party. 'I told you once, fuck off!' "

"Did she really say that?" Davis asked.

"What she said was, 'I'm sure you're a very nice fellow, but I'm just not interested.' "

"I still think it's worth a try," Davis said. "Two or three tries. She's our best shot at the Chenowith Group."

"Okay," Matt said. "I'll give it a shot."

"We don't expect her to lead you to the rendezvous, Payne," Leibowitz said. "We don't even expect you to find out where she's meeting these people. All we want from you is to call us — which means Special Agent Matthews — when you have reason to believe she is going to meet them. Just tell us where she is at that moment. We'll take it from there."

Matt's mouth ran away with him.

"Tail her, you mean? The way you tailed me? If she spots you as quickly as I did — and I suspect she'd be looking for a tail, and I wasn't — this is all going to be an exercise in futility."

Davis glowered at him. Wohl looked amused.

"We will have assets in place, Detective Payne," Leibowitz said, "that will permit us — providing you give us enough time to deploy those assets — to keep the Reynolds woman under surveillance without being detected."

"I hope so," Matt said.

"Matty," Chief Coughlin said. "I hope you

heard what Mr. Davis and Leibowitz said about how they want to arrest these people?"

"Yes, sir."

"They don't want to run any risk of these people being injured, or their resisting arrest," Coughlin went on. "You understand that?"

"Yes, sir."

"Consider that an order from me," Coughlin said. "If you should run into this Chenowith fellow and the other man and the two women skipping down North Broad Street at high noon, all you are to do about it is tell the FBI. You take my meaning?"

"Yes, sir."

If I see any of these scumbags, Detective Payne thought, his mind full of the faces of the eleven innocent people who had been killed, *and I think I can put the arm on one of them — or all of them — without getting myself hurt, I will, and no one will ever remember that I got that order.*

Eleven

When Matt rang the bell at Number 9 Stockton Place, it was opened by a muscular man in his late thirties. Matt was startled, not so much by the man opening the door instead of Daffy herself, or one of the ever-changing parade of maids, but because the man smelled of cop. That instant reaction was immediately confirmed when Matt saw the unmistakable bulge of a pistol in a shoulder holster.

"Who are you?" Matt blurted.

"Who are *you,* sir?" the man said with exaggerated courtesy that rubbed Matt the wrong way.

"Are you on the job?" Matt demanded.

"Who was that at the door?" Chad Nesbitt called down from the second floor.

"The gentleman was just about to give me his name, sir," the man said, offering Matt a patently insincere smile. That was enough to tell Matt that he was facing a rent-a-cop.

"Household Finance, Mr. Nesbitt," Matt called, raising his voice. "We want our money or the television."

"Shit." Chad chuckled. "Let him in."

"Yes, sir," the rent-a-cop said, and stood back to let Matt pass.

"Let him in anytime," Chad added. "He's safe. As a matter of fact, he's a cop. Forgive me, a *detective.* Which probably means, come to think of it, that we'll have to count the silver after he leaves."

"You can go up, sir."

"Wachenhut?" Matt asked the man.

The Wachenhut Security Corporation provided the rent-a-cops for the Stockton Place complex.

"Nesfoods Security, sir," the man said.

"You've got a permit to carry, concealed?"

"Of course, sir."

Matt started up the stairs.

"Your name, sir?" the security man asked, and before Matt could reply, explained, "For your next visit, sir."

"Payne," Matt said. "Matt Payne."

"Did I understand Mr. Nesbitt to say you are a police officer, sir?"

"Yes, he did, and yes, I am," Matt said.

"Thank you, sir."

Matt went up the stairs.

Chadwick Thomas Nesbitt IV, in a sweat suit, was holding Penelope Alice Nesbitt in his arms.

"I have trouble believing you are responsible for that," Matt said.

"For what?"

"That beautiful child," Matt said. He leaned close to the baby and touched her cheek with his finger. "Fear not, sweet child, your godfather will protect you from these terrible people."

"Fuck you," Chad said. "To what do we owe the honor?"

"I thought I would take you out and buy you dinner," Matt said. "I had La Bochabella in mind."

244

La Bochabella was an upscale Italian restaurant in the 1100 block of South Front Street, not far from Stockton Place.

"What did you do, get into it with Daffy again?" Chad asked suspiciously.

"Her, too, if she wants to go," Matt said.

Chad laughed.

"If she wants to go where?" Daffy said, walking into the room. She was also wearing a gray sweat suit.

"He wants to take us to La Bochabella," Chad said.

"By way of making up for what?" Daffy said, taking the baby from her husband.

"Actually, I hoped that by the time they came around with the check, your husband would figure, after what you did to me, Daffy, with the virgin's mother, that the least he could do was buy me dinner."

"For all you know, wiseass, Susan may *be* a virgin," Daffy said. "Why not? I'll need to shower first, of course."

"I can't imagine why," Matt said. "What's with the sweat suits?"

"She's trying to get her figure back," Chad said.

"Where did it go?" Matt asked, innocently.

". . . so we put in a little exercise room," Daffy said.

"You know, to keep in shape," Chad said. "You want to see it?"

"No. Not really. But while you're sharing all the sordid secrets of your married life with me, what's with the rent-a-cop?"

"He's not a rent-a-cop. He's from the company."

"What's he doing?"

"The Old Broads got together," Chad said. "The grandmothers. They went to the Old Man."

"I don't understand."

"They're worried about Penny's safety," Daffy said. "And mine, too."

"Did something happen?" Matt asked, now concerned.

"You ever hear, 'an ounce of prevention,' et cetera?" Chad said.

"You're really worried?" Matt asked. "In here?"

"Daffy's alone a lot," Chad said, a bit defensively. "With the baby."

"And a nanny, and at least one maid," Matt said. "Not to mention the rent-a-cop at the gate keeping the riffraff out."

"And now a security guy from the company," Chad said. "All right? It makes the Old Broads feel better and it makes me feel better, too, okay?"

"That guy's going to be here around the clock?" Matt asked.

"Not *that* guy," Chad said. "He's a supervisor. He's a retired Jersey state trooper. He used to bodyguard the governor. What he's doing is seeing what has to be done. But yeah, there will be security people here around the clock."

"You should know better than most people, Matt," Daffy said, "what goes on in the city. And that the police can't stop things from happening."

"There's only so many cops, Daffy," Matt said,

now defensively. "They can't be everywhere at once."

"My point exactly," Chad said.

"I like the idea of La Bochabella," Daffy said. "Exercise makes me hungry."

She handed the baby back to her husband.

"I'll shower first," she said.

"Give me the urchin," Matt said mischievously, "and you can shower together."

Chad took him seriously.

"Yeah," Chad said, and handed him the baby. "Good thinking. One of the perks of married life. You should try it, buddy."

"Don't drop her, Matt!" Daffy said.

"She will be a good deal safer with me, madam, than she would be in her mother's arms," Matt said solemnly.

"You're up to something, Matt," Daffy said. "I don't trust you."

"I have no idea, madam, of what you're accusing me."

"Fix yourself a drink," Chad said. "You know where it is."

"Yeah."

Fixing himself a drink proved more difficult than he thought it would be. When he went to the bar, holding the baby, it became immediately apparent that he could not easily, one-handed, either open a scotch bottle or get ice from the refrigerator.

He walked to the couch and, with infinite tenderness, laid his goddaughter down on it, far enough away from the edge so there was no chance of her falling off.

He was halfway back to the bar when Penelope Alice Nesbitt expressed her displeasure at being laid down by howling with surprising volume for someone her size.

She stopped howling the moment she was picked up again, and he carried her back to the bar, where, with great difficulty, he made himself a drink. Then he carried the baby back to the couch and sat down.

After a moment, he propped the baby up at the junction of the back and arm of the chair, and watched to see if she would start to howl again. She didn't. She liked that. She smiled and made a gurgling noise.

"Would Penny and I have made something like you, sweetheart?" Matt asked softly as he extended his finger to the baby. She took his finger in her hand.

Matt became aware that his eyes were tearing and his throat was very tight.

"Shit!" he said, and took a deep swallow of his scotch on the rocks. The emotional moment passed.

Surprising him, Daffy returned first, dressed to go out.

"You should have gotten yourself a date," she said. "It would be like old times."

"You mean, you and Chad in the backseat of the car, making elephants-in-rut–type noises?"

"Screw you, you know what I mean," Daffy said. "Are you seeing much of Amanda these days?"

He shook his head, "no."

"Why not? She's a really nice girl."

"We never seem to be free at the same time," Matt said.

"Yeah," Daffy said, and changed the subject: "Well, since we all can't fit in your car, I'd better see about ours."

"Either this child has terminal B.O., or it needs a diaper change," Matt said.

Daffy picked up her baby and walked out of the room with her. Chad appeared a moment later, walked to the bar, poured whiskey in a glass and tossed it down, then held his finger in front of his lips in a signal that Daffy was not to know he had a little predinner drink.

Daffy reappeared, and they went down the stairs. The rent-a-cop was not in sight, and Matt wondered where he was.

When they went outside, the rent-a-cop was standing beside an Oldsmobile 98 sedan, the doors of which were open.

Daffy and Chad got in the backseat, the rent-a-cop got behind the wheel, and Matt got in the front passenger seat beside him.

"You know the La Bochabella restaurant?" Chad asked.

"Yes, sir."

"Where'd you get this?" Matt asked when they were inside. "It's new, isn't it?"

"Yeah," Chad said. "Tell him, Mr. Frazier."

"The statistics show," Frazier announced, very seriously, "that there are far fewer incidents involving Oldsmobiles and Buicks than there are involving Cadillacs and Lincolns. Presumably, they don't attract the same kind of attention from the wrong kind of people."

"You're telling me your old man is going to turn in his Rolls Royce on an Olds?" Matt asked. "To avoid an *incident?*"

"No." Chad laughed. "But he's stopped going anywhere in it alone."

"You seem to feel this is funny, Matt," Daffy said. "I don't. *We* don't."

"Straight answer, Daffy?"

"If you can come up with one."

"As a cop, I'm a little embarrassed that Chad's father, and your mothers, and you really feel it's necessary."

"That brings us back to my ounce of prevention," Chad said.

Matt confessed to the maître d' of La Bochabella that he didn't have a reservation, and asked how much of a problem that was going to be.

The maître d' consulted his reservations list at length, frowning, and shaking his head.

If this son of a bitch is waiting for me to slip him money, we'll be here all night.

"I'm afraid, sir . . ." the maître d' began.

A chubby, splendidly tailored man in his late twenties walked up to the maître d's stand.

"Ricardo," he announced, "Mr. Brewer just phoned and canceled his reservation." He looked at Matt. "If you're willing to wait just a few minutes, sir, we'll be happy to accommodate you."

"Thank you," Matt said.

"And your name, sir?"

"Payne," Matt said. The maître d' wrote that

250

at the head of his list of reservations.

"Initial?" the splendidly tailored chubby fellow said.

"*M,*" Matt said.

"Perhaps you'd like to wait at the bar," the splendidly tailored chubby fellow suggested. "It will be a few minutes."

"Thank you," Matt said, and led the way to the bar, which occupied most of the left side of the corridor leading from the door to the dining room. When he had slid onto a stool, he saw Frazier sitting at the end of the bar, near the door.

He wondered, idly, what Frazier was drinking.

Can you sit at the bar of an expensive place like this and drink soda? Or does a rent-a-cop on duty order a scotch straight up with soda on the side, and not drink the scotch? Or pour it on the floor, when no one's looking?

The bartender appeared.

"I'll have what that gentlemen is drinking," Matt said, indicating Frazier.

"The gentleman is drinking soda with a lemon slice, sir," the bartender said.

"In that case, I think I'd better take a look at the wine list," Matt said. "We can take a bottle to the table later, right?"

"Of course, sir."

"What are we celebrating, Matt?" Daffy asked.

"Nothing, so far as I know. Why?"

"I don't trust you when you are charming. *You* asking for the wine list?"

"Then screw you, baby! You don't get no wine."

She smiled.

"Better. That's the old Matt, the one I have always loathed and despised."

Chad chuckled.

The chubby, splendidly tailored man in his late twenties, whose name was Anthony Joseph Desidiro, waited until he saw that Mr. Payne and party had taken seats at the bar, and then he walked to the rear of the dining room. Against the rear wall was a table shielded by a light green silk screen. The screen's weave was such that people seated at the table could see the dining room but people in the dining room could not see who was sitting at the table.

There were two men at the table. One was Mr. Desidiro's cousin, a large, well-muscled, equally splendidly tailored gentleman whose name appeared on the liquor and restaurant licenses of La Bochabella as the owner. His name was Paulo Cassandro. His mother and Mr. Desidiro's mother were sisters. Mr. Cassandro had provided his cousin Tony with both his tuition at the Cornell School of Hotel & Restaurant Administration, and a generous allowance while he was there so he would be able to devote his full time to learning the hotel and restaurant administration profession.

On his graduation, Mr. Desidiro spent two years working — he thought of it as an internship — at the Ristorante Alfredo, another of Philadelphia's more elegant Italian restaurants, on whose liquor and restaurant licenses Mr. Cassandro was also listed as owner.

Two months before, Mr. Desidiro had been

named manager of La Bochabella. He had told his cousin Paulo that it was his plan that La Bochabella would become known as the best Northern Italian restaurant in Philadelphia, catering to the social and economic upper crust of Philadelphia.

He wanted to raise prices sufficiently to discourage the patronage of those who thought Italian cuisine was primarily sausage and peppers and spaghetti and meatballs, and that fine Italian wine began and ended with Chianti in raffia-wrapped bottles.

"You got eighteen months, Tony," Cousin Paulo had told him. "Mr. S. thinks maybe you got a good idea. You got eighteen months to make it work."

Mr. S. was what his intimates called Mr. Vincenzo Savarese, and Mr. Desidiro was aware that Cousin Paulo's name on the licenses notwithstanding, Mr. Savarese had the controlling interest in both La Bochabella and Ristorante Alfredo.

Mr. Desidiro thought it was fortuitous that Mr. Savarese had chosen tonight to have dinner in La Bochabella with Cousin Paulo — he came in only every couple of weeks, and then mostly for lunch, not dinner — and he would thus have the opportunity to prove to Mr. Savarese that his philosophy for the successful operation of the restaurant was bearing fruit.

He stepped behind the curtain. Both Cousin Paulo and Mr. Savarese interrupted their meal to look at him.

"Is everything all right?" Mr. Desidiro asked. "Do you like the lamb, Mr. Savarese?"

"Very much," Mr. Savarese said. "The garlic — how do I say this? — is delicate."

"We throw garlic buds, crushed but in their skins, directly on the coals when the leg is still raw," Mr. Desidiro said. "It delicately infuses the meat with the flavor, I think. I'm pleased that you like it."

"Very nice," Mr. Savarese said.

"Yeah, Tony," Cassandro said.

"You know who we have outside, waiting for a table?" Mr. Desidiro said, and went on before a reply could be made. "Mr. and Mrs. Nesbitt the Fourth, of Nesfoods International."

"Yes," Mr. Savarese said. "I saw them. I was going to have a word with you about them."

Mr. Desidiro tried not to show his surprise that Mr. Savarese recognized the heir to Nesfoods International and his wife.

"Yes, Mr. Savarese."

"They have a friend with them," Mr. Savarese said.

"A Mr. Payne," Mr. Desidiro said.

"Yes, I know," Mr. Savarese said. "You should be very careful around him, Tony."

"Yes, sir?"

"He is not only a policeman, but he shoots people in the head," Mr. Savarese said. "Isn't that so, Paulo?"

"That's right, Mr. S.," Paulo agreed.

"You remember that crazy man, Tony, who was kidnapping and then doing sexual things to women in Northwest Philadelphia?" Mr. Savarese asked.

"Yes, I do. A policeman shot him?"

254

"That policeman," Mr. Savarese said.

"Right in the head, Tony," Cassandro said, miming someone shooting a pistol. "Ka-pow! Ka-pow!"

"Very interesting," Mr. Desidiro said, wondering what a cop was doing having dinner — Mr. S. had said "a friend" — with the guy whose father owned Nesfoods International.

"If Mr. Payne should ask for the check, Tony," Mr. Savarese said, "please tell him that it has been taken care of by a friend — make that 'an admirer.' "

"Right, Mr. Savarese. 'An admirer.' "

"Please have the courtesy to let me finish, Tony," Mr. Savarese said.

"Excuse me, Mr. Savarese," Mr. Desidiro said. "I beg your pardon."

"You should learn to listen, Tony," Mr. Savarese said.

"Jesus Christ, Tony!" Cassandro snapped.

"If young Mr. Payne asks for the check, please tell him that it has been taken care of by an admirer of *his father,*" Mr. Savarese said.

"Of his father," Mr. Desidiro said. "Right, Mr. Savarese."

And then he had a question, which, after a moment, he spoke aloud.

"And if Mr. Nesbitt should ask for the check, Mr. Savarese?"

"Then give it to him," Mr. Savarese said. "I am not indebted to his father."

"Right, Mr. Savarese."

"You understand, Tony," Cassandro said. "You don't mention Mr. S.'s name?"

255

"Right. Of course not."

"I'm going to Harrisburg," Matt Payne announced after they had all ordered, at the suggestion of the waiter, roast lamb with roasted potatoes, a spinach salad, and were waiting for the shrimp cocktail they had ordered for an appetizer.

"I didn't know anyone went there on purpose," Chad said.

"I am *being sent* to Harrisburg," Matt corrected himself.

"Susan lives outside Harrisburg," Daffy said.

"You do something wrong?" Chad said, reaching for the bottle of Merlot.

"Of course not," Matt said. "I am known in the department as Detective Perfect. Yeah, that's right, isn't it? She told me that."

"Shit!" Chad said. "Who told you what?"

"Susan Whatsername told me she lived in Harrisburg."

"Camp Hill," Daffy corrected him. "Outside Harrisburg."

"What are you being sent to Harrisburg for?" Chad asked.

"They are having a crime wave, and require the services of a big-city detective to solve it."

"Bullshit."

"You remember reading about the lieutenant the Department threw in the slammer for protecting the call girl ring?"

"Yeah."

"Not for publication, I'm tying up some loose ends on that," Matt said.

"A call girl ring?" Daffy said. "Right down your alley. You should love that."

"I'm looking forward to it."

"You really should call her," Daffy said.

"Call who? Any call girl? Or do you have a specific one in mind?"

"Susan, you ass."

"Your pal Susan shot me down in flames, you will recall."

"If at first you don't succeed," Daffy said.

"I have her phone number," Matt said. "You gave it to me."

"Call her. If nothing else, it'll keep you out of trouble with the call girls," Daffy said.

"I don't know," Matt said doubtfully.

"Call her, damn you. She's a very nice girl."

A very nice girl, Matt thought, *who is aiding and abetting four murdering lunatics.*

"Are you going to be talking to her?" Matt asked.

"I don't know," Daffy replied. "I can. Why?"

"I don't suppose you would be willing to tell her you were only kidding when you told her what an all-around son of a bitch I am?"

"I wasn't kidding. But, okay, I'll call her and put in a good word for you. *If* you promise to call her when you're there."

"If I can find the time," Matt said.

"Find the time," Chad said.

"She's really a very nice girl," Daffy said.

Now, if you call our Susan and tell her, or let her surmise, that my calling her was your and Chad's idea, and I'm not thrilled about it, that just may allay her suspicions that I might have a professional interest in her activities, and this charade will not have been in vain.

"Ah," Matt said. "Here comes the shrimp. Can we change the subject, please?"

"Take her to the Hotel Hershey," Daffy said. "That's romantic as hell."

"All I want to do with her, Daffy," Matt said, sounding serious, "is get her in bed. I didn't say a word about . . ."

"You bastard!" Daffy said, smiling at him. "Now I *will* call her. Susan may be just the girl to bring you under control."

Philip Chason, a slightly built fifty-five-year-old who walked with a limp, turned his three-year-old Ford sedan off Essington Avenue — sometimes called "Automobile Row" — and onto the lot of Fiorello's Fine Cars.

It was one of the larger lots; Chason figured there must be 150 cars on display, ranging from year-old Cadillacs and Buicks down to junkers one step away from the crusher.

Chason was not in the market for a car. And if he was going shopping for one, he wouldn't have come here. Joe Fiorello was somehow tied to the mob. Chason didn't know exactly what the connection was, but he knew there was one. And Chason had a thing about the mob; he didn't like the idea of them getting any of his money.

Chason had spent twenty-six years of his life as a Philadelphia policeman, and eighteen of the twenty-six years as a detective, before a drunk had run a red light and slammed into the side of his unmarked car. That had put him in the hospital for six weeks, given him a gimp leg that hurt whenever it rained, and gotten him a line-of-duty-injury pension.

After sitting around for four months watching the grass grow, Phil Chason had got himself a private investigator's license, made a little office in the basement of his house, put in another telephone and an answering machine, and took out an ad in the phone book's yellow pages: "Philip Chason, Confidential Investigations. (Retired Detective, Philadelphia P.D.)."

It was not a quick way to get rich in any case, and it had been tough getting started at all. But gradually jobs started coming his way. Too many of them were sleaze, like following some guy whose wife suspected he was getting a little on the side, or some dame whose husband figured she was.

He got some seasonal work, like at Christmas at John Wanamaker's Department Store, helping their security people keep an eye on shoplifters and seasonal employees. And Wachenhut called him every once in a while to work, for example, ritzy parties at the Philadelphia Museum of Art, or a big reception at one of the hotels, keeping scumbags from ripping people off.

Both Wanamaker's and Wachenhut had offered him a full-time job, but the money was anything but great, and he didn't want to get tied down to having to go to work every day, especially when the leg was giving him trouble.

He got some work from the sleazebags who hung around the courts and called themselves "The Criminal Bar," but there were two things wrong with that: he didn't like helping some scumbag lawyer keep some scumbag from going to jail, and they paid slow.

And he'd done a couple of jobs for Joe Fiorello before this one. Fiorello had called him out of the blue about a year ago, said he'd seen the ad in the yellow pages, and needed a job done.

Chason had told Joey his "initial consultation fee" was fifty bucks, whether or not he took the job. He knew who Fiorello was and he had no intention of doing something illegal. Joey had told him no problem, that he should come by the used-car lot and he'd tell him what he wanted done, and Chason could decide whether or not he wanted to do it.

What Joey wanted the first time was for Chason to check out a guy he was thinking of hiring as a salesman. The guy had a great reputation as a salesman, Joey said, but there was *something* about him that didn't smell kosher, and before he took him on, he wanted to be sure about him, and how much would that cost?

Chason had told him it would probably take about ten hours of his time, at twenty-five dollars an hour, plus expenses, like getting a credit report, and mileage, at a dime a mile, and Joey thought it over a minute and then said go ahead, how long will it take, the sooner the better.

That time, Chason had found out the guy was what he said he was, what his reputation said he was, a hardworking guy with a family, who paid his bills, didn't drink a hell of a lot, went to church, and even, as far as Chason could find out, slept with his own wife.

Chason couldn't figure why a guy like that, who already had a good job as sales manager for the used-car department of the Pontiac dealer in Willow Grove, would want to work in the city for Fiorello. The answer to that was that he didn't. The second time Joey Fiorello called Chason, to do the same kind of a job on another guy Joey was thinking of hiring, Chason asked him what happened to the first guy, and Joey told him he'd made the guy an offer that wasn't good enough — the guy wanted an arm and a leg, Joey said — and that hadn't worked out.

The second time had been like the first job. Only this time the guy was selling furniture on Market Street, and thought he might like selling cars. Another Mr. Straight Citizen. Wife, kids, church, the whole nine yards. And he either came to his senses about what a good job he already had, or somebody whispered in his ear that Joey Fiorello wasn't the absolutely respectable businessman he wanted everybody to think he was. Anyway, he didn't go to work for Fiorello Fine Cars, either.

This last job was something else. This one was a young guy, from Bala Cynwyd, who was a stockbroker. Chason thought there was something fishy about a stockbroker wanting to be a used-car salesman right from the start. Usually, it would be a used-car salesman trying to get into something more classy, like being a stockbroker, not the other way around.

Once he started nosing around, Chason thought he understood why. This guy was a real sleaze, too sleazy even to work for a sleazy greaseball like Joey Fiorello.

One of Joey's salesmen, a young guy wearing an open-collared yellow sport shirt with a gold chain around his neck and a phony Rolex on his wrist, came out of the office with a toothy 'Hello, sucker!' smile on his face.

"Can I be of some assistance, sir?"

"Mr. Fiorello around?"

"Yes, sir," the salesman said. "But I believe he may be tied up at the moment. Is there something I can do for you?"

"No, thanks," Chason said, and walked around the guy and into the office.

Joey's secretary, a peroxide blonde with great breasts who Chason had learned wasn't as dumb as she looked, smiled at him, then picked up her telephone.

"Mr. Chason is here, Mr. Fiorello," she announced, listened a minute, and then hung up.

"Mr. Fiorello said he'll be right with you, Mr. Chason," she said. "How have you been?"

"Can't complain," Chason said. "How about yourself?"

"Well, you know," the blonde said. "A little of this, a little of that."

A moment later, the door to Joey's office opened and a guy who looked like another salesman came out. Then Joey appeared in the door.

"Hey, Phil, how's the boy? Come on in. You want a cup of coffee, or a Coke or something?"

"I could take some coffee," Chason said.

"Helene, how about getting Mr. Chason and me some coffee. How do you take yours, Phil?"

"Black would be fine," Chason said as he shook

Joey's extended hand and walked into the office.

He had to admit it, Joey had a classy office. Nice furniture, all red leather, and a great big desk that must have cost a fortune. The walls were just about covered with pictures of classy cars and of Joey and his family on his sailboat. There was a model of the sailboat, sails and everything, in a glass case.

The blonde delivered two mugs of coffee. The mugs said, "Fiorello Fine Cars. We sell to sell again!"

Joey waited until the blonde had closed the door behind her, then asked, "You got something for me, Phil?"

"I don't think you're going to like it, Joey."

"I pay you to find things out. Who said anything about me having to like it?"

"Mr. Ronald R. Ketcham is a sleazeball, Joey," Chason said.

"How is he a sleazeball?"

"You understand I can't *prove* anything, Joey. I mean, if I was still a cop, I don't have anything I could take to the district attorney."

"Tell me what you found out," Joey Fiorello said. "That's good enough for me."

"Okay. The truth is, he is a stockbroker. For Wendell, Wilson and Company, in Bala Cynwyd. Before that, he was a stockbroker with Merrill, Lynch, here in the city. He told Wendell, Wilson he wanted to leave Merrill, Lynch so he wouldn't have to come into the city every day. The truth is, he resigned from Merrill, Lynch about five minutes before they were going to fire him."

"Fire him for what?"

"For one thing, he didn't go to work very often, and for another, there was talk that when he did show up for work, he did a lot of business his customers didn't know about. You know what I mean?"

Joey shook his head, "no."

"Stockbrokers work on commission. The more stocks and bonds and stuff they buy and sell, the more money they make. So, if they aren't too ethical, they call their customers up and suggest they sell something he hears is going to go down, and buy something else he hears is going to go up, and maybe his information isn't so kosher. He did a lot of that at Merrill, Lynch, but that isn't all. If they have customers that are buying and selling a lot, so their monthly statements are pretty complicated, what some of those guys do — what Ketcham got caught doing — is making trades their customers didn't order."

"Explain that to me," Joey said.

"Like you own five thousand shares of, say, General Motors. Ketcham would sell, say, a thousand shares one day, and buy it back the next. And get a commission selling it, and another commission buying it back."

"The customers don't notice?"

"A lot of the customers don't keep good records," Chason explained. "They get their statement, it says they sold a thousand shares at fifty bucks, and then, a day later, they bought a thousand shares at forty-seven-fifty, which means they picked up twenty-five hundred bucks less the commissions, why ask questions?"

"What if they sold the stock at forty-seven-fifty,

and then bought it back at fifty, and they *lost* twenty-five hundred? Don't that ring bells that something ain't kosher?"

"From what I hear, believe it or not, most people don't catch on right away. The company itself catches more salesmen doing stuff like that than the customers do. And that's what happened to Mr. Ketcham at Merrill, Lynch. The company — they call the people who do it 'internal auditors' — caught him."

"But they didn't fire him?" Joey asked. "You said he resigned, right?"

"Like I said, I can't prove this happened to him at Merrill, Lynch, but this is the way something like this works, all right? The internal auditors catch a guy doing something like this, what can they do? If they fire the guy because he's been making unauthorized trades for his customer, and they tell the customer, the customer is going to be pissed, right? And take his business some other place, and tell all his friends what Merrill, Lynch, or whoever, has done to him."

"Yeah," Joey said, considering that. "So what do they do?"

"They call the guy in, tell him that they have enough on him to get him kicked out of the stockbroker business for life, and that the smart thing for him to do is have his desk cleaned out by five o'clock, keep his mouth shut, and if he gets another job, to straighten up and fly right. You get the picture."

"Jesus, you just can't trust anybody these days, can you?" Joey said.

"There's more crooks out of jail than in," Chason said.

"So he went to this company in Bala Cynwyd, you're telling me, and started this shit all over?"

"No. Not exactly. He's about to get canned from Wendell, Wilson for not producing. That means not selling or buying enough for his customers. The reason he's not producing enough is that he comes to work late, leaves early, or doesn't come to work at all. You can only get away with telling the boss you were 'developing business' on the golf course, which is why you weren't at work, if you actually produce the business."

"If he's not 'producing business,' what's he living on, if he's working on commission?"

"That's what I wondered," Chason said. "He lives good. He pays a lot of money for his apartment, drives a fancy car, dresses good, and he's got a girlfriend who probably costs him a lot of money."

"You mean a hooker?"

"No, I mean one of those Main Line beauties, who expect to be taken to expensive restaurants, and weekends at the shore. Like that."

"How do you know about the girlfriend?" Tony asked.

Chason took a small notebook from his pocket.

"Her name is Cynthia Longwood," he said. "Her father is Randolph Longwood, the builder."

"I heard the name," Joey said.

"Anyway, they have been running around for some time. So I wondered how he was paying for all this, and started asking some questions around. I got to tell you again, Joey, that I can't prove any of this, it's just . . ."

Joey Fiorello indicated with his hands that he understood the caveat.

"If I was a betting man, Joey, which I don't happen to be, I'd give odds that this sleazeball is into drugs. Maybe not big time, but not small time, either."

"No shit?"

"It all fits, if you think about it."

"You tell me."

"If somebody has an armful of that shit, everything is rosy. You don't give a shit about anything. You don't feel like going to work, you don't go to work. Everything will be all right. And if you do go to work, you put some shit up your nose, it turns you into a fucking genius. You're too smart to get caught buying and selling stocks and bonds nobody told you to. You understand?"

"I'm getting the picture."

"You get your hands on, say, twenty thousand dollars' worth of heroin, or cocaine, any of the high-class stuff, if you know where to get it and where to sell it, you keep out what you need to shove in your own arm, or up your own, and your girlfriend's, nose —"

"You think his girlfriend is a junkie?"

"I didn't hear anything like that. But I would be surprised if she didn't do some 'recreational drugs.' That's pretty common among people like that. You heard what happened to the Detweiler girl, her father owns half of Nesfoods?"

Joey Fiorello shook his head, "no."

"I know who they are," Joey said. "What about the girl?"

"She stuck a needle in her arm in Chestnut Hill and was dead before she could take it out."

"No shit?"

"Killed her like that," Chason said, snapping his fingers. "Anyway, after you put aside whatever shit you need for yourself and your girlfriend, you sell the rest. You put away enough money to buy another twenty thousand worth later on, and you live good on what's left over."

"And you think Ketcham is doing this?"

"Like I said, I can't prove it, but yeah, Joey, I'd bet on it."

"Can I ask you a personal question, Phil?"

"You can ask," Chason said. "But I won't promise to answer."

"You're a retired police officer," Joey said. "You get this feeling about somebody like this, dealing drugs, doing what you think he's doing with the stockbroker business, you feel you got to tell the cops?"

"No," Chason said. "For one thing, like I said, I can't prove any of this. And for another, if I did, they'd probably tell me to mind my own business."

"What do you think his chances are of getting caught dealing drugs?"

"He'll get caught eventually," Chason said. "If he don't get killed first, in some drug deal gone bad, or kill himself, the way that Detweiler girl did."

"Well, one thing for sure," Joey said. "We don't want this son of a bitch walking around the lot, do we?"

"I wouldn't if I was you, Joey," Chason said.

"Phil, I don't want anybody to know I was even *thinking* of giving this son of a bitch a job. It would be embarrassing, if you know what I mean."

"What I do, Joey, like it says in the phone book, is *confidential* investigations. What I told you, you paid for. It's yours. I just forgot everything I told you."

"I appreciate that, Phil," Joey said.

Chason nodded his head.

"How long did it take you to come up with all this, Phil?"

"No longer than usual. I'm going to bill you for ten hours, plus, I think, about sixty bucks in expenses."

"Two things, Phil. First of all, I think it took you like *twenty* hours," Joey said. "And I figure you had maybe two hundred in expenses."

"You don't have to do that, Joey."

"Don't tell me what I have to do, Phil, please, as a favor to me. Second thing, how would you feel about being paid in cash, instead of with a check? Are you in love with the IRS?"

"I don't have a thing in the world against cash, Joey."

"That's good, because I just happen to have some cash the IRS don't know about, either," Joey said.

He got up from his desk and went into what looked to Phil Chason like a closet. He returned in a minute with an envelope.

"You want to check it, to make sure it's all right?" Joey asked.

"I'm sure it is, Joey," Chason said, and put the envelope in his suit jacket pocket.

Joey offered him his hand.

"We'll be in touch," Joey said.

Chason started out of the office.

"Phil, you want to get out of that piece of shit you're driving, I'll make you a deal on something better."

"Not right now, Joey, but I'll consider that an open offer."

"It's an open offer," Joey said.

Chason left the office. Joey went to the venetian blinds and watched through them until Chason had left the lot.

Then he left his office.

"I've got to see a man about a dog, Helene," he said.

He went out and got into a red Cadillac Eldorado Convertible and drove off the lot. Six blocks away, he pulled into an Amoco station and stopped the car by an outside pay phone.

He dropped a coin in the slot and dialed a number from memory.

"This is Joey. I need to talk to him," he said.

"Yes?" a new voice responded a minute later.

"This is Joey, Mr. S.," Joey said. "I just left the retired cop. I think we had better talk, if you have time."

"Come right now, Joey," Vincenzo Savarese said.

Twelve

Chief Inspector Dennis V. Coughlin looked up from the mountain of paper on his desk and saw Michael J. O'Hara sitting on his secretary's desk.

"How long have you been out there, Mickey?" Coughlin called.

"You looked like you were busy," O'Hara said.

"I told him I'd let you know he was out here," Veronica Casey, Coughlin's secretary, said.

"Never too busy for you, Mickey," Coughlin said, motioning for O'Hara to come into his office.

"Oh, you silver-tongued Irishman, you," O'Hara said, and slumped into one of the two armchairs in the room. "What's going around here you don't want me to know about?"

"There's a long list of things like that," Coughlin said. "You have something specific in mind?"

"Actually, what I had in mind was that you and I should go somewhere and have a little sip of something. Maybe two sips. Maybe even, if you don't have something on, dinner. You got plans?"

"No," Coughlin said. He looked at his watch. "I didn't realize it was so late." He raised his voice. "Go home, Veronica!"

"You sure?"

"I'm sure. Put this stuff away, and we'll start again in the morning."

"Okay," she said, coming into the office and

gathering up the papers on Coughlin's desk. "He skipped lunch," she said to O'Hara, "so eat first before you do a lot of sipping."

"Okay," O'Hara said. He waited until she had left the office, and then said, "She's in love with you. Why don't you marry her?"

"She has a husband, as you damned well know."

"What's that got to do with anything?"

"Go to hell, Mickey," Coughlin said, laughing. "But she's right. I didn't have any lunch. I need to put something in my stomach."

"Fish, fowl, or good red meat?"

"Clams and a lobster comes to mind," Coughlin said.

"Bookbinder's?"

"That's close," Mickey said.

"Too far to walk," Coughlin said. "Where's your car?"

"In the No Parking zone by the door," Mickey said. "I'll bring you back here, if you like."

Michael J. O'Hara's Buick was indeed parked in the area immediately outside the rear door of the police administration building, in an area bounded by signs reading "No Parking At Any Time."

The joke went that there were only two people in the City of Philadelphia who would not get a parking ticket no matter where they left their cars, one being the Hon. Jerome H. Carlucci, the mayor, and the other being Mickey O'Hara.

That wasn't exactly true, Coughlin thought as he got into O'Hara's car. But on the other hand, it was close. He himself didn't dare leave his car parked where Mickey had parked the Buick, confident he would not find a parking ticket stuck under his wiper blade when he returned for it.

Mickey enjoyed a special relationship with the Police Department of the City of Philadelphia shared by no other member of the press. Coughlin had often wondered why this was so, and had decided, finally, that while some of it was because he was a familiar sight at funerals, weddings, promotion parties, and meetings of the Emerald Society (and, for that matter, at gatherings of the German, black, and Jewish police social organizations as well), it was basically because he was trusted by everybody from the guy walking a beat to Jerry Carlucci.

He never broke a confidence, and he never published anything bad about a cop until he gave the cop a chance to tell his side of the story.

And while he did not fill his columns with puff pieces about the Philadelphia Police Department, he very often found space to make sure the public learned of some unusual act of kindness, or heroism, or dedication to duty of ordinary cops walking beats.

And that was probably, Denny Coughlin thought, because Mickey O'Hara, in his heart, thought of himself as a cop.

Not that Mickey ever forgot he was a journalist. Denny Coughlin had thought of Mickey as a personal friend for years, and he was sure the reverse was true. But he also understood that the reason Mickey had appeared at his office to offer to take him to dinner was less that they were friends than that Mickey had questions he hoped he could get Coughlin to answer.

The door chimes sounded, playing "Be It Ever So Humble, There's No Place Like Home."

"Who the *fuck* is that?" Inspector Peter Wohl wondered aloud, in annoyance that approached rage.

Amelia Alice Payne, M.D., who had been lying with her head on his chest, raised her head and looked down at him.

"Oh, my *goodness!* Are we going to have to wash our *naughty* little mouth out with soap?" she inquired.

"Sorry," Wohl said, genuinely contrite. "I was just thinking how nice it is to go to sleep with you like this. And then that *goddamned* chime!"

Amy was not sure whether he meant naked in each other's arms, or sexually sated, but in either case she agreed.

She kissed his cheek, tenderly, and then, eyes mischievous, said innocently, "I wonder who the fuck it could possibly be?"

"What am I doing? Teaching you bad habits?" Peter asked, chuckling.

"Oh, yes," she said.

She pushed herself off him and got out of bed, then walked on tiptoes to peer out through the venetian blinds on the bedroom window.

There was enough light, somehow, for him to be able to see her clearly.

"My God, it's Uncle Denny!" Amy said.

What the hell does Denny Coughlin want this time of night?

"We had the foresight, you will recall," Peter

said, chuckling, "to hide your car in my garage."

"You think he wants to come in?" Amy asked, very nervously.

On the one hand, Amy, you march in front of the feminist parade, waving the banner of modern womanhood and gender equality, and on the other, you act like a seventeen-year-old terrified at the idea Uncle Denny will suspect that you and I are engaged in carnal activity not sanctioned for the unmarried.

"No," Peter said. "I'm sure all he wants to do is stand outside the door."

He got out of bed.

"You just get back in bed and try not to sneeze," Peter said. "And I will try to get rid of him as quickly as I can."

"I'll have to get dressed," Amy said.

"Why bother?" Peter said as he put on his bathrobe. "If he comes in the bedroom, I don't think he'll believe you were in here helping me wash the windows. Maybe you *could* say you were making a house call, Doctor."

"Screw you, Peter," Amy said. "This is not funny!"

But she did get back into the bed and pulled the sheet up over her.

Peter turned the lights off, then left the bedroom, closing the door.

Then he turned and knocked on it.

"Morals squad!" he announced. "Open up!"

"You bastard!" Amy called, but she was chuckling.

Peter turned the lights on in the living room, walked to the door, and opened it.

Chief Inspector Dennis V. Coughlin — who,

in the process of maintaining his friendly relationship with the widow of his pal Sergeant John
F. X. Moffitt, had become so close to the Payne
family that all the Payne kids had grown up thinking of him as Uncle Denny — stood at the door.

In a cloud of Old Bushmills fumes, Peter's nose
immediately told him.

"I was in the neighborhood, Peter," Coughlin
said, "and thought I would take a chance and see
if you were still up."

Peter had just enough time to decide, *Bullshit,
twice. I don't think you were in the neighborhood,
and even if you were, you got on the radio to get my
location, and if you did that, you would have asked
the operator to call me on the phone to see if I was
up,* when Coughlin added:

"That's bullshit. I wanted to see you. Radio
said you were home. I'm sorry if I got you up.
You got something going in there, I'll just go."

Does he suspect Amy is in here with me?

"Come on in. I was about to go to bed. We'll
have a nightcap."

"You're sure?" Coughlin asked.

"Come on in," Peter repeated.

Coughlin followed him into the living room,
sat down on Peter's white leather couch — a
remnant, like several other pieces of very modern
furniture in the apartment, of a long-dead and
almost forgotten affair with an interior decorator
— and reached for the telephone.

As Peter took ice, glasses, and a bottle of James
Jamison Irish whiskey from the kitchen, he heard
Coughlin on the telephone.

"Chief Coughlin," he announced, "at Inspector Wohl's house," and then hung up.

Peter set the whiskey, ice, and glasses on the coffee table in front of the couch and sat down in one of the matching white leather armchairs.

Coughlin reached for the whiskey, poured an inch into a glass, and took a sip.

"This is not the first I've had of these," he said, holding up the glass. "Mickey O'Hara came by the Roundhouse at six, and we went out and drank our dinner."

"There's an extra bed here," Peter said, "if you don't feel up to driving home."

And then he remembered that not only was Amy in his bed, where she could hear the conversation, but that the moment she heard what he had just said she would decide he was crazy or incredibly stupid. Or, probably, both.

If Denny Coughlin accepted the offer, there was no way he would not find out that Amy was here.

Coughlin ignored the offer.

"The trouble with Mickey is that he has a nose like a bird dog, and people tell him things they think he would like to know," Coughlin said. "And he thinks like a cop."

"He would have made a good cop," Peter agreed.

He poured whiskey in a glass and added ice.

"After he fed me about four of these," Coughlin said, "he asked me whose birthday party it was we were all at at the Rittenhouse Club."

"We meaning you, me, Matt, and the FBI?"

Coughlin nodded.

"What did you tell him?"

"I told him that Matty had had a little run-in with a couple of FBI agents, and you and I were pouring oil on some troubled waters."

"Did he buy it?"

"He said he was naturally curious why a couple of FBI agents who don't even work in Philadelphia were following Matty around in the first place."

"He knew they had been following him? God, he does find things out, doesn't he?" Wohl said.

"Including some things that you and I didn't know," Coughlin said. "Like when those two FBI agents were waiting in the Special Operations parking lot to see if Matty was coming out, a Highway Patrol sergeant — Nick DeBenedito — thought they looked suspicious and went and tapped on their car window and asked them who they were."

Coughlin smiled, and Wohl laughed.

"It's not funny, Peter," Coughlin said. "And it gets worse. The FBI guys showed Nick their identification, and told him they were on the job, surveilling the guy driving the Porsche, and did Nick know what he was doing inside. Nick asked why did they want to know, and they told him it was none of his business. So Nick goes inside, tells the duty officer, who calls the FBI duty officer and asks him what a couple of FBI agents, one of them named Jernigan, are doing parked in the Special Operations parking lot, and the FBI duty officer says he doesn't have an agent named Jernigan. So Nick and the duty officer go back to the parking lot, and the FBI guys are gone. Then they go see Matt, who's working upstairs, and ask him what's going on, and Matt tells them not to worry about it, the FBI thinks he's a kidnapper they're looking for."

"Oh, God!" Wohl said, laughing. "So within thirty minutes, it's all over Special Operations. The FBI with egg on its face again."

"That's funny, I admit. But what's not funny is, of course, that somebody couldn't wait to tell Mickey, and he put that and us being in the Rittenhouse Club together and came up with the idea that something's going on he doesn't know about, and the way to find out is to ask me."

"What did you tell him?"

"I told him I didn't feel free to tell him until I'd first checked with you."

What do you call that? Passing the buck?

"So he's going to come see me?" Wohl asked. "First thing in the morning, no doubt?"

"Probably, since he didn't beat me here," Coughlin said, smiling. He held up his whiskey glass. "I told you, we mostly drank our dinner. I don't like to make decisions when I do that. I figured telling Mickey he'd have to ask you would give us time to think how much we're going to tell him. We're going to have to tell him something."

Wohl didn't reply.

"So I decided to come here," Coughlin said. "And on the way I had a couple of other unpleasant thoughts."

"Oh?"

"Do me a favor, Peter, and don't decide before you think it over that this is the whiskey talking."

"I wouldn't do that, Chief," Peter said.

"Yes, you would. I would too, if you showed up at my place at this hour of the night with half a bag on."

Their eyes met for a moment, and then Coughlin went on.

"I'm worried about Matty," he said. "I'm sorry I went along with this 'cooperation' with the FBI business."

"I don't think you had much choice."

"I could have said no, and then gotten to Jerry Carlucci before Walter Davis did and told him why I said no."

"What would you have told him?"

"That these animal activists are really dangerous people, and that Matt's not experienced enough to deal with them."

"As I understood it, he isn't going to deal with them. Just see if he can, by getting close to the Reynolds woman, positively locate them for the FBI. And the FBI will deal with them."

"Did you see what was in his eyes when I gave him that order?" Coughlin asked. "And I made that order as clear as I could."

"I remember. What about his eyes?"

"There was a little moving sign in them. Like that sign in Times Square. You know what it said?"

Wohl shook his head again.

"Yeah, right. Say what you want, old man, but give me half a chance, and I'm going to put the arm on these people, make the FBI look stupid, and get to be the youngest sergeant in the Philadelphia Police Department. Just like Peter Wohl."

Wohl was torn between wanting to smile at the image, and a sick feeling that Coughlin was right.

"Chief, for one thing, Matt knows an order when he hears one."

"Ha!" Coughlin snorted.

"And he's both smart and getting to be a pretty good cop. He won't do anything stupid."

"He's too smart for his own good, he thinks he's a much better cop than he really is, and what would you call crawling around on that ledge on the Bellvue-Stratford twelve stories above South Broad Street? That wasn't stupid?"

"That was stupid," Wohl admitted.

"And how would you categorize his using a boosted passkey to go into the Reynolds girl's room in the hotel? The behavior of a seasoned, responsible police officer?"

Wohl didn't reply.

"Not to mention taking the FBI on a wild-goose chase in North Philly?"

"Well, under the circumstances, I might have done that myself," Wohl said. "But I see your point."

"There's a lot of his father in Matty," Coughlin said. It took Wohl a moment to understand Coughlin was not talking about Brewster Cortland Payne. "Jack Moffitt would still be walking around if he had called for the backup he knew he was supposed to have before he answered that silent alarm and got himself shot. And Dutch Moffitt would still be alive, too, if he hadn't tried to live up to his reputation as supercop."

"Chief," Wohl said, "I'm sure Matt has thought about what happened to his uncle Dutch and his father. And learned from it."

"You don't believe that for a second, Peter," Coughlin said. "When did he think about it? Before or after he climbed out on that twelfth-floor ledge? And if Chenowith or any of the other lunatics show up in Harrisburg, you think he's going to think about what happened to Dutch and his father? Or try to put the arm on him — or all of them?"

Wohl shrugged and didn't reply for a moment.

"Well, what do you think we should do?" he asked finally.

"How's he going to check in?"

"Twice a day. With either Mike Weisbach or Jason Washington, or Weisbach's sergeant, Sandow. Or whenever — if — he finds something."

"Take the call yourself. Have a word with him. He just might listen to you. He thinks you walk on water."

"I'd already planned to do that," Peter said.

Coughlin met Wohl's eyes. He looked for a moment as if he was going to say something else, but changed his mind. He picked up his glass and drained it.

"I'll let you go to bed," he said. "Thanks for the drink."

"Anytime, Chief. You know that," Wohl said.

"If I interrupted anything," Coughlin said, nodding toward the closed door of Peter's bedroom, "I'm sorry."

Jesus Christ, is he psychic? Or did Amy cough or something and I didn't hear her and he did? Or did he take one look at my face and read on it the symptoms of the just-well-laid man?

"You didn't interrupt anything, Chief," Wohl replied.

"Good," Coughlin said.

He reached for the telephone and dialed a number.

"Chief Coughlin en route from Inspector Wohl's house to my place," he said, and hung up.

Then he walked to the door. He put out his hand to Wohl.

"A *strong* word when you talk to our Matty, Peter."

"As strong as I can make it," Wohl said.

Coughlin nodded, then opened the door. Peter watched to make sure he made it safely down the stairway, then went inside the apartment, locked the door, and went into his bedroom.

"I gather he's gone?" Amy said. "He didn't accept your gracious invitation to spend the night?"

"Sorry about that," Peter said. "He's gone. How much did you hear?"

"Everything," she said.

"He's very fond of Matt," Wohl said. "And he had a couple of drinks."

"I hardly know where to ask you to start," Amy said. "Why don't we start with the twelfth floor ledge of the Bellvue-Stratford? That sounds very interesting."

"It wasn't as bad as it sounds, Amy. That ledge was two feet wide. And I really read the riot act to him when I heard about it."

"Two feet wide and twelve stories off the ground, right? Let's have it, Peter."

"You read in the papers where a Vice Squad lieutenant was taking money from a call girl madam?"

Amy nodded.

"A lot of it took place in the Bellvue. Matt was on the surveillance detail. They put a microphone on a hotel-room window with a suction cup. The cup fell off. Matt went out on the ledge and put it back in place."

"He risked his life so you could arrest a call girl madam?"

"We were really after the police officers involved. And don't get mad at me, Amy. I didn't tell him to do it. And I ate his ass out when I found out about it."

Amy snorted.

Peter started to take his bathrobe off.

"Just hold it right there," Amy said. "This isn't pick-it-up-where-we-left-it-when-we-were-so-rudely-interrupted time. Who are these people Denny Coughlin is afraid Matt will try to arrest by himself?"

"I can't get into that," Wohl said. "I'm sorry."

"What's that supposed to mean?" Amy flared, parroting, " 'I can't get into that'?"

"It's a highly confidential underway investigation."

"And you never talk about highly confidential underway investigations to the bimbo you're banging, right?"

"Is that what you think you are to me? Some bimbo I'm banging?"

"Don't try to change the subject, Peter," Amy said.

284

"And what am I to you, Amy?" Wohl heard himself asking, wondering where the sudden rage had come from. "A convenient stud? Once or twice a month, when the hormones get active, call the stud and ask if you can come over?"

"How did we get on this subject?" she asked uncomfortably. "Is that what you really think?"

"I don't know what to think," he said.

Amy exhaled audibly.

She met his eyes.

"What do you want me to say? That I think I'm in love with you?"

"If that were the truth, that would be a nice start."

"My patients, I am forced to conclude, are not the only ones who try to avoid facing the truth."

"What's that supposed to mean?"

"In this case, the truth I seem to have been avoiding facing is that I am in love with you."

Peter didn't reply.

"No response to that?" Amy asked after a long moment.

"You're so matter-of-fact about it," he said.

"There's something wrong with that?" Amy asked.

Peter shook his head, "no."

"I'll tell you what happens now," Amy said. "If it's the truth, it would be a nice start if you said, 'I love you, too, Amy.' "

"I love you, too, Amy."

"Okay, step two. Now you can take off your robe and come to bed, and after we do what people in love do, step three, you tell me all about this highly confidential underway investigation you've got my little brother involved in."

"Can I suggest step one-A?"

"Suggest."

"I have a bottle of champagne in the refrigerator I've been saving for a suitable occasion."

"Very good. Go get it. Perhaps this love affair of ours isn't going to be as hopeless as logic tells me it's going to be."

"You think it's hopeless?"

"We'll have to wait and find out, won't we, Peter?"

He left the bedroom to fetch the champagne. As he was standing by the sink, unwrapping the wire around the cork, Amy came out of the bedroom and went to him and wrapped her arms around him from the back.

"It's true," she said, almost whispering. "When I saw you walking out of the bedroom, I suddenly realized, My God, I really do love that man."

It took Matt Payne ten minutes to get through the system set in place to protect Harrisburg's chief of police from unnecessary intrusions on his time by the public and to his second-floor office in the police headquarters building, but once he got that far, he found that his passage had been greased.

"The chief's on the phone, Detective Payne," his pleasant secretary greeted him with a smile, "but he's been expecting you. Can I get you a Coke or a cup of coffee?"

"Coffee would be nice. Thank you."

She was pouring the coffee when the red light indicating the chief's line was busy went out, and she stopped pouring the coffee and picked up one of the phones on her desk.

"Detective Payne just came in," she announced.

A moment later the door to the chief's office opened and a stocky, ruddy-faced man in uniform came through it, his hand extended, and a smile on his face.

"Sorry to keep you waiting," the chief said. "The damned phone. You know how it is. Agnes take care of you all right?"

"Yes, sir," Matt said, as he took the Chief's hand and nodded toward the coffee machine.

"Pour one of those for me and bring them in, will you, Agnes?"

"Yes, sir."

"Come on in, Payne, and we'll see what we can do to make things a little easier for you."

"Thank you, sir," Matt said.

A highly polished nameplate on the chief's desk identified him as A. J. Mueller. At each end of the plate was a deer's foot, and there were two deer's heads hanging from the walls. One wall was covered with photographs, about half of them showing the chief shaking hands with other policemen and what looked like politicians — one showed the chief shaking hands with the governor and another with the Hon. Jerome H. Carlucci — and the rest showing the chief, in hunting clothes, beaming, holding up the heads of deer he'd apparently shot.

A glass-doored cabinet held an array of marksmanship — mostly pistol — trophies and four different target pistols with which he had presumably won the trophies.

"I hope you didn't check into a hotel yet?" Chief Mueller asked, motioning for Matt to sit in one of the armchairs facing his highly polished desk.

"No, sir. I came directly here."

"Good. I called the Penn-Harris — that's the best in town — and got you a special rate."

"That was very kind of you, sir," Matt said.

"Well, not only does Walter Davis speak highly of you, but — maybe I shouldn't tell you this — an old friend of mine, Chief Augie Wohl, called and said he heard you were coming out here, that you were not only a pretty good cop but a friend of his, and he'd be grateful if I'd do what I could for you."

"That was very nice of Chief Wohl, sir."

"I'm a little curious how come you know Chief Wohl. To look at you, I'd guess — no offense — Augie retired when you were in grammar school."

"I work for Chief Wohl's son, sir. Inspector Peter Wohl."

"Peter's an inspector? God, I remember him in short pants. Really. We had a convention of the National Association of Chiefs of Police in Atlantic City. I'd just made chief, and it was my first convention. Anyway, Augie brought Peter along. In a cop suit. He was a cute little kid, serious as all get-out."

Matt was unable to restrain a smile at a mental image of a cute little kid named Peter Wohl dressed up in a cop suit.

"Yes, sir. He commands the Special Operations Division."

288

Agnes delivered the coffee and left, leaving the door ajar. Chief Mueller got up from his desk, walked to the door, and closed it.

"Does Chief Wohl know about this — what do we call it? — 'cooperative effort' you're doing with Walter Davis?"

"I don't know, sir. I don't think so, but Inspector Wohl may have told him."

"He didn't mention it on the phone, so we'll presume he doesn't know. Okay?"

"Yes, sir."

"That means on this police force I'll be the only one to know. It's been my experience, generally, that when more than one person knows something, you can forget about it being a secret."

"Yes, sir."

Mueller walked back to his desk, opened the drawer, took out a business card, wrote something on it, and handed it to Matt.

"In case you have to get in touch with me in a hurry," he said. "The first number is my unlisted number at home, and the second is the number of the officer in charge of the radio room. They always know where I am."

"Thank you, sir."

"It might be a good idea if you called in here at least once a day. The third number on there is Agnes's private line. If I have any messages for you — you get the idea."

"Yes, sir. I'll check in with Agnes at least once a day."

"Now, before I call Deitrich in here, let's make sure we have all our balls lined up in a straight line. Officially, what you're doing here is looking

289

for dirty money the Vice Squad lieutenant may have stashed up here. Is that about it?"

"Yes, sir."

"Are you really going to do that, or is that just for public consumption?"

"I'm going to be doing that, sir."

"I guess I don't have to tell you that if he does have money, or anything else, hidden up here it doesn't have his name on it?"

"No, sir. I have a list of names of people who might be cooperating with him."

Chief Mueller nodded.

"I hope you find something," Mueller said. "It rubs me the wrong way when crime pays. Especially when the bad guy used to wear a badge."

"I'm sure that's the reason Inspector Wohl sent me up here, sir," Matt said.

"And then this cooperation with Walter and the FBI just came along?"

"That's about it, sir."

"Well, I hope that works, too. For the same reason. It also rubs me the wrong way when people who've killed people just thumb their noses at the rest of us. And get away with it."

"Yes, sir."

"If you need anything, Payne, to help you along, all you have to do is ask."

"Thank you very much, sir."

Mueller went back to his office door and opened it.

"See if Lieutenant Deitrich's got a minute, will you, please, Agnes?" he ordered, and then turned to Matt. "Deitrich, a good man, heads up our White Collar Crime Division. He can get you into the banks."

Deitrich, a very large, nearly bald man in his forties, came into Mueller's office two minutes later.

"Paul, say hello to Detective Matt Payne of the Philadelphia Police Department," Chief Mueller said.

Deitrich examined Matt carefully before putting out his enormous hand.

"How are you?" he said.

His handshake was surprisingly gentle.

"You remember reading in the papers about that dirty Vice lieutenant — what was his name, Payne?"

"Meyer, sir," Matt furnished.

Deitrich nodded his head, confirming Matt's snap decision that Lieutenant Deitrich was a man who didn't say very much.

"The Philadelphia Police Department thinks that ex-Lieutenant Meyer may have some money and/or some property hidden up here," Mueller went on. "And sent Payne up to see if he can find it."

Deitrich nodded again.

"That's a righteous job so far as I'm concerned, so I have offered him our full support."

Deitrich nodded again.

"And Detective Payne comes with a first-class recommendation from a mutual friend of ours. You getting the picture, Paul?"

Again the massive head bobbed once.

"And, for the obvious reasons, he wants to do this as quietly as possible," Mueller said.

"I told him, for openers, that you can get him

into the banks," Mueller went on, "and — I just thought of this — you have friends in the county courthouse if he wants to check property transfers."

"When do you want to start?" Deitrich asked.

"How about tomorrow morning?" Chief Mueller answered for him. "Get him a chance to get settled in his hotel. The Penn-Harris."

The massive head bobbed.

"I'll make some calls this afternoon," Deitrich said.

"Thank you."

"You'll be moving around," Mueller said. "What kind of a car are you driving?"

"A Plymouth."

"Yours, or the department's?"

"An unmarked car."

"What year? Does it have official plates?"

"A new one," Matt said. "Blue. Regular civilian plates."

"They must like you in Philadelphia," Deitrich said. "Before you leave, get me the plate numbers. I'll have the word put out that a suspicious, not-one-of-ours unmarked car is to be left alone."

"Thank you."

Deitrich wordlessly took a business card from his wallet and handed it to Matt.

"Thank you," Matt repeated.

"Nine o'clock?" Deitrich asked.

"Nine's fine with me."

Deitrich looked at Mueller to see if there was anything else.

"Thank you, Paul," Mueller said.

Deitrich nodded first at Mueller and then at

Matt and then sort of shuffled out of the room.

Mueller waited until he was out of earshot, then said, "Paul doesn't say much. When he does, listen."

"Yes, sir."

"Why don't you let me welcome you to Harrisburg with a home-cooked dinner?" Mueller asked.

"That's very kind, sir. But could I take a rain check?"

Mueller looked at Matt, his bushy eyebrows raised. Then he nodded.

"I hope she's pretty," Mueller said.

"She is," Matt said.

Mueller put out his hand. The meeting was over.

"I meant what I said about if you need anything, anytime, you have my numbers."

"Thank you, sir," Matt said, "for everything."

The Penn-Harris hotel provided Detective Payne with a small suite on the sixth floor at what Matt guessed was half the regular price. There was a bedroom with three windows — through which he could see the state capitol building — furnished with a double bed, a small desk, a television set, and two armchairs. The sitting room held a couch, a coffee table, two armchairs, and another television set.

While he was unpacking, he opened what he thought was a closet door and found that it was a kitchenette complete to a small refrigerator. To his pleased surprise, the refrigerator held a half-dozen bottles of beer, a large bottle of Coke, and a bottle of soda water.

He decided this was probably due more to Chief Mueller's wish to do something nice for a friend of Chief Inspector (Retired) Augustus Wohl than to routine hotel hospitality, particularly for someone in a cut-rate room.

Matt finished unpacking, then took a bottle of beer from the refrigerator, settled himself on the sitting-room couch with his feet up on the coffee table, and reached for the telephone.

Jason Washington's deep, vibrant voice came over the line.

"Special Operations Investigations. Sergeant Washington."

"Detective Payne, Sergeant Washington, and how are you on this warm and pleasant afternoon?"

"How good of you to call. We were all wondering when you were going to find the time."

"I just got here," Matt protested, and then asked, "Did something come up?"

"I have had three telephone calls from Special Agent Matthews asking if we had heard from you. Weren't you supposed to liaise with him, Matthew?"

"I'm not sure I know what that means," Matt said. "Anyway, I don't have anything to tell him. I just got here."

"So you said. And how were you received by our brothers of the Harrisburg police?"

"By the chief. Nice guy. He said Chief Wohl had called him."

"That's interesting."

"Yeah, I thought so. Anyway, Chief Mueller

set me up with their White Collar Crimes guy, a lieutenant named Deitrich, who's going to get me into both the banks and the hall of records in the courthouse."

"Where are you, Matthew?"

"Six twelve in the Penn-Harris," Matt said. He took a close look at the telephone and read the number to Washington.

"I will share that with Special Agent Matthews," Washington said. "Is there anything else, in particular anything concerning your — what shall I say, 'social life in romantic Harrisburg' — that you would like me to tell him?"

"I haven't called her. I will when I get off the phone with you. And that one telephone call may be, probably will be, the end of that."

"And how is that?"

"You were there when I told Davis that her eyes glazed over when I told her I was a cop."

"If at first you don't succeed, to coin a phrase. You might try inflaming her natural maternal instincts, and get her to take pity on a lonely boy banished to the provinces far from home and loved ones."

Matt chuckled.

"If you were she, would you be eager to establish a close relationship with a cop?"

"That might well depend on the cop," Washington said. "Think positively, Matthew."

"I'll let you know what happens."

"Would a report at, say, eight-thirty in the morning be too much to ask? I would so hate to disappoint Agent Matthews should he call about then, as I'm sure he will."

"I'll call you in the morning," Matt said.

"I will wait in breathless anticipation," Washington said, and hung up.

Matt took the telephone number for the Reynolds home Daffy had given him from his wallet, read it aloud three times in an attempt to memorize it, and then dialed it. As the phone was ringing, he looked at the scrap of paper in his hand, decided this was not the time to rely on memory tricks — even one provided by Jason Washington — and put it back in his wallet.

"The Reynolds residence," a male voice announced.

Jesus, they have a butler!

Why does that surprise me? Dad said her father was an "extraordinarily successful" businessman, and that's Dad-speak for really loaded/stinking rich.

"Miss Reynolds, please. Miss Susan Reynolds. My name is Matthew Payne."

"One moment, please, sir."

It was a long moment, long enough to give Matt time to form a mental image of Susan being told that a Mr. Matthew Payne was on the line, taking a moment to wonder who Matt Payne was, to remember, *Oh, that cop at Daffy's!* and then to tell the butler she was not at home and would never be home to Mr. Payne.

"Hello?" a female voice chirped.

"Susan?"

That doesn't sound like her.

"No," the female voice said, coyly. "This is not Susan. This is Susan's mother. And who is this, please?"

"My name is Payne, Mrs. Reynolds. Matthew

Payne. I met Susan at Daffy . . . Daphne Nesbitt's —"

"I *thought* that's what Wilson said!" Mrs. Reynolds cried happily. "You're that *wicked* young man who kept Susan out all night!"

Christ, she's an airhead. In the mold of Daffy's mother, Chad's mother, Penny's mother. What is that, the curse of the moneyed class? Or maybe it's the Bennington Curse. The pretty young girls grow up and turn into airheads. Or otherwise go mad. Like those who believe in being kind to dumb animals by blowing buildings up. Or at least aid and abet those who think that way.

"I think you have the wrong man, Mrs. Reynolds."

"Oh, no, I *don't,* Matthew Payne. Daphne Browne — now she's Daphne Nesbitt, isn't she? — told me all about you! You're a *wicked* boy! Didn't you even think that we would be worried *sick* about her! *Shame* on you!"

"Yes, ma'am."

"Well, she's not at home. I mean, she's really not at home. She's at work."

"I'd like to call her there, at work, if that would be possible."

"That's not possible, I'm afraid. They don't like her to take personal calls at work. Could I give her a message?"

"What I was hoping to do was ask her to have dinner with me."

"When?"

"I thought perhaps tonight, if she didn't have previous plans."

"In Philadelphia?" she asked incredulously.

"No. Not in Philadelphia. Here. Harrisburg."

"You're in Harrisburg?"

"Yes, ma'am. On business."

"I really thought for a minute that you wanted to have dinner tonight with Susan in Philadelphia."

"No, ma'am. I'm here. And I thought she might be willing to have dinner with me."

"Well, I'll tell you what," Mrs. Reynolds said, and there was a long pause. "You come here and you can have dinner with Susan's daddy and me. And, of course, Susan."

"I wouldn't want to impose," Matt said.

"Not at all," she said. "And I want to get a look at you, and give you a piece of my mind. You will come to supper, and that's that."

"In that case, thank you."

"You may change your mind about that after Susan's daddy lets you know what he thinks about you keeping Susan out all night."

"Yes, ma'am."

"We eat at seven-thirty sharp when we're at home. Is that convenient?"

"Yes, ma'am."

"Do you know where we are?"

"No, ma'am. Just that you're in Camp Hill."

"I'll give you directions. They're not as complicated as they sound. Have you a pencil?"

"Yes, ma'am."

Thirteen

Matt was in the shower when the telephone rang, and walked, dripping, to the telephone, wondering both who was calling him and why he had bothered to wrap a towel around his waist when he was alone in the suite.

"Hello?"

"It took you long enough to answer the phone," Peter Wohl said.

"There's no phone in the shower," Matt said.

"Denny Coughlin suggested I call you," Wohl began. "Actually, he suggested I talk to you when you checked in. According to Weisbach, you haven't found time in your busy schedule to do that."

"I checked in with Jason Washington the minute I got to the hotel. What's up? Some —"

"Washington didn't say anything to me," Wohl said, just a shade defensively.

"Boss . . ."

"Okay. Sorry I jumped on you."

"Your father called out here," Matt said.

"My father called out there? What did he want?"

"I don't know. He called Chief Mueller —"

There was a knock at the door.

"Come in!" Matt called.

There was a rattling of the doorknob, but the door remained closed.

"Hold it a minute," Matt said. "There's somebody at the door."

"Room service, no doubt," Wohl said. "Go ahead."

Matt put the phone down and walked to the door, standing behind it when he opened it, so that only his face would show to whoever was in the corridor.

"Jesus H. Christ!" Matt said in genuine surprise when he had opened the door. "Sorry, I gave at the office."

The wit sailed two feet over the head of Miss Susan Reynolds.

"May I come in?" she asked icily.

"There are several problems with that, as delighted as I am to see you," Matt said. "One of them being I'm wearing only a towel."

"Put your pants on," Susan said. "I'll wait."

"Don't go away," Matt said, and rushed into the bedroom, pulled on a pair of slacks, and trotted quickly back to the half-open door.

"Come in, please," he said, opening it wide.

Susan stepped inside the room, and closed the door.

"Problem two is that I'm on the phone," he said.

"Go ahead," Susan said, and went to the couch and sat down.

Matt picked up the telephone.

"I don't suppose I could call you back?" he said.

"What's going on?"

"I'd rather not say."

300

"It will have to wait," Wohl said. "This won't take long."

"Yes, sir."

"What Denny Coughlin wanted me to say to you — and incidentally, I agree with all of this — is that he thinks what he ordered you — the operative word here is 'ordered' — to do about Chenowith went in one ear and out the other. Do you remember that order?"

"Yes, sir."

"Prove it. What did he say?"

"This is a very bad time for that, Inspector," Matt said.

"What did he say, Matt? What did he order you to do?"

"I'd really rather call you back when I have a chance to refresh my memory," Matt said.

"You're telling me you've forgotten?" Wohl asked incredulously.

"No, sir."

Wohl suddenly caught on.

"She's there?" he asked, even more incredulously.

"That's the long and the short of it, Inspector."

"In that case, call me back when you have a free minute. In the meantime, Matt, for Christ's sake, remember those people are dangerous."

"I'll keep that in mind, sir," Matt said.

The phone went dead.

Matt looked at Susan. The way she was sitting with her legs crossed on the couch gave him a good view of a shapely calf, moving in what looked like annoyance or impatience, and a view of her upper leg halfway up her dress.

Whatever she looks like, she doesn't look dangerous.

"Sorry," he said. "That was my boss."

"You want to tell me what's going on here?"

"You mean with him and me, or you and me?"

"What are you doing here?"

"Working," he said.

"Working?" she repeated.

"I've been sent up to look into some bank records," Matt said. "Lieutenant Deitrich of White Collar Crimes is going to get me into the banks."

"What kind of bank records?"

"What are we doing, playing Twenty Questions?"

"I'm curious, all right?"

"There were some not very nice people in Philadelphia who had what we call ill-gotten gains, which we suspect they have hidden out here in the provinces. I have been sent to see if I can find said ill-gotten gains."

"Not very nice white-collar people?"

"Actually, this is not at all a nice character. What this character is is what you could call a White Shirt with a dirty collar."

"Why do I have the feeling we are talking two different languages?"

"There was a call girl ring in Philadelphia, who had a Vice lieutenant on the payroll. In the quaint cant of the police trade, lieutenants and up are called 'White Shirts,' possibly because their uniform shirts are white."

"You do a lot of this sort of thing?" she asked.

"Jobs like this are handed out to junior detectives," Matt said. "I am a very junior detective. Before I was promoted to do things like search bank records, I spent a lot of time investigating recovered stolen motor vehicles. That is the bottom rung of my profession, like Chad going into grocery stores and begging them to buy two more cases of Nesbitt's World Famous Tomato Soup."

That earned him another smile.

"I have trouble really believing you're a cop."

"So do a lot of people," Matt said. He decided it was time to change the subject. "I am of course delighted to see you. If I had known you were coming, I would have had champagne on ice. But I am just a little curious."

"I have to talk to you," Susan said.

"I may be a junior detective, but I am a brilliant junior detective, so let me demonstrate my Sherlock Holmes–like deductive skills: There has been a change in plans, and your mother's kind invitation to break bread has to be withdrawn."

"I wish it was that simple," she said. "I need a big favor from you."

"I suppose I could let you have a couple of bucks until payday. Presuming you have some sort of collateral."

"Aren't you ever serious?"

"Only when there is no possible alternative. How may I assist you, fair lady?"

"You can let my parents think we were out until very late listening to Dixieland jazz."

"But we weren't, were we? Your words, which broke my heart, are burned in my memory: 'I'm sure you're a very nice fellow, but I'm just not

303

interested. Okay?' I cried myself to sleep that night."

She shook her head in amazed disbelief.

"I'll tell you what I'm going to do, Susan, since I am a Boy Scout and we are sworn not to lie to girls' mothers. You call your mother, and tell her we're going to have dinner in town. That way, I don't have to lie to your mommy, or eat alone."

"I meant it when I said I'm just not interested," Susan said. "There's somebody else."

And would his name, perchance, be on the FBI's Most Wanted List?

"Really?"

"You're not making this easy for me, are you?"

"Well, *my* father's lawyer didn't call *your* father, demanding to know what *you* had done with the family virgin."

"I'm sorry about that, I really am."

"You can't imagine how humiliating that was, to walk into my home and have my mommy and daddy waiting for me, wringing their hands, looking at me with sad eyes, to ask what terrible things I had done with *your* daddy's precious baby. That pissed me off, just a smidgen."

"I said I was sorry."

"Tell me about 'someone else.' "

"You don't know him."

I hope to rectify that situation in the very near future.

"That's what this whole thing was all about," Susan went on. "My parents don't like him, can't stand him."

I can't imagine why not. What is this bullshit, anyway?

"And he didn't want me to go to Daffy's party," Susan said, and met Matt's eyes. "And we fought about that. So he came to Philadelphia, and when I left the party he was waiting for me in the lobby of the Bellvue. And we went to my room. And had a fight. And made up. And I didn't call my mother, the way she expected me to, and when she called the hotel — I knew it had to be her, who else would call me at half past two? — she was the last person in the world I wanted to talk to — how could I, with him there? — so I didn't answer the phone. And that started everything else that happened. Mother called Daffy —"

"You were in your room the whole time?"

"Yes."

"With Whatsisname?"

"Yes."

"What's Whatsisname's name?"

"None of your business, is it, really?"

Christ, Wohl was right. These people are dangerous. She looked me right in the eye and lied through her teeth. Or is that indicative of anything more significant — that, as a general rule, females are good liars?

"Just curious, is all. I thought maybe if we became pals, I could learn something from him."

"Like what?"

"Man stuff," Matt said. "I mean, what the hell, I struck out with you in about twenty seconds flat, and this guy, well, he really captured the fair maiden's heart, didn't he? Right up to the room, spend the night. You didn't even want to talk to Mommy."

"Daffy said you could be a prick," Susan said.

305

"Guilty. But just to prove Daffy wrong one more time, I'll call your mother and tell her something's come up, and I won't be able to come to dinner after all."

She looked at him a long moment.

"You don't know my mother. She's determined to meet you. If you don't come tonight, she'll ask about tomorrow night, and the night after that. And if that doesn't work, she'll come to Philadelphia after you."

"Well, that's understandable. I am a very eligible bachelor. There is a long list of mothers with family virgins they're trying to get rid of after me. She'd have to take a number and wait in line."

"You son of a bitch, you're unbelievable," Susan said, and laughed. "Will you?"

"Will I what?"

"Be a good guy. Go along with we were out late listening to Dixieland. I'd really appreciate it."

"How much? What's in it for me?"

"What's that supposed to mean?"

"Well," Matt said, and he heard Jason Washington's melodious voice in his mind, "if I do this for you, it would seem only fair that you take pity on a lonely boy banished to the provinces far from home and loved ones and have dinner with me. A couple of times. Several times. I really hate to eat alone."

"You're serious?"

"I'm always serious."

"But I don't like you."

"Then why did you stay out until the wee hours

with me? Or didn't you?"

"I don't want to get involved with you. You understand that?"

"Women have been known, I'm told, to change their minds."

"This one won't."

"Time will tell. Your choice, Susan."

"You like having something to hold over me, don't you?"

"Truth to tell, I find it interesting."

"Okay," Susan said. "If you get your kicks from something like this, okay. So long as it's clearly understood we're talking about dinner. Period."

"Meaning what?"

"I'm not going to bed with you."

"I don't recall making the offer. And how could I hope to compare with good ol' Whatsisname who made you forget to call Mommy? And what *about* ol' Whatsisname? What are you going to tell him about us going out?"

"He's not here. He's out of town. That won't be a problem."

Casing his next bank robbery, no doubt.

"Good."

"Don't slip tonight, and let on that I came here," she said, and pushed herself off the couch.

"Rest assured, my dear Susan, your deepest, darkest secrets are safe with Matt Payne. At least for the moment."

"Inspector," Officer Paul O'Mara announced, sticking his head in Wohl's office door, "Detective Payne is on Three."

"Tell him to hold on," Wohl said.

He looked at the people in his office with him — Captains Mike Sabara and David Pekach and Lieutenant Jack Malone, with whom he had been discussing the plans for the retirement party of a Highway Patrol sergeant — shrugged his shoulders, said, "Sorry. I'll be as short as I can," and motioned them out of his office.

He waited until the door was closed, then picked up his telephone.

"Go ahead, Matt."

"She just left, boss."

"Then that *was* our lady friend — in your room?"

"Yes, indeed. Your timing was perfect."

"What did she want?"

"After I talked to Jason, I called her house. She wasn't there, but her mother invited me to dinner. And then she apparently called Susan and told her I was coming, and obviously that I'm at the Penn-Harris. So she came here to ask me to go along with the story that we were out all night in Philadelphia."

"She gave you a reason?"

"Looked me right in the eye, with those beautiful, innocent blue eyes, and told me there is a boyfriend, no name given, of whom her parents disapprove —"

"You think she's talking about Chenowith, or the other one? What's his name?"

"Edgar L. Cole. No, for one thing that acne-faced scumbag is hardly her type. I think *this* boyfriend was invented — along with the rest of the story — after her mother called and told her to guess who's coming to dinner."

"Okay. Go on."

"It was quite a story. She told me that she and the boyfriend had a fight about her going to Chad Nesbitt's party. When she went anyway, so goes her tale, he followed her to Philadelphia. When she returned to the Bellvue, the boyfriend was waiting for her in the lobby. They went to her room, fought some more, and then made up. She implied — without any detectable embarrassment — that they sealed the peace in a carnal fashion, and were having at it with such enthusiasm that she forgot to call her mother, and then, when Mommy called, she didn't want to play coitus interruptus by answering the phone."

"No chance that might be true?"

"Peter, her bed was not slept in."

The reason he knows that not only germane, but important-to-this-investigation, information, Wohl thought, resignedly, *is that he went into her room. This is obviously not the time to jump on his ass for a technical illegality.*

"Was she suspicious about you suddenly appearing in Harrisburg? In a cop sense, I mean?"

"At first, yeah. But I explained it."

"You gave her the story you're looking for hidden money? And she bought it?"

"I think so."

"Now what happens?"

"I made a deal with her," Matt said. "I go along with the she-was-with-me story for her parents, and she goes to dinner with me, keeps me company while I'm all alone in Harrisburg, so to speak."

"You blackmailed her, in other words?"

"Yeah. Sort of."

"You don't think pushing yourself on her will make her suspicious?"

"Only that I'm trying to get into her pants."

"Are you?"

"I am prepared to make any sacrifice in the line of duty," Matt said.

"That would really be stupid, Matt," Wohl said.

"Hey, that was a joke. You really think I'm that stupid?"

"I hope not."

"I'm not," Matt said firmly.

"Okay. Matt, if it should ever come up, I just now gave you a long, firm lecture on the price you would have to pay for disobeying Denny Coughlin's clear order to you that you're not to do anything but locate Chenowith and friends for the FBI."

"Okay," Matt said. "Lecture received and duly noted."

"Don't misunderstand me. I'm just trying to save time. You disobey that order and I'll have your ass, Matt. Coughlin's serious about this, and so am I."

"Yes, sir," Matt said.

"I'll bring you up on charges, Matt. Understand that."

The trouble with that dramatic threat is that Matt knows that it's empty. If he gets lucky and grabs these people, or any one of them, it'll be in all the papers, and we're not going to discipline a policeman for doing something the public expects policemen to do; that gets in the papers, too.

"Yes, sir," Matt said.

"Keep in touch," Wohl said. "Have a nice dinner."

He hung up.

Matt found the Reynolds house, following Mrs. Reynolds's instructions, with little trouble. She had neglected to tell him it wasn't visible from the street, and it took him two trips down Schuler Avenue before his headlights picked up a sign by a driveway reading "Reynolds."

The house, when he'd driven several hundred yards up a macadam drive though a wooded area to it, was a large brick colonial with a house-wide verandah. It looked, however, Matt thought, more like the house of an assistant vice president of Nesfoods International than a house one would expect the chairman of the board, president, and chief executive officer of a Fortune 500 company to own.

As he stopped the Plymouth, two large brass fixtures on either side of the double front door went on, and just as he got close to the door, it was opened.

"Good evening, sir," the butler — a middle-aged man wearing a gray cotton jacket — greeted him.

"Good evening," Matt replied. "My name is Payne."

"Yes, sir, you're expected," the butler said. "This way, please, sir."

The house was larger inside than it had appeared from the outside. The entrance foyer was large, and stairways on either side of it rose to a second-floor balcony.

The butler led him to a set of double doors under the balcony and opened one of them.

"Mr. Payne, sir," he announced, and waved Matt inside.

Inside looked like a combination living room and library. Three of the walls held ceiling-high bookcases. The fourth was a wall of sliding glass doors opening onto a patio. Beyond the patio was a lawn stretching down to what Matt supposed was the Susquehanna River.

A stocky, blond-haired man in his fifties, in a well-tailored double-breasted nearly black suit, rose from what looked like *his* chair and advanced on Matt with his hand extended.

"Matt Payne, I presume?"

"Yes, sir."

"Did you see the movie?"

"Sir?"

"*Guess Who's Coming to Dinner?*"

"Let me clear the air," Matt said. "All I want is a free meal."

Thomas Reynolds laughed.

"Is taking a little nip among your vices?"

"Among my lesser vices, yes, sir."

"I was about to make myself another," Reynolds said, taking Matt's arm and leading him to a sideboard laid out with bottles and cocktail-hour impedimenta. "What's your pleasure?"

"A little of that Famous Grouse would go down nicely, thank you."

"The same family's been making that stuff for six generations. Did you know that?"

"No, sir."

"I've been drinking it since college," Reynolds said as he poured.

"So has my father," Matt said. "That's why I drink it, I suppose."

Reynolds handed Matt a glass.

"There's ice and water and soda," he said.

"A little water, please," Matt said.

When that was done, Reynolds tapped his glass against Matt's.

"Welcome," he said.

"Thank you."

"I admire your courage."

"Excuse me?"

"Didn't Susie tell you her mother is furious?"

"Oh. Well, my conscience is clear. I wasn't the one supposed to call home."

"And here she is!" Reynolds cried.

Mrs. Thomas Reynolds, who looked, in her simple black dress and single strand of pearls, as if she had been cast from the same mold as Mrs. Soames T. Browne, Daffy's mother, came into the room from a side door.

"Here he is, Grace," Reynolds said. "His horns are apparently retracted, so be nice to him."

"You're a wicked young man," Grace Reynolds said.

"My mother doesn't think so," Matt said.

"And a smarty-pants to boot!"

"Grace, leave him alone!" Thomas Reynolds ordered.

"I'm only kidding, and he knows it."

"Yes, ma'am."

"But whatever were you thinking about, keeping her out until all hours?"

"Well, we got pretty tied up in conversation," Matt said. "I don't often meet girls with such an intimate knowledge of hog belly futures. Time just flew!"

"Susan doesn't know —" she began to protest, in confusion.

Reynolds laughed again, interrupting her. "He's telling you, politely, to mind your own business, Grace. You may finally have met your match."

"This is an occasion," Grace Reynolds said, cheerfully changing the subject. "I think I'll have a martini."

Reynolds turned to make her one.

"Susan'll be down in just a minute or two, Matt — you don't mind if I call you by your Christian name, do you?"

"No, ma'am."

"Susan's having her shower," Mrs. Reynolds went on.

A quite clear image of Susan in her shower popped up in Matt's brain.

Cool it. For one thing, she is not at all interested, and Wohl was right. It would be really stupid.

"That's nice," Matt said.

"I called her at work. I'm not supposed to do that, unless it's important, but after I asked you to join us, I didn't want her running off to the movies with a girlfriend, or anything."

"And she was no doubt thrilled to hear I was coming?"

"Actually, it was more surprise than anything else, to tell you the truth," she said.

Her husband handed her a martini, and then,

suddenly, a warm smile appeared on his face.

"Princess!" he said.

Matt turned and saw Susan coming toward them. She was dressed like her mother, Matt thought, and then amended the thought: simple black dresses and single strands of pearls were very nearly a uniform for females of her age and social position.

Susan smiled — it looked genuine — and gave him her hand.

"A pleasant surprise, Matt," she said.

"Ten thousand horsemen," Matt said, very seriously, "and all the king's men could not have kept me away."

"Jesus Christ!" Susan said, shaking her head in disbelief.

"Susie!" her mother said, in shock.

"If you're going to blaspheme like that, Susie, we'll just have to call the whole thing off," Matt said piously.

Susan's father laughed, and her mother looked confused.

"I should have warned you, Daddy, he's an idiot."

"So far, I like him."

"Daddy, could I have a scotch?" Susan said.

"Well, as Mommy said, this is an occasion," he said. "Why not?"

"Give her a weak one," Matt ordered, "and only one. Two drinks and she'll want to stay up until the sun comes up."

"Is that what really happened?" Mrs. Reynolds asked. "Susie had too much to drink?"

"I did not," Susan protested automatically.

"How much?" Mommy demanded to know.

"Not much, really," Matt said, "I mean, after the martinis — and, of course, the champagne — at Daffy's, all you had was a couple of tequila surprises in the Mexican place, and then no more than three, well, maybe four, beers in the Dixieland place."

"What's a 'tequila surprise'?" Mrs. Reynolds asked.

"They call them that because after the second tequila surprise, nothing surprises you," Matt said seriously.

"Mommy," Susan protested. "He's pulling your leg."

If I called Mother "Mommy," she'd throw up.

"I didn't believe him for a second," Mrs. Reynolds said.

"Are you a golfer, Matt?" Mr. Reynolds asked.

"Yes, sir."

"Did you bring your clubs?"

"No, sir."

"What I was thinking was that I could call the club, and get you a guest membership while you're here."

"That would be very kind of you, sir."

"How long will you be here?"

"That'll depend on how long it takes me to get what I'm after. A week, or ten days, anyway."

"Then I'll call the club and set you up," Reynolds said.

A middle-aged woman in a black dress with a white maid's apron appeared in the door.

"Anytime you're ready, Mrs. Reynolds," she announced.

"Thank you, Harriet," Mr. Reynolds said. "We'll be right in."

The dining room was so small that Matt decided there must be another, larger one, and that they were dining *en famille.* Confirmation of that came immediately when Mr. Reynolds asked him if "he would like to watch a master of the broiler at work."

"Yes, sir."

"We can finish our drinks out there," Reynolds said.

Reynolds led Matt out to the patio, where a gas charcoal grill was giving off clouds of smoke. What looked like a London broil was on a large white plate.

"It's one of the unanswered questions of my life," Reynolds said as he opened the grill's top, "whether women are congenitally unable to cope with a charcoal grill, or whether they are all united in a conspiracy to give that impression, and have the men do their cooking for them."

"I would bet on the conspiracy theory," Matt said.

Reynolds threw the slab of beef on the grill, closed the top, and pushed a button on the stainless-steel Rolex Chronograph on his wrist.

"I don't know," Reynolds said. "I think it's significant that until very recently, there have been very few females among the great chefs of the world. I think it has to do with the difference in the way men and women think."

"How so?"

"Women are always changing, and improvising. Men solve a problem — for example, how long over a fire of a certain temperature one broils a London broil. In this instance, four minutes on one side, three and a half on the other for medium rare — is that how you like your broil, Matt?"

"Yes, sir."

"And once we have solved the problem, that's it. We go on to other problems. Females, on the other hand, cannot resist tampering. If you're a chef, feeding, say, fifty people in the course of an hour, you can't tamper. A certain efficiency is required, and, generally speaking, most women just don't have it in them to be efficient."

"I suppose that could be true," Matt said.

"I *know* it's true," Reynolds said. "You start thinking about it — I don't mean just tonight, I mean over the next six months or so, and you'll find plenty of examples to prove I'm right."

"I'll give it a shot," Matt agreed.

Reynolds consulted his watch, and at what was presumably precisely four minutes, opened the grill and flipped the broiler. Then he reset his watch.

"Do you cook, Matt?"

"I'm a bachelor," Matt said. "Sometimes it's necessary."

"You should give it a shot," Reynolds said. "It's really quite rewarding."

"I don't have much of a kitchen," Matt said.

"Then get one," Reynolds said. "There are three things that give a man contentment in life. Good shoes, a good mattress, and a decent kitchen."

"How about a good woman?"

"That's a given," Reynolds replied. "Of course a good woman."

At what was presumably precisely three minutes and thirty seconds after he had flipped the London broil, Reynolds removed it from the grill with an enormous stainless-steel fork and laid it on the plate.

Then, with Matt following, he marched back into the small dining room, laid the platter on the table, and motioned for Matt to take a seat.

"The final step," he announced, "is to let the meat stand for five minutes before slicing. That gives the juices a chance to settle, and while that's happening, to have a little glass of wine to cleanse the taste buds. I asked Harriet to open some cabernet sauvignon, to let it breathe. I hope that's all right with you?"

"That's fine with me," Matt said. He smiled at Susan. "Do you cook, Susie?"

Her mother answered for her.

"Daddy's tried to teach her. But Susie really doesn't seem to care much about it."

"My mother was always telling my sister that the way to a man's heart was through his stomach," Matt said.

"That would be useful information," Susan replied, "presuming one was looking for the way to a man's heart. Did your sister pay attention?"

"Of course."

"Well, perhaps she saw her future as a wife and homemaker."

"As opposed to doing something useful — say, being a social worker?"

"Something like that. Nothing wrong with being a wife and homemaker, of course. Each to his own," Susan said.

"Actually, my sister is a physician. A psychiatrist, as a matter of fact," Matt said.

"He got you, Princess!" Mr. Reynolds said, obviously pleased.

Susan smiled.

What is that, Susie, the smile to freeze a volcano?

Mr. Reynolds filled their glasses.

"To friends old and new," he said, raising his.

He consulted his watch, had another sip of wine, consulted his watch again, and, the requisite five minutes apparently having passed, skillfully sliced the London broil with an enormous French chef's knife.

The meat was perfectly done, and Matt said so.

"What I was saying before, Matt. Solve a problem, file the answer away for future use, and go on to the next problem."

"Yes, sir."

"Daddy," Susan said, "I was just thinking. I'm sure Matt — he's here working, not on vacation — doesn't want to make a long evening of it."

"I get by on very little sleep, actually," Matt said.

"And," Susan went on, ignoring him, "he doesn't know where the club is. What I was thinking, Daddy, was that after dinner, he could follow me there in his car, we could have our coffee there, and he would know how to find the club."

"Good idea," her father said. "How's that sound to you, Matt?"

"Sounds fine to me," Matt said.

"Then it's done," Reynolds said. "On to the next problem to be solved, right?"

"Yes, sir."

"Matt, you haven't told us what you're doing in Harrisburg," Mrs. Reynolds said.

"No, I guess I haven't," Matt said.

Reynolds laughed.

"I didn't mean to be nosy," Mrs. Reynolds said in a hurt tone.

"I'm looking for ill-gotten gains," Matt said.

"If I didn't think you'd think me nosy, I'd ask what that means," Mrs. Reynolds asked.

"There was a police officer in Philadelphia who took money he shouldn't have taken," Matt said. "We suspect he may have hidden it up here."

"Really?" Reynolds asked.

"I don't really expect to find it," Matt said. "But someone has to look, and I am the junior man on the totem pole."

"I think you're being far too modest, Matt," Mr. Reynolds said.

"Sir?"

"On the night in question," Reynolds said, making the cliché a joke, "and immediately thereafter, when we were still thinking of you as the ogre who had run off with the Princess, I asked Charley Emmons about you, and he said that you were — you had earned the right to be — the fair-haired boy of the Philadelphia Police Department."

"Really?" his wife said. "You didn't say anything to me, Daddy."

"Among other things, Charley said your father told him you ranked number two on the detectives' exam when you took it. First time out."

"Among what other things, Daddy?" Susan asked.

"Well — there's no need for you to feel embarrassed, Matt; you didn't mention any of this yourself — he's been in two gun battles, and won both of them. Killed both criminals who were trying to kill him. He has two citations for valor, and one for outstanding performance of duty."

"Really?" Mrs. Reynolds asked.

"I'm impressed," Susan said. "You want to tell us about the gun battles, Matt?"

"No," Matt said simply.

"I can understand that," Mr. Reynolds said. "And I don't think you should push him about that, Princess. But my whole point here is that I really don't think Matt was sent here because he's low man on the totem pole. His superiors, I am sure, sent him here because they think he can find whatever he's looking for. He's a very highly regarded detective."

Matt looked at Susan and saw something — more likely alarm rather than surprise — that hadn't been in her eyes before.

Thanks a lot, Daddy, for triggering Princess Susie's alarm.

Christ, have you — goddamn you, Daddy — blown this whole thing?

Quick, change the subject.

"How do you like your Porsche, Susie?"

That wasn't brilliant, but it certainly is a change of subject.

"I like it fine," she said. "How did you know I have a Porsche?"

"Mommy and I really wish she didn't," Daddy said. "That's really too much car for a girl."

"Oh, I agree," Matt said.

"How did you know I have a Porsche?" Susan repeated. "And it is not too much car for a girl. Sometimes, Daddy!"

"Daffy told me," Matt said. "Daffy said, 'You'll like Susie. She has a car just like yours.' "

"You have a Porsche?"

"Uh-huh. A silver 911."

"Susie's is fire-engine red," Mommy said. "She's always getting speeding tickets."

"They — Porsche 911s — are known in the law-enforcement community as AHN cars," Matt said.

"Excuse me?" Daddy said.

"Arrest Him — or of course, Her — Now. If he — she — is not speeding now, he — she — will be in the next ten minutes."

"That's terrible," Mommy said.

"Unfortunately, it's probably true," Susan said.

"Would you like some more broil, Matt?" Daddy asked.

"No, thank you, sir. I've really had enough. And Susie's right. I really should be on my way."

"Well, remember what I taught you. Four minutes, flip, three and a half minutes, and then let it stand for five."

"Yes, sir, I will."

Mommy and Daddy came out onto the verandah with them. Susan went to the garage for her car.

Mommy gave Matt her cheek to kiss, and said

she hoped to see him soon again. And then she said she had something she had forgotten to tell Susie, and ran toward the garage after her.

Daddy shook Matt's hand and said he was sure Matt knew Susie had to be at work early.

"Yes, sir, I know."

"I'm going to call the club now, so they'll expect you. I want you to feel free to use it. The food's good."

"Maybe Susie would go to dinner with me there," Matt said.

"All she can say is no. But I think she'd like that."

The garage door opened and Susan's Porsche emerged.

Matt shook Daddy's hand again and got into his Plymouth.

Susan drove off down the driveway so fast that Matt wondered for a moment if she was trying to lose him. On reflection, under the circumstances, that didn't seem likely.

Five minutes later, by which time Matt had decided Princess Susie had a really heavy foot, the red and blue lights of a bubble-gum machine appeared in his rear window.

Shit! That's all I need!

He flicked on the turn signal, slowed, and moved to the shoulder of the road.

The patrol car — there was a reflective Harrisburg police sign on the trunk — went by him without slowing. Matt pulled back onto the pavement and saw, five hundred yards or so down the road, that the uniform had pulled the Porsche over.

He drove the five hundred yards and pulled in behind the patrol car. He took his ID folder from his jacket pocket and got from behind the wheel, holding the ID so the badge would be visible.

The uniform looked concerned. When he walked toward Matt, he had his right hand where it could quickly unholster his pistol.

Susan, Matt saw, had not gotten out of her Porsche.

Matt held out the ID so the uniform could see it.

"What can I do for you?" the uniform — a football-tackle type, with a ruddy complexion — asked after he had given the ID and Matt a good look.

"Philadelphia, huh?" the uniform said, then looked back at Matt's car and added, "Blue Plymouth. We got the word on you."

"What word is that?"

"That you're up here looking for some money some dirty cop in Philadelphia's trying to hide up here, and we should leave you alone."

"Guilty."

"This is part of that?"

"No. This is personal. You are about to ruin my romantic evening. How does the Harrisburg Police Department feel about professional courtesy?"

"You know how fast she was going?"

"Too fast for me to take my eyes off the road to look for speed-limit signs."

"Sixty-five. This is zoned forty."

"I understand. If you feel that duty requires you toss her in the slam and ruin the best chance

I've had in six months, I will understand."

The uniform laughed.

"If you put it that way, how could I run her in?"

"You could be a prick like my corporal when I was in Highway."

"Have a word with her," the uniform said, chuckling.

"I will," Matt said, and put out his hand. "Thanks, I appreciate it."

"Good luck," the uniform said, and got back in his car.

Matt walked up to Susan's car. The window was down, but she didn't say anything. She looked a little frightened.

"I just got you off," he said. "Say, 'Thank you, Matthew.' "

"I heard," she said. "Everything. I think I'd rather have gotten the ticket."

"You're welcome," Matt said.

The window whooshed up.

"Drive slow," Matt muttered a little bitterly and then walked back to the Plymouth.

When he flicked the Plymouth's headlights, the Porsche moved off the shoulder and down the road and he followed it.

He had a sudden insight:

She was not being routinely rude. She was frightened. But why? I just got the uniform not to pinch her. And she knew that. She said she "heard everything."

In which case, she heard the uniform verify my story about why I'm in Harrisburg. That should have put her mind at rest about me, if indeed Daddy had turned on her alarm system and she was wondering if I was really here looking for hidden money.

But if I was involved in something like she is, and a police car with its bubble-gum machine flashing pulled me over, I'd be pissing my pants, too. And while Wohl is probably right — Chenowith, who robs banks with a sawed-off shotgun, and the scumbag with the acne are dangerous — from what I've seen tonight, Susan is more a Presbyterian Princess who calls her parents "Mommy" and "Daddy," than a cold-blooded terrorist.

She didn't blow up the Biological Sciences building. If she had, the FBI would have said so. Helping those lunatics makes her an accessory after the fact, sure, but it doesn't mean she's as cold-blooded as they are.

Can I use that somehow?

Fourteen

If he saw it at all, Mr. Ronald R. Ketcham paid little attention to the black GMC Suburban truck parked near the elevator in the basement garage of his garden apartment building on Overbrook Avenue.

The truck was inconspicuous, and intended to be that way. It was painted black, and all but the windshield and front-seat windows had been painted over. There were no signs on its doors or sides indicating its ownership or purpose; it was classified as a "Not For Hire" vehicle, and none were required by law.

The inconspicuous Suburban was normally used to carry the remains of the recently deceased from their place of death — usually a hospital, but sometimes from the Medical Examiner's office, if the deceased had died at home, or for some other reason was subject to an official autopsy — to a funeral home.

Larger undertaking establishments often had their own discreet vehicles for the purpose of collecting bodies and bringing them to their places of business, as they had their own fleets of hearses, flower cars, and limousines to carry the dear departed, his/her floral tributes, and his/her mourners to his/her final resting place. But many — perhaps most — of Philadelphia's smaller funeral homes had found it good business to take advantage of the corpse pickup service and delivery service offered by Classic Livery, Inc., which owned the Suburban Mr. Ketcham did not notice as he drove his Buick into his garage.

Even the larger undertaking establishments, when business was good, often used one of the four black Suburbans Classic Livery had made available to the trade, as they similarly availed themselves of hearses, flower cars, and limousines from Classic Livery's fleet when their own equipment was not sufficient to meet the demands of that particular day's service to the deceased and bereaved.

Classic Livery, Inc., also owned the black Lincoln sedan parked among the rows of cars in the basement garage of Ketcham's garden apartment, and the four men in it — who had been waiting for Ketcham for two hours before the shit-ass finally showed up — were longtime employees of Classic Livery.

Ketcham parked his Buick coupe in the place reserved for it, got out, reached in and took his briefcase from the rear seat, and walked toward the elevator.

As Ketcham did so, everyone in the Lincoln sedan except the driver got out, and the driver of the remains-transporting Suburban started his engine.

The three men from the Lincoln reached the door to the elevator at about the time Ketcham reached it. One of them, a well-dressed thirty-five-year-old of Sicilian ancestry, smiled at Ketcham and waved him into the open elevator door. When Ketcham had entered the elevator, the three men got into it with him.

The elevator door closed.

The driver of the black Suburban drove to the door of the elevator and backed up to it. The doors were opened from the inside.

The elevator door opened again not quite a full minute later. Ketcham, the upper part of his body now concealed in an overcoat, and staggering, as if he had been subjected to some sort of blow to the head, emerged from the elevator, supported by two of the three men who had entered the elevator with him.

Ketcham was assisted into the Suburban, and one of the three men from the Lincoln got in with him. Ketcham was dragged toward the front of the Suburban — all but the front seat, of course, had been removed, so there would be room for a cadaver — where he lay upon his stomach. The doors were closed.

The other two men walked unhurriedly back to the Lincoln and got in. When the black Suburban drove away from the elevator door toward the entrance of the garage, the Lincoln followed it.

"What the hell's going on here?" Ketcham asked, his voice somewhat muffled by the overcoat over his head and shoulders.

The man who had opened the doors from the inside, and was now half sitting on a small ledge in the side of the Suburban, kicked him in the face.

"Shut your fucking face," he said.

He then proceeded to wrap two-inch-wide white surgical — or perhaps "morticians and embalmers" — white gauze around Ketcham's neck, in such a manner that the overcoat would not become dislodged.

Next, he used the tape to bind Ketcham's wrists together, and then his ankles.

Approximately five minutes later, Ketcham, who sounded close to tears, said one word: "Please . . ."

This earned him two sharp kicks, one in the ear from the man in the front, and a second in the buttocks, delivered by the man who had smiled at him as he had entered the elevator and who had gotten into the Suburban with him.

Ketcham said nothing else during the rest of the journey, which took approximately forty minutes, and neither did either of the two men with him in the rear of the remains-transporting Suburban.

Ketcham tried to recognize, and make sense of, the sounds and noises he heard during the trip. From the frequent stops and starts, and the sounds of automobiles accelerating and shifting gears, Ketcham deduced they were in traffic somewhere.

He searched his memory, very hard, in an attempt to guess who was doing this to him and why, but to no avail. The first thing that occurred to him, perhaps naturally, was that it had something to do with Mr. Amos J. Williams.

At first — Ketcham was understandably upset and not thinking too clearly, although the two lines of cocaine he had nasally ingested in the men's room of the Blue Rock Tavern on his way home gave him a feeling of euphoria about all things, including a sense that his mind was really firing on all twelve cylinders — that seemed the most logical inference to draw.

Williams — and his thugs — had been arrested at the Howard Johnson motel on Roosevelt Boulevard, and I wasn't. That damned well might have made him suspicious, maybe made him think I had set him up with the police. And his getting arrested had also caused him to lose the cocaine he had intended to sell me. Even if he had paid only half of what he was going to sell it to me for, that's still ten thousand dollars, and he would be very unhappy about losing that much money.

And if he has decided — he's not intelligent, obviously, so he's liable to decide anything — that I had something to do with his arrest, then this may be my punishment for that.

Unlikely. The first thing he would do — intelligent or not, he has a certain criminal cunning — would be to recoup his losses. At least the ten thousand he had invested, and possibly the entire twenty I had agreed to pay him. Once he had done that, he might well kill me. But what would be the purpose?

If it's money he wants, I'll promise to get it for him. Under these circumstances, I will be certainly motivated to find it somewhere.

But wait a minute! If this, whatever this is, has something to do with Amos Williams & Company, he would have sent his man Baby Brownlee. The people who are doing this to me are white men!

Could this be a case of mistaken identity?

For that matter, could I be hallucinating? This does feel like a bad dream. Am I going to wake up in just a minute?

Or could I really be hallucinating? I did a couple of lines . . . what, forty minutes ago? Was it bad stuff?

No. That was from my next-to-last packet of emergency supplies. I've been into it twenty, perhaps thirty, times without anything unpleasant happening.

Ketcham became aware that the sound of the vehicle's passageway over the roadway had changed. For one thing, he sensed that they were moving more slowly than they had been.

The vehicle stopped.

Ketcham heard the sound of the vehicle's door opening, and then it moved as if someone had gotten out.

He heard a metallic screech and decided, after a moment, that it was the sound of a door opening, and then changed that to suspect strongly that it was the sound a gate in a Cyclone fence — as those surrounding a tennis court — makes when being opened.

The vehicle moved a short distance forward. Ketcham heard the sound of the squeaking gate again. The vehicle tilted as if someone had gotten in the front seat. The door slammed shut and the vehicle drove off.

Ketcham sensed that they were no longer on a paved road, and confirmation of this came when the vehicle, moving slowly, encountered one hole in the road after another.

What are they doing? Taking me out in the woods someplace to kill me?

But if they wanted to kill me, they had ample opportunity in my garage.

If they're not going to kill me, then what? They must want something from me. What?

If this is a case of mistaken identity, which seems as likely an answer as anything else I've been able to come up with, then there will be the opportunity to clear things up, to let them know I'm not who they are looking for.

Or, even if it's not a case of mistaken identity, if they want something from me — maybe they know I'm a stockbroker, and think we keep large amounts of cash around the office. They're Italian, they could be the Mafia. That sounds like something the Mafia would do. And they might not know the only cash around the office is in the petty-cash box, and I don't even know of any negotiable instruments at all. Anyway, if they do want something from me, there will certainly be an opportunity to talk, to negotiate.

Those thoughts made Ketcham feel better.

After two or three minutes of lurching down what Ketcham was now convinced was an unpaved road, the vehicle moved onto a solid, flat, and thus presumably paved surface and stopped.

There was the sound of two doors being opened, the sense of shifting as if two persons had left the vehicle, and the doors slammed shut.

Then Ketcham heard the rear doors of the vehicle being opened.

"Cut that shit off his legs," a voice ordered.

There was a clicking sound, which Ketcham decided just might be the sound of a switchblade, and a sensation of sawing around his ankles. He felt the pressure that had been holding his ankles together go away.

Ketcham was dragged out of the Suburban and set on his feet. He felt a hand on each arm, as if there was a man on each side of him.

He was pushed into motion. Without quite knowing why, he sensed that he had entered some kind of a building. The sense grew stronger as he was guided down what he now believed to be a corridor, and confirmation came when he was stopped, and heard the sound of a door — a heavy metal door, he deduced. *Where am I? In a factory? Or a garage?* — being opened.

Ketcham was pushed through the door, led fifteen feet inside, and stopped.

"Cut his hands loose," the same voice ordered, and again there was the sort of slick clicking sound a switchblade knife made, and again the sawing sensation, this time at his wrists.

And then they were free.

"Without taking the coat off your head, take off your clothes," the same voice ordered.

"What?" Ketcham asked incredulously.

This earned him a blow in the face.

That wasn't a fist. That was something hard. A stick perhaps. Or perhaps a gun.

"Without taking the coat off your head, take off your clothes," the same voice repeated.

The one thing I cannot afford to do, Ketcham told himself, *is lose control of myself. They want me to take off my clothes, very well, I will take off my clothes — meanwhile, waiting patiently, and carefully, for my opportunity.*

With some difficulty, Ketcham removed the jacket of his dark blue, faintly striped blue suit. Without thinking what he was doing, he held the suit jacket out, as if waiting for someone to take it from him and hang it up.

A snicker made Ketcham realize that no one

was going to take the jacket from him. He let it slip from his fingers.

Ketcham next removed his necktie, and tried to drop that on top of his suit jacket. Then he pushed his braces off his shoulders, loosened the snap and opened the fly of his trousers, and somewhat awkwardly removed his trousers, which he then attempted to drop atop his jacket, tie, and shirt.

"I won't be able to remove my undershirt," he began, trying to sound as polite and reasonable as possible.

Ketcham was then struck upon the face again, which caused him to lose his balance and fall backward onto the floor.

"What he means," a new voice said, "is that he can't get his undershirt off without taking the overcoat off his head."

"Fuck the undershirt, then," the first, now familiar voice replied. "Take off your shorts and your shoes and socks."

Ketcham complied. He was now naked save for the overcoat over his head and upper body, and his undershirt, sitting on the floor. The floor was cold.

From its consistency, Ketcham decided the cold floor was concrete, which tended to buttress his suspicion that he was in a garage, or a factory of some sort.

"Get up," the familiar voice ordered.

Ketcham complied.

"Hold your hands out in front of you, together," the familiar voice added.

Ketcham complied, and almost immediately

felt his wrists again being tied together.

There was a short burst of derisive laughter.

"Christ, look at his cock," a third voice, previously unheard, said. "Angelina's Chihuahua's got a bigger cock."

There were chuckles of agreement.

"Shut your fucking mouth!" the familiar voice said.

I will remember that when this is over and I'm out of here, Ketcham decided with some satisfaction. *One of these thugs has a wife, or girlfriend, named Angelina, who has a Chihuahua.*

Then nothing happened, except for what Ketcham believed to be the sound of shuffling feet, and what could have been the sound of the door being closed.

It was cold wherever he was, and Ketcham felt himself start to shiver.

That should really please the thug who thinks my penis is funny, when he sees me standing here naked and shivering.

I will not lose control. I will wait until whatever is going to happen happens.

Five minutes later, very carefully, Ketcham uttered one word.

"Hello?"

There was no reply.

Thirty seconds after that, Ketcham spoke again:

"Hello? Is anyone there?"

There was no reply.

Obviously, there is no one here. If there was, and I was not supposed to have spoken, they would have hit me again.

Will someone be coming back?

What would they do to me if they came back and found that I had somehow been able to remove the overcoat over my head?

Two minutes after that, after having debated the question with himself carefully, Ketcham decided to attempt to remove the overcoat that covered his head and upper body.

Doing so was easier than he thought it would be. By maneuvering his shoulders while holding one side of the coat with his bound-together hands, he was able to get the coat off first one shoulder and then the other, and when that was done, he was able to untie the tape holding the coat around his neck.

But when Ketcham had removed the coat, he could see absolutely nothing. There was no light of any kind whatever in the room. He suddenly felt faint and dizzy, and dropped to his knees, and then moved to a sitting position. The floor under his buttocks was rough and cold.

Ketcham raised his wrists to his mouth, and with some difficulty, using his teeth, he managed to untie the tape binding his wrists together. That done, he groped for the overcoat, found it, and put it on. It was too small for him; he could button only a few of the buttons, and the cuffs were six inches off his wrists.

Ketcham then went back on his hands and knees and began looking for the clothing he had been forced to remove and had dropped onto the floor.

It was not where he remembered having dropped it, and Ketcham decided that he had become disoriented when he had felt faint and dizzy, and decided he would have to search for it methodically.

Ketcham crawled on his hands and knees until he encountered a wall. Then he moved along the wall hoping to find a door, or something else. He didn't, but eventually he found a corner. He moved from the corner to the next, and estimated that the room was about fifteen feet in that dimension. Then he followed that wall until the next corner, and the next. Along that wall, to one end of it, he encountered a door.

He stood up then and ran his hands over the door. He found a hole, which presumably had at one time held a doorknob. Ketcham put his index finger in the hole and felt around, but encountered nothing. Next Ketcham ran his hands over the concrete on both sides of the door. His fingers encountered a square box, a shielded cable running to it, and then, on the box itself, two toggle switches.

Ketcham closed his eyes so that he would not be blinded by any sudden light. He threw both switches several times, but there was no light.

Walking erect now, Ketcham proceeded along the wall until he came to the corner from which he had started. Then he made another circumnavigation of the room, walking erect and rubbing his hands in slow wide arcs over the cold rough concrete. Midway down one wall, he encountered another shielded cable, and followed it to a plug box near the floor. There was a similar arrangement on the next wall.

Ketcham realized that while he was, literally

speaking, still totally in the dark, he was no longer in complete ignorance of his surroundings. He was in a room he estimated to be probably fifteen feet by twelve. There was one door, no handle, and electrical circuits that were dead — or alive. Someone could have removed the bulbs from the light fixture — fixtures; there were two switches — they controlled.

There were no windows, which meant that he was more than likely in some kind of basement.

But they didn't lead me down any stairs, and the truck or station wagon, or whatever that was, didn't descend an incline; I would have sensed that if it had.

So where the hell am I?

Where are the people who brought me here?

Why did they bring me here?

What happens next?

Ketcham began to shiver again.

Where the hell are my clothes?

Ketcham dropped to his knees and began a methodical search of the room, rubbing his hand over the concrete in wide arcs. His confidence that it would be just a matter of time until he found his clothing took a long time dying, but eventually, after twenty passes, he gave up.

Ketcham rested his back against the wall.

His fingertips, and the palms of his hands, and his knees were raw from the concrete.

And I have to take a leak!

Jesus, what do I do about that?

Ketcham got to his feet and moved along the wall until he came to a corner.

I will piss here. This corner will be the toilet.

What the hell am I going to have to do when I

have to take a crap?

Ketcham held the too-small overcoat out of the way and voided his bladder. Moments after he had begun to do so, he felt warm urine on his bare feet. He spread his legs as far apart as he could until he finished.

Fuck it, I'd rather get beaten up than put up with any more of this shit!

Ketcham made his way to the door and shouted "Help" and "Hello" and beat on the door with his fists, which caused the door to resound like a bell.

No one responded.

Ketcham made his way to the corner opposite from the toilet, and rested his back against the wall, and started to weep in the darkness.

The parking lot of the country club was nearly full, and Matt lost sight of Susan's Porsche while finding a place to park the Plymouth. After three minutes of wandering around the parking lot, he found the car, but not Susan.

"Thank you ever so much for waiting for me," he muttered, and headed for the brightly lit entrance to the clubhouse.

He found Susan in the center of the large entrance foyer, talking to a man whose dress and manner made Matt guess — correctly, it turned out — that he was the steward, or manager.

"Good evening," Matt said, smiling.

"Matt, this is Mr. Witherington, the manager."

"Claude Witherington," the man said as he put out his hand to Matt. Then he was unable to resist making the correction: "*Executive* Manager, actually. Welcome to River View, Mr. Payne. We hope you'll enjoy our facilities."

"Thank you very much," Matt said.

"After Mr. Reynolds called," Witherington said, "I had your guest card made out." He handed it to Matt.

"Thank you," Matt said.

"This is a no-cash club," Witherington said. "I thought I should mention that."

"How am I going to pay?"

"Have you a home club?"

"I belong to Merion, in Philadelphia, if that's what you mean."

"Splendid. Merion, of course, is on our reciprocal list. Actually, had I known that, I wouldn't have had to issue a guest card at all. In any event, all you will have to do is sign the chit, and if you think of it, add 'Merion, Philadelphia.' "

"Actually, I think it's *in* Merion," Matt said. "What should I do, write 'Merion, Merion'?"

Susan Reynolds shook her head, but there was the flicker of a smile on her lips. Mr. Witherington looked distressed, but after a moment smiled happily.

"You just sign your name, Mr. Payne, and I'll handle it from there. You'll be billed through your club."

"You're very kind, thank you very much."

"Not at all," Witherington said. "Enjoy, enjoy!"

He walked off.

Susan put out her hand.

"Good night, Matt."

"Good night?"

"Good night."

"That wasn't our deal, fair maiden. Our deal was that I help you deceive your parents — and that was difficult for me; they're nice people — and in return you keep me from being overwhelmed by loneliness here in the provinces. I kept up my end of the deal, and I expect the same from you."

"Matt, if you go into the bar, and hold your left hand up so that people can see you don't have a wedding ring, a half dozen — what did you say, 'fair maidens'? — will fall over themselves to get at you."

"I know, that happens to me all the time. But I'm not that sort of boy. I don't let myself get picked up by strange young ladies. And I don't kiss on the first date. Besides, if you went home now, so soon, your daddy and mommy might get the idea our romance is on the rocks."

"We don't have a romance."

"You wouldn't want to break your mommy's heart, would you? From the way she was looking at me, she's already making up the guest list for our marriage."

"That's not true!"

" 'The truth is a shattered mirror strewn in myriad bits, and each believes his little bit the whole to own,' " Matt quoted, and when Susan gave him an incredulous look, added, "That's from the Kasidah of Haji Abu el Yezdi — in my judgment, one of the wiser Persian philosophers."

"You're unbelievable!"

"So my mother tells me," Matt said.

"What do you want to do?"

343

"Let's go in the bar and have a couple of quick stiff ones," Matt said. " 'Candy is dandy, but liquor is quicker.' I believe Mr. Ogden Nash said that."

Susan shook her head again. "One drink," she said.

"Three. We can then compromise on two."

Without replying, she walked toward what turned out to be the bar. It was a large, dark, and comfortable room, with a bar along one paneled wall, and tables with red leather-cushioned captain's chairs scattered around the room.

Matt did not miss the eight or ten attractive young women in the room, sitting in groups of two or three at tables and at the bar.

Maybe I should have let her get away. I think the odds to make out in here look pretty good. My chances with Susie range from lousy to zip.

Not that I would, anyway. Could, anyway. Peter was right about that.

I will not, Boy Scout's honor, make that mistake.

A waiter appeared as soon as they sat down.

"Good evening, Miss Reynolds," he said.

"What do you drink, Matt?" Susan asked. "Let your imagination run loose. Da— my father will expect me to make this my treat."

"Daddy's going to pay?" Matt asked.

"That's what I said."

"Would you bring us the wine list, please?" Matt said.

"The wine list?" Susan asked incredulously.

"It's a list of the available fermented grape juices," Matt said seriously, "generally stapled into some kind of artificial leather folder."

"Miss Reynolds?" the waiter asked in confusion.

"Go get the wine list," Matt ordered. "If the lady's going to welsh on her offer to spring for the booze, I'll pay for it myself."

"Get the wine list, please," Susan said.

"Yes, ma'am."

Susan looked at him.

"I don't think your insanity comes naturally," she said. "I suspect you actually think you're amusing, and really work on your crazy-man routine."

"I'm disappointed that you can see through me so easily," Matt said. "But now that you know my darkest secrets, are you going to tell me yours, to even the playing field?"

"Would it crush you even more if I told you I wouldn't give you my phone number, much less tell you my darkest secrets?"

"I already have your phone number," Matt said.

"Unfortunately," she said.

"When did you first realize you were falling in love with me? At Daffy's?"

"Oh, how I wish I had never seen you at Daffy's!"

"Then it must have been when some primeval force, stronger than both of us, brought you to my hotel-room door."

"Do you ever stop?"

"Not when I'm on a roll."

The waiter laid a wine list in front of Matt.

Matt looked at Susan.

"You never saw one of these before?" he asked

innocently. "They're quite common in Philadelphia."

"Jesus Christ!"

"What's your pleasure, Susan?" Matt asked.

"Whatever you like," she replied.

Matt looked at the waiter.

"Have they got any Camembert in the kitchen? Or Roquefort?"

"I'm sure there's Roquefort, sir. I'm not sure about the other."

"Okay. Well, ask, and bring us one or the other, preferably both. And some crackers, and of course a cheese knife, and a bottle of this Turgeson Napa Valley cabernet sauvignon. And a couple of glasses, of course."

"Yes, sir."

"We just had dinner," Susan said when the waiter had gone.

"But — you were so anxious to be alone with me — no dessert."

"I was anxious to get you out of the house as soon as possible."

"Isn't that what I just said?"

"Before you said something you shouldn't have."

"Not fair, fair maiden. I held up my side of the bargain."

After a moment, she said, "You're right. You did. Thank you."

"You're welcome," Matt said. "That brings me to the other 'thank-you' you owe me."

"For what?"

"For talking that Harrisburg uniform out of giving you a ticket for going sixty-five in a forty-mile-per-hour zone, thereby offending the peace and dignity of the Commonwealth of Pennsylvania."

"Is that what you call them, 'uniforms'?"

Matt cupped his hand behind his ear, signaling he was waiting to hear 'thank you.'

She smiled.

"Okay, thank you. Now answer the question."

"Yes."

"Isn't that a little condescending?"

"Not at all. It's simply an identifying term."

"I have trouble picturing you in a policeman's uniform."

"I'm dashing. Within a two-mile circle, girlish hearts flutter," Matt said, and then added, "Actually, I've hardly worn my uniform."

"How's that?"

"I went, right out of the Academy, to a plainclothes job."

"How did you arrange that?"

"It was arranged for me. My father has friends in high places, one of whom believed — with my father — at the time that I would quickly come to my senses, resign from the cops, and go to law school. My father's friend, he's a chief inspector, arranged for me to be assigned as the administrative assistant — sort of a secretary in pants — to Inspector Peter Wohl. The idea was that in this manner, until I came to my senses, I would not get myself hurt."

"But you didn't resign. Why not? Why are you a cop in the first place?"

"Why are you a social worker? That doesn't look like much fun to me, and I would be surprised if the pay's any better."

"I'm doing something important."

"The police are important. Try to imagine life without us."

"I don't have to shoot people," Susan said.

Shooting people is a no-no, right? But blowing them up — or at least aiding and abetting those who do — is OK, right?

"I only shoot people who are trying to shoot me," Matt said. "Or run me over with a truck."

"Is that what happened?"

"That's what happened."

"Did it bother you to have taken someone's life?"

Be careful what you say here, Matthew. Think before you open your mouth. I think the answer here is going to be important.

"Well, did it?" Susan asked, somewhat impatiently.

"I got psychiatric advice," Matt said.

"You went to a shrink?"

"My big sister is a shrink. She came to me."

"And?"

The waiter appeared with the wine and a plate holding crackers and a triangular lump of Roquefort cheese. While the waiter opened the bottle, Matt put cheese on half a dozen crackers.

He sipped the wine, nodded his approval, waited for the waiter to pour into first Susan's glass and then his own, then popped one of the crackers into his mouth and immediately took a sip of wine.

"What are you doing?" she asked in clear disapproval.

She had to wait until he had finished chewing for his reply.

"Don't tell me you never saw anyone do that before?"

"I never saw anyone do that before," she said. "It's gross!"

"But it tastes so good," he said. "Don't knock it until you've tried it."

"No, thank you."

"Oh, go on, take a chance. Live dangerously. Escape your mundane social worker's life."

She looked very dubious and did not reply. Matt popped another Roquefort-on-cracker into his mouth, added some of the wine, chewed, and smiled with pleasure.

Curiosity got the better of her. She shrugged and reached for one of the crackers and then the wine. She took a tentative chew, then smiled. When she had finished, she confessed, "That's good."

"And you didn't want to have a couple of snorts with me. You would never have learned that — something you can use for the rest of your days — from good ol' Whatsisname."

Her eyes showed she didn't like that.

"You were telling me what your sister the shrink told you," she said.

"You really want to know?"

"Yeah," Susan said thoughtfully. "I suppose I do."

"She said that I should remember that what I did was an act of self-preservation, rather than an act of willful violence. And that self-preservation is one of the basic subconscious urges, right up there with sexual desire, over which man has very little control."

I just made that up. I must be getting to be a pretty good liar. Or, more kindly, actor. When Amy came to me in her Sigmund Freud role after I shot the late Mr. Warren K. Fletcher in the back of his head, I told her to butt out.

And Susie seems to be swallowing it whole.

"And, of course, in that case, the act of homicide had an undeniably desirable social by-product."

"And what does that mean?"

"When he tried to run me over he had a naked housewife tied up with lamp cord under a tarpaulin in the back of his truck."

"Come on!" Susan said, almost scornfully.

Matt held up his right hand, pinky and thumb touching, the others extended. "Boy Scout's honor," he said. "And there was no moral question in that woman's mind whether or not I should have shot him. He had been telling her all the interesting things he was going to do to her just as soon as they got out of town."

"In other words, so far as you're concerned, it's morally permissible to take human life under certain circumstances — for a greater good?"

Matt bit off the answer that started to form on his lips, and instead said, "Have another cracker, Susan."

"We're changing the subject, are we? What happened, did you run out of sardonic witticisms?"

Yeah, for some reason I sensed that it was time to

change the subject. I have no idea how, but I knew that line of conversation was dangerous.

"I guess so. You can go home to Mommy and Daddy, Susan. I don't like the conversation anymore."

Her face colored, and for a moment Matt thought she was about to push herself out of her chair and march out of the room.

But she didn't.

"Sorry, I — I just never had a chance to ask . . ."

" 'How does it feel to kill somebody?' " Matt furnished, not very pleasantly.

She nodded.

"I'm sorry, Matt."

Why don't you ask your pal Chenowith? Wouldn't you say that blowing up eleven innocent people would make him more of an expert?

Jesus, she didn't! She has never talked to Chenowith about what he did! How do I know that? I don't know how I know, but I know.

"What was it? Feminine curiosity?" Matt asked.

"I said I was sorry."

"Like I said, have another cracker," Matt said, and made her another one.

She took it, put it in her mouth and added wine, and chewed. And smiled.

"That is good."

"I'm surprised your father doesn't do it. He takes his food seriously."

"What you really said was 'Go home, Susan,' " she said.

"I can't believe I said something like that," Matt said. "Not when we still have half a bottle of wine and two pounds of cheese."

She smiled.

"I'm sorry I said that," Matt said. "I apologize. I really don't want you to go home."

"I'm going to have to. I have to go to work tomorrow. And so do you."

"Have another cracker," he said, and made her another one.

She took it.

"I learned something about you tonight I didn't know," she said. "That may have had something to do with my uncontrolled curiosity."

"Like what?"

Susan looked into his eyes. "I never connected you with Penny before," she said.

"I don't recall mentioning Penny," Matt said. "Oh, that's right. You're another product of Bennington, aren't you?"

"We were friends," Susan said.

"How did you come to connect me with Penny?"

"This is awkward," Susan said.

"Go ahead. If we're going to spend the rest of our lives together, we should have no secrets from each other."

She smiled at him again.

"Oddly enough, I seem to like you better when you're playing the fool," she said.

"Thank you very much," Matt said.

"When I went to get my car from the garage? And my mother came to the garage?"

Matt nodded.

"Mommy told you?"

"*Mommy* said I should be especially nice to you

because of your tragic loss," Susan said. "So I naturally asked, 'What tragic loss?' "

"Okay. So are you going to be nice to me?"

"What happened to her?"

"You don't know?" Matt asked. "She got some bad shit, stuck it in her vein, and 'So Long, Penelope Detweiler.' "

"You sounded like a policeman just then."

"I am a policeman."

"I mean instead of her fiancé."

"We never got quite that far," Matt said. "Close, but not that far."

"But it hurt, right?"

"It was a tragedy. She had everything going for her —"

"Including you?" Susan interrupted.

"That was a possibility. But she couldn't leave it alone. The drugs, I mean. Her parents sent her to a place in Nevada, but it didn't work."

"How did she get started on it?"

"She started running around with a gangster named Anthony J. DeZego, also known as Tony the Zee. I have no idea how that happened — she was probably looking for a thrill. But I'm sure he's the bastard that got her hooked."

"And he's still around?"

"No, he's not. The mob, for reasons still unknown, blew him away. That's why Penny wasn't Daffy's maid of honor when she married Chad. Penny was with Tony the Z when they hit him. Shotgun. When Chad and Daffy were married, Penny was in Hahnemann Hospital, full of number eight shot, wrapped up like a mummy.

Mummy with a *U;* as in Egyptian."

"My God!"

"You didn't go to the wedding? It gave everybody something to talk about."

"I couldn't get away," Susan said.

"No, of course you weren't at the wedding. If you had been, I would have remembered."

She looked at him uncomfortably.

"This is all new to me."

"Daffy didn't tell you?"

"Daffy told me drugs were involved in Penny's death. I didn't pry."

They lapsed into silence. Finally, Susan stood up.

"I really have to go," she said.

Matt scrawled his name on the check.

"I'll walk you to your car."

"That's not necessary," Susan said. "Stick around. The hunting looks good."

"Not to me," Matt said.

"I told you, Matt, I'm just not interested."

"I remember," he said.

She shrugged.

They walked out of the club and to her Porsche.

She unlocked the car and stood by the open door and held her hand out. He took it.

"Drive slow. That uniform may have a quota of tickets to pass out."

"I will," she said. "And thank you for being a good guy at the house tonight."

"Good ol' Whatsisname would never know," Matt said.

"Know what?"

"If you gave me the briefest, most platonic possible kiss good night."

"I don't *want* to," Susan said. "Can't you get that into your head?"

"A teeny-weeny, absolutely innocent kiss that not even the Pope could object to, much less Mommy and Daddy."

"Oh, Jesus," she said, and moved her head very quickly and brushed his lips.

Then she stood back and they looked at each other in something close to amazement.

Jesus H. Christ! Matt wondered. *What the hell was that? Lust at first touch?*

Susan quickly crawled into the Porsche, slammed the door closed, started the engine, and drove quickly out of the parking lot without looking at Matt again.

Matt watched until the car disappeared from sight, exhaled audibly, and went looking for the unmarked Plymouth.

Mrs. Reynolds came into Susan's room as she was undressing.

"Did you have a good time?"

"Yes, as a matter of fact, we did. He taught me to put Roquefort on a cracker and then take a swallow of wine."

"Daddy used to do that," Mommy said.

"Did he really?"

"He seems to be a very nice young man," Mommy said.

"For a cop," Susan said.

"What's that supposed to mean?"

"Nothing."

"At least he's working, and according to Mr. Emmons, very highly regarded in his chosen profession."

"And what else did Mr. Emmons have to report?"

"He's very comfortable. I mean, personally, now. And the Paynes are more than comfortable."

"Where do you think we should be married, Mommy?" Susan said.

"Don't be like that, Susie, you asked!"

"Sorry."

"Are you going to see more of him?"

"I'm afraid so."

"I think you like him."

"Good night, Mommy."

Mrs. Reynolds turned as she passed through Susan's door.

"Mary-Ellen Porter called," she said.

"Who?"

"Mary-Ellen Porter. She said you were together at Bennington."

Since I never heard the name Mary-Ellen Porter until this moment, then it has to be either Jennie or Eloise.

"Oh, of course. *Mary-Ellen.* What did she want?"

"She said she would call you at work tomorrow. I told her they didn't like that, but she said she had to talk to you in the morning."

"I wonder what she wants?" Susan asked, more or less rhetorically.

Fifteen

"Good morning, Lieutenant," James C. Chase said. "It's always a pleasure to see you. How can we be of assistance this morning?"

The brass sign on Chase's large, highly polished desk in his glass-walled office off the main room of the First Harrisburg Bank & Trust Company identified him as "Vice President."

Matt had instantly decided that Chase was the exception to the general rule that most banks had as many vice presidents as they did tellers, and that the title had come in lieu of a pay raise and carried with it very little authority.

This man — fifty-something, gray-haired, very well-tailored — had the look and bearing of someone in authority, used to making decisions.

"This is Detective Payne, of the Philadelphia Police Department," Lieutenant Deitrich said.

The announcement visibly surprised Chase, but he quickly recovered and offered Matt his hand.

"How do you do?" he asked.

"How do you do, sir?" Matt replied.

"Payne, you said?"

"Yes, sir."

"I was in school with a chap from Philadelphia named Payne," Chase said. "Brewster C. Payne. I don't suppose there's any chance —"

"He's my father, Mr. Chase," Matt said.

"Then I really am delighted to meet you. How is your father? I haven't seen him in several years, I'm afraid."

"Very well, thank you, sir."

Well, I just got handed the keys to the bank didn't I?

"You make sure to give him my very best regards."

"Yes, sir, I will."

Wait a minute!

If this guy is really an old pal, why didn't Dad at least mention him when I told him I was coming to Harrisburg?

If Chase really is a good friend — and I think he thinks he is, which doesn't mean Dad reciprocates, of course — not mentioning him wasn't *an inadvertent oversight. Because Dad doesn't think of him the same way? No. He would have warned me about something like that.*

Maybe because Dad didn't want to lean on his old school chum on behalf of the cops? Or because he knew that it would quickly come to Chase's attention that a Philadelphia detective named Payne wanted to nose around his bank? And that Chase would either ask — as indeed, he just did — or call Dad and ask.

In the latter instance, that got Chase off the hook. If he wants to be nice to the son of his old buddy, fine and dandy. If he doesn't, he doesn't have to, and since Dad didn't ask Chase didn't have to say "no." No hard feelings.

You are *a smart one, Dad! Clever. Subtle. A real class act.*

It's amazing, as the saying goes, that the older I get, how much smarter you get.

And what was it you told me about banks? "Most bank presidents are figureheads, who spend their time talking to the Kiwanis and the Rotary and drumming up business on the golf course. Banks are run by their boards of directors, through the secretary or treasurer of the corporation, or sometimes a vice president."

Why do I suspect that I have just met that "sometimes vice president"? And that Lieutenant Deitrich damned well knows where Mr. Chase fits into the power structure around here?

"Now, how may I be of assistance?" Chase asked.

"We have reason to believe that someone engaged in criminal activity in Philadelphia has moved money to Harrisburg," Matt said. "Concealing it."

"And you're here to see if you can find it? And obviously with the blessing of Chief Mueller, or Lieutenant Deitrich wouldn't be with you."

Deitrich nodded.

"Yes, sir," Matt said.

"Are you at liberty to tell me the source of the funds?"

"One of our officers has been suspended, and indicted for taking money from a madam who was operating a call girl ring in Center City," Matt said.

"That's one of the more lucrative 'occupations,' I understand. Do you have a search warrant?"

"For the property of the officer concerned. His name is Seymour Meyer. He was a lieutenant."

"I suppose it would be too much to hope he would have an account, or a safe-deposit box, in his own name, wouldn't it?"

"Yes, sir," Matt said. "I have a list of names of relatives, friends —"

"Well, we'll look first — we might get lucky — for any accounts in this man's name. Or a safe-deposit box in his name. Your warrant — you have it with you?"

Matt reached into his jacket and came out with the warrant. Chase read it.

" 'Wherever located,' " he read aloud. "Good. That will give you access to either the details of his account or the box. If we find either. But as far as boxes in another name, or the details of someone else's account . . ."

"Yes, sir. I understand. If, however, there is an account — are accounts — matching the names on my list, I understand the courts have held that it is not a violation of the client's confidentiality if a bank were to review the account and tell me if there were unusual deposits, or unusual activity. Without divulging the amounts involved, of course. With that, something out of the ordinary, I'm sure we can go back to the judge and get additional search authorization."

"You know your business, don't you?" Chase asked, and went on without giving Matt a chance to reply. "What I'll do, Mr. Pay— Would you mind if I called you by your first name?"

"Not at all, sir. 'Matt.' "

"What I'll do, Matt, is get you a desk, and then I'll get a list of our account holders and box holders, and you can start your search."

"That's very kind of you, sir."

"May I see your list of names?"

"Yes, sir, of course," Matt said, reached in his pocket for it, and handed it to him.

"I'll have my girl make a Xerox of this, and start the process rolling."

"I think you're set up here, Payne," Deitrich said. "When you finish here, give me a ring, and I'll take you around to First National."

"Thank you, Lieutenant," Matt said.

"Mr. Chase," Deitrich said, nodded at the banker, and left the room.

When he was out of earshot, Chase looked at Matt and smiled.

"He doesn't talk very much, does he?"

"No, sir."

"But he's a good man. We've had some — what do I say, 'business'? — together, and I must confess I was very impressed with him."

"He gives me that impression, too, sir."

"Ordinarily, Matt, I'd install you in a small room off the lobby, but I think I can, for my old friend's son, do a little bit better than that."

He walked to the glass door of his office and waved Matt through. Then he walked ahead of Matt across the lobby to another glass-walled office like his own, but somewhat smaller.

A middle-aged woman sat at a desk outside it.

"Dolores," Mr. Chase said, "I can't believe you'll find anything, but would you have a quick look for anything of a confidential nature in Mr. Hausmann's desk? This is Mr. Payne, who will be using it for a while while Mr. Hausmann is in Boston."

"I'll check," she said, getting up and smiling at

Matt. "You're from First Chicago, Mr. Payne?"

"No, ma'am."

"What Mr. Payne is doing here is confidential, Dolores."

"I see," she said. "Well, this won't take me a moment. Mr. Hausmann is very careful about things of a confidential nature."

She went into the office and came out in less than a minute.

"Nothing on top, and everything else is locked."

"Thank you," Chase said. "Now, I'm sure that you would have done everything you could to make Mr. Payne welcome, even if I didn't tell you his father and I are old friends. Classmates, as a matter of fact."

"Of course."

"In that case, I'll leave him with you, and try to make the bank some money."

She laughed dutifully.

"Matt," Chase said, as if he had just thought of this. "How long do you think you'll be here?"

Matt smiled.

"Until I either get what I came for, or know that it was never here in the first place."

"Where are you staying?"

"At the Penn-Harris."

"That's the best place. Room all right?"

"Very nice, sir."

"Good. Do you play golf?"

"Yes, sir."

"Would you like me to call out to River View and get you a guest card?"

"That's very kind, sir. But a friend's father, Mr.

Reynolds, already did that for me."

"Tom Reynolds?"

"Yes, sir."

"Well, in that case, I won't have to ask what was going to be my next question."

"Sir?"

"Which was going to be, 'Would you like me to see if I couldn't find a nice girl to introduce you to?' "

Matt chuckled.

"That won't be necessary, sir. But thank you very much."

Chase touched Matt's shoulder and walked back to his office.

"Can I get you a cup of coffee, Mr. Payne?" Dolores asked.

"That would be very nice," Matt said. "And may I use the phone?"

"Of course. Just make yourself comfortable."

She waved in the direction of Hausmann's desk. Matt walked into the office, settled himself in the comfortable green leather high-backed chair, took a look at a silver-framed photograph presumably of Mr. and Mrs. Hausmann and the four little Hausmanns, and then reached into the credenza behind the desk for the Harrisburg telephone book.

He found what he was looking for and dialed the number. He had to go through a switchboard, but in less than a minute, he heard:

"Appeals, Reynolds."

"My, don't we sound businesslike? I'm sure, hearing that no-nonsense voice, that the taxpayers of Pennsylvania are getting a good day's work for a fair day's pay out of you."

"Oh, God! What do you want?"

"There are several things on my mind, actually."

"Make it quick. They don't like personal calls around here."

"Okay. First and foremost, I wanted to assure you that I haven't washed my face."

"What?"

"I may never wash it again, as a matter of fact."

"Oh," Susan said, finally taking his meaning. "Jesus! Grow up, Matt!"

"You mean you washed your face?" he asked incredulously.

"Of course. . . . What's on your mind, Matt?"

"I think you already know."

"God!" she responded in what she hoped was an expression of disgust and disbelief.

"If you have a pencil, Susie, I'll give you the telephone number of my new office. Very classy. It gives me a splendid view of the polished marble floors and ornate bronze fixtures of the lobby of the First Harrisburg Bank and Trust Company. In case you want to call me in the next couple of hours."

"I don't think that's likely."

"You never know when you're going to need a cop, and in case you do, you'll have my number right at your fingertips."

"Next?"

"Where are we going for lunch?"

"Nowhere."

"Then where are we going for dinner?"

"Nowhere."

"I thought maybe we could drive out to Hershey and have dinner in the Hotel Hershey."

"No."

"Well, any place you like is fine with me. What time shall I pick you up?"

"You don't know how to take 'no' for an answer, do you?"

"We have a deal, fair maiden."

"I don't know what you've got in your mind, Matt —"

"Really? No feminine intuition at all? I find that difficult to believe."

"Damn you!"

"I seem to have offended you. Since — my intentions being so pure and noble — I can't imagine how, what I am obviously going to have to do is call your mommy, tell her how sorry I am, and ask her if she can't try to fix things up between us."

There was a chuckle. Not a very pleasant chuckle, more one ringing of resignation.

"And you really would, wouldn't you, you son of a bitch?"

"You can take that to the bank. The First Harrisburg Bank and Trust."

"I'll pick you up in front of the Penn-Harris at half past six. We'll have a quick and early dinner."

"To start," Matt said. "You won't have any trouble spotting me. I'll be the handsome devil with the look of joyous anticipation in his eyes."

"Oh, God," Susan said, and hung up.

Matt put the phone in its cradle and only then noticed a mousy-looking female in her thirties standing in the office door. She held a deep metal

365

tray full of strange-looking forms — bank records, probably, he decided — in both hands.

"Mr. Payne?" she asked.

Matt nodded. She came into the office and, with a grunt, laid the gray metal tray on the glass-topped desk.

"These are the safe-deposit box access records," she said. "When you're through with them, would you please tell Dolores, and I'll come and get them."

"Thank you," Matt said, and smiled at her.

He ran his fingers down the forms. Each form was metal-topped, and designed to hang from the reinforced side of the tray. Each form was for one box, and listed not only the names and addresses and social security numbers of every person authorized access to that particular box, but at what time, on what date, someone had the box, and for how long.

What I thought Chase was going to get for me was a list of names of box holders matching — at least the last name — the names on my list. This tray obviously holds a card for every safe-deposit box in the bank.

Is giving me more information than I even asked for, crossing over the confidentiality line, the way they always "cooperate" with the police in a situation like this?

Or only when they trust the cop doing the looking?

Or because of my father's relationship with Chase?

What difference does it make? Never stick your finger in a gift horse's mouth.

He had finger-walked his way through perhaps half a dozen of the records when the skinny woman came back, this time carrying a tray in which another kind of bank records lay flat.

"These are the accounts in which you may be interested, Mr. Payne," the skinny woman said. "Through 'D.' The sooner I can have them back, the better. So if you would just ask Dolores to Xerox the ones you're interested in, then you could send them back. I'd really like it better not to bring you 'E' through 'H' until you're through with these. Would that be all right?"

"That would be fine," Matt said. "Thank you very much."

Matt picked up the top record in the tray. It was a complete record, going back four years, of the banking activity — the dates and times of deposits; withdrawals; interest payments; and service charges — in a savings account of an individual whose last name — only — matched one of the names on the list Matt had prepared in the Personnel Office in the Roundhouse.

The form (actually three forms, stapled together) under the first was a record of the same activity in the individual's checking account.

If I get one of these — two of these — for every account holder in this bank with the same last name as the names on the list I gave Mr. Chase, I'll be in Harrisburg for a month.

Which, considering the rockets that went off when I kissed Susie last night, might not be entirely a bad thing.

For Christ's sake! What the hell's the matter with you? Get that stupid idea out of your mind, once and for all!

He reached for the telephone, dialed the operator, and placed a collect call to Sergeant Jason Washington.

"Matthew, my boy! How are things in the capital of our great Commonwealth?"

"Well, I am into the bank."

"So, apparently, is the opposing side," Washington replied.

"Excuse me?"

"You first. You seemed surprised."

"The . . . *level of cooperation* is much more than I expected."

"Perhaps it's your charm," Washington said. "I understand you were to take someone to dinner last night. Did that happen?"

"Yeah."

"Was the evening fruitful? In a professional sense?"

Was that a dig? Or was he just being clever?

"I think so."

"But nothing specific to report?"

"No."

"Are you somewhere where you can conveniently and confidentially telephone? There's someone else you really should talk to."

"Wohl?"

"Matthews."

"I'm in a glass-walled office off the lobby of the Harrisburg Bank and Trust Company," Matt said. "It's private enough, but I would have to call him collect."

"Give me the number — I should have thought of that anyway — and I'll suggest he call you. The unattractive lady bandito has apparently struck again."

"Really? Where?"

"I have only the most rudimentary facts. But I suspect Jack Matthews is happily anticipating providing you with every last detail."

Matt read the telephone number and the extension off the phone to Washington.

"I am sure that you will be hearing from Matthews within minutes," Washington said. "And there is one more thing, Matt."

"What?"

"Peter Wohl is concerned that you might do something foolish. So am I. Allow Mr. Matthews's associates to deal with this beyond the limitations of what you were ordered to do."

"Okay."

"If you were to disobey your orders, and Wohl, so to speak, threw the book at you, he would have my complete support."

"You have made your point."

"I devoutly hope so," Washington said, and hung up.

Three minutes later, Dolores, after first knocking, put her head into the door of the office.

"There is a Mr. Rogers of the Philadelphia Savings Fund Society on line three for you, Mr. Payne. Do you want to take it?"

"Thank you," Matt said, and picked up the telephone. "Payne."

"Can you talk?"

"Didn't you just hear me talking?"

"Christ, Matt!"

"What can I do for you, Mr. Rogers? Don't tell me I'm overdrawn again?"

He could hear Matthews sigh.

"The Farmers and Merchants Bank of Clinton, New Jersey, was held up yesterday morning. We just heard about it, and I just talked to our Newark office — they have jurisdiction. Same modus operandi as the Riegelsville job. Same description of the perpetrator. This time, the haul was nearly sixty thousand dollars."

"Hairy legs and all?"

"That wasn't mentioned. But the unattractive, heavy makeup, earrings, et cetera, et cetera. For reasons I can't understand, Newark sent the surveillance-camera film to Washington — to the Anti-Terrorist Group; I suppose they issued a 'Report Similar Events' notice — *before* they processed it. I called Special Agent Jernigan, and he's promised to send me whatever the camera shows by wire as soon as it's processed. I'll be very surprised if it turns out to be someone else."

"Sawed-off shotgun, too?"

"No. That's the one thing that doesn't fit the modus. This time it was a sawed-off carbine."

"Explain that to me, please?"

"One of the witnesses — the bank guard — got a good look at it. The stock had been cut off behind the pistol grip, and then rounded with a file. And the barrel was cut off back to where the forearm whatchamacallit holds it. You understand?"

"What's the purpose?"

"Concealability, obviously. And presumably our friend thinks he now has the latest thing in terrorist machine-pistols. Those were M2 — fully automatic carbines — they stole from Indiantown Gap."

" 'Presumably our friend thinks'?" Matt quoted.

"I fired a carbine modified very much like this one on the FBI range at Quantico. They look great, very menacing, but —"

"I've fired one, too," Matt interrupted. "And also at Quantico. But on the Marine Corps' known-distance range."

"Okay. Then, knowing that there's a good deal of recoil in a carbine, you'll understand how hard this 'modification' would be to control, even single shot, without the stock. If he tries to fire it full automatic, he just couldn't control it. The danger here is —"

"If he should try to take a shot at a cop, or one of you guys, he'd be more likely to hit a civilian," Matt finished for him.

"Right."

"What is this clown doing, acting out a fantasy?"

"That bombed building was no fantasy, Matt."

"No," Matt agreed. "Anything else?"

"How did your dinner with the girlfriend go?"

"What do you mean, 'girlfriend'?"

"Chenowith's, not yours, of course."

"I must have missed something. I thought the Ollwood woman was his girlfriend."

"Right. So what?"

"Yes or no?"

"No. I have carefully gone through everything. I have had plenty of time, you see, waiting patiently by my telephone to hear from you —"

"Screw you, Jack," Matt said amiably.

"— and there is nothing to suggest that the Reynolds woman is, or has been, romantically

371

involved with either male."

" 'Either *male?*' "

"I didn't mean to suggest that. But who knows? These people don't consider themselves bound by the usual conventions of society. If it feels good, do it."

Christ, is that a possibility? There is no boyfriend. Has been no boyfriend . . .

"How did dinner go?" Matthews asked.

Well, pal, we had dinner with Mommy and Daddy, and Daddy taught me how to cook a London broil, and then we went to the country club. En route, the female suspect got pinched for speeding, and I talked a local uniform out of writing the ticket. At the country club, I taught the female suspect to eat Roquefort on crackers with a sip of cabernet sauvignon, and we talked about mutual friends, and then the female suspect kissed me for approximately one-tenth of second, whereupon my heart nearly jumped out of my chest. Moments later, my wang tried very hard to break through my zipper. And then I tossed and turned most of the night, thinking about it.

"All right," Matt said.

"Are you gaining her confidence? Do you think she suspects you're in Harrisburg for any reason but the cover story?"

"Yes and no. That was two questions."

"Are you sure she's not suspicious? That's a clever female, Matt. She might be able to conceal her suspicions from you, to see what you're really up to."

"Hey, I was told to liaise — whatever the hell that means — with you, not have you question my conclusions."

"What's the matter with you?" Matthews asked, sounding shocked.

"Nothing. Why should there be?"

There was a pause, then Matthews asked, "What happens next? Are you going to see her again?"

"Dinner, tonight."

"You haven't picked up on anything?"

"Our relationship is not yet at the point where I can ask, 'Hey, Susie, by the way, what do you hear from your friend, the bomber and bank robber?' But I'm working on it."

"You will, of course, call me if you do pick up on anything? I mean, presuming you got out of the right side of bed that morning?"

"Yeah. Of course I will. But for Christ's sake, don't expect miracles."

"Be careful, buddy."

"I will."

Matthews hung up.

Ten minutes after her conversation with Matt Payne — while part of her mind was still occupied with wondering why she somehow just hadn't been able to tell him that not only would she not have dinner with him tonight, but that the fun and games was over, period, don't call me anymore, period — Susan Reynolds received a telephone call from Jennifer Ollwood.

"Hi," Jennie began.

Susan gave her a telephone number and hung up. She rose from her desk and put her head in the door of Appeals Officer, Grade IV, Veronica Haynes.

"Cover for me, will you, Veronica? I'll be back in fifteen minutes."

"Make it half an hour," Veronica replied. "Fifteen minutes isn't really long enough for an early-morning quickie, is it?"

"Is that all you ever have on your mind?"

"Yeah," Veronica said, after appearing to have given the question serious thought. "What's more important?"

"I can think of some things."

"Some things that are as much fun?"

"Yeah," Susan said, after appearing to give Veronica's question as much serious thought as Veronica had given hers.

"Have fun," Veronica said. "Keeping one eye on the clock, of course."

Susan rode the elevator to the lobby and left the Department of Social Services Building. She walked to a car wash three blocks away. That morning, on her way to work, knowing Jennie — or less likely, Eloise Anne Fitzgerald — was going to call, she had had her Porsche washed.

While it had been going through — she hadn't liked to think what the brushes and felt washing pads were going to do to the Porsche's paint job, but doing this seemed necessary — she had walked to the corner, where there was a pay telephone booth, and written down — and later memorized — the number.

She entered the phone booth, took the handset off its hook, held the hook down with her finger, and pretended to be having a conversation until the phone rang.

"Hi," Jennie said again.

"Hi, yourself. How are you?"

"Well, you know. Fine. Why shouldn't I be?"

Being a fugitive from justice, wanted for murder, and that son of a bitch you're living with comes immediately to mind.

"And the baby?"

"He's just wonderful!"

And what's going to happen to him when Mommy and Daddy are hauled away in handcuffs?

"Jennie, is something wrong? I don't think these telephone calls, so many of them, are really smart."

"Why don't you come see the baby?" Jennie asked cheerfully.

"First of all, I don't think — I was just there — that's such a smart idea. As much as I'd like to, Jennie."

"Bryan has something he wants you to keep for us," Jennie said.

What? Another bag full of money he stole from a bank?

"Really?"

"Like the last package, only a little bigger," Jennie said. There was a touch of pride in her voice.

My God, don't tell me he actually did rob another bank!

I'll have to get a larger safe-deposit box. The one I have is nearly full of money he stole.

"Jennie, I really don't think coming there so soon again makes sense."

"Bryan wants you to," Jennie said. "He says you know why."

If he's arrested — when he's arrested — he doesn't

want to be found in possession of money the cops will suspect came from one or more so far unsolved — or is the word "successful"? — bank robberies. He wants the money to pay for his defense.

I sometimes think that Bryan really would like to be caught, and put on trial. He thinks that with a good lawyer — and himself skillfully playing the role of noble young intellectual courageously standing up for moral principle — he will not only walk out of the courtroom a free man, but into a role as Hero of the New Order.

And, of course, Jennie has been mesmerized into going along with his fantasies. She thinks the father of her baby is the Scarlet Pimpernel.

"Jennie, there are reasons I can't come there anytime soon. You're just going to have to tell Bryan that, and to put the package someplace safe where you are."

"What reasons?" Jennie asked, almost indignantly.

"Good and sufficient reasons, Jennie. I'm sorry."

"You better tell that to Bryan yourself," Jennie said.

"I don't want to tell him —"

"Just a minute, Susie," Jennie interrupted. "Hang on."

The son of a bitch is there. Probably sitting in his car. Let Jennie do the work.

What I should do is just hang up. But if I do that, he'll make her call the office, or the house. What the hell am I afraid of? If he comes on the phone, I'll tell him why I don't want to go get his "package" for him.

Bryan's voice came over the line. "Hey, Susie, what's going on?"

"I told Jennifer there are reasons I can't meet her."

"So she said. What are the reasons?"

"One of them is that the last time I spoke to you on this subject, you told me that was the last time."

"You know we need money," he said, "and this was too good to pass up."

"You don't need the money. You have enough now."

"Good lawyers are very expensive, Susie," Bryan said reasonably.

"You've got more than enough for a good lawyer," Susan said. "I can't get away so soon again without having people ask questions."

"Think of something. You're an intelligent girl. And we're in this together, Susie."

What is that, a not so lightly veiled threat?

"I'm not going to debate this with you," Susan replied. "There are reasons I can't make a trip there anytime soon."

"I'm waiting to hear them."

"Well, for one thing, I've got a cop on my back."

That comment obviously set him back. There was a perceptible pause before he replied:

"Don't you think you should tell me about that, Susie? What makes you think the cops are onto you? Why should they be? Are you suffering from paranoia?"

"I didn't say 'cops,' I said 'cop,' singular."

"Where did he come from?" Bryan asked, and

Susan detected concern in his voice.

As hard as the macho son of a bitch is trying to hide it.

"Philadelphia," she said.

"A Philadelphia cop in Harrisburg?" Bryan asked doubtfully, and then went on patronizingly: "Susie, Philadelphia cops have no authority outside Philadelphia."

"Is that so?"

"Yes, that's so. You're sure he's a cop, and not FBI? How did he get onto you, anyway?"

"He's a Philadelphia cop. Actually, a detective. I met him at Chad Nesbitt's birthday party."

"What was a *cop* doing at Mr. Canned Chicken Soup the Fourth's birthday party?"

"He's Mr. Canned Chicken Soup the Fourth's oldest friend, and godfather to their baby."

"And he's a cop?" Bryan asked dubiously again.

"Detective."

"Susie, this sounds unreal."

"It feels unreal. But there it is. Every time I look in the mirror, there he is, on my back, making sophomoric jokes."

"He came on to you?"

"He came on to me, and I put him down, and then — to hell with it. It's a long story. The last chapter is that the Philadelphia police sent him here on some kind of an investigation —"

"So he says," Bryan interrupted. "That could be a story. I suppose it did occur to you that he may not be what he says he is?"

"Now who's sounding paranoid? I have good reason to believe he's here for the reason he gives."

"We can't be too careful," Bryan said seriously. "The FBI is not always as stupid as generally believed."

"Anyway, he called the house and my mother invited him for dinner. And I'm going to have dinner with him tonight. There was no way I could get out of it."

"How hard did you try?"

"Go to hell, Bryan," Susan said. And then, before he could reply, Susan went on, "I've got to get off the phone. All you have to understand is that with the cop on my back, I can't go anywhere near you."

"Susie, let's think about —" Bryan responded.

Susan hung up on him.

Sixteen

Susan Reynolds had to stop for a red light near the Penn-Harris hotel, and saw Matt Payne before he saw her. And when she saw him, her heart jumped.

He was leaning on the brass sign next to the revolving door, legs crossed, reading the newspaper. He was wearing a very well-cut glen plaid suit, a crisp white button-down-collar shirt, and gleaming loafers.

The son of a bitch is good-looking, she thought. *And that is a very nice suit. Whatever he looks like, he doesn't look like what comes to mind when you hear the word "cop."*

The light changed and she drove toward the hotel, then blew the horn to attract his attention.

She saw him lower the newspaper to look around, and then he saw her. A wide smile appeared on his face, and she remembered what he had said about her not having any trouble spotting him: "I'll be the handsome devil with the look of joyous anticipation in his eyes."

She told herself: *Don't hold your breath, Matt Payne, waiting for the satisfaction of your joyous anticipation. That just isn't going to happen.*

She pulled to the curb, and he opened the door and got in.

"Hi," he said.

"Hi." She pulled into traffic.

I have no idea where we're going.

"It smells good in here," Matt said.

"And you just love women who wear French perfume, right?"

"I was talking about the smell of the leather," Matt replied. "Peculiarly Porsche, so to speak."

My God! He either thinks very quickly, or he really was talking about the damned leather.

He leaned close to her and sniffed.

"But now that you mention it, I do *love* women who wear French perfume."

And I can smell him, too. I don't know what that aftershave is, but he didn't get a large economy bottle of it for ninety-eight cents in Woolworth's.

And he's freshly shaven. He probably took a shower and a shave, getting all ready for the big date.

I wonder what he looks like in the shower?

What's the matter with you? Stop that!

"Is where we're going far?" Matt asked. "More than, say, two miles?"

"I haven't made up my mind where we're going. Only that it's not going to take long."

"Whatever you decide is fine with me, fair maiden. But keep in mind the two-mile limitation."

"What's with two miles? What are you talking about."

"These are marvelous machines, fair maiden, the *ne plus ultra* of German automotive engineering. But even a 911 requires what the Germans call, I think, 'petrol.' Or, maybe, *essence.* It's needed, you see, to make the pistons go up and down."

Susan dropped her eyes to the dashboard. The

red FUEL WARNING light was blinking, and the needle on the gas gauge pointed below Empty.

"Shit!" Susan said, and started looking for a gas station.

"These are a real bitch to start after you've run them completely dry," he said matter-of-factly.

"Among your many other qualifications, you're a Porsche expert, right?" she snapped.

"Maybe 'journeyman craftsman' would be more accurate."

"I'm touched by your modesty," she said.

"And well you should be," he said.

She pulled into a gas station and stopped at a line of pumps. Matt opened the door and got out.

The attendant appeared.

"You mind if I do it myself?" Matt asked.

"Help yourself," the attendant said.

"How about getting me a little rag? I want to check the oil, too."

"You got it."

"The oil's fine," Susan said.

"An ounce of prevention is worth several thousand dollars' worth of cure," Matt proclaimed solemnly. "Pop the lid, fair maiden."

"Shit," Susan said, and got out of the car to check the oil herself.

"The way you do that," Matt called to her from the gas pump, "is that there's a long thin metal thing that fits in a hole."

"Screw you, Matt."

"Who taught you all the dirty words? Good ol' Whatsisname?"

She pulled the dipstick, wiped it, dipped it again and looked at it in disbelief, and dipped it again. And again there was only a trace of motor oil on it.

"How much does it need?" Matt asked, and when she looked at him, he added, "I was watching your face."

"A lot," she confessed.

"What do you run in it?" he asked.

"Pennzoil 10W-30," she said.

"Good stuff," he said. He turned to the attendant. "Two, and possibly three, quarts of your very best Pennzoil 10W-30, please."

"You got it," the attendant said, smiling at him.

Or, condescendingly, Susan wondered, *at a stupid female who doesn't have enough brains to check the oil? Well, if that's it, I deserve it. Not checking the oil was stupid.*

Matt put the oil in. It took three quarts, and half of a fourth.

"It was just a little low, I would say," Matt said.

"Okay. You were right and I was wrong. I've had a lot on my mind lately, I guess, and just didn't check."

"I have a sister who does the same sort of thing," he said with a smile.

"Anyway, thank you."

"You're welcome," he said. "Can I make a request?"

"Request."

"A truce until after dinner? Hostilities can resume immediately after the second cup of coffee."

"Okay," she said after a just perceptible hesitation.

Why not? What's playing the bitch with him

going to accomplish?

"Deal?" Matt asked.

He put out his hand and, without thinking about it, she took it. His hand was warm and strong.

"Deal," Susan said. She was aware her voice sounded strange.

"Good," he said. "Then pay the man, fair maiden, and we'll be on our way."

He got behind the wheel and closed the door.

"What makes you think I'm going to let you drive?" Susan demanded.

"Because we are in a state of truce," Matt replied. "And also maybe because you are grateful I kept you from running out of gas."

Why not? Same reason as before.

She gave the attendant her credit card, signed the form, and got in beside him. She was a trifle amused at the care with which he adjusted the driver's seat.

He pulled out of the station, and she saw that he was better working the gears than she was.

"Where are we going?" she asked.

"To the only decent restaurant I know around here. Except, of course, the Penn-Harris. They gave me a very nice breakfast. My lunch was a disaster."

"Where is this only decent restaurant?"

"Little town called Hershey," Matt said. "They make chocolate there, you know."

"I don't want to go all the way out to Hershey."

"Not to worry, fair maiden. We now have a full tank of petrol. And I'm driving."

Susan elected not to make an issue of it.

384

He got on U.S. 422 and immediately pushed harder on the accelerator.

"You're going to get a ticket," Susan said.

"Fear not, fair maiden."

The speedometer was indicating seventy-five when there was the sound of a siren and the image of the flashing lights of a bubble-gum machine on a state trooper's car in the rearview mirror.

Matt immediately slowed, but did not pull off the highway onto the shoulder. The state trooper pulled alongside. Matt held his identification folder up for the trooper to see.

The trooper made a slow-it-down gesture. Matt nodded his willingness to do so. The trooper's car slowed and fell behind. Susan turned and looked out the window. The trooper had pulled his car off the road, and was about to make a U-turn back toward Harrisburg.

Back to give a ticket to some ordinary citizen for going five miles over the speed limit.

"That's outrageous!" Susan said indignantly.

"That's what's known as professional courtesy," Matt said. "You know, like sharks don't eat lawyers?"

"It's an abuse of power!"

"It's legal," he said. "Traffic officers have the option of issuing a citation or a warning. He opted to give me a warning."

"Jesus!" she said in contempt.

Five minutes later, with the speedometer indicating sixty-five — fifteen miles over the posted limit — Matt said:

"I really like the smell in here. And I am not talking about the leather."

385

Susan didn't reply.

He drove into the town of Hershey. The delightful smell of cocoa beans overwhelmed the smell of her perfume, and he told her so.

"That may not be a bad thing," he said. "Have you ever thought of rubbing a Hershey bar behind your ears? Or someplace more feminine? You might be able to save some money that way. What you're wearing has to be awfully expensive."

"No," she said as sternly as she could manage. But she had to smile.

He pulled into the parking lot behind the Hotel Hershey.

Susan started to open the door.

"Wait a minute," Matt ordered.

She turned and looked at him, and obediently slumped back into her seat.

He turned, so that his back was resting on the door. His hand and arm came to rest on the back of her seat. She could feel the warmth of his hand.

But it's not as if he's trying to put his arm around me or pull me over to him or anything.

"What?" she asked.

"It could have been one of those unexplained phenomena one hears about, something that happens only once in ten thousand years," Matt said.

He's talking about that damned kiss. Goddamn him, he knows what it did to me.

"What could?"

"On the other hand, it could well be a harbinger of heaven on earth," Matt said.

"Harbinger of heaven on earth"? My God! Give credit where it's due. That's one hell of a line.

"I think, before we have our supper, in the

386

interest of scientific research, let the chips fall where they may, so to speak, we should attempt the experiment again."

"Matt . . ."

"You agree?"

God, if he puts his hand on my shoulder, if he touches me, I don't know what I'll do.

"Matt . . ."

Matt pushed himself away from the door far enough so that he could reach her right shoulder with the balls of his fingers.

"Matt, I don't want to kiss you, I'm not going —"

And then she was on his side of the Porsche, the gearshift jabbing her painfully in the back. She was breathing heavily, looking up at him, seeing that his face was really smeared with her lipstick.

"Well," Matt said. "Now we know, don't we?"

"The gearshift," Susan said.

"Oh! Sorry!" he said, and she was aware they had moved on the seat, and that they were now close enough to conduct the experiment again.

And she became aware that his hand was under her blouse.

Why don't I slap his face, or at least push his hand away?

"Don't," she ordered, and heard in her voice that it was a lie.

He kissed her again.

I've got to stop this! Why don't I just push him away?

And then she was looking at his face again,

aware that she was breathing heavily. And then she was horrified to hear herself challenging, bitchily, "Well, you seem to have recovered very well from your tragic loss of Penny, haven't you?"

"I've thought about that," he replied immediately, matter-of-factly.

God, was he thinking about that, too?

"I don't think I ever loved Penny. She needed me. She was really fucked up. I got sucked into that. It was the, quote, decent, unquote, thing to do. Doing the right thing keeps getting me in trouble."

What did he say? "She needed me. She was really fucked up. I got sucked into that"?

He looked down at her again.

"Don't be a bitch, Susan."

"Sorry," she heard herself say, and that sounded very honest to her ears.

He kissed her again, and this time she became aware that the hand that had been on her breast was now between her legs.

Oh, God, I'm all wet! He'll know!

She freed herself violently, and sat erect in her seat and put her clothes in order.

My bra is loose. Did he unfasten it?

"I am not going to do this in a car," she said righteously.

"Sorry, I got carried away," he said.

That sounded sincere.

Matt opened his door and got out of the car.

What's this? What's he doing?

He walked around the rear of the Porsche and opened her door.

If he thinks I'm just going to go in there and have dinner . . .

She swung her feet out of the Porsche and got out.

She looked at his lipstick-smeared face, then for a moment into his eyes, and then quickly averted hers.

I'm not going in there with him looking like that!

She took the crisp white handkerchief from the breast pocket of his suit jacket and rubbed at his lips. When the lipstick didn't want to come off, she spat on his handkerchief and resumed rubbing with it.

I can't believe I did that.

"All right," she said finally.

He nodded and took her elbow and led her through a rear entrance into the hotel building, and down a corridor into, finally, the lobby. She saw a green neon arrow and the word "Restaurant."

God, my hair must be a mess, and my face is probably as smeared with lipstick as his was and everybody in the restaurant will see.

"Wait," Matt ordered.

He left her.

Where's he going? God, he's going to the desk. He doesn't actually expect me to go to a hotel room with him. I can't believe that this is happening. I won't let it happen. I'll just go back to the car . . .

Two minutes later, he was back, swinging a hotel key.

"We have a small suite overlooking the tenth green," he announced.

Susan nodded her head.

He took her arm and led her to the elevator. *I can't believe I'm doing this!*

The elevator operator, an old man, held his hand out to look at the key. When the elevator stopped and the door opened, the old man said, "To the right, sir. About halfway down."

"Thank you," Matt said, and waved Susan out of the elevator in front of him.

He unlocked the door to the suite, went inside, found and snapped on the lights, and turned to Susan, still standing in the corridor.

Their eyes met, and again she averted hers, and then went through the door.

She stopped six feet from the door and looked at him.

"What did you say about Penny?" Susan asked.

He looked confused, searched his memory, and shrugged.

"I don't know what you're talking about," he said.

"You said Penny needed you. That she was really fucked up. That you got sucked into it."

"Yeah, I said that. It's true."

"And that doing the right thing keeps getting you in trouble."

"Shut up, Susan," Matt ordered with a smile.

He crossed the few steps to her, put his hand on her cheek, and tilted her face up to look at him.

Their eyes met, and this time she didn't avert hers.

She felt his fingers working the buttons of her blouse. Her breasts, because he had unfastened her brassiere, were not restrained by it.

When he put his hand on her breast, then his mouth on her nipple, she heard herself saying, softly and plaintively, "Matt, I have to sit down. Lie down."

He picked her up and carried her into the bedroom, where, with one hand, he jerked the cover off the bed. Then he lowered her onto it, and as they looked into each other's eyes, took off the rest of her clothing.

Mr. Paulo Cassandro, the owner of record of Classic Livery, Inc., and its president, a 185-pound gentleman who stood six feet one inches tall, who had been summoned nevertheless, entered the living room of Mr. Vincenzo Savarese very carefully, and was immediately pleased that he had.

Mr. Pietro Cassandro, who was carried on the books of Classic Livery, Inc., as its vice president, immediately looked up at Paulo and made a gesture indicating that Paulo should wait and say nothing.

Pietro, who was twenty pounds heavier than Paulo, two inches taller, four years older and equally well-tailored, was not, however, quite as bright. For that reason, Mr. Savarese had some years before decided that Paulo was better equipped to direct Classic Livery and Pietro was better suited to function as a companion, which translated to mean that Pietro served Mr. Savarese as a combination chauffeur, bodyguard, and guardian of Mr. Savarese's privacy.

Paulo saw why Pietro had held up his hand, fingers extended in a warning to say nothing and wait until Mr. S. was ready for him.

Mr. S. was sitting slumped in a very large, comfortable-appearing armchair, his highly polished shoes resting on its matching footstool. His eyes were closed, and his right hand was moving in time with tape-recorded music being reproduced through a pair of five-foot-tall, four-feet-wide stereophonic loudspeakers.

I know that, Paulo thought with just a little pride. *That's* Otello, *by whatsisname, Verdi.* Giuseppe Verdi. And that's the part where the dinge offs the broad.

Paulo had three times accompanied Mr. S. to the Metropolitan Opera in New York City to see a performance of the opera. He could see it now in his mind's eye.

He very carefully backed up to the wall and leaned on it, to wait for Mr. S. to have time for him.

Three minutes later, Mr. Savarese pushed himself away from the cushions of his chair, causing Paulo concern that he might have inadvertently made a noise, distracting Mr. S. from his enjoyment of the opera.

Mr. S. did not seem annoyed with him.

Maybe he turned around to see if I was here yet.

Confirmation of that seemed to come when Mr. S. turned the volume off all the way.

"Pietro, rewind the tape carefully, please, and put it away."

"You got it, Mr. S.," Pietro said.

"Thank you for coming, Paulo," Mr. S. said. "Will you have a glass of wine?"

"That would go nice, if it wouldn't be an inconvenience, Mr. S."

"Get a bottle of wine and some glasses, Pietro, please," Mr. Savarese said, then motioned Paulo into one of the chairs surrounding an octagonal game table.

"Thank you, Mr. S.," Paulo said.

"If there had been any activity with the man, you would have told me, Paulo?"

"I had one of the guys ride by there every forty-five minutes, no less than once an hour. Nothing, Mr. S."

Pietro took a bottle of an Italian Chablis from the sterling-silver cooler where it had been kept ready for Mr. S. in case he wanted a little grappa, opened it, and set it on the table. He added two glasses.

"You'll have a glass, too, Pietro," Mr. S. said, "when you have finished with the tape."

"Thank you, Mr. S."

Savarese nodded and smiled at him, then turned to Paulo.

"I have been thinking that I would like to be there when you talk with this man," he said.

"You don't mean you want to go there, Mr. S.," Paulo said in surprise.

"I think that would be best, under the circumstances," Savarese said. "I would like to personally hear what he has to say."

"What I meant, Mr. S., is that you don't want to go *there*, do you? I mean, I can have him at the garage, for example, or anyplace else, thirty minutes after you give me the word."

Mr. Savarese poured wine in two glasses and handed one to Paulo.

"*Salute,*" he said.

"*Salute,*" Paulo repeated.

Mr. Savarese took a small, appreciative sip of the wine.

"That would involve moving him," he said. "I would rather that he not be moved. I think that would be better."

"Whatever you say, Mr. S."

"Paulo, he is in a certain state of mind after having been where he has been, under those circumstances, for twenty-four hours. If we move him, that would, I think, break the spell, so to speak."

"You're right, Mr. Savarese. I didn't think about that."

Paulo was frequently reminded, when dealing with Mr. S., that if he was one and a half times as smart as Pietro, Mr. S. was like five times, *ten* times as smart as he was.

"There'll be no problem, nothing to worry about," Paulo said. "I'll get enough people to guard that place like fucking Fort Knox!" When he saw the pained look on Mr. S.'s face, his own colored quickly. "Sorry about that, Mr. S."

Mr. S. did not like either profanity or obscenity.

Mr. S. accepted his apology with a curt nod of the head.

"This man is strong and dangerous. Paulo?"

"No, Mr. S. He's not. Not at all."

"And there is no question in your mind that you and Pietro can deal with him in any circumstance that you can think of?"

394

"I don't even need Pietro, Mr. S."

"Nevertheless, I want Pietro to go along with us."

"Right, Mr. S."

"I don't want this man to see me, for obvious reasons," Mr. S. said. "Or to hear my voice."

"No problem, Mr. S."

"Although I doubt it very much, he may have had nothing to do with the problems my granddaughter is having. I don't want to close any doors that might have to later be opened, you understand?"

"Absolutely, Mr. S."

"And, of course, we don't want to be interrupted while we are talking with him."

"I understand."

"I wondered if someone saw the vehicle you previously used there if it might not cause curiosity."

"I see what you mean, Mr. S. Let me think a minute."

Mr. Savarese waited patiently.

"How about a Chevy station wagon, Mr. S.? We got a couple of them. At a big funeral, we use them to haul flowers ahead of the procession, you know, enough to cover the phony grass by the grave —"

"They are black, like the Suburban?" Mr. Savarese interrupted him.

Paulo nodded. "And they don't have any signs painted on them or anything."

"I was thinking of something more on the order of a utility vehicle."

Again he waited patiently for Paulo to give

that some thought.

"What we do have is a Ford pickup, Mr. S. We keep it around with a jack and a couple of spare wheels and tires in the back, in case a hearse or a flower car has a flat."

"Does that happen often, Paulo?"

"No, Mr. S. But sometimes, you know, you get a bad tire or pick up a nail."

"Yes," Mr. Savarese said, understanding. Then he gave a dry chuckle. "The final indignity of life, Paulo, a flat tire on your way to your last resting place."

"Yeah, I see what you mean, Mr. S."

"Is there room for the three of us in this flat-tire truck?"

"You know, it's a regular pickup truck. It would be a tight squeeze. And it's sometimes dirty."

"The upholstery, you mean?"

Pietro finally came to the table and sat down.

"You heard what we have been talking about, Pietro?" Mr. Savarese asked.

"We could put a blanket or something on the seats, if they're dirty, Mr. S.," Pietro said.

"You understand, Mr. S.," Paulo explained, "we get a call there's a flat, one of the mechanics drops whatever he's doing and jumps in the pickup —"

Mr. Savarese held out his hand in such a manner as to indicate that a further explanation was not necessary.

"What I think we should do," Mr. Savarese said, "unless this interferes with your plans, Paulo . . ."

"My time is your time, Mr. S., you know that."

". . . is send Pietro to the garage, where he will clean this flat-tire truck up as well as he can, and if necessary, as he suggested, put a clean blanket over the dirty seats, and then bring it here. By then it will be dark."

"Good thinking, Mr. S.," Paulo said.

"And in the meantime, you and I will discuss what you're going to talk to this man about."

"Right, Mr. S.," Paulo said.

Paulo Cassandro's prediction that it would be a tight squeeze in the front of the Ford pickup truck proved to be true, and the blankets — he had sent one of the Classic Livery mechanics to a dry goods store to get two nice ones — proved to be hot and slippery when installed over the greasy upholstery, and Paulo knew Mr. S. was uncomfortable.

But Mr. S. hadn't said anything. Paulo interpreted this to be another manifestation of Mr. S.'s being fair. Mr. S. knew that he was the one who had ordered the pickup, so it wouldn't be right to bitch about what happened when he got what he asked for.

At five minutes to eight, the pickup stopped outside a ten-foot-high hurricane fence in a field south of the Philadelphia International Airport. There were metal signs reading, "U.S. Government Property. Trespassing Forbidden Under Penalty of Law" attached at twenty-five-foot intervals to the fence.

As they had driven up to the fence, Mr. Savarese had seen where there once had been provision for floodlights to illuminate the entire perimeter of the fenced-in area. They were no longer in use. Neither was what had been contained inside the fence: a battery (four launcher emplacements) of U.S. Army antiaircraft weaponry.

During a particularly tense period of the Cold War, the installation had been one of many such batteries surrounding Philadelphia and from which, should the Russian bombers have come, NIKE rockets would have been launched to blow them out of the sky.

Roughly in the center of the four launcher emplacements (their launching mechanisms long since removed) was a windowless concrete building. Its thick concrete walls had been designed to resist anything short of a direct hit from a low-yield nuclear weapon. When the site had been active, the building had held, in four interior rooms, an additional dozen NIKE rockets, as well as some maintenance supplies and equipment.

The dozen NIKEs were to be used to reload the four launchers, a process that would take — presuming the launchers and their crews were still intact after the first Russian assault — about twenty minutes. The possibility had occurred to the planners that the shock waves generated by the first bombs dropped would almost certainly put any elevator system bringing the spare NIKEs from underground storage out of whack, even if there was, immediately post-strike, any electricity to power the elevator.

So the spare NIKEs were stored at ground level, behind thick concrete walls and heavy steel doors, in rooms from which they could be man-handled to the launchers.

Paulo Cassandro was impressed — but not sur-prised — when Mr. Savarese had told him about the NIKE sites, and how he thought they might come in useful at some time for some purpose. Mr. S. had said he thought they would be around for some years, deserted but in reasonably intact condition.

Wherever possible, Mr. S. had told him, they had been built on land that was cheap, which meant that no one could see much that could be done with it, and for which there was still not much demand. Now that use of the areas would require the demolition — very expensive demo-lition — of thick, steel-reinforced concrete before anything else could be erected on it, the land was even less desirable.

But what he had found really interesting about the NIKE sites, Mr. S. had told him, was that they were federal property, much like Fort Dix over in New Jersey. Local police did not have authority on federal property. Which meant not only that the Philadelphia police would not be patrolling the NIKE sites, but also that the federal authorities, with nothing to protect but empty, and practically indestructible, buildings, would not be giving them very much attention, either.

Mr. Savarese had told Paulo to put an eye on several of the NIKE sites and determine which of them could be put to use while attracting the least attention. And after that, to *keep* an eye on it, in case anything should change.

After making a careful survey of the abandoned

NIKE sites, Cassandro had come up with two that seemed to meet about equally the criteria Mr. Savarese had set up. They were in reasonably remote areas, and not readily visible from the streets and highways. He had gone to Mr. Savarese and suggested that while it would obviously take twice as much manpower to keep an eye on both sites, he recommended this course of action, as it would give them two convenient places. Mr. Savarese had agreed to this, with the caveat that he did not wish to use the sites routinely, but rather as sort of emergency support, and therefore he wished to be consulted before either of the sites was used at all.

Mr. Savarese had given permission to use the sites only twice. The first time was to store a hijacked tractor-trailer load of whiskey for five days until the heat was off. In this case, the driver of the truck had been a fucking fool who had gotten brave, and when struck in the head with a crowbar suffered more severe cranial injuries than was planned, which in turn caused more police attention than was anticipated.

The second site, near Chester, had been used once for a similar purpose, this time a tractor-trailer load of sides of beef. The police seemed to be paying an unusual amount of attention to the cold-storage locker where such a cargo would normally be taken, so Mr. Savarese authorized the use of the NIKE site until distribution of the meat could be arranged. Even the sound of the diesel engine powering the refrigeration system of the insulated trailer attracted no attention in the three days and nights the trailer was at the

NIKE site. But, of course, one had to consider that looking for that tractor trailer was not a high police priority.

Pietro Cassandro drove the Ford pickup to the rear (most distant from the road) gate in the hurricane fence and stopped. Paulo Cassandro got out and swung the creaking gate open and flat against the fence itself, reasoning that it would be better to have the gate open, in case a rapid departure became necessary, even if the open gate — improbably, in the dark — attracted attention.

He then walked to the building, taking from his pocket as he walked a full-face ski mask and pulling it over his head.

Pietro Cassandro drove the Ford pickup to the rear of the building, turned it around so that it was headed toward the open gate, and then got out.

"This won't take long, Mr. S.," he said.

Mr. Savarese nodded, and arranged himself more comfortably on the seat.

Pietro pulled a similar full-face ski mask over his head, then took two battery-powered floodlights from the tool bin in the bed of the truck. Then he joined his brother at the steel door to the building.

They opened the door, stepped inside, closed the door, turned on the floodlights, and walked down the corridor to the room in which, twenty-four hours before, they had left Mr. Ronald R. Ketcham to his thoughts in the dark.

The door was closed with two locking levers much like those used to secure hatches on vessels.

Pietro Cassandro opened both quickly and

pushed the door inward. Paulo Cassandro, his floodlight in his left hand and a crowbar in the other, went quickly into the room.

His floodlight quickly found Ketcham, who was cowering in a far corner of the room, the too-small overcoat not quite concealing his nakedness under it. Ketcham shielded his eyes against the painful glow of light.

"On your feet, cocksucker!" Paulo ordered.

Ketcham pushed himself erect by sliding up the wall behind him.

"Can we talk?" Ketcham asked.

"Oh, we'll talk," Paulo said.

"Jesus Christ," Pietro said in disgust, "it smells like shit in here. We can't bring —"

"Shut your fucking mouth," his brother admonished him, and then addressed Ketcham. "Take the coat off and put it over your head, asshole!"

"I really think there's been some kind of misunderstanding."

"The next time you open your mouth without being told to, you're going to eat the fucking crowbar!"

Ketcham removed the overcoat and placed it over his head as directed.

Paulo indicated the two-inch-wide white surgical — or perhaps "mortician's and embalmer's" — white gauze Ketcham had removed and which was now lying on the concrete floor, and indicated to his brother that it should be reused to make sure the overcoat over Ketcham's head did not become dislodged.

Pietro did as his brother ordered.

"Just stand there, motherfucker," Paulo ordered.

He then left the room, walked down the corridor, and opened the door to another of the NIKE storage rooms. He flashed his floodlight around it, saw nothing that bothered him, and then returned to the room where Ketcham stood naked with an overcoat over his head.

He went to Ketcham, put his hand on his arm, indicated with his finger that his brother take the other arm, then started to lead Ketcham out of the room.

"You said we could talk," Ketcham said plaintively.

"I also told you to shut your fucking mouth," Paulo replied.

They led Ketcham into the center of the other room and turned him around. Ketcham's situation was almost identical to what it had been in the first room, except in this room there was no odor of feces and urine.

Paulo wordlessly indicated to his brother that he was going after Mr. Savarese, handed his crowbar to his brother, and left the room.

He returned in two minutes, politely ushering Mr. Savarese into the room ahead of him. Mr. Savarese stood perhaps six feet from Ketcham, his delicate, fragile-looking hands folded together in front of him. He nodded his permission to Paulo to commence the conversation.

Paulo reclaimed his crowbar from his brother and walked across to Ketcham. He extended the crowbar to Ketcham's groin, gently touching both his penis and his scrotum with it.

"Oh, Jesus Christ!" Ketcham said.

"Okay. Now we'll talk," Paulo said. "Tell me about drugs."

"What drugs?" Ketcham responded, sounding genuinely confused.

Cassandro's crowbar touched Ketcham's scrotum and penis again, somewhat less gently.

"Tell me what you want to know, and I'll tell you," Ketcham said, sounding desperately determined to be agreeable.

"You know fucking well what I want to know," Paulo said. "I want to hear it from you."

There was a long pause.

"I swear to God," Ketcham finally said, "that I had nothing to do with the cops being there."

"Bullshit," Cassandro replied.

"I swear to God," Ketcham repeated. "They must have followed, been following, Williams."

"Bullshit," Paulo repeated.

Mr. Savarese held up his hand to signal the conversation should be interrupted. Paulo went to Mr. Savarese, who, very softly, asked, "Williams?"

"I think a dinge drug dealer. I'll make sure," Paulo whispered in Mr. Savarese's ear.

"I had no reason to go to the cops," Ketcham said.

"But you would turn in a drug dealer like Amos Williams to save your miserable ass, wouldn't you?" Paulo asked reasonably.

"I didn't turn him in. I swear to God, I didn't. We had a long-standing business relationship."

"So you tell me what happened, then."

"I don't know. All of a sudden, there's cops

all over the motel."

"Why do you think that was?"

"I swear to God, I don't know. Except they must have been following Williams."

"What was the name of this motel?"

"You don't know?" Ketcham blurted.

Paulo picked up Ketcham's scrotum with his crowbar.

"I ask, you talk," he said.

"The Howard Johnson on Roosevelt Boulevard," Ketcham said quickly.

"Maybe your girlfriend turned you both in, is that what you're saying?"

"No. Christ no! She didn't even know what was going on."

"She was there with you, wasn't she?"

"She didn't even go in the motel. She waited outside in the car."

"You expect me to believe your lady didn't even know what the fuck you were doing?"

"She didn't," Ketcham said firmly.

"Right. Like she don't use shit herself, right?"

"She doesn't. I mean, every once in a while, a couple of lines, but she's not addicted."

"Bullshit!"

"She doesn't. She's a nice girl, from a good family."

"Who does a couple of lines every once in a while, right, and goes with you to meet with this drug dealer? Bullshit."

"It's the truth, so help me God!"

"Maybe we're talking about two different people," Paulo said. "What's this lady's name?"

"Cynthia Longwood," Ketcham said.

Paulo turned to look at Mr. Savarese, who was sadly shaking his head from side to side.

"If she was waiting outside in the car, and didn't set you and the dealer up with the cops, then what's she so upset about?"

"Why do you think?" Ketcham blurted.

This earned him a short but painful jab in the scrotum, which caused him first to double over in agony, then fall backward into a sitting position on the floor. Paulo then kicked Ketcham in the head.

"Answer the fucking question, motherfucker!"

"What the hell was I supposed to do?" Ketcham said. "The cop had just ripped me off of twenty thousand dollars, and I was handcuffed to the toilet. You think I liked what the cop did to her?"

"What cop? Did he have a name?"

"I don't know what his name is," Ketcham replied. "He was an undercover narc. Probably from that special squad of narcs."

"And what did he do to your lady that made her so upset?"

"He made her blow him," Ketcham said.

Cassandro looked at Mr. Savarese. His face was expressionless, but tears ran down both cheeks. When he saw Paulo looking at him, he gestured with his hand for him to continue.

"He made her what?" Cassandro asked.

"First he made her take off her clothes, and then he made her blow him."

"What did this cop look like?" Paulo asked.

"I don't know," Ketcham began, and then, quickly, to ward off another kick to the head or jab at his scrotum, went on. "White guy. Thirty years old. Average size —"

"What's his name, motherfucker?"

"I told you, I don't know. I never saw him before."

Paulo Cassandro, sensing movement, turned to look at Mr. Savarese. Mr. Savarese was walking out of the room.

Cassandro went after him. Mr. Savarese stopped walking halfway down the corridor, took the white Irish linen handkerchief from the breast pocket of his suit, and dabbed at his eyes and cheeks with it.

"What do you want me to do with this bag of shit, Mr. S.?"

"Nothing," Mr. Savarese replied.

"Nothing?" Cassandro parroted incredulously.

"Get Pietro. Make sure we will leave nothing behind that belongs to us, and then close the door."

"Whatever you say, Mr. S.," Paulo said.

Mr. Savarese nodded, then walked down the corridor toward the door and the Ford flat-tire truck outside.

They were almost back at Classic Livery, Inc., before Paulo finally understood what Mr. S. had in mind for Ketcham.

Nothing didn't mean nothing. Nothing meant that the miserable fucking cocksucker who had dishonored Mr. S.'s granddaughter would have a long fucking time in the fucking dark to think over what he had done before he died. And there wasn't even anything in that fucking room he could use to kill himself, unless maybe he could bang his fucking head against the

407

fucking wall until his brains came out.

That's really better than what I was going to do to the bastard.

Paulo Cassandro had taken the crowbar with him, thinking it would be the thing to use to break Ketcham's fingers and arms and kneecaps and legs before he put an ice pick in his ear.

He considered Mr. Savarese's decision on how to properly deal with Ketcham one more proof of Mr. Savarese's profound wisdom.

Seventeen

After a long time in the bathroom — much of it looking at her reflection in the mirror, as if there was going to be some kind of answer there — Susan finally came out, wrapped in a hotel-furnished terry-cloth robe.

Matt was propped up against the headboard of the bed, naked except for a corner of the sheet over his groin, the telephone to his ear.

Matt said "Thank you" into the telephone and hung it up and looked at her.

"Who were you talking to?" Susan asked.

"Room service. You were in there so long, I got hungry. I told them to send up oysters and a bottle of champagne."

Been watching a lot of Cary Grant movies, have you, Matt? A little elegant counterpoint to hot and heavy sex?

"Oysters and champagne?"

"Yeah. It seemed appropriate under the circumstances."

"I don't like oysters," Susan said.

He reached for the telephone and dialed. The sheet over his groin was dislodged.

He either didn't notice or doesn't care.

"This is Mr. Payne," he said. "If it's not too late, make that one dozen oysters."

He hung up and moved back to his propped-up-against-the-headboard position and looked at

409

her. He did not pull the sheet over his nakedness.

Why does that annoy me so much? What is he doing, exposing himself like that? Saying, "Now that I know what a hot-blooded bitch — what a good fuck — you are, why worry about decency?"

"You apparently have a lot of experience in *circumstances* like this," Susan heard herself say.

"Actually," he said wryly, "I have absolutely no previous experience in a circumstance even remotely like this one."

"Would you mind covering yourself?" she heard herself ask in the voice of a bitch.

"Sorry," he said, and grabbed for the sheet.

"I can't believe I did this," she said.

Matt shrugged. The shrug — his whole attitude — infuriated her.

He made it worse by asking, "You ever hear the expression 'These things happen'? Or, 'Sex is what makes the world go around'?"

"Goddamn you!" Susan said.

He looked at her without expression.

"What if I'm pregnant?" she heard herself blurting.

That surprised him.

"You're not on the pill?"

She felt herself blushing as she shook her head, "no."

"Why not?"

"I don't need it."

"That was an admission, in case you weren't aware of it, that there is no good ol' Whatsisname, the boyfriend your parents can't stand."

"Yes, there is —"

"Stop the bullshit, Susan," he interrupted her

410

rather unpleasantly. "We don't have time for it. It'll only make things worse than they are. If that's possible."

"What's that supposed to mean?" she challenged.

He patted the bed beside him.

He's ordering me to shut up and get back in bed! Goddamn him!

"What makes you think we're going to do that again? Ever?"

"I told you we don't have time for bullshit. Sit down," he said, and then went on, "I said 'sit,' not 'lay.' "

Not knowing why she decided to give in, Susan went to the bed and sat on the edge. Matt took her hand in his.

For a moment, thinking he was going to put her hand on him under the sheet, she debated jerking her hand free. But she sensed, somehow, that having her fondle him was not — at least for the moment — on his mind.

"You were a little surprised about this, right?" Matt asked seriously. "What's happened to us?"

"That's the understatement of the century," she said.

"Well, me, too, fair maiden. This is the last thing I expected to happen, or wanted to happen."

"That's not the impression you gave me."

"The cops are onto you, fair maiden."

"And what the hell is that supposed to mean?"

He shrugged again, and again it infuriated her.

"Truth time," Matt said, "For example, to clear the air: When you were not in your room

411

in the Bellvue with the nonexistent boyfriend, you were off meeting a guy named Bryan Chenowith and/or one or more of his fellow fugitives."

"Oh, my God!"

"Yeah," Matt said. "In other words, the jig is up. You are what is known in the criminal statutes, state and Federal, as an accessory after the fact. And actually, I want to be sure about the after the fact."

"You son of a bitch! You went to my house! You had dinner with my parents. And all the time —"

"You left out 'made love to me.' Guilty on all counts. And I'm going to take great pleasure in seeing your pal and his friends hauled off to the slammer without possibility of parole for the rest of their natural lives. My problem is what to do about you."

She looked at him with horror in her eyes, but didn't speak.

"I don't want you to go to the slam, fair maiden. That would distress me terribly."

"Why should that bother you, Mr. Detective?" Susan flared, and started to get off the bed. She wondered if she was going to throw up.

He held her wrist, and he was too strong for her.

"I'm not through," he said, not very pleasantly.

"What are you going to do now? Rape me before you arrest me?"

"Come on, Susan, you know better than that. Get it through your head that right now I'm the best friend you've got."

"How often have you used that line? What do

they call that, putting the suspect at ease?"

"That's what they call it," Matt agreed. "The difference is, this is the first time I've used the technique on an interviewee I think I'm in love with."

Her heart jumped when he said that.

"In love?" she asked, witheringly sarcastic. "You don't expect me to believe that, do you?"

"Well, maybe what happened affected me more than it affected you, but that's how I'm forced to look at it."

"Oh, come on, Matt!"

"If I didn't come to realize, when you were in the bathroom all that time, that what's wrong with me is that I'm in love with you, then what would have happened was that we would have torn off another couple of pieces, had our dinner, and I would have taken you home and been not at all upset about the inevitability of you going off to the slam."

"My God, you're serious!"

"Were you listening when I said we don't have time for bullshit?"

There was a knock at the door.

"Who's that?" Susan asked, as if frightened.

"Probably the waiter. When I checked in, I told them to cool a couple of bottles." He raised his voice. "Just a moment, please, I'm in the shower."

He let go of her wrist and got out of bed.

"Is there another one of those in there?" he asked, making reference to the hotel's terry-cloth robe and gesturing toward the bathroom.

"I only saw this one," Susan said.

"Then you better give me that one," Matt said. "And wait in the bathroom. Or get under the blankets."

She looked at him doubtfully, then looked around for her discarded clothing.

"Where's my clothes?"

"I kicked them under the bed," he said matter-of-factly, then smiled and went on. "Come on, give me the robe. The cow already got out of the barn. I know what you've got hidden under there."

She turned her back on him, unfastened the robe, and, aware that she was blushing again, shrugged out of it and ran to the bathroom.

"What do you want to eat?"

"What do I want to *eat?*" she parroted incredulously. "Eat?"

"They do a nice standing rib," he said. "Okay?"

"I just don't give a damn," she confessed, and closed the bathroom door.

Feeling dizzy and a little faint, but no longer nauseous, Susan leaned against the closed bathroom door. This gave her a view of herself in the mirrors over the sink.

For a moment, she seriously considered that she might be having a bad dream. That was obviously not the case.

But I can't believe any of this is happening! Either what happened in the car, or that I came to the room, or what happened here. Anything that happened here, from letting him undress me through what happened after he did, to that clever little unbelievable line, "The cops are onto you, fair maiden."

She was vaguely conscious of hearing him order

dinner — New England–style clam chowder, not the kind with tomatoes, medium-rare beef, baked potatoes, asparagus, and a large pot of coffee — and couldn't believe that, either.

How the hell can he even think of food at a time like this?

And then he was trying to push the bathroom door open against the weight of her body.

"Hey, you all right, Susan?" he asked, and there was concern in his voice.

"What do you want?"

"I thought you might want the robe back."

"Just a minute," she said, and pushed herself off the door and went after a towel.

Before she reached it, he had pushed the door open. Susan tried to cover herself modestly with her hands.

"Ta-ta!" Matt cried. "The Mad Flasher strikes again!"

Using both hands, he pulled the bathrobe open wide.

Under it, his private parts were now concealed by his shorts.

"You're insane," she said, but she smiled and reached for the robe as he shrugged out of it.

"Your maidenly modesty is really a waste of effort, you know. I have seen what I have seen, and it is burned indelibly for all eternity on my brain."

"You really are insane, aren't you?" Susan said.

Why am I pleased that he liked what he saw? And for that matter, why am I not really all that embarrassed about him seeing me naked?

Matt went back into the bedroom, and as she

415

fastened the robe around her, she saw him going into the sitting room. She combed her hair as best she could, then went into the bedroom.

Where she found that he had indeed kicked her clothing under the bed. The first thing she retrieved was her brassiere.

And saw he had torn it off: the buttonhole on the strap between the cups was ripped open.

She found her underpants and pulled them on under the terry-cloth robe and went into the sitting room.

He was pouring champagne. He picked up both glasses and held one out to her.

"I'm not sure I want this," she said.

"What shall we drink to?" he asked, ignoring her.

"What is there to celebrate?"

"Us, maybe? Or am I really alone in thinking that something really special happened to both of us in the last twenty-four hours?"

"Matt, I'm afraid to believe you about . . . what you said," she said.

"I told you I think I love you after I told you that bullshit time is over," he said. "You can believe that."

"I don't know what happened to me," Susan said.

"The question is was it special for you? Half as special, maybe, as it was for me?"

"What do you think?" she asked softly.

"I don't know what to think. That's why I asked."

"The last time somebody put his hands in my pants in a car was when I was in high school. I hit him with a flashlight and knocked out two of his teeth."

"Is that a yes?"

"I came up here with you, didn't I? And you know what happened."

"In that case, we have just taken step one," Matt said. "Which I think we should commemorate with a swallow of the bubbly, and, if you're so inclined, with a friendly kiss."

"A *friendly* kiss?"

"Boy Scout's honor," he said, and stepped close to her.

She looked into his eyes for a long moment, then kissed him, very chastely, on the lips.

That was and that wasn't. It was closed-mouthed and gentle, but I felt it all the way down to my crotch.

If he kisses me again, or puts his hand inside the bathrobe, we'll be back in the sack again.

Matt touched his glass to hers.

"Well, at least we have our priorities right. First the kiss, and then the champagne."

"And now what?" Susan asked.

"We wait for dinner to be delivered," he said. "And meanwhile, we try to start to find some kind of a solution to our dilemma."

"And how do we do that?"

"You start by trusting me," he said, looking into her eyes. "You really don't have any choice, but I want you to really understand that."

She averted her eyes by lowering them.

"Are you constantly in that state?" she blurted.

"I just kissed you," he said. "And it happened." He snapped his fingers. "Just like that. *Ah-ten-*

hut! And then, feeling noble as hell, I resisted the enormous urge to pick you up and carry you back to bed."

"That wouldn't be smart, would it?" Susan asked, raising her eyes from his erection to his eyes.

"Not right now, but you could easily talk me out of that position."

"Maybe that's all it is," she said. "Unbridled lust. On both sides."

"Maybe," he said very seriously. "I think there's more, but if that's all there is, that's enough."

"I don't really know what you mean by trust you," she said.

"Well, that means I'm going to ask you questions, and you're going to answer them. The truth, the whole truth, and nothing but the truth. You're not going to hold anything back. You've just changed sides, Susan. Chenowith and his friends are now the bad guys."

"I'm not sure I can do that," she said very softly.

"You don't have any choice, honey. What I'm trying to do is find some way to keep you from going down the toilet with them."

"What did you call me?"

"What?"

"You called me 'honey.' "

"I guess I did," Matt said. "Does that bother you?"

"No," she said after a just-perceptible hesitation. "No, Matt, it doesn't."

"I would be amenable to reciprocation," he

said. "Does 'precious beloved' come easily to your lips?"

"No," she said, smiling. " 'Precious beloved'? My God!"

"There are many other possibilities," he said. "Think it over. Whatever makes you happy."

"All I can think of is 'honey,' " she said. "And that's awkward."

"Give it a shot."

"Honey," she said.

"Sounds great to me," he said. "Let's go with that for a while, until you think of something better."

She sensed that he was about to kiss her again, and turned her back to him.

"Matt, I can't betray them," she said.

"What happened to 'honey'?" he asked lightly, and then, his voice changing, added: "Get it through your head, honey, that they're going to jail. If they're lucky, the feds will let Pennsylvania try them. We don't often send people to the chair."

" 'We' don't?"

"We, the citizens of the Commonwealth of Pennsylvania," he said, rather unpleasantly. "Okay, first question. Did you have any prior knowledge that Chenowith was going to blow up the Biological Sciences building at the University of Pennsylvania?"

Susan shook her head and said, softly, "No."

"No knowledge of any kind? He — and when I say 'he,' read Chenowith, the scumbag with the acne, and either of the women. Or any friends we don't know about — never discussed this with you, even in idle conversation, with a couple of drinks in him? 'What we should do is blow up the building'?"

"I told you no, Matt," she said, then added, "God, you sound like a policeman."

"I am a policeman," he said. "I have to be absolutely sure of this, honey. Let me ask it in another way. When they blew up the Biological Sciences building, were you surprised, or did you sort of expect something like that to happen?"

"Matt, would you believe me if I said I'm sick about the Biological Sciences building? I was sick then, and I'm sick now."

He looked at her carefully, and she realized he was making up his mind whether or not to believe her. And then she saw in his eyes that he did.

"That wasn't the question, honey. The question was, did the bombing of the Biological Sciences building come to you as a surprise, or not?"

"I really didn't even know Bryan Chenowith when that happened," she said.

"Then how the hell did you get involved with these people? Has he got something on you?"

"Now he does," she said.

"What?"

"I know what he did, and that the police are looking for him. Isn't that what you said — I'm an accessory after the fact, for helping him?"

"What's he got on you?"

"That I've been helping him."

"*Why* have you been helping him?" Matt asked impatiently.

"Room service!" a cheery voice announced, and there was a knock on the door.

"Just a minute," Matt called.

He gestured for her to give him the robe again. When she did, he saw that she was wearing underpants.

"What did I do? Shame you back into maidenly modesty?" he asked.

"Don't you ever shut your mouth?" she snapped.

"Go hide in the bathroom like a good girl," he said, stuffing his arms into the sleeves of the robe.

She went into the bathroom and closed the door, and listened while he dealt with the waiter, and to the sound of furniture moving, and metallic clanks she presumed were the plate and dish covers that come with room-service meals. But when the noise died down, he didn't come to the bathroom door. She wondered if the waiter was still there, or if there was some other reason.

Curiosity finally got the best of her. She opened the bathroom door carefully and walked quickly to the door to the sitting room.

Matt was sitting at the table, wearing the terry-cloth robe, putting an oyster on a cracker.

"Pity you don't like oysters. These are first-rate," he said.

"I've been waiting for my robe," she said indignantly, walking across the room to him, concealing as much of her breasts as she could with her arms.

"*Our* robe," Matt corrected her. "And you were standing behind the door, right, so that you could put your hand — only — through the door and snatch it from my hand so that I wouldn't get to see anything?"

"Give me the damned robe," she said, tugging at the neck of it.

He got out of the chair, shrugged out of the robe, and held it out so that she could put her arms in the sleeves.

"I cannot tell a lie," he said. "I'm glad I did that. You wearing nothing but your underpants and a look of high indignation is truly a sight to see."

"What are you?" she said, furious with herself for blushing. "Some kind of a pervert?"

"No. I don't think so. I'm in love. Or maybe lust. Or both. I think 'all's fair in lust and war' is also true."

She shook her head and then, robe modestly belted, looked at him.

"That can't possibly be true," she said.

"What can't?"

"Love."

"Why not? You hear about it all the time. Love at first sight, and they lived happily thereafter."

"That's the . . . bullshit . . . you keep talking about. Things like that just don't happen."

"Well, I think it happened to me. With my luck, it probably won't be reciprocal, but I'm willing to settle for half a loaf."

She looked at him with a strange look on her face.

"I'll be damned if I don't think you're serious."

"I have never been more serious in my life," Matt said.

Susan suddenly had a very strong urge to cry.

"Can I have one of your oysters?" she asked, her voice sounding strange.

"I thought you didn't like oysters?"

"I was being a bitch. You bring that out in me."

He turned to the table and picked up an oyster in its shell and handed it to her.

She ate it from the shell.

"Very good," she said.

"I told you. Shall I get you a dozen? I ate most of —"

"There won't be time," she said.

"Why not?"

"This one's already working," she said.

"Meaning what?" he said, and then took her meaning. "Oh, really?"

She raised her eyes to his and nodded solemnly. He unfastened the belt on the robe and she shrugged out of it.

"You want to go out there?" Matt asked. "Or should I try to roll that cart in here?"

"You weren't thinking of food two minutes ago."

"That was two minutes ago."

"Since we have only one bathrobe between us, I don't think I want to go out there. I've had enough new experiences for one night. Eating dinner in the nude will have to wait for another time."

"In other words, roll in the tray?"

"*I'm* not all that hungry. Why don't you just bring in one plate, and we'll share it?"

"Okay. I'll get a plate. I'm delighted you didn't think of the other option: Getting out of bed and getting dressed."

"I wish that I could spend the rest of my life

in this bed," she said.

"Oh, really?"

"Yes, really."

He got out of bed and went into the sitting room. And returned pushing the cart. Susan raised her eyebrows questioningly.

"I wanted to bring the champagne, too," he said. "And there's two oysters left. I didn't want them to be wasted."

She felt herself blush again.

"We can't spend the rest of our life in this bed," she said.

"Not this one. Maybe in another one," he said.

He handed her a napkin, silverware, and a plate of roast beef. Then he poured champagne in a glass and got in bed with her, sitting cross-legged across from her.

"While you're cutting me a piece of that," he said, "and while I'm chewing it, tell me how in the hell you got involved with these people."

Susan exhaled audibly, looked at Matt, then dropped her eyes to the slab of pink roast beef on the plate between her legs and started cutting it.

"Jennie —" she began.

"Jennifer Downs Ollwood," Matt interrupted. "Five feet four inches, 130 pounds, brown eyes, black hair worn in bangs, got herself kicked out of Bennington for taking free speech a step too far by assaulting a campus police officer, then transferred to the University of Pittsburgh. What about her?"

"You seem to know everything about her."

"Come on, honey. I'm just trying to save time.

We still have to take you home to Mommy and Daddy sometime tonight."

"Until you said that," Susan said, "I completely forgot about having to go home. What time is it?"

He looked at his watch.

"Half past ten."

"It seems like much later," she said.

"Well, didn't you notice? A lot's happened tonight."

"We're going to have to go soon."

"Not until we're finished," he said, and then smiled. "I already have a reputation for keeping the Reynolds family virgin out all night. Mommy would probably be surprised, even disappointed, if I brought you home early."

"I guess that means I don't get arrested tonight, if you're going to take me home," Susan said, making what she instantly realized was a bad little joke.

"Not by me. Not ever by me," Matt said seriously. "But I can't speak for the rest of the law-enforcement community."

"Matt, I'm scared."

"Well, you should be. What about the Ollwood woman? Did she meet Chenowith at the University of Pittsburgh? Or were they already planning armed revolution and rebellion at Bennington?"

"I don't know where she met him," Susan said. "But you have to understand about Jennie, Matt."

"What do I have to understand?"

"She is no more capable of blowing up a building than I am."

"The fact is that she did. There's no question

425

about that, honey."

"You have to understand her."

"Understand what, Susan?"

"Her family is a disaster," Susan said. "Her mother's a drunk, on her fourth husband. Her father doesn't give a damn about her. She's all alone, Matt, and always has been. Until, of course, Bryan came along. Whatever she did was because of Bryan."

"That's bullshit, honey," Matt said gently. "She might have been strongly attracted to this character, that's understandable. But once she found out that he was seriously considering doing something like blowing up a building — there's a hell of a difference between hitting a campus cop with your 'Fair Play For Animals!' sign and robbing a National Guard armory to get explosives and weapons —"

"You know about that?" Susan interrupted.

"We even know the serial numbers of the carbines they stole. And that your friend Chenowith —"

"He's not my friend, Matt!"

"— has chopped down one of them into a movie-style terrorist's machine pistol to use when he robs banks."

"Well, that answered another question I had. You know about the banks."

"Yeah, we know about the banks. And it's only a question of time before Robin Hood decides he has to use that machine pistol, and other innocent people get killed."

She met his eyes and then looked away.

"You want to hear about Jennie?" she asked softly.

"Yeah," Matt said. "I do. I left off saying that she had a choice to make when she understood that he was about to do some very terrible things, and she made the wrong one. I can't work up much sympathy for your friend, honey, drunken mother on her fourth husband or not."

"You said, in the car, that you were . . . 'sucked into' your relationship with Penny Detweiler. That she was really fucked up, and really needed you."

"I wondered why you picked up on that," Matt said. "That's how it is with you and the Ollwood woman?"

Susan nodded.

"After — what happened at the Univer—"

"Let's knock off the euphemisms," Matt said. "What happened was that your friend actively assisted Chenowith in the placement and detonation of an explosive device in a building on a college campus, and caused the deaths of eleven innocent people."

"All right," Susan said, her voice choked. Tears formed in her eyes and ran down her cheeks.

"Say it, honey," Matt said gently but insistently.

She sighed.

"After Bryan . . . blew up the building, and the police started looking for him, Jennie called me. She was hysterical. Desperate. I felt so sorry for her. And she said she absolutely had to have some money . . ."

"And you gave it to her," Matt finished. "And as you were aware she was involved in blowing up the science building, that made you an accessory after the fact."

"I didn't think about that," Susan said, and looked at him through tear-filled eyes. "My friend was all fucked up, Matt. She had nobody else to turn to. I had to help."

"Where did you get the money?" he asked, ignoring her.

"It was mine," she said.

"Where did you get it? Specifically, did you take it out of the bank? Is there a record of you making a substantial" — *Of course there isn't. If there was, the FBI would have known about it, and told me* — "withdrawal —"

"No," Susan said. "I had it. I had a quarterly dividend check from Chrysler that day, and I had just cashed it — I was going shopping — and I gave her the money."

"No, you didn't," Matt said.

"What?"

"You will swear on a stack of Bibles that you didn't give her any money. I don't think the FBI knows about that, and we don't want them to know. You cashed the check to go shopping, didn't buy anything, and just kept the money around and pissed it away on routine expenses. How much was it?"

"Three thousand and change," Susan said, very softly. "Matt, I'm not a very good liar."

"Well, you fooled me, honey. You told me you were just not interested, and I believed you."

"Oh, Matt!"

"I'm serious. You're a good liar, which is a good thing."

"Matt, there is something about money. . . ."

"What?"

"I'm holding some money for Bryan."

"From the bank jobs?"

She nodded.

"Jesus Christ, why?"

"Because he asked me to. Or he got Jennie to ask me to. Same thing."

"Did he tell you why?"

"Against the possibility of his being arrested —"

"The inevitability," Matt interrupted.

"— to hire a good lawyer."

"Shit," Matt said. "He's stupid. For one thing — let me explain how this will work — for one thing, the FBI knows all about the bank robberies. He did another one a couple of days ago, in Clinton, New Jersey. Dressed up like a woman, by the way."

"Jennie called me — my God, that's only this morning — and asked me to come visit her and the baby."

"What baby?"

The FBI doesn't know anything about a baby. An infant in arms considerably cuts into the number of wanted females meeting a physical description. I would have been told. It would even have been in their movie.

"They have a baby boy."

"Jesus H. Christ! Wouldn't you consider that a little irresponsible, considering their circumstances?"

"Maybe it happened to them the way it could have happened to us just now," Susan said.

"Stop finding excuses for her, Susan," Matt said. "If you're facing life in prison, you don't get pregnant."

"Okay," she said. "I told you, she's all fucked up."

"Okay. Where were we? I was telling how this will go down. You're on the FBI's list. The moment they arrest Chenowith, they'll have you picked up as an accessory after the fact. The same day, probably, if they don't have one already, they'll get a search warrant for your house, your office, the place in the Poconos. . . . Where is the money?"

"In my safe-deposit box," she said. "In the Harrisburg Bank and Trust Company."

"And for that," Matt said. "They will find the money, and since you have no other explanation for it, and there is evidence that you have been meeting with Chenowith, it will (a) be seized as recovered loot from bank robberies, and (b) used as evidence that you are an active accessory after the fact."

"Oh, God!"

"For both, probably," he went on as he thought about it. "I think they'll probably try to make you an accessory to the bank robberies, too."

"Why bother, if they are going to send me to prison for life for helping Jennie?"

"You, and Poor Little Jennie, and Bryan Chenowith, and the guy with the acne — Edgar Leonard Cole — and the other female. What's her name? Eloise Anne Fitzgerald," he said.

"Where are they, by the way?"

"I don't know, Matt."

"You don't know, or you're overwhelmed with compassion because they had unpleasant childhoods?"

"I don't know, Matt," she said, half crying, looking at him. "I don't know if I'd tell you if I did, but I don't know."

Then she started to cry.

"Jesus, please don't do that," Matt said.

Once she started, she couldn't stop. It was soft, almost a moan, as she hugged her breasts and her chest heaved with sobs.

Matt moved to her, spilling the plate of roast beef, and put his arms around her.

"Come on, honey," he said. "That's not going to do any good."

"I wish I was dead," she spluttered.

"What is that, a commentary on our lovemaking?"

"You bastard!"

"Two things have happened," he said.

"What two things?" she said, sobbing.

"I have asparagus in my pubic hair, au jus on my balls, and holding you like this is making me horny."

She pushed herself away from him and looked. It was all true.

Half crying, half giggling, she shook her head.

"Go take a bath," she said.

"You got some of it, too," he said, pointing. "Come with me."

"Take a shower with you?"

"Why not? Or would you rather sit here in the

roast beef and blubber?"

She put her hand out and touched his cheek.

"My God, I think I do love you," she said.

"You wash my back, and I'll let you have the asparagus," Matt said, and took her hand and pulled her out of the bed.

"We have to get that money out of your safe-deposit box," Matt said as he was toweling himself in the bathroom and shamelessly watching Susan do the same.

"What did you say?" Susan asked, her voice muffled by the towel she had over her head.

He didn't repeat the statement; he had thought of something else.

"Just before we came in here, you said Poor Pathetic Jennie called you. What did she want?"

She took the towel off her head and looked at him.

"Do you have to call her that?"

He shrugged but didn't reply directly.

"What did she want?"

"She said she had another package she wanted me to keep for her —"

"From the Farmers and Merchants Bank of Clinton, New Jersey, no doubt," Matt interrupted. "And when did you tell her you were going to meet her?"

"I told her I wouldn't," Susan said. "I told the both of them that. She put him on the phone."

"Why not?"

"I thought, so soon after I was in Philadelphia, that it would be suspicious. And I told them I had a cop on my back."

"Jesus! But you said you didn't —"

"At the time, I believed you," Susan said. "At the time, I thought you were what your friends told me you were."

"Which friends? What did they tell you I was?"

"Your two old school pals at Daffy's party. They told me you were a mixed-up screwball playing at being a cop. To prove your manhood. You're not, are you? You're really a cop, and what you're playing at is being a screwball. It's a good act. It had me fooled."

"And now that my facade has been torn away, what do you think?"

"I'm afraid about how much I like what I see," she said. "I'm afraid that it's going to be taken away from me."

"You want to go back in the shower?" Matt asked.

"No. God, I can't believe we did that. I didn't think it was possible."

"Well, I wouldn't want you to spread this around, but that was a first for me, too."

"Really?"

"Of course, I never had a woman look for asparagus bits in my —"

"Stop!"

"Yeah. We have to stop," he said seriously. "But let's finish Poor . . . What happened when you were on the phone with Jennifer and Chenowith?"

"That's it. He asked about you. He said you might really be an FBI agent, and I assured him you were just a cop."

"When are you going to meet with them?"

"I'm not," she said. "I told him I wasn't going to do it, and when he started to argue, I hung up on him."

"But you told him about me?"

"I just told you I did," she said. "That was before you pointed out to me the many benefits of changing sides."

"Don't start playing the bitch again. We don't have time for that."

"I'm sorry," she said, sounding genuinely contrite. "Forgive me. Matt, so much has happened —"

"Whatever happened to 'honey'?"

"I'm sorry, honey."

"You think he took 'no' for an answer? Or will he call again?"

"He'll probably call again."

"If he does, stall him again. I don't know how yet, I'll have to think about it, but maybe we can put his wanting to hide the bank money to our advantage."

"Matt, I don't want to betray them!"

"For the last fucking time, Susan, get it through your head that you don't have any options. They're going down, and all we can hope for is that I can figure out some way to keep you from going down with them!"

She met his eyes but didn't reply.

He angrily tossed his towel on the floor and walked out of the bathroom.

After a moment, she went after him.

He was on his hands and knees, reaching under the bed, and he pulled his and her clothing out from where he had kicked it. And something else.

434

A snub-nosed revolver in a holster.

"Did you really think you would have to use that on me?" Susan asked.

"I'm a cop. Cops carry guns," he said somewhat abruptly. He tossed the clothing and then the pistol onto the bed, and reached for his shorts.

"Honey, I'm sorry," Susan said. "I really don't want you to be angry with me."

"I'm not angry."

"Yes, you are."

He looked at her.

"You're too goddamned smart to be stupid," he said. "And we can't afford it."

"I like the way you said 'we,' " she said softly.

That made him smile.

He made the sign of the cross. "I grant you absolution. Go, and be stupid no more."

"I'll try," she said.

She started to dress.

"Did you see what you did to my bra?" she asked a moment later, and showed it to him.

"I did that?"

"Yes, you did that."

"What's Mommy going to think when you come in the house flopping all over?"

"I'll keep my coat on."

"What are you going to do with it?"

"The bra? Throw it away. It's beyond repair."

"Can I have it?"

"What are you going to do with it?"

"Make a trophy out of it. A little foam rubber, so it looks lifelike, and a brass plate reading, 'Susan, 34B, Hotel Hershey,' and the date. Then I'll mount it on the wall, with all the others."

"Damn it, I'm serious."

He met her eyes.

"I don't know why I want it," he said. "I just do."

She held it out to him. When he put his hand out, she caught it and kissed it.

"For the record, it's a 34C," she said.

She let go of his hand, and he took the brassiere and stuffed it in his trousers pocket.

"Thank you, honey, for wanting it," Susan said.

When Phil Chason came home from Captain Karl Beidermann's retirement party, it was half past two in the morning and he was half in the bag, and he almost didn't go into his basement office to see if there were any messages for him on the answering machine.

Phil and Karl Beidermann had gone through the Academy together, had had their first assignment — to the Central District — together, and had done a hell of a lot of things together on the job, although Karl had liked working in uniform (he retired as commanding officer of the 16th District) and Phil had decided he'd rather be — and stay — a detective, who with overtime took home as much money as a captain anyhow.

And it was good to see a lot of the people at the party. Once you went off the job, you didn't see people very much, and that was sort of sad. On the way home, Phil had thought that if he had to do it all over again, he still would have become a cop. He had had a good twenty-six years on the job, and no real complaints.

As he started up the stairs to his bedroom, he

remembered about the answering machine downstairs in the office, and decided, fuck it, even if there was something on it, it would most likely be somebody trying to sell him a house in Levittown or just begging for money, and not somebody who needed the professional services of Philip Chason, retired Philadelphia Police Department detective.

But halfway up the stairs, he decided that he might as well check the son of a bitch, or otherwise he would stay awake all goddamn night wondering what might be on it.

He stopped, turned around on the stairs, and went back down them and then into the basement.

When he opened the door, the little red light indicating that somebody had called was flashing, so he flipped on the light switch, waited for the fluorescent light fixtures to take their own goddamned sweet time to come on, then sat down at the desk and pushed the Play switch.

"Phil, this is Joe Fiorello."

Fuck you, Joey Fiorello. Now I'm sorry I came down here.

"I'm really sorry to call this late, but at least, since I got your answering machine, I didn't wake you up, right?"

Get to the fucking point, Fiorello!

"Well, I guess you can guess why I'm calling, right, Phil? I got another job for you."

I figured you called me because you love me, asshole.

"So as soon as you get this message, you want to give me a call, Phil?"

It's half past two in the morning, Joey. You mean you want me to call you at half past two?

"This is important, Phil. And I would consider it a favor if you would get back to me just as soon as you can."

If it's important to you, then whatever it is, it's going to cost you through the nose, you sleazeball.

"I guess you've got the numbers, but just to be sure, I'll give you my private line at the lot and my number here at the house."

Fiorello recited the numbers slowly, then repeated them.

What I really should do is call you at your house and wake your greasy ass up!

Fuck it! I never should have come down here in the first place!

Phil stood up and walked to the door, turned off the flickering lights, and closed the door.

When he got to his bedroom, Mrs. Irene Chason greeted him by saying she knew he must have had a good time, because his breath smelled like a spittoon.

Eighteen

"Seven-C," Mrs. Loretta Dubinsky, RN, answered the telephone on her desk. Ward 7C was the private-patient section of the Psychiatric Division of University Hospital. Mrs. Dubinsky, a slight, very pale-skinned redhead who looked considerably younger than her thirty years, was the supervisory psychiatric nurse on duty.

"Dr. Amelia Payne, please," the caller said.

"Dr. Payne's not on the ward."

"I got to talk to her. Do you know where I can find her?"

"I suggest you try her office. In the morning."

"I got to talk to her tonight."

"I can give you the number of Dr. Payne's answering service."

"I got that. They don't know where she is."

Mrs. Dubinsky knew better than that. The way the answering service worked, they never said they didn't know where someone was, they asked the caller for their number, and said they would try to have Dr. Whoever try to call the caller back. Then — unless the caller said it was an emergency, and especially at this time of night; it was half past two — they would make a note on a card and keep it until Dr. Whoever called in for his messages.

If the caller said it was an emergency, same procedure, except that they would call the numbers Dr. Whoever had given them, where he could be reached in an emergency.

"Then I'm afraid I can't help you, sir," Mrs. Loretta Dubinsky, RN, said.

"Look, I got an important message for her."

"Then I suggest you call her in the morning."

"This won't wait until morning."

"I'm afraid it's going to have to, sir. There's nothing I can do to help you."

"Who are you?"

Mrs. Dubinsky replaced the telephone in its cradle.

Two minutes later — Paulo Cassandro having worked his way through the hospital switchboard again — the telephone rang again, and Nurse Dubinsky picked it up.

"Seven-C."

"Look, lady, you don't seem to understand. This is important."

"Sir, I told you before," Mrs. Dubinsky said, her pale skin coloring, "that Dr. Payne is not on the ward, and that I have no idea where she is."

"I got to get a message to her."

"What is it?"

"Who are you? This is private, personal."

"My name is Dubinsky. I'm the nurse-in-charge."

"There's no doctor around there?"

"You want to give me the message or not?"

"Let me talk to a doctor," Cassandro said.

"I'm afraid that's not possible," Mrs. Dubinsky said.

"Let me talk to a goddamn doctor!"

Mrs. Dubinsky again replaced the handset in its cradle.

And two minutes later, the telephone ran again.

"Seven-C."

"Look, lady, I'm sorry I lost my temper. But this is really important."

"I will try to get a message to Dr. Payne. What is it?"

"I need to talk to a doctor. Could you please get one on the line?"

"I told you, sir, that's just not possible."

"Jesus Christ, will you get a goddamn doctor on the phone?"

Mrs. Dubinsky again replaced the handset in its cradle.

And two minutes later, the telephone rang again.

"Seven-C."

"You might as well get it through your goddamn head that I'm gonna speak to a goddamn doctor if I have to call every two minutes until the goddamn sun comes up!"

Mrs. Dubinsky, her facial skin now blotched with red spots, started to replace the handset in its cradle again, but at the last moment instead laid it on the plate glass on her desk.

Shaking her head, she got out of her chair, left the nurses' station, and walked down the corridor to her left, where she entered a room about halfway down. She walked to the bed, where a very small, thin, brown-skinned man in a medical smock was sleeping under a sheet.

She gently pushed his arm, and when he showed no sign of waking, pushed harder.

"Doctor?" she said.

Juan Osvaldo Martinez, M.D., opened his eyes and sat up abruptly.

"Sorry," Nurse Dubinsky said.

"There is a problem?"

"There's a nut on the phone who insists on speaking to a doctor."

Dr. Martinez's eyebrows rose in question.

"He won't give up, Doctor. He calls every two minutes."

He nodded his understanding, swung his feet off the bed, and sort of hopped to the floor.

He retraced his steps to the nurses' station and picked up the telephone.

"Dr. Martinez," he said.

There was no reply. He looked at Nurse Dubinsky and shrugged helplessly.

"No one on the line."

"Hang up. He'll call back," Nurse Dubinsky said with certainty.

Dr. Martinez hung up the phone. The two of them stared at it for two long minutes. It did not ring.

"Well," Dr. Martinez said, and shrugged again.

That figures, Nurse Dubinsky thought, after *I wake this poor young man up,* then *this bastard decides to hell with it, he'll wait 'til morning.*

"I'm sorry, Doctor."

"It is not a problem," Dr. Martinez said, and started back down the corridor.

He had taken a half-dozen steps when the telephone rang.

He picked it up.

"Seven-C, Dr. Martinez."

"You're a hard man to get on the goddamn phone, Doctor."

"How may I help you?"

"I have a message for Dr. Amelia A. Payne."

"She's not here," Dr. Martinez said.

"The nurse told me that. That's why I wanted to talk to you."

"What is the message?"

"You got a pencil and paper?"

"Yes," Dr. Martinez said, although in fact he did not.

"Okay. Now, get this right. You ready?"

"Ready."

"To Dr. Amelia A. Payne. Your patient, Miss Cynthia Longwood . . . Am I going too fast for you?"

"No. Go ahead," Dr. Martinez said.

He had looked in on 723 just before going to an empty room to try to catch a little sleep. She had been awake. Privately, Dr. Martinez disagreed with her attending physician, Dr. Payne. If the Longwood girl had been his patient, he would have prescribed at least a mild sedative to help her through the night. She had recurring, and very disturbing, dreams, the consequence of which was that she slept very badly, did not get enough sleep, and thus dozed through the day.

If she had been his patient, he believed it would be best to have her rested when he spoke with her, trying to get to the root of her problem. But she was Dr. A. A. Payne's patient, not his. And he was a resident, and Dr. Payne was not only an adjunct professor of psychiatry, but held in the highest possible regard by the chief of Psychiatric

Services, Aaron Stein, M.D., former president of the American Psychiatric Association.

Despite that, and his own genuine respect for her, Dr. Martinez felt that Dr. Payne was wrong when she told him that in cases like this the best sedation was the least sedation, and it was her call.

"Okay," the caller said. "She was stripped naked and orally raped by a policeman under circumstances that were themselves traumatic. You got that?"

"No. You were going too fast for me," Dr. Martinez said as he gestured to Nurse Dubinsky that he wanted to write something.

She pushed an aluminum clipboard to him, and when she saw that he was having trouble finding his own pen or pencil, handed him her own ballpoint.

"Miss Cynthia Longwood was stripped naked and orally raped," the caller began, very slowly, making it clear to Dr. Martinez that he was reciting — probably reading — what he was saying, "by a policeman under circumstances that were themselves traumatic. You got it all now, Doc?"

And what he had recited — probably read — didn't sound as if it had been written by the man on the telephone.

"I've got it now, thank you," Dr. Martinez said.

"Read it back to me."

"Miss Cynthia Longwood was stripped naked and orally raped by a policeman under circumstances that were themselves traumatic," Dr. Martinez recited.

Nurse Dubinsky's eyebrows rose, and she shook her head.

"That's it. You make sure Dr. Payne gets that."

"Of course. Just as soon as she comes in. And who should I say called?"

The caller laughed. "Nice try! Fuck you, Doc."

There was a click and the line went dead.

Dr. Martinez and Nurse Dubinsky looked at each other.

"Interesting," Dr. Martinez thought aloud.

"You believe that?"

"I don't believe the man who called wrote the message," Dr. Martinez said. "I think he was reading it."

"Yeah," Nurse Dubinsky agreed. "He didn't sound as if he would say things like 'orally raped' or 'traumatic circumstances.' "

Dr. Martinez looked at his watch and wrote down the time.

"If I happen to be asleep —"

"You mean, 'are not at the moment available,' " Nurse Dubinsky interrupted him.

"Thank you, but no thank you," Dr. Martinez said. "What is it you say up here about 'calling a shovel'?"

"A spade a spade," she corrected him. "It's from playing cards."

"If Dr. Payne should come here in the morning, and I am sleeping, please wake me. I want to talk to her about this. I think we both should be available to her."

"Of course," Nurse Dubinsky said.

"This is very interesting," Dr. Martinez said.

"I wonder who that man was? Not the policeman, certainly."

"That poor girl," Nurse Dubinsky said.

When Matt woke up, the first thing he saw was Susan's brassiere, which he had placed with the other contents of his trousers and jacket pockets on the bedside table.

He sat up in bed and reached for it, feeling more than a little chagrined. Taking it did not seem nearly so much a fine idea in the light of day as it had the night before.

"Jesus," he said aloud.

He examined the torn buttonhole on the strap.

Was I "mad with passion"? Or did that just happen, because we were like two squirming snakes on the seat of the Porsche?

He raised it to his nose and sniffed it. There was a very faint odor of Susan — or her perfume? Same thing? — on it.

Do I really love her? Or do I have a fatal case of penis erectus?

How could I possibly love her? Christ, I hardly know her. And what we've done most of the time is either fight or lie to each other.

But if I don't love her, where did this Susie-and-me-against-the-whole-goddamned-world feeling come from?

And does she love me? Or is this because she knows I'm onto her and fucking the cop, under the circumstances, seems a more logical thing to do than docilely putting out your wrists to have them cuffed?

And where is Susie now? Waking up and getting ready to go to work, to wait for my call, or already

446

on an airplane headed for San José, Costa Rica, having stopped only long enough to call Chenowith from a pay phone in the airport to tell him the cops are onto him for his bank jobs?

Could she have been faking what happened to us in the car? Or in bed?

Why not? I got my sex education from two sources. Dad telling me about how not to knock up some decent girl, and Amy telling me the important stuff, including that because the female is smaller and weaker than the male, nature has equipped them with superior mental mechanisms to even things up. They lie much better than men, according to Amy. And, Amy said, they are entirely capable of allowing themselves to get knocked up if that's the only way they see to get the male of their choice to the altar. And to do that, they are entirely capable of pretending a far greater physical fascination with, sexual reaction to, the male than is actually the case. They can and do fake orgasms.

Was that what Susie was up to? Convincing me that I was the greatest thing since Casanova in the sack because that made more sense than getting herself hauled off?

It is entirely possible, Matthew the Innocent, that you have been played like a violin by a really tough female who had trouble not laughing out loud at your naïveté.

Particularly when I wanted to keep her brassiere. Jesus!

Am I that fucking stupid? Face it, you are.

And how am I going to explain this to Peter Wohl? "Sorry, boss. I was thinking with my pecker. You know how it is"?

Will I be allowed to resign? Or are they going to

prosecute me for being an accessory? They'll prosecute me. And they damned well should. I have betrayed that oath I took. What cops are supposed to do is get the bad guys, not help them walk from a multiple murder. I forgot that oath until just now.

And if all this is true, and logic tells me that it is, why don't I believe it? Why do I think that when, after carefully casing the First Harrisburg Bank & Trust Building to make sure the FBI doesn't have somebody watching the safe-deposit-box vault, and I call her office, she will be there, waiting for my call to come get the bank loot she's holding for Chenowith?

Because I am the fucking fool of fame and legend, thinking with my dick?

Or because I think that she loves me, and I love her, and she's the best thing that's ever happened to me?

Well, Matthew Payne, if you're going to go down in flames, you're really going to go down in flames. You're going to play this little scenario out to the end, believing what you saw in Susie's eyes — not only that she didn't know Chenowith was going to blow up the science building but, more important, that she loves you back — until Special Agent Leibowitz puts the cuffs on your wrists and starts reading you your Miranda rights.

He put Susan's brassiere back on the bedside table and picked up the telephone. He ordered orange juice, milk, coffee, a breakfast steak, two eggs sunny-side up, hash brown potatoes, and an English muffin.

"Since I know you are going to rush this right up, which means I will be in the shower, I will leave the door ajar," he said, and hung up. And

448

then he added, aloud, "After all, the condemned man is entitled to the quick delivery of his last meal."

While he was shaving, he heard the sound of the cart being rolled into the room. He stuck his head out the bathroom door and called to the waiter, "Forge my name and add fifteen percent for the tip."

When he had finished shaving and combing his hair, he left the bathroom naked, and en route to the chest of drawers for his underwear lifted the cover over the steak and eggs.

"To hell with it," he announced to himself. "I'm hungry."

And then he pulled a chair to the cart and sat down naked.

He had just dipped the first piece of steak into one of the egg yolks when there was a knock at the door.

"Shit," he muttered, got up, stood behind the door and opened it.

Maybe it's the newspaper.

It was Miss Susan Reynolds. She smiled at him somewhat shyly, met his eyes momentarily, and then looked away.

I love her. It's as simple as that. Otherwise, I couldn't possibly be this happy — maybe "thrilled" is a better word — to see her.

"Come in my parlor, my beauty, as the spider said to the fly."

"I wasn't sure if you'd be up," she said as she walked into the room. The first thing she saw was his reflection in a mirror, and then the room-service cart.

"My God!" she said.

"A little birdie told me you were coming, and I wanted to be ready."

"I was talking about the food," Susan said. "But now that you mention it, put your pants on."

"Do I have to?"

"Do you always eat that much for breakfast?"

"My mother taught me that the most important meal of the day is breakfast," Matt said solemnly.

"I'm surprised you're not as fat as a house."

"May I offer you a little something while I put my pants on?"

"All I had at the house was a glass of orange juice," she said.

"Help yourself," he said, and started for the chest of drawers.

He saw, reflected in the mirror, that she was watching him. He put an innocent look on his face and covered his crotch with both hands. Susan shook her head and smiled.

The telephone rang.

He sat on the bed and picked it up.

"Hello?"

"I hope you were sound asleep," Jack Matthews's voice said.

"Why, Special Agent Matthews of the FBI!" Matt said. "What a joy it is to hear your melodious voice!"

Susan looked frightened, decided Matt was pulling her leg again, shook her head in resignation, and then, when he nodded, signaling that he was indeed talking to an FBI agent, looked frightened again.

Matt signaled for her to come to the bed.

"Are you alone? Can you talk?"

"I am alone and I can talk," Matt said.

He swung his feet into the bed to give Susan room to sit down. She took one of the pillows and laid it over his midsection. Then she sat on the bed. Matt held the handset away from his ear so that Susan could hear Matthews.

"Were you out with the Reynolds woman last night?"

"Indeed I was."

"What times?"

"Jack, you're not my mother."

"Just answer the question, for Christ's sake, Matt."

"She picked me up at the hotel about half past six and dropped me back off here just before midnight. We drove out to Hershey, to the hotel. We had clam chowder, roast beef, and asparagus. Did you know, Jack, that asparagus is an aphrodisiac?"

"Don't tell me it worked. You're not doing anything really stupid with that woman, are you, Matt?"

"No," Matt said, and looked into Susan's eyes. "I'm not doing anything stupid with that woman, Jack. Did you call up for a report on my sex life, or did you have something on your mind?"

"You didn't call."

"I had nothing to report. I have nothing to report now, so, if you will excuse me, Jack, I will return to my breakfast. The eggs are getting cold."

"The Ollwood woman called the Reynolds

451

woman twice last night. Called herself 'Mary-Ellen Porter.' Called at six fifty-five and again at eleven thirty-two."

"If she called herself 'Mary-Ellen Porter,' how do you know it was the Ollwood woman?"

"We ran a voiceprint, of course," Matthews said, just a trifle condescendingly.

"Excuse me," Matt said. "I should have known. *A voiceprint.*"

"And she called the Reynolds woman at her office yesterday morning. At 9:44."

"You've got a tap on the Reynolds woman's office phone?"

"Well, sort of."

"What exactly does 'sort of' mean?"

"We have an agent in her office. Not on this, something else. But she's an agent —"

"*She's* an agent?" Matt interrupted.

"I'm not supposed to bring you in on any of this, Matt."

"What the hell, I'm only a lousy local cop, right? Tell me as little as possible?"

"There's a lot of fraud in the welfare system. Including some people in the Department of Social Services on the take. The programs are federally assisted, so that makes it fraud against the government. So we have somebody in there. What's she's done is rig a simple tap, a small recorder."

"Has the amateur wiretapper got a name?"

"*That,* I'm not going to tell you. Sorry, Matt, that's none of your business."

"Good-bye, Jack."

"Shit!" Matthews said. "Don't hang up!"

"What's her name, Jack?"

"Veronica Haynes," Matthews said.

Susan exhaled audibly. Matt put his hand on her shoulder, and somehow Susan wound up lying beside him, with her face in his neck.

"Well, maybe this is your business after all," Matthews said. "What happens is the Ollwood woman calls the Reynolds woman, who gives her a number. Almost certainly of a phone booth. Always a different one — you'd be surprised how many phone booths there are within a five-minute walk of the Department of Social Services Building. She uses some kind of code for the number, so we never can find it until too late. Anyway, once she gives her the number, the Reynolds woman goes to the phone booth, and the Ollwood woman calls her there."

"So you can't get a tap on the phone booth?"

"No. I told you. We never can locate it until too late."

"So you don't have a tape recording of what they talk about?"

"Obviously not."

"They could be talking about anything? Something innocent? Like babies, for example?"

"Where are you going? We know goddamn well what they're talking about. Setting up a meeting."

"What I'm driving at is that you have nothing incriminating in these telephone calls, right?"

"I guess you're right," Matthews said after a moment's hesitation. "So what? It's not as if we need it."

"What exactly have you got to tie the Reynolds

453

woman to the bombing?"

"Accessory after the fact. You know that."

"Did she have anything to do with the bombing itself?"

"She doesn't have to. If she willingly aided the bombers, same thing. Why are you asking?"

"Maybe she could be reasoned with," Matt began.

"Forget it. (a) They're determined to try all of these people. And (b) you're not authorized to make any kind of a deal."

"Right. All I am is the local cop who does only what he's told to do, right?"

"That's it, Matt. You understood that going in."

"So what did the Ollwood woman say on the phone, if anything?"

"Nothing worth anything. What we think is significant is that she's called so often. Twice last night. What you have to do is alert us when you think she's going to meet these people. We'll take it from there."

"Put a tail on her? Like those two clowns who tailed me?"

"What the hell is the matter with you? Why are you so belligerent?"

"Nothing personal, Jack. I guess I just don't like the Imperial FBI telling me only those things you decide the dumb local cop can handle."

"It's not that way, Matt, and you should know it."

"That's what it feels like. Now, unless there's something else, can I finish my breakfast?"

"You will call me if you learn anything, right?"

"Yeah, but don't hold your breath. I'm not getting close."

"All you have to do is stick as close to her as possible, and call me when you even suspect she's going to meet with Chenowith."

"Yeah, that I remember."

"Are you going to see her today?"

"Probably."

"Try."

"Yes, sir."

"Watch yourself, buddy. Behind that innocent face and those magnificent teats is a really dangerous bitch."

"Good-bye, Jack."

Matt pushed himself up far enough so that he could hang up the telephone, then lay back down again. Through the entire process, Susan didn't move her face from his neck.

"Magnificent teats?" Susan quoted Jack Matthews. She seemed close to tears.

"Like I said, fair maiden," Matt said, gently, "the cops are onto you."

"You sounded like you and that man are friends," Susan said.

"We are. Jack's a good guy."

"They have the telephones in my house tapped?"

"Yes, they do. And the local cops are watching your place in the Poconos. I didn't know about the tap on your office phone, or that they had an agent in your office. It's lucky I didn't call over there and say something indiscreet."

"Do you think I am, Matt, 'a really dangerous bitch'?"

"You can't blame Jack for that, honey," Matt replied. "He knows you're helping these people. And he knows they're dangerous. And he hasn't, the FBI hasn't, been able to lay a hand on you so far. In his mind, you're dangerous."

"You have any second thoughts last night, Matt?"

"About us?"

"Yes."

"Not last night. I woke up wondering whether you would be in the office when I called there this morning, or on a plane to San José, Costa Rica."

"San José, Costa Rica?"

"Foreign country of choice for fleeing felons," Matt said. "They don't believe much in extradition."

"And what are you thinking now?"

"That we don't have much time. We have to get that bank money out of your safe-deposit box right away. Do you talk to this FBI woman? Is she curious about where you go, and why?"

"Until three minutes ago, I thought it was simple feminine curiosity. Why?"

"Tell her you're going to have lunch with me. I'm sure those bastards told her about me. If not vice versa. Then come to the bank, get the money out of the box, and give it to me. I don't think, if they're onto you having the money in the bank, that they will think you'd try to move it when you were going to be with me."

"What are you going to do with it?"

"I haven't figured that out yet. One thing at a time. I'll buy a briefcase before I go to the bank.

They gave me an office to use, and we can move it from your purse to my briefcase in there. That way, you won't have the money if they should grab you as you leave the bank. I don't think that's likely, but I wouldn't be surprised if that lady agent coincidentally had to cash a check about the time you'd be here."

Susan nodded, almost absently, her acceptance of that.

"If I tell you where you can find Bryan, will you help Jennifer get away?"

"No," Matt said. "I can't do that, honey."

"You said Costa Rica doesn't believe in extradition?"

"I won't let you let yourself in for another aiding-and-abetting charge," Matt said. "For one thing, it would tie you closer to the bombing and the bank robberies, and there's a chance — not much of a chance, but a chance — that maybe we can do something about that. And if you helped her in getting out of the country, they'd learn about it, and really go after you. I can't let you do anything like that."

"I just can't turn Jennie in!" she said.

"Does she trust you?"

"Of course."

"Then tell her to turn herself in. A good lawyer, and a babe in arms, might get her out of the murder rap."

"She'd never betray Bryan."

"Tell her to start thinking about her baby. They take babies away from women doing life without possibility of parole."

"You mean when she calls?"

" 'I can't meet you, Jennifer, because I don't want to be responsible for them taking your baby away from you.' Something like that. Sow the seed."

"I don't know," Susan said doubtfully.

"Have you any better ideas?"

She shook her head, then started to cry.

"That's not going to do any good. And I don't want that lady FBI agent to get on the phone and tell her boss you came to work looking like you'd been crying. They might interpret that as meaning something. "

That speech had the precisely opposite reaction to the one Matt had hoped for. It seemed to open a floodgate.

He tried to comfort her, fully aware as he did so that comforting a weeping woman was not among his social skills.

When she was finished, she pushed herself away from him, sat up and knelt on the bed. There was a box of Kleenex on the bedside table, and she blew her nose loudly.

"Sorry," she said.

"Honey, you're just going to have to get used to the idea that your friend Jennifer is beyond salvation."

"I know," Susan said. "That's not what I was crying about."

"Then what?"

"Us," she said. "Where the hell were you, my precious beloved, when I needed you? To deliver that Jennie-made-the-wrong-choice speech, to tell me 'I won't let you get yourself in for an aiding-and-abetting charge'?"

"I wish I had been there," Matt said. "Jesus, I can't believe how someone as intelligent as you are has fucked yourself up like this!"

"Truth, they keep saying, is stranger than fiction," Susan said.

Matt didn't reply.

"What are you thinking now?" Susan asked.

"You don't want to know."

"Yes, I do. I thought about that in the wee hours last night. I've got to start thinking about how things really are, not how I wish they were."

"That's a start," he said.

"So what were you thinking just now?"

"How things really are?" he asked. "The naked truth?"

She nodded.

"I want to take your clothes off," Matt said.

"Just like that?"

"You asked."

She pushed herself off the bed and stood up.

"I'll take them off," she said. "You tend to rip them."

"If you don't want —" Matt began, now chagrined.

"When I was crying, honey," Susan interrupted, "I was thinking, *Why doesn't he put his hand up my dress when I desperately want him to, need him to?*"

Matt had a sudden, unpleasant thought.

What that could be is, "I will fuck a gorilla and pretend I love it if it will keep me from going to the slam."

Three minutes later, as he lay spent on top of her, he knew that wasn't true and was deeply ashamed of himself.

Officer Paul Thomas O'Mara stood in the door to Inspector Peter Wohl's office, waited until Wohl had finished speaking on the telephone, and then announced, "There's a Dr. Payne on three, Inspector. You want to talk to her?"

"I think I can find time to work the good doctor into my busy schedule, Tommy," Wohl replied. "Thank you very much, and please close the door."

Then he picked up his telephone and punched the Line Three button.

"Peter?"

"I have this problem, Doctor," he began. "I wake up in the morning, alone in my bed —"

"You want to buy me lunch?"

"You have the same problem, do you? Your place or mine?"

"Here."

"You're at home?"

"I'm at the hospital."

"The last time we ate there, as I recall, the guy playing the violin was on strike, the champagne was warm, and they were out of everything but dry sandwiches and ice cream in little paper cups. Doesn't Ristorante Alfredo seem a much better idea?"

"You have trouble remembering that I work for a living, don't you?"

"I've offered to take you away from all that."

"This is serious, Peter."

"You haven't had another case of introspection, have you? While I'm gnawing on a dry sand-

460

wich, you're not going to give me that 'this is just not going to work out, Peter' speech, are you?"

"I don't think I will," she said chuckling, "but that's not what I want to talk to you about."

"Okay, Doc. What time?"

"When can you get away?"

"Anytime from right now."

"You could come right now?"

"The never-ending war against crime will have to wait. My lover calls."

"God, you're as bad at Matt."

"If this is about him, I don't have anything to tell you. I just finished talking to Jack Matthews — I was talking to him when you called — and he said that as of half past seven this morning, Matt had nothing to report."

"It's not about Matt. Can you come right now?"

"You sound serious. Yeah. I can be there in fifteen minutes."

"Please, then, Peter."

"No farewell declaration of affection?"

"I'll be in my office."

"I guess not," Peter said. "But nevertheless, I will come instantly, borne on the wings of love."

"Oh, God," Amy said and hung up.

Inspector Wohl swung his feet, clad in highly polished loafers, off his desk and left his office. Officer O'Mara stood up at his desk.

"Until further notice, I'll be with Dr. Payne at University Hospital," Wohl told him. "You have her number. Try to keep everybody in Special Operations from knowing that."

"Yes, sir. You're unavailable."

"I didn't say that, Tommy," Wohl said patiently. "Just use a little discretion. Don't tell *everybody* who calls where I am."

"Yes, sir."

Detective Harry Cronin of South Detectives, who had been on the job for nineteen years, and a detective for thirteen, cleverly deduced it was going to be a bad day when he went into his kitchen at approximately 10:30 A.M. and found the kitchen table bare, not even a tablecloth.

Normally, before she went to work, Mrs. Cynthia Koontz Cronin, to whom Detective Cronin had been married for eighteen years, set the table for his breakfast. Patty was a technician in the Pathological Laboratory of Temple University Hospital, and left the house at half past six or so.

Normally, the *Bulletin* would be neatly folded beside the table setting, there would be a flower in a little vase Patty had bought at an auction house on the boardwalk in Atlantic City, and there would usually be a little note informing him there was scrapple, or Taylor ham, in the fridge.

Detective Cronin was more than a little hungover — when he'd gone off the job at midnight the night before, he had stopped off at the Red Rooster bar, run into Sergeant Aloysius J. Sutton of East Detectives, and had had several more belts than had been his intention — and further cleverly deduced that his coming home half in the bag probably had something to do with the bare kitchen table.

He opened the refrigerator door. The one thing he decided he could not face right now was taking

462

an unborn chicken from its shell and watch it sizzle in a frying pan. Neither did he completely trust himself to slice a piece of Taylor ham from its roll without taking part of a finger at the same time.

He reached for a bottle of Ortlieb's. It would settle his stomach.

He carried it into his living room and looked around for the *Bulletin*. It was nowhere around, which he deduced indicated that Patty was really pissed.

What the hell, he decided, he'd lie on the couch and see what was on the tube, and get up around noon, go get a cheese steak or something for lunch, and return to the house prepared to apologize to Patty for having run into Sergeant Sutton and having maybe one more than he should have.

"Good morning," Peter said when Amy waved him into her comfortably furnished office.

The sunlight coming into her office from behind her showed him that beneath her white nylon medical smock, Amelia A. Payne, M.D., was wearing only a skirt and underwear.

The psychiatric wing of University Hospital was often overheated, and this was not the first time he had noticed this was her means of dealing with it.

He found this erotically stimulating, but from the look on her face he knew that he should not mention it.

"Good morning," she said and did not get up from her desk.

"Why do I suspect that you're not going to

throw yourself in my arms?"

"Because I'm not. Peter, this is a hospital."

"Love, I have heard, cures all things."

"The medical term for what ails you is 'retarded mental development,' " she said but she smiled for a moment, then pushed a sheet of paper across her glass topped desk toward him.

He picked it up and read, "Miss Cynthia Longwood was stripped naked and orally raped by a policeman under circumstances that were themselves traumatic."

He looked at her, his eyebrows raised questioningly.

"I'm on thin ice ethically with this, Peter," she said. "Please don't push me. Right now, I'm wondering whether I should have gone to Denny Coughlin with this."

"I'm glad you came to me," he said seriously. "Okay, Doctor, tell me more, starting with, is this your medical opinion?"

"No. But I believe it."

"Where did this come from?" he asked, waving the sheet of paper.

"It was left as a telephone message for me at quarter to two this morning," Amy said.

"By whom?"

Amy shrugged.

"This woman is a patient of yours?" Peter asked, and when Amy nodded, thought out loud: "Then it obviously came from someone who (a) knew that and (b) was not a relative or family friend — they would have told you — and (c) is trying to be helpful — maybe — without getting himself involved — certainly."

464

Amy nodded and said simply, "Yes."

"You think this happened?" Peter asked.

"Yes."

"You want to tell me why?"

"Just before I called you, I spoke with Cynthia."

"And she said she had been . . ."

"I raised the subject obliquely," Amy said. "Very obliquely. That was enough to send her back to square one. I had to sedate her, and I really didn't want to."

"How do you define 'square one'?"

"Hysteria, drifting in and out of catatonia. The problem here, Peter, is that this is a precursor to schizophrenia. Once that line is crossed, it's often very difficult to bring people back. That's what I want desperately to avoid here."

"In other words, you've got a sick girl on your hands."

"Who — this is where I'm on thin ethical advice, telling you this — was already living with something pretty hard to deal with before this happened to her."

"You going to tell me what?"

"Peter, this might be, very probably is, a violation of physician patient confidentiality. The only reason I decided I could tell you is because she doesn't know I know."

"Know what?"

"Cynthia Longwood is your typical Main Line Presbyterian Princess. From Bala Cynwyd. Her father is Randolph Longwood, the builder. She doesn't remember it, but I've seen her at the Rose Tree Hunt Club."

"So, being a very nice girl, the . . . oral rape . . . really affected her?"

"Whose maternal grandfather is Vincenzo Savarese, the gangster."

"Jesus!" Wohl said genuinely surprised. "How do you know that?"

"Another confidentiality about to be violated," Amy said. "When they brought her in here, I thought, God forgive me, that she was the typical Main Line Princess who had a fight with her boyfriend, and whose parents wanted nothing but the best, damn the cost, for their lovesick princess. I had really sick people to try to help, and declined to attend her."

"I don't quite follow that, honey."

From her face, Peter saw that this was not the time to address A. A. Payne, M.D., using a term of endearment.

"When her grandfather heard about that, he showed up in Dad's office and begged him to beg me to see her. He did — he called me, he didn't beg — and out of either a desire to do Dad a favor, or out of morbid curiosity, I agreed to see her."

"I'll be damned!" Peter said. "Do you think that call came from Savarese?"

"I think that's possible, don't you?"

"What do you want from me, Amy?"

"In the best of all possible worlds, I would be able to go tell Cynthia that the bastard who did this to her has been arrested and will never bother her again. She has recurring nightmares, in which I really think she relives the horror of this over and over again. And the brain, protecting itself, keeps trying to push the memory into a remote corner. And the result of that could damned well be schizophrenia."

"I can't really offer much hope on that score. Presumably she hasn't given you a description of the 'traumatic circumstances,' much less a description of the cop?"

"No. But — and here we go again, violating physician-patient confidentiality — her blood workup showed traces of morphine, or its derivatives."

"She's an addict?"

"How do you define that? Was Penny Detweiler an addict? Two days before she put that needle in her arm, I did her blood, it came back clean, and I was able to tell myself she was past the worst of her addiction. Possibly Cynthia is psychologically addicted. Sniff a couple of lines and it doesn't seem to matter that Grandpa is a gangster and that all your friends are likely to find that out tomorrow. Or today. And your life will be ruined."

"You like this girl, don't you?"

"Yeah, and I'm not supposed to. I'm supposed to be professionally detached."

"You think the 'already traumatic circumstances' had something to do with drugs?"

Amy shrugged.

"That would seem to make sense, wouldn't it?"

"Who took the message?"

"The supervisory nurse and the resident. You want to talk to them?"

"Yeah."

"I thought you might want to. I asked them

to stick around."

"I'd like your permission to talk to Denny about this, Amy."

"Thank you for asking my permission," she said. "I was afraid you'd feel you have to go to him, with or without my permission."

"Denny can be trusted, honey," he said. "I don't know if we can find the animal who did this, but we'll damned well try."

She shrugged resignedly. "Now that I've told you, I feel better. Not comfortable, but better."

"Is there a boyfriend? A girlfriend?"

"There is — maybe was — a boyfriend. I don't know his name. And he hasn't been to see her. Or even called."

"That's interesting. Maybe if I can find him, and that shouldn't be hard, I can get something out of him."

"All I want you to do, Peter, is remember that I have a very sick girl on my hands to whom irreparable damage can be done if —"

"Honey, I understand," Peter said.

"You want to see Dr. Martinez and Loretta Dubinsky now?"

Peter nodded.

"They're crapped out in a room down the hall," she said. "I'll take you."

" 'Crapped out'? Doctor, you really should watch your mouth!"

"Fuck you, Peter," she said.

"I love it when you talk dirty," he said.

"I know," she said. "That's why I do it."

She got up from behind her desk and started

for the door. He waved her ahead of him. She stopped and touched his cheek.

"And, goddamn it, I don't want to, but I guess I do love you."

Nineteen

It took Irene Chason even longer than she thought it would to wake her husband up.

But finally, he rolled over on his back and looked up at her in mingled indignation and concern.

"What's up?"

"You plan to get up today, or what?"

"I'm a little hungover, all right? Get off my back, Irene."

"There's some guy on the phone for you."

"Some guy?"

"This is the third time he's called," Irene said.

"What's he want?"

"He didn't say."

Fiorello. It has to be Joey Fiorello. What's with him?

"Is he still on the phone?"

"Yeah," she said and lifted the handset from the bedside-table telephone and handed it to him.

"Philip Chason."

"Joey Fiorello, Phil."

"What can I do you for?"

"I got a quick, good-paying job for you, if you're interested."

"Joey, I'm up to my ass in alligators."

"You heard what I said about good-paying?"

"What does that mean?"

"This is important to me."

470

"What does that come out to in round figures? And for what?"

"Phil, you're hurting my feelings. You know that I pay good. I thought we were friends."

"What do you want from me, Joey?"

"I want you to ask a few quick, discreet questions."

"Ask who a few quick, discreet questions?"

"Look, Phil, are you going to help me out on this or not?"

"I told you, Joey, I'm up to my ass in work. Whether I can help you depends on what you want me to do, and how much it's worth to you."

"Let me put it to you this way, Phil. You come to my office in the next hour, and let me explain what I want you to do for me, and that'll be worth two hundred to me, whether or not you can help me out."

"Two-fifty, Joey," Phil said.

"Jesus. And I thought we were friends," Joey Fiorello said obviously pissed. "Okay. Two-fifty. I'll be expecting you. Thank you, Phil."

The line went dead in his ear.

"What was that all about?" Irene asked.

"I don't have a goddamn clue," Phil said as he swung his feet out of bed.

The warm smile on Joey Fiorello's face when Phil Chason walked into his office at Fiorello's Fine Cars forty-five minutes later, was, Phil thought, about as phony as a three-dollar bill.

I wonder why he didn't tell me to go fuck myself when I held him up for two-fifty? And he must need me; otherwise, he would have.

471

"Thank you for coming, Phil," Joey said. "I appreciate it."

"So what's up?"

"Can I have Helene get you a cup of coffee? Or a Danish? *And* a Danish?"

"Yeah. Thank you. You said this was important, so I came right away without my breakfast."

"I appreciate that," Joey said and raised his voice: "Helene!"

The magnificently bosomed Helene put her head in the door.

"Honey, would you get Mr. Chason a cup of coffee and a Danish, please?"

"Be happy to. If there's any Danish left."

"If there's no Danish left, honey, send one of my so-called salesmen after some."

"Yes, sir, Mr. Fiorello," Helene said.

Joey reached into his pocket and peeled five fifty-dollar bills off a wad held together with a gold paper clip and handed them to Phil.

"If I can't get you a Danish, the least I can do is pay what I owe you," he said with a smile.

"Thank you," Phil said. "Like the man said, money may not be everything, but it's way ahead of whatever's in second place."

"Absolutely," Joey said.

"So, what's on your mind, Joey?"

"I'm sure I can trust you to keep what I'm about to tell you to yourself."

"That would depend on what you want to tell me," Phil said. "Let me put that another way. As long as it's legal, you can trust me."

"Absolutely goddamned legal," Joey said. "Je-

472

sus Christ, Phil, what do you think? I'm a businessman."

What I think is that you're in bed with the mob, is what I think.

"No offense, Joey. But we should understand each other."

"I agree one hundred percent," Joey said. "And you have my word I would never ask you to do anything that would in any way be illegal."

"Okay. Fine."

"The thing is, Phil, I'm a silent partner in the Howard Johnson motel on Roosevelt Boulevard. You know where I mean?"

Phil nodded.

Why don't I believe that?

"Nice, solid investment. You know, people trust a place with Howard Johnson's name on it."

"Yeah, I guess they do."

"You know how that works, Phil? I mean, it's a franchise. We pay them a percentage of the gross. We get to use the name, and they set the standards. They got inspectors — you never know who they are — who come and stay in the place, and eat in the coffee shop, and check things . . . see if the bathrooms are clean, that sort of thing. You understand?"

Phil nodded.

"They insist that we run a high-class operation," Joey said. "A nice, clean, respectable place, a family place, by which I mean that a Howard Johnson is not a no-tell motel, you know what I mean?"

"I understand," Phil said.

"The way the contract is drawn, we don't keep

the place up to standard, they have the right to do one of two things: either make us sell the place, or take down the sign."

"Is that so?"

"Which would cost us a bundle. Which would cost me, since I have a large piece of that action, a large bundle, if Howard Johnson should decide to pull our franchise."

"And you're worried about that happening, is that what you're driving at?"

"I am worried shitless," Joey said.

"Why?"

"Can you believe there was a drug bust at the Howard Johnson last Thursday night? Can you believe that?"

"Drugs are all over, Joey, you know that."

"Not in my fucking Howard Johnson motel, they're not supposed to be."

"Those things happen, Joey."

"Like I said I'm a silent partner. I put up the money, and the other partners run the place. Which means they hire the manager."

"Okay."

"He's a brother-in-law of one of the partners. His name is Leonard Hansen."

"And?"

"So far as I know, he's as honest as the day is long."

"Okay."

"So far as I know, is what I said."

Helene came into the office with two mugs of coffee and a half-dozen Danish.

She gave Phil — maybe innocently, maybe not — a good look down her dress as she put his mug and the Danish on the coffee table in front of him.

"No calls, and make sure nobody walks in here on Mr. Chason and me, Helene," Joey said.

"Yes, sir, Mr. Fiorello."

Joey waited until she had left the office and closed the door.

"Where was I, Phil?"

"You were saying that so far as you know, the manager of the Howard Johnson is honest."

"Right. And, so far as I know, he knows how to run a motel. We take a nice little profit out of that place."

"Okay."

"Okay. Now, maybe I'm wrong, and I hope to Christ I am, but two things worry me."

"Such as?"

"The drug bust, of course. And then me not hearing about it for three days. Not until last night, and it happened on Thursday."

"Why does that worry you?"

"Like I said, I really hope I'm wrong, but with the amount of money we're talking about, hope don't count."

"I'm not sure where you're going, Joey. You think the manager has something to do with the drugs?"

"What I'm saying, Phil, is that we don't pay him a whole hell of a lot of money. I don't really know what I'm talking about here. But drugs in a Howard Johnson motel?"

"What are you thinking?"

"I don't have any idea how it could have gotten started, but hear me out. You got a guy making peanuts, like Leonard Hansen. He finds out that he can pick up a couple of hundred tax-free by loaning somebody a motel-room key for a couple of hours. You beginning to see where I'm coming from?"

"Yeah."

"And all of a sudden, it comes out — I have the highest respect for the detectives who work Narcotics — that my Howard Johnson motel *is* a no-tell motel. Not hookers, but much fucking worse — as far as the Howard Johnson people are concerned — drugs. That's all Howard Johnson would have to hear. So long, franchise. They'd pull that franchise so quick . . ."

"I see your point. So you want me to check this Leonard Hansen out?"

"I really hope you find him as clean as a whistle," Joey said. "But you understand, Phil, why I have to know?"

"I understand your problem, Joey."

"And discreetly, Phil. Like I said, he's a brother-in-law of one of my partners. He would get pissed in a second if he heard I'd asked you to check this guy out."

"I understand."

"I'll give you fifty an hour, plus all your expenses, if you can get on this right away, Phil."

"I told you, Joey, I'm up to my ass —"

"This is important to me, Phil, but I would hate to think you're trying to hold me up. We have a good relationship here. . . ."

"I wasn't talking about money. I was talking about other jobs I have, Joey."

"No offense, Phil."

"No offense taken, Joey. I'll get on it as soon as I can."

"I appreciate that, Phil," Joey said.

He got up behind his desk and put out his hand.

"You get me something on this guy I can take to my partners, something solid, and there'll be a bonus in this for you, Phil."

"If there's something there, I'll find it," Phil said.

"Jesus, I just had a thought," Joey said.

"What?"

"Let me throw this at you. I don't know why I didn't think of it before."

"Think of what before?"

"If anybody knew if my Howard Johnson motel is being used as a fucking drug supermarket, it would be the narcotics cops, right?"

"Maybe."

"Maybe, my ass. They did one drug bust there. They had to have a reason, a suspicion, that something was going on there."

"So what?"

"Could you ask them? You know any of them?"

"No, and no. I don't know any of them, and if I did know one of them, and asked him something like that, he'd tell me to go fuck myself."

"I thought you cops got along pretty well," Joey said visibly disappointed.

"I'm a retired cop, which is the same thing as saying, so far as they're concerned, that I'm a civilian. They don't tell civilians anything. So far as that goes, they don't tell other cops anything."

"If they knew — even suspected; we wouldn't need any proof — about something going on at my motel, that would settle this thing in a hurry. Which is what I'm after, Phil, finding out yes or no in a hurry."

"I told you, Joey, if the Narcotics Unit *knew* that drug deals were going on every hour on the hour at your motel, they wouldn't tell me."

"You couldn't explain the situation to them?"

"Jesus, you don't know how to take 'no' for an answer, do you?"

"Not when I'm about to lose a lot of fucking money, I don't," Joey said. He paused. "The bonus I was talking about would kick in, of course."

Phil shook his head, "no."

"Well, how about this? Get me a couple of names of detectives in the Narcotics Unit. Get me *two* names of the detectives who did the drug bust at my motel last Thursday. I'm a very reasonable guy. I can talk to them, explain my problem."

"I'll see what I can do," Phil said. "No promises."

"One promise. You get me two names, I pay you for ten hours of your time, and throw in the bonus."

"I'll see what I can do, Joey," Phil repeated.

From the glass-walled office that had been loaned to him by Vice President James C. Chase of the First Harrisburg Bank & Trust Company, Detective Matthew Payne of the Philadelphia Police Department devoted a good deal of his attention throughout the morning to the bank's employees and customers.

He was looking for someone who might be an FBI agent, on surveillance duty, and charged with keeping an eye on the safe-deposit box leased by Miss Susan Reynolds, who was aiding and abetting the Chenowith Group in their unlawful flight to escape prosecution for murder and their participation in a series of bank robberies.

It had been agreed between them that in the event Matt saw someone who might be the FBI, he was to signal Susan cleverly — with a negative shake of the head — on her arrival in the lobby. If he gave such a signal, she was not to go to her safe-deposit box but, instead, come directly to his office, from which they would go to lunch.

If he did not give her a negative shake of the head, she would go to her safe-deposit box, take out the bank loot, and then come to Matt's office. After transferring the money to his brand-new hard-sided attaché case, they would then go to lunch.

The only person he saw who even remotely looked like a police officer of any kind was the gray-uniformed bank guard, who was about seventy years old and had apparently learned to sleep on his feet with his eyes open. Matt didn't think he would notice if someone walked into the lobby and began to carry out one of the ornate bronze stand-up desks provided for the bank's clientele.

There was something unreal about the whole thing, starting with the fact that someone like Susan would even know someone who robbed banks, now with a homemade movie-style machine pistol. And it was, of course, absolutely unbelievable that, in violation of everything that, before the Hotel Hershey, he had believed was really important to him, he was actively involved in the felony of concealing evidence in a capital criminal case.

Or as unbelievable as what had happened — or at least how many times it had happened — in his hotel room that morning, before Susan finally got out of bed and put her clothes back on just in time to go to work.

But that was true, and so was the fact that he was a yet-undetected criminal.

He wondered, idly, once or twice during the morning if this detachment from reality was the way it was for real criminals — he changed that to "other criminals" — and might explain the calm, *I don't give a shit* behavior many of them manifested.

And then, at ten to twelve — Susan said she would probably be at the bank at 12:05 — he spotted a familiar head walking across the marble floor to the bronze gate to the safe-deposit room door.

The familiar head needed both a shave and a haircut. The man was wearing blue jeans and a woolen, zippered athletic jacket.

Not what one expects from the usually natty FBI. Which means that not only are they surveilling the safe-deposit boxes, but using an undercover agent to do it.

He felt bile in his mouth.

Christ, we're going to get caught! What made me think we could get away with this?

And then he realized, with mingled relief, chagrin, and surprise, that while the unshaven man

480

in the jeans and athletic jacket was indeed a law-enforcement officer, he was not in the employ of the Federal Bureau of Investigation.

He gets his paychecks from the same place I do. That son of a bitch is Officer Timothy J. Calhoun of the Five Squad of the Narcotics Unit!

Matt's mind made an abrupt right turn: *Christ, there's four paychecks in my desk. I've got to find the time to go to the goddamn bank and deposit them!*

And then returned to the lobby of the First Harrisburg Bank & Trust Company. He lowered his head and raised his hand to shield his face.

He won't expect to see me here, of course, but the son of a bitch is a cop, and he just might recognize me. He gave me a long hard look the last time I saw him.

That flashed through his mind. He had been startled then, too, to recognize Calhoun, the first time he had ever laid eyes on him. He'd just come from going through the personnel records of Five Squad, which had included a photograph of clean-shaven Officer Calhoun taken on his graduation from the Academy.

But that had been enough for him to recognize unshaven undercover officer Calhoun in the Roundhouse parking lot. He had followed him into the building and watched as he and somebody else — Coogan, Officer Thomas P. — had processed prisoners into Central Lockup.

And the both of them looked at me long and hard when they saw me later in the parking lot. If he sees me here, he will recognize me!

But what the hell is he doing here?

I've already cross-checked the names I got from his

481

record against the names of people who rent safe-deposit boxes here, and there wasn't a match.

Which means either I was not doing my job well — which seems possible, since I have had other things on my mind — or that the box is rented in the name of somebody whose name I don't have.

I have to find out what box he's going into.

Calhoun was no longer in sight.

Matt looked across the lobby toward the office of Vice President James C. Chase. It was empty.

He quickly scanned the desktop looking for a list of telephone numbers under the plate glass. There was none. He pulled out first the left, then the right, shelf on the desk, and on the right found a list of telephone numbers.

Chase, James C. was not on it.

Of course not, stupid. The guy whose desk this is damned well knows the boss's extension number by heart.

He punched one of the buttons on the telephone and punched in the numbers listed on the phone.

"Good morning, First Harrisburg!"

"Mr. Chase, please."

"Mr. Chase's office."

"My name is Matthew Payne. . . ."

"Oh, yes, Mr. Payne. How can I help you?"

"I'd like to speak to Mr. Chase, if that's possible."

"Oh, I'm so sorry, but it's not. Mr. Chase won't be in until this afternoon. Is there anything I can do for you?"

"It'll wait. Thank you very much."

"Mr. Chase left instructions that you're to have

anything you need."

Somehow, I don't think that includes asking you to walk across the lobby and find out what box the guy in the blue jeans and athletic jacket is going into.

And, Christ! They keep a record of who goes into what box, and the time. I don't need her.

"It's not important," Matt said. "It'll wait. Thank you."

"I'll tell him you called."

"Thank you," Matt said and hung up and looked at his watch. It was five to twelve.

He looked at the door through which Calhoun had disappeared. No Calhoun. He looked through the lobby.

Susan was at one of the stand-up desks, looking — nervously — his way.

What do I do? Send her in there with him? They're liable to both come out at the same time, and being normal, Calhoun will take a look at her tail, and then maybe spot me in here.

He fixed what he hoped was a smile of confidence on his face and winked at Susan.

She smiled in relief, and his heart melted.

What did you tell her about Poor Pathetic Jennie? That when Jennie knew what was going down was really wrong, she had a choice to make, and made the wrong one? Does that have an application here?

He watched Susan until she disappeared from sight, then got out the list of names of relatives of Officer Timothy J. Calhoun and stared at it, wondering again whether he had screwed up, or the name of the box Calhoun was going into wasn't one of his names.

He looked up, from behind the hand shielding

his face, and saw Calhoun coming back into the lobby. Calhoun looked quickly around the lobby — a little nervously, Matt thought — and then walked out of the bank.

But I've got you, you son of a bitch!

Said Detective Payne, literally in the middle of the commission of a felony, with monumental hypocritical self-righteousness.

He shrugged, and reached for the telephone.

"Special Operations Investigation, Sergeant Washington."

"Officer Calhoun, Timothy J., just went into — at 11:54 — a safe-deposit box at the First Harrisburg Bank and Trust."

"I am almost as glad to hear that as I am to hear your voice, Matthew. You have the number of the box? That will permit me to have the search warrant all ready for the signature of a judge at the auspicious time."

"Not yet."

"I'm sure I don't have to tell you that banks keep records in minute detail of the time their clients gain access to their boxes?"

"That's right. You don't. But I want to get it — I want the guy from the bank to get it for me. He'll be in this afternoon."

"And you will relay the number to me immediately after you have it?"

"Yes, sure."

"And how are other things going in Harrisburg, Matthew? Mr. Matthews tells me you had dinner in Hershey."

"That's going slowly."

"And carefully, Matthew? I devoutly hope care-

484

fully. You've heard the gentleman has added gunsmith to the long list of his other skills and accomplishments?"

"Matthews told me."

"Then let 'caution, caution, *toujours* caution' be your creed, Matthew."

"That's *audacity,* not caution. *'L'audace, l'audace, toujours l'audace.'* "

"Don't correct me, please. I'm a sergeant, and sergeants are never wrong. And the one thing I absolutely *do not* want from you is audacity. I will, with more or less bated breath, await your next call."

"Sometime this afternoon," Matt said.

The line went dead.

Matt hung up and looked into the lobby.

Susan, looking uncomfortable, was walking across the lobby toward his office.

He started to get up, then changed his mind. His newly acquired attaché case was in the well of the desk. He planned — while he hoped anyone looking would think he was tying his shoe — to transfer the bank loot from Susan's purse there.

"Ready for lunch?" Susan asked at the door.

"Come into my office, my dear, and I will explain why the bank *has* to repossess your Porsche."

He waved her into the chair beside the desk. She put her purse on the floor in front of her. Matt bent over, grabbed the purse, and put it into the desk well. Then he opened the attaché case, went into Susan's purse, and moved the money, noticing as he did that some of the stacks of currency were bound with paper strips bearing the names of the banks from which they had been stolen.

These people are really stupid! Those currency wrappers would really tie them to the robberies. Didn't Chenowith think about that? Or did he simply assume that Susan would take care of getting rid of the wrappers and she was too stupid to do it?

He closed the briefcase and ran his finger over the combination lock.

Jesus, if the combination wasn't set at 000, I'm going to have to break the lock to get back into it. That wasn't too smart, Matthew!

He slid Susan's purse back across the floor to her, then straightened up.

"Done," he said and smiled.

She nervously smiled back.

Not too stupid to get rid of the currency wrappers; she's not stupid. Naive. That's the word. Naive.

"Well, let's go," Matt said. "For some reason, I'm starved."

"That's because you didn't eat any breakfast," she said.

"After you left, I did," Matt said. "It was cold, but I needed the strength of good red meat."

He waved her ahead of him out of the office.

When they passed Mr. Chase's office, his "girl" — she was at least forty — smiled approvingly at them.

"I wish I had more time, Peter, to enjoy this," Chief Inspector Dennis V. Coughlin said indicating the Rittenhouse Grill Room's "Today's Luncheon Specials" — a mixed grill — a waiter had just set before them.

That's not a simple expression of regret, Wohl thought, *that he is a busy man who had trouble fitting lunch with me at the Rittenhouse Club into his busy schedule. I don't know what the hell he really means, but let's get whatever the hell it is — from half a dozen possibilities — out in the open.*

"I belong here now," Peter said.

"I thought that might be the case when you invited me here," Coughlin said.

"Matt's father — maybe I should say Amy's father — called me up and said he would like to put me up for membership. I told him I'd like to think it over, and then I thought it over, and decided, what the hell, why not? It is a good place to have discreet little talks . . . like now. So I told him, 'Yes, thank you.' "

Coughlin nodded.

"You should have said 'Matt and Amy's father,' " Coughlin said. "The background of that is Matt went to his father about getting you in here. He didn't want it to look as if he had his nose up your rear end. Amy went to her dad, and asked him what about getting you in here like I'm in here, what do they call it? — *ex officio,* it comes with the job."

"I didn't know that."

"So Brewster Payne came to me and said he'd be delighted to get you in, provided you never found out that Matt asked him, or that it wouldn't get you in trouble with the department. For being too big for your britches, in other words. There's a lot of chief inspectors who don't get to join. As a matter of fact, it's only me and Lowenstein. He said that he's been thinking about it, aside from

487

Matt and Amy, for some time. He said there's a lot of people, including him, who think that somewhere down the pike, you should be police commissioner . . ."

"Jesus!" Peter blurted.

". . . and he wondered if getting you in here, now, would help or hurt that. He also said he didn't want you to get the idea he was doing it to make points with you about Matt. He asked me to think it over and get back to him. So I thought it over, and I got back to him, and told him I thought it was a good idea, and that I felt sure you would come to me, ask me about it, and I would tell you that."

"Chief . . ."

"It's a good idea, Peter," Coughlin said.

"I didn't want to put you on a spot," Wohl said.

"I gave you the benefit of that doubt. So far I've seen no signs that you're getting too big for your britches. But I think there are — I know there are — some people in the department who do, and will take you being in here as proof of that."

He sliced off a piece of his lamb chop and put it in his mouth.

"Before you tell me what you want to tell me, Peter, did you hear this Chenowith character has got himself a sawed-off fully automatic carbine?"

Wohl nodded. "I heard."

"Presumably Matty has been told?"

"He's been told."

"You think he's going to obey his orders?"

"You read the riot act to him, I read the riot

488

act to him, and Washington read the riot act to him. I've been telling myself we are the three people whose orders he's most likely to obey."

Coughlin nodded.

"He called Washington first thing this morning," Wohl went on, "and told him he had just seen Officer Timothy J. Calhoun of Five Squad going into the safe-deposit box vault of the First Harrisburg Bank and Trust."

"I . . . I was about to say I don't think Calhoun's about to take a shot at him, but remembering that telephone call to the Widow Kellog, maybe I shouldn't. I'm more concerned about this Chenowith character. He knows he's facing life anyway, so why worry about shooting a cop? And he's crazy."

"So far as I know, Matt is still trying to gain the Reynolds woman's confidence. I think he understands the situation."

"I hope you're right. What happens next with Calhoun?"

"Matt's supposed to call later with the name of the safe-deposit box number. Jason's going to do everything about a search warrant but hand it to a judge for his signature."

Coughlin nodded.

Wohl handed him the sheet of paper on which Dr. Martinez had written, "Miss Cynthia Longwood was stripped naked and orally raped by a policeman under circumstances that were themselves traumatic."

Coughlin's eyebrows went up, and he looked at Wohl for amplification.

"Amy gave me that this morning," Wohl said.

Coughlin went off on a tangent.

"You've been seeing a lot of Amy, haven't you?"

"How do you define 'a lot'?"

"You know how to define 'a lot,' " Coughlin said. "Does Amy believe this?"

Wohl nodded.

"This is a patient of hers?"

Wohl nodded again, and added, "And she's Vincenzo Savarese's granddaughter."

"I heard his daughter had married a Main Line guy," Coughlin said "but I didn't make the connection until just now. Longwood is the builder, right?"

Wohl nodded.

"You think Savarese knows about this?"

"I think that message — it was phoned in to the hospital for Amy in the wee hours this morning — *came* from Savarese."

"Savarese called the hospital?"

"More likely one of his goons. I talked to the doctor and the nurse who talked to them. Both agreed the guy on the phone didn't use the kind of vocabulary in the message."

"Anything else?"

"Amy is concerned about violating medical ethics, and when I told her I was going to talk to you about this, asked me to tell you this girl is about to get shoved off the cliff into schizophrenia, and please be careful."

"That's all?"

"She found traces of hard stuff in the girl's blood, making her — and me — think there's a drug connection."

Coughlin grunted, read the message again, then raised his eyes to Wohl.

"You thinking what I'm thinking, Peter?"

"I hope so," Wohl said.

Coughlin made a "give it to me" gesture with his hand.

"There was a drug bust. That's the 'already traumatic circumstances.' Then this animal did this to her, and let her go. What is she going to do? Walk into a district and tell the desk sergeant, 'I was making a buy, and one of your cops' . . . ?"

"You think Savarese has also figured that out?"

"No one has ever accused Savarese of being slow."

"Anybody but you know about this?"

"Washington."

Coughlin's eyebrows rose in question.

"There's a boyfriend. He has not called the hospital. I told Jason to find out who he is."

"But not to talk to him?"

"Not to talk to him."

"And next?"

"That's what I wanted to talk to you about, Chief. How do I handle this?"

"You talk to the boyfriend. Do you think Washington has anything yet?"

"He's had two hours. Let me find a phone, and I'll find out."

He started to push himself away from the table. Coughlin waved him back into it.

"Now that you've joined the upper crust, Peter," Coughlin said smiling at him, "let me show you how the upper crust finds a telephone."

He twisted around in his chair, caught a

waiter's eye, and put his balled fist next to his ear, miming someone holding a telephone. The waiter nodded and immediately brought a telephone to their table, plugging it into a socket on the table leg.

"Thank you," Coughlin said smiling at Wohl, then dialed a number from memory.

Wohl thought it interesting that Coughlin had not found it necessary to ask for Washington's number.

He either has a great memory — which is of course possible — or he has been calling that number frequently.

"How much were you able to learn about the boyfriend?" Coughlin began the conversation without any other opening comment.

Wohl smiled. He knew that Jason Washington had begun his police career walking a beat in Center City under Lieutenant Dennis V. Coughlin. They had been friends — and mutual admirers — ever since. Polite opening comments were not necessary. Washington would immediately recognize Coughlin's voice and know what Coughlin wanted to know.

Coughlin, in an automatic action, had taken a small leather-bound notebook and a pencil from his pocket. He scribbled quickly on it as Washington replied.

"Sit on it until I get back to you. I'm with Wohl," Coughlin said and hung up.

Now it was Peter Wohl's turn to look at Coughlin with a question on his face.

"One boyfriend," Coughlin said. "Ronald R. Ketcham, twenty-five, five-ten, brown hair, 165

492

pounds, no record except for traffic violations, lives in one of the garden apartments on Overbrook Avenue near Episcopal Academy . . .”

He looked at Wohl until Wohl indicated he knew the garden apartment complex, and then went on:

“. . . works for Wendell, Wilson, the stockbrokers in Bala Cynwyd. Has not been to work for three days, and has not been seen around his apartment. His car, a Buick coupe, is locked up in the garage. There are no signs of forcible entry into his apartment, and no signs of any kind of a struggle inside the apartment. He could, of course, be in Atlantic City.”

“Or passed through Atlantic City on his way to swim with the fishes,” Peter said.

“You think?”

“If Savarese found out this guy was with his granddaughter when she was raped.”

“How could Savarese know that?” Coughlin asked.

“How could he know she was raped?” Peter countered.

“Maybe he found this guy before Jason did.”

“If that’s the case . . .” Peter said.

“Yeah,” Coughlin said. “Savarese is now looking for the cop.”

“I’m tempted to say let him have him,” Peter said.

“You don’t even want to start thinking things like that, Peter,” Coughlin said almost paternally.

“The other thought I have been having, if this went down the way I think it did, was that —”

“It sounds like something an already dirty Five

Squad cop would do?"

Wohl nodded.

"Knowing that another dirty cop would not turn him in," Coughlin agreed.

Both of them fell silent for nearly a full minute.

"You open to suggestion, Peter?" Coughlin finally asked.

"Wide open," Wohl said.

"Okay. Tell Jason to find out what else he can about Mr. Ketcham. I'll put out a Locate, Do Not Detain on him. And I will think about what to do about our friend Vincenzo."

"For example?"

"I know that you think it would probably be a good thing, but we really can't permit Savarese to cut the limbs off this scumbag one at a time with a dull knife," Coughlin said.

"My mouth ran away with me," Peter said.

"So long as it wasn't your heart," Coughlin said.

"I wish we had more than 'seems likely' to tie somebody on Five Squad to the oral rape —"

"We don't even have 'seems likely,' all we have is 'could be,' " Coughlin interrupted. "What are you thinking?"

"We go into Calhoun's safe-deposit box in Harrisburg. And then Jason explains to him that not only do we now have him with money he can't explain, but that we are about to find out who raped this girl, and in his own best interests, he should tell us about everything."

"Too many 'ifs.' There may be nothing in that box to incriminate him about anything. And if we go into the box, then they know we're looking at them. And they shut down. And what if Calhoun is the scumbag who did that to the girl?"

"Then Jason tells him who the girl is, and that unless he goes along, we tell Grandpa."

Coughlin looked at him.

"Maybe you will get to be police commissioner," he said. "I am seeing in you a certain amoral ruthlessness I never noticed before."

He met Peter's eyes, then stood up.

"For the time being, only you, me, and Jason. Agreed?"

"Yes, sir."

"Thank you for lunch, Peter."

"Chief, I'm sorry I didn't ask you before I accepted . . ."

"No problem. But there is one."

"Sir?"

"Does your dad know?"

Peter shook his head, "no."

"The problem is you're going to have to tell him before he finds out, for one thing. And when he finds out, he'll think you just might be getting a little too big for your britches."

"Yeah."

"Good. You've got that message?"

"Loud and clear, sir."

"Okay. Then I will take pity on you and tell you I already told him I was going to tell you to accept. But now you know how the phones work in here, I'd get on it. Call him and ask him what he thinks. Even money he'll say go ahead."

"And if he doesn't?"

"Thanks again for lunch, Peter," Coughlin said and walked out of the Grill Room.

Susan led Matt three blocks from the First Harrisburg Bank & Trust to a Pennsylvania Dutch restaurant.

The place was spotless, and the waitress, a tall blonde about as old as Susan looked, Matt thought, like a visual definition of innocent and wholesome. She wore a starched white lace hat on top of her blond hair, which was parted in the middle and done up in a bun at her neck. Her white cotton blouse — buttoned to the neck — was covered with an open black sweater. Her black skirt was more than halfway down her calves, and her starched white apron matched the cap. No makeup, of course.

She smiled gently, and apparently sincerely, at Susan and Matt.

I wonder what she would do if she knew she was about to serve two felons?

"Are you going to have lunch with us?" she asked. There was a Germanic accent to her speech.

"That depends on what you have," Matt said.

She looked at him curiously.

"Please," Susan said and kicked him under the table.

When the waitress left, Matt asked, "Did I say something wrong?"

"She's Amish, I think," Susan said. "But whatever, she's what they call plain people, and she would not understand your smart-ass wit."

"How am I going to order lunch if I don't know what's on the menu?"

Susan inclined her head toward the waitress,

who was pushing a large-wheeled cart toward their table.

"What a big-city sophisticate like you would probably call prix fixe," Susan said. "As much as you want, all one price. But don't be a pig; take only what you intend to eat. It hurts them when you don't eat everything on your plate. They think you didn't like it."

"Yes, Mother," Matt said.

There was an enormous display of food in bowls and on platters arranged on the cart.

Matt took roast pork, beef pot roast, potatoes au gratin, lima beans, apple sauce, beets, succotash, two rolls, butter, what looked to him like some kind of apple pie, iced tea, and coffee.

The wholesome waitress smiled at him approvingly, then served Susan approximately one-third as much food.

"Did you hear what I said about eating everything?" Susan said when the waitress had rolled the cart away.

"I intend to," Matt said.

She shook her head in disbelief.

"Do you know what happened when you put that briefcase under your desk?"

"No," Matt said, curious and therefore serious, "what? I think it's safe there, if that's what you mean."

"That's not what I mean," she said. "You had a choice to make, and you made one. Have you thought about that?"

"I didn't have any choice," he said. "You know that."

"Could you put yourself in Jennifer's shoes?

497

Did she have any choice?"

"Oranges and lemons, Susan," Matt said. "And how did Jennifer manage to intrude herself on what I thought until sixty seconds ago was going to be a nice lunch?"

"She called this morning. Just before I went to the bank."

"And?"

"I told her I was busy and that she would have to call back."

"How much of the conversation did your pal from the FBI hear? Or record?"

"All of it. But there's nothing —"

"It was one more call in a series of recent calls. They'll think that something is about to happen. If I were in charge, I would tighten surveillance. We don't need that."

"What do I tell her? She'll keep calling until I talk to her."

"Tell her to call you tomorrow," Matt said.

"And what do I tell her tomorrow?"

"Between now and then, we'll think of something."

"What are you going to do with the mon— the briefcase?"

"Take it to my room."

"And then?"

"I don't know. I've been kicking the idea around that maybe we can — somehow, but don't ask me how — use your returning the loot to our advantage. It would at least show a change of heart. I don't know how much good that would do."

She looked at him but said nothing.

"Eat your succotash, like a good girl," Matt said. "Another option, of course, is to get rid of it. Then —"

"You mean destroy it?"

Matt nodded, and went on: "Then it would be your word against Chenowith that you ever had it."

"His and Jennifer's," Susan said. "She'll go along with whatever he says."

"Against her faithful friend?" Matt asked sarcastically.

"Yes."

"Then why do you give a damn about her?"

"I do, Matt. I can't help that."

Matt raised a forkful of pot roast toward his mouth, then lowered it.

"You don't know that," he said.

"I don't know what?"

"From everything you've told me, Jennifer is a really weak sister."

"I told you about her, why she's that way," Susan said.

"So she goes along with Chenowith because he's strong, right? Or at least she sees him that way."

Susan nodded.

"What are you driving at?"

"Don't take this as anything but me thinking out loud," he said. "Tell me about the drunken mother. Is she going to spring for a lawyer — a good lawyer — when they arrest Jennifer?"

"I don't know. Probably. But if she doesn't, I will. Do you know one?"

"I know two of the best, but I don't think

they'd take her case."

"I thought they were supposed to represent people no matter what they did."

"Let's skip that for the moment," Matt said. "For the sake of argument, Jennifer has a good lawyer. By definition, a lawyer argues. A good lawyer offers strong arguments."

"I don't understand you."

"Little lady, you have a choice. You either stick with your murdering boyfriend, in which case they will take your baby away from you, and you will never see it again, or you go tell the FBI everything you know, and after you do that, you go into that courtroom and convince people you stayed with him out of fear for your life, and that of the baby."

"I don't know, Matt," Susan said.

"We're back to have you got any better ideas?"

"Let me think about it," Susan said.

"Throw this in the equation," Matt said. "*Don't* do it. Just think about it. You tell her you'll meet her but you want to meet her alone. Set up the meet. I'm there. I arrest her. Then we tell the FBI where to find Chenowith. You tell Jennifer not to say one goddamn word until she has a lawyer. Then the lawyer delivers his little speech to her."

"I'll think about it. Matt, it doesn't sound credible."

"I'm still thinking out loud. If she had the money — all the money, what you have and what you think she's going to give you —"

"They wouldn't believe that."

"It doesn't matter what they believe, or, for

500

that matter, what they know. They have to convince the jury, and that's not as easy as it looks in the movies. Maybe they'd let her cop a plea. Prosecuting a young mother with a baby in her arms isn't easy. And they want to win this bad."

Susan looked at him intently. He saw that she was beginning to accept the argument.

"What I said Susie, is that I'm thinking out loud, and that's all."

"I understand," she said.

"Changing the subject," Matt said. "You want to go back out to Hershey tonight for our anniversary? Or would you rather have a quiet evening at home with room service in the Penn-Harris? I know the Penn-Harris has oysters."

She blushed, which he found both sweetly touching and somehow erotic.

"At home, unfortunately. My home."

"Christ, no!"

"You've met Mommy. Mommy thinks you should come to dinner, so you're coming to dinner. You know what she's like."

"Yeah, I know what she's like. Penny's mother is just like her. And so is Chad's mother. And Daffy's. Bennington apparently has a required course in how to be a three-star bitch."

"Right now, we can't afford to antagonize her, Matt."

"And afterward?"

"Mommy had a motherly word of advice for me when she telephoned to tell me we're having dinner at the house. After dinner, when you are sure to suggest we go to the club or someplace, I'm to politely turn you down. Leave them wanting more, Mommy said. The worst thing a girl can do when she's really interested in a boy is appear too interested."

"Christ! Why do I have this sickening feeling you're dead serious?"

"Because I am. What do you want me to do?" Matt shrugged in annoyed helplessness.

"I could get off an hour early," Susan said, her fresh blush telling him he had correctly interpreted what she meant. "If you could."

"I don't know," Matt said doubtfully. "They're pretty strict, at the bank, about people taking off before the books are balanced to the last penny."

"You bastard!"

"How about an hour and a half early? For that matter, how about taking the afternoon off?"

Shit, what if she says yes? I've got to see Davis about what box Calhoun went into.

"Maybe a little more than an hour. But not much," Susan said seriously.

"I'll leave a candle burning in the window," Matt said.

"My girl said you wanted to see me, Matt?" Mr. James C. Chase said as he came into Matt's borrowed office two minutes after Matt returned from lunch.

"Yes, sir," Matt said and quickly decided the way to handle Chase was to tell him exactly what he wanted. "At eleven fifty-four this morning, one of the men we're interested in went into the safe-deposit section —"

"You recognized him?"

"Yes, sir. But none of the names on my list of

502

his relatives and acquaintances matches any of the names of your safe-deposit-box holders."

"And you would like me to find out what box he went in, without drawing attention to you?"

"Yes, sir, that's exactly what I hoped you could do for me," Matt said.

"I'll be right back," Mr. Chase said and walked out of the office.

Well, I couldn't ask for anything more than that, could I?

Chase came back into Matt's office a few minutes later, wearing a look of confusion.

"Matt, are you sure of the time?"

"Yes, sir."

"According to Adelaide's records —"

"Adelaide?"

"Adelaide Worner, she's been in charge of the safe-deposit vault for . . . God, I don't know, at least ten years, and is absolutely reliable; there were only two people who went into their boxes between eleven forty-five and twelve-fifteen. One of them was a man I've known for years, who makes nearly daily visits to his box, and who I don't think could possibly be involved in the sort of thing you're interested in. And the other was a young lady with whom I believe you're acquainted, Susan Reynolds, Tom Reynolds's daughter."

"We had lunch," Matt said.

Shit. This smells. I know Calhoun went in there. But I can't tell Chase that Adelaide Worner, his faithful tender of the safe-deposit vault, is either mis-

taken or — worse! — might be involved with Calhoun.

"I don't know what to tell you, Matt," Chase said.

"When all else fails, tell the truth," Matt said with a smile. " 'Matt, you were obviously wrong.' "

"It looks that way, doesn't it?" Chase said. "Did you have a nice lunch?"

"Susan took me to a Pennsylvania Dutch place a couple of blocks from here."

"Christianson's?"

"They wheel enough food to feed a family of ten to your table."

"Christianson's," Chase confirmed. "I was going to recommend it to you."

"Very nice place. I ate too much."

"That's why people go to Christianson's, to eat too much."

"Yes, sir."

"If there's anything else you need, Matt?"

"No, sir. I'm sorry to have wasted your time."

"Don't be silly."

Matt waited until he saw Chase enter his office across the lobby and then called the number Lieutenant Deitrich had given him. There was no answer. Matt let it ring long enough first to decide that it was Deitrich's private number — otherwise someone would have answered it — and then to have the thought *Shit, is good old Adelaide Worner going to be suspicious about Chase's interest in her records and ring the warning bell to Calhoun?* and then hung up.

He called Chief Mueller.

"Chief, I really need to talk to Lieutenant Deitrich," Matt said. "And his phone doesn't answer."

"Time important, Payne?"

"Yes, sir."

"Give me your number. I'll get back to you."

Three minutes later, the telephone rang.

"Deitrich will pick you up on the corner — turn right when you leave the bank — in five minutes," Chief Mueller announced, without any preliminary greeting.

"Thank you very much."

"Happy to do it."

Almost exactly five minutes later, a pea-green unmarked Ford with Deitrich at the wheel pulled up at the corner. He signaled Matt to get in.

"You got something?" Deitrich asked.

Matt recited the chain of events as they drove through traffic.

Deitrich nodded his head.

"One of the troubles you have when dealing with banks is that nobody in a bank wants to believe that honest somebody could possibly have his, or especially her, hand in the till," he said. "I guess you already learned that."

I have just been complimented.

"I'll check this Adelaide Worner out. Where are you going to be?"

"At the bank. Tonight I'm going out to dinner."

"Eight o'clock at the Penn-Harris too early for you?"

"No, sir. Thank you very much."

505

Deitrich pulled to the curb, and Matt understood he was to get out.

"Thank you, sir."

Deitrich nodded at him but did not speak.

Matt got out. He had no idea where he was, and had to ask directions to get back to the First Harrisburg Bank & Trust.

He called Jason Washington, was told he was not available, then tried Staff Inspector Weisbach's number and was told he was out sick with a cold. Finally, he called Inspector Peter Wohl.

I really don't want to talk to Wohl.

Wohl listened to his recitation of Calhoun going into a box without there being a record of it, and what he had done about it.

"Call in when you have something," Wohl said.

"Yes, sir."

"I had lunch with Chief Coughlin," Wohl said. "I told him that I felt sure you were not going to do anything stupid in Harrisburg. Don't make a liar of me, Matt."

"I'll try not to."

"Anything happening with your lady friend?"

"No, sir."

Jesus, I hate to lie to him. It makes me want to throw up.

"Take care, Matt," Wohl said and hung up.

Matt hung up, then leaned back in the high-backed executive chair.

His foot struck the attaché case half full of stolen money and knocked it over.

He sat there another minute or two, considering the ramifications of what he had done, and what he was doing.

And then he stood up, reached under the desk for the attaché case, picked it up, and walked out of the bank with it.

Twenty

While Mr. Michael J. O'Hara of the Philadelphia *Bulletin* enjoyed a close personal relationship with many — indeed, almost all — of the senior supervisors of the Philadelphia Police Department, the White Shirts, as a general rule, did not provide him with the little tidbits of information from which Mr. O'Hara developed the stories in which his readers were interested.

The unspoken rules of the game were that if Mr. O'Hara posed a question to a senior White Shirt based upon what he had dredged up visiting the various districts and the special units of the Philadelphia Police Department, he would either be given a truthful answer, or asked to sit on the germ of a story, and they would get back to him later — and more important, first, before his competitors — when releasing the information would be appropriate.

The unspoken rules were scrupulously observed by both sides. The White Shirts would indeed get back to Mickey O'Hara first as soon as they could. And on his part, even if Mr. O'Hara himself uncovered the answers to the questions-on-hold, he would not print them without at least asking for the reasons he should not, and in nine occasions of ten, having been given a reason, would sit on the story until he was told it would be appropriate to publish it.

The White Shirts were aware that no manner of stern admonition to lower-ranking police officers would stop them from furnishing Mr. O'Hara with facts they thought would interest him. Ninety-five percent of the uniformed police officers of the Philadelphia Police Department thought of Mr. O'Hara as one of their own.

In each of Philadelphia's police districts, the day-to-day administrative routines are under the supervision of a corporal. The corporal is always assisted by a "trainee," which is something of a monumental misnomer, as the term would suggest to the layman a bright-eyed, bushy-tailed, very young police officer.

Quite the reverse is true. Many trainees are veteran police officers with many years on the job, who for a variety of reasons, but often their physical condition, are not up to walking a beat, or riding around in a radio patrol car for eight hours. They don't wish to go out on a pension, and being designated a trainee both gives them something important to do and gives the district the benefit of their long experience.

Michael J. O'Hara knew every trainee in the Philadelphia Police Department by his first name, and just about every trainee felt privileged to consider himself a friend of the Pulitzer prize–winning journalist.

When Mickey O'Hara went into the 1st District Headquarters at 24th and Wolf streets in Southwest Philadelphia, he caught the attention of the corporal behind the plate glass window and mimed drinking from a coffee cup. The corporal smiled, gave Mickey a thumbs-up, and pushed the button that activated the lock on the door that carried the caveat, ABSOLUTELY NO ADMITTANCE — POLICE PERSONNEL ONLY.

Mickey went into the room, helped himself to a cup of coffee, and put a dollar bill into the coffee kitty.

"Shit, Mickey, you don't have to do that!" the trainee, a portly, florid-faced fifty-year-old with twenty-six years on the job, said.

"I am simply upholding the reputation of those of Gaelic extraction as perfect gentlemen," Mickey replied.

(In truth, this was not entirely a benevolent gesture. The dollar would be reported on Mr. O'Hara's expense account as "Coffee and Doughnuts for three, 1st Police District, $8.50.")

The corporal and the trainee laughed, then laughed even louder when Mickey told them the story of the cop in the 19th District who, after he'd had a couple of belts on the way home, realized it was not only three A.M. when he got there, but that he probably smelled of perfume which was not that of his wife. Knowing that if he tried to take a shower, his wife would hear the water and wake up for sure, he needed a better idea, and found one. He tiptoed into the bathroom, remembering not to turn on the lights, because that would wake the wife. Then he stripped and sprayed himself liberally all over with deodorant. When he sniffed himself, he thought he could still smell perfume, so he sprayed himself again, and then tiptoed into the bedroom and eased himself into bed without waking his wife.

"That took him about ninety seconds," Mickey finished. "Just long enough for the wife's hair spray — what he thought was deodorant — to glue his wang to his left leg and his balls to the other."

The laughter emanating from the office was of such volume as to attract the attention of the district commander and the tour lieutenant, who looked into the office, saw Mr. O'Hara, and entered the office to say hello.

Mickey repeated the story for their edification and amusement, and they chatted about mutual acquaintances for several minutes. The district captain told Mickey he and the lieutenant were going to ride around — which he knew meant take a look around the 1st District — and invited him to join them.

He declined with thanks. They shook hands, and the White Shirts left the office.

Neither the corporal nor the trainee thought it out of the ordinary — or inappropriate — when Mickey went to a clipboard containing the most recent communications from the Roundhouse, took it off its nail, and started reading them.

He found one of interest.

A Locate, Do Not Detain had been issued on one Ronald R. Ketcham, white male, twenty-five, five-ten, brown hair, 165 pounds, of an address on Overbrook Avenue, which Mickey recognized as being near the Episcopal Academy. The bulletin said he might be driving a Buick coupe, and gave the license number. The cooperation of suburban police departments was requested.

What attracted Mr. O'Hara's attention was that

511

the Locate, Do Not Detain ordered that any information generated on Mr. Ketcham be immediately furnished directly to ChInsp. Coughlin or Insp. Wohl or Sgt. Washington — it gave their telephone numbers — rather than be reported through ordinary channels.

Mickey carried the clipboard to the trainee.

"Pat, what's this, do you think?"

"Yeah, I noticed that. The last I heard, Denny Coughlin wasn't running Missing Persons. I don't have a clue."

"Name doesn't ring a bell?"

Pat shook his head, "no."

"Probably some ambulance chaser took off for Atlantic City with his squeeze, and the wife came home from Mama's before she was expected."

"Probably," Mickey said, although he didn't think so.

He thought about it a minute, then decided he would not call Denny Coughlin and ask him what it was all about.

Paragraph 11.B. of the Unspoken Rules required that, in a situation like this, he make inquiries of the senior White Shirt whose name he had, to avoid putting the subordinates on the spot about what to tell him. Denny Coughlin would tell him, of course. But that would use up a favor, and Mickey liked to have Denny Coughlin in his debt, rather than the other way around.

So Mickey didn't call Chief Inspector Coughlin, but instead filed Ronald R. Ketcham away in a corner of his mind, to be retained until he heard something else.

Officer Tommy O'Mara put his head into Captain Michael Sabara's office.

"Sir, there's a civilian who wants to talk to you."

"To me, personally?"

"Yes, sir."

"Did this civilian say what he wants?"

"No, sir."

Sabara picked up the telephone, punched the flashing button, and, somewhat impatiently announced: "This is Captain Sabara. How can I help you?"

"My name is Phil — Philip — Chason, Captain. Does that ring a bell?"

Sabara quickly searched his memory.

"I'm afraid not, Mr. Chason. How may I help you?"

"I was with you last night, Captain, at Captain Beidermann's retirement party. I was hoping you'd remember."

"Oh, of course," Sabara lied kindly. "My memory is failing."

"I used to be a detective," Chason said. "I went out on medical disability after twenty-six years on the job."

"How can I help you, Mr. Chason?"

"Karl and I went to the Academy together. I just found out that he meant it when he told us last night he was going to Florida in the morning. Otherwise, I would have gone to him."

"Oh?"

"I've stumbled onto something that bothers me. And I don't want to go to Narcotics with it.

513

Or Major Crimes. Or Intelligence."

"Stumbled onto what?" Sabara asked, a trifle impatiently.

"I was hoping you'd have fifteen minutes to hear me out."

"This concerns Narcotics? This is Special Operations, we don't deal —"

"Narcotics and the mob," Phil said. "I really think I wouldn't be wasting your time."

"You want to see me now, is that it?"

"I'd like to, yes."

"You know where I am?"

"Frankford and Castor?"

"Right. I'll be expecting you."

"Thank you."

Sabara hung up and then raised his voice: "Tommy!"

Officer O'Mara appeared.

"Just for your general information, Officer O'Mara, that unnamed civilian who called me has a name."

"Yes, sir?"

"His name is Chason," Sabara said. "And he's coming to see me. When he comes in, bring him right in."

"Yes, sir."

"Mr. Chason is actually Detective Chason, Retired, Tommy."

"Yes, sir?"

"Do you know where your father was last night, Tommy?"

"Yes, sir. He was at Captain Beidermann's retirement party. They were classmates at the Academy."

"Then your father was also a classmate of Detective Chason, Tommy. And he was also at Captain Beidermann's retirement party. Now, don't you think you could have at least picked up a little bit of that information regarding Detective Chason before you told me a nameless civilian was on the phone?"

Officer O'Mara considered that.

"Yes, sir. I suppose I should have."

"Good boy!" Sabara said.

"Thank you, sir," Officer O'Mara said, pleased to have been complimented.

"Thank you for seeing me, Captain," Phil said when Officer O'Mara — after telling Chason who his father was, and that he understood they were Academy classmates — had taken him into Sabara's office.

"Any friend of Karl's . . ." Sabara said. "He and I went to Wheel School together. He was a sergeant . . ."

He waved Chason into an upholstered chair.

"Now that I'm here," Chason said, "I'm beginning to wonder if this was such a hot idea."

"You said you wanted fifteen minutes. You've got it."

"All I've really got is that a guy I suspect — can't prove — has ties to the mob wants — is willing to pay a thousand dollars for — the names of some narcs, and told me a complicated bullshit story to explain why."

"Who's the guy you think has ties to the mob?"

"Joey Fiorello," Phil said. "He runs a car lot on Essington Avenue —"

515

"I know who Joey is," Sabara interrupted. "Why does he want the names of the narcs?"

"I don't know, but the story he gave me is bullshit."

"You want to start at the beginning?" Sabara said. "How did you come into contact with Joey Fiorello?"

"Well, I went out on medical disability. I got bored, so I got myself a private investigator's license and put an ad in the yellow pages. About a year ago, Fiorello called me, said he saw the ad."

"Called you to do what?"

"What I guess you could call a background investigation. He said he was thinking of offering a guy a job as a salesman, sales manager, and wanted to know about him. I checked out the first one, he was a solid citizen. A couple of months later, same story. Another solid citizen. And he called me a third time, just a little while ago. This time the guy was a real sleazeball, a stockbroker named Ketcham."

"What was that name?"

"Ketcham, Ronald R. You know it?"

"Tommy!"

Officer O'Mara put his head in the door.

"See if Sergeant Washington is upstairs, will you? If he is, here, now, Tommy."

"Yes, sir."

"Who's Sergeant Washington?" Phil asked.

"Great big black guy? Used to work Homicide? The Black Buddha?"

"Jason's here, and a sergeant?"

"I don't how he feels about being a sergeant,

516

but he doesn't like being here."

Officer O'Mara reported that Sergeant Washington was not in the building but Detective Harris was.

"Ask him to join us, please, Tommy," Sabara said.

"Tony Harris, too?" Phil asked.

"Equally unhappy at not being in Homicide," Sabara said.

Tony Harris came into the office two minutes later.

"Jesus, look what the tide washed up. The poor man's Sam Spade."

"Fuck you, Tony!" Phil replied.

Sabara was pleased. Obviously, Harris and Chason were friends. That spoke well for Chason, who had spent twenty-six years on the job, but whom Sabara could not remember ever having seen before he walked into his office.

"Mr. Chason was just telling me that he was engaged just a few days ago to investigate Mr. Ronald R. Ketcham," Sabara said.

"No shit?" Tony asked, looking at Phil.

Phil nodded.

"How did you know we're looking for him?"

"I didn't, but I'm not surprised. He's a sleazeball."

"You didn't see the Locate, Do Not Detain?" Sabara asked, just to be sure.

"No, I didn't."

"Who hired you to check Ketcham out?" Tony asked.

"Joey Fiorello," Phil said.

Tony grunted.

"You don't happen to know where he is, do you, Phil?"

"Sorry."

"The other interesting thing Mr. Chason had to say, Tony, was that Fiorello is also interested in learning the names of some other narcotics officers."

"Narcotics Five Squad officers?" Tony asked quietly.

"I don't know about that, but there was a drug bust at the Howard Johnson motel last Thursday. . . ."

"That's interesting," Sabara said.

"Can I ask what's going on?" Phil asked.

"That's a tough one," Sabara began. "Mr. Chason, we're working on something — I can't answer that question. You understand."

"Horseshit," Tony Harris said. "Mike, I've known Phil for twenty years. If there are two honest cops in the whole department, Phil's the other one. The more he knows about what we're trying to do, the more useful he's going to be."

That was a clear case of insubordination. Not to mention using disrespectful language to a superior officer. And, for that matter, Harris was clearly guilty of being on duty needing a shave and a haircut.

But on the other hand . . .

"The *other* honest cup? You mean you and him?"

"Well, maybe Washington and Wohl, too," Harris said. "That would make four, but I'm not so sure about Wohl. . . ."

"For the record, Tony, I told you not to tell him . . ."

"So report me."

". . . so I will tell him," Sabara finished. "With the understanding none of this leaves this room, Mr. Chason?"

"Yes, sir."

"Vincenzo Savarese's granddaughter is in the psychiatric ward of University Hospital, in pretty bad condition," Sabara began. "Somebody called up there and said she had been orally raped."

"I don't get the connection," Phil said.

"Ronald R. Ketcham is the girl's boyfriend," Tony said. "And no one seems to know where he is."

"Ketcham must be a ladies' man," Chason said. "What I heard was he was carrying on hot and heavy with a Main Line — Bala Cynwyd — princess named Longwood."

"Same girl, Phil," Tony Harris said.

"And she's Savarese's granddaughter? And this guy raped her? Don't hold your breath until you find him, Tony," Phil said and then had a chilling thought.

"Oh, shit! And I told Joey Fiorello, who told Savarese . . ."

"How were you to know?" Tony Harris said. "Phil, let's start at the beginning again. Maybe there's something there."

"About a year ago," Phil began.

Despite his intention to rise at noon, Detective Harry Cronin had woken a little after three P.M. to the sound of cooking utensils banging in the

519

kitchen. He rose from the couch and went into his kitchen.

"Hi, baby!" he said to Mrs. Cronin.

She gave him a sadly contemptuous look but did not reply.

"I'm sorry about last night, honey. What happened was I went by the Red Rooster —"

"And got plastered," Patty finished for him.

He accepted the accusation with a chagrined nod.

"Just because you're back on nights, Harry," Patricia said, "does not mean you're going to start going to the Red Rooster and —"

"It was a one-time thing, baby."

"It better have been, Harry," Patty said, then closed the conversation by adding, "You better take a shower and a shave. It's time for you to go to work."

"Right," Harry agreed.

When he came back downstairs, shaved, showered, and ready both to go to work and apologize, sincerely, to Patty for his lapse, she wasn't in the house.

So there had been nothing to do but go to work, and he had done so.

It turned out to be a slow night, and there had been a chance for him about ten o'clock to go into a drugstore and buy Patty a large box of assorted Whitman's chocolates as sort of a let's-be-friends-again peace offering.

Patty was always pleased when he bought her a box of Whitman's. She might forgive him. On the other hand, for the next two weeks or whatever, until the chocolates were gone, whenever she ate one, she would be reminded of why he had given them to her.

What the hell, he decided. *She has a right to be pissed. Buy the chocolates anyway.*

Later, he was pleased with his decision. There was no place he could have conveniently bought flowers — which would last only a couple of days — and flowers would have been a confession he had *really* fucked up, not only had a couple more drinks than he should have had.

At five minutes after midnight, he got into his four-year-old Chevrolet full of resolve not to go to the Red Rooster, but home, where he would fix things up with Patty.

His route took him past a deserted NIKE site.

He slowed and took a good long look. There was nothing. No lights. No sign of activity. Zilch.

But Harry Cronin knew that something was going on in that goddamn NIKE site.

He had absolutely nothing to support this belief except the intuition that comes to intelligent men with nineteen years on the job, thirteen of them as a detective.

He had had this feeling about the NIKE site from the time the Army had moved out, although at that point it was more a logical suspicion that — deserted buildings attract illegal activity — some kind of illegal activity would take place in the future.

But the feeling Harry had then was not the feeling he had now. Now he *knew* something wrong was going on at the NIKE site, and he *knew* that it was something more than somebody talking his girl into going into one of the buildings with mutual criminal intent to violate the still-on-the-books statutes prohibiting fornication.

And Cronin didn't think it was dope. Dope dealers need a reasonably discreet location to serve their clientele. A string of people making their way through the hurricane fence from the street to the buildings and then back out would attract unwanted attention.

Philadelphia police officers had no authority inside the fence, but the moment someone walked back out through the gate in the fence, with that day's supply of joints, or whatever, they would again fall under Philadelphia police authority.

What went on inside the hurricane fence with the now-getting-a-little-rusty "U.S. Government Property. Trespassing Forbidden Under Penalty of Law" warning signs attached at twenty-five-foot intervals to the fence was absolutely none of Detective Harry Cronin's business, and he knew it.

Having reminded himself of all this, he decided to go with his gut feeling, even if that meant he would be a little late getting home and Patty would sniff his breath the minute he walked in the door.

He slowed even further, and made a U-turn and drove back to the gate in the hurricane fence.

When he got out of the car and opened the gate, it occurred to him that, in the eyes of the feds, he was probably an illegal trespasser. And with his luck, some overpaid federal bureaucrat, to make a little overtime, would make one of his twice-a-year four-hour detailed inspections of the property right about now.

That meant he would drive past the place probably faster than Harry had, without stopping. That would be four hours on his overtime time sheet.

Harry almost had second thoughts.

But there was a place scraped free of rust on the gate hinges.

Somebody's been in here, and recently. Fuck it. If I don't go in, I'll be up all night wishing I had.

He drove slowly around the compound, flashing his flashlight into dark corners, wishing that he had with him the six-cell flashlight he carried in his unmarked car, rather than the little two-celler he kept in the glove compartment of the Chevrolet.

Zilch.

But then the headlights, not the flashlight, picked up tire tracks in the mud. The mud hadn't had a chance to dry completely.

Harry deduced, *Some son of a bitch has been in here, and in the last couple of days.*

Probably the bureaucrat.

But maybe not.

He stopped the Chevrolet and got out and examined the tire tracks sufficiently to determine they were truck tires, light truck tires. From a pickup truck, not passenger tires.

What the hell is going on around here?

He walked to the nearest building and shone his light on the exposed hinges of the steel door. Bright scratches in the rusted metal told him the door had recently been opened.

He pushed the door open and went inside.

He walked down the corridor.

The smell of feces and urine assailed his nostrils.

Some fucking bum is in here. Or was in here. I hope was. The last thing I want right now is to find some dead bum in here. I'd never get home tonight. What a smart man would do would be turn around and get his ass out of here.

There were three doors opening off the corridor. Two of the doors were open.

In one of the rooms, his nostrils found the source of the smell of feces.

And a pile of clothes.

Nice clothes. Not a bum's clothes.

What the hell is going down in here?

The third door was closed, with latches that reminded Cronin of his time as Fireman First Class, USN.

The last time he had been in here, all the doors had been open.

Harry worked the levers and pushed the door inward.

Somebody's taken a dump in here, too.

What the fuck is that?

"Listen, we have to talk!" a naked man sitting against the wall with an overcoat over his shoulders said plaintively. "Please, let's talk!"

"I'm a police officer," Harry said. "Everything's going to be all right."

"Thank God!" the man said.

"You want to tell me what happened?"

"You're a policeman?"

"Detective Cronin, South Detectives."

"Look, all I want to do is go home. Where's my clothes?"

"What did you say your name was?"

"All I want to do is go home."

"I don't think that's going to be possible right now," Harry said. "Now, what did you say your name was?"

"I don't have to tell you a goddamn thing!" the naked man said with absolutely no confidence, but a certain desperation, in his tone.

What the fuck do I do now? I'm off-duty. I've got no authority inside that fucking fence. And, since I'm in my own car, I don't even have a goddamn radio to call this in!

Matt Payne, who had been watching a program of television commercials interrupted by three-minute segments of a John Wayne leading the cavalry against the Chiricahua Apache movie, jumped out of bed when there was a knock at the door, went to it, stood behind it, and pulled it open first a crack, then all the way.

"It's not that I am not delighted to see you, but does your mommy know where you are, little girl?"

"I hope not," Susan said. "Would it be too much to ask you to put your shorts on?"

"Don't trust yourself, eh?"

"Oh, God!"

"What did you do, sneak out?"

He went to the chest of drawers, found a pair of Jockey shorts, and pulled them on.

"Okay?"

"Thank you."

"Under the circumstances, I suppose a blow —"

"I've heard that before, Matt — my God, you can be vulgar! — and I don't think it's funny."

"Why do I have this unpleasant feeling that we are about to have a very serious conversation?"

"Because we are," Susan said. "I've been thinking."

"Pure, asexual thoughts only, obviously."

"I've been thinking about what you said at lunch."

"I said a lot of things at lunch," Matt replied. "You mean about letting me arrest Jennifer?"

Susan nodded. "Would that work?"

"It's iffy, honey," Matt said now serious. "Starting with the first premise, that she can get away from Chenowith."

"She met me alone the last time. Behind a restaurant in Doylestown. And she had their baby with her."

"And if she doesn't bring the baby this time?"

"Matt, this was your idea in the first place."

"I'm trying to think of all the things that can — and probably will — go wrong."

"Tell me what will happen from the moment you arrest her."

"Well, I put the cuffs on her — and there's problem one, because I don't have any handcuffs."

"Excuse me?"

"My handcuffs are in Philadelphia. When you first go on the job, you carry your handcuffs with you all the time. After a while, you realize (a) that not only aren't you using them very much — in my case, never — and (b) that they're uncomfortable to carry around, so you start leaving them at home, which is where mine are."

"Is that important?"

"Yeah, it's important. From what you tell me, Jennifer is not going to go to the slammer willingly. I'm going to have to immobilize her."

"Can you buy a pair of them here?"

"I don't know. I'll have to do something."

"And then what?"

"Well, I could put her arm behind her back, and physically restrain her — which isn't as easy as it looks in the movies — until I can get on the radio and call for the local cops. I'm not sure, problem two, if the Doylestown cops are on one of my frequencies. We'd have to play that by ear."

"I'm confused."

"Presuming she will meet you in Doylestown, we won't know if I can call the cops on the radio until we get there and I can try it. Let me put it this way. Best possible situation. I put handcuffs on her, throw her in the back of the car, and drive her to the Doylestown Police Station. They'll hold her for me — I think — if I identify myself as a Philadelphia cop who has made an arrest in their jurisdiction. . . ."

Matt stopped, obviously having had another, distressing, thought.

"What?" Susan asked, picking up on this.

"If the Doylestown cops, or the state police, see you, they'll wonder who you are. So we can't let them see you. And . . ."

He stopped again, and then, after a long moment, shrugged.

527

"What's that shrug of resignation all about?" Susan asked.

He met her eyes.

"My orders are quite clear," he said. "I am not to do anything but inform the FBI when I think you are about to go meet any member of the Chenowith Group. I am not supposed to try to make the collar by myself. I've been told that by everybody but the mayor."

"So you'll be in trouble?"

He nodded.

"And you don't want to do it, now that you've thought it over?"

"I didn't say that," he said. "What we're doing now is talking. The money is another problem. My priority is to get you out of this mess. I'm trying to figure the best way to do that. And the thing we have to keep in mind is what Lincoln said."

"What *Lincoln* said?"

" 'You can fool all of the people some of the time, and some of the people all of the time, but you can't fool all of the people all of the time,' " Matt quoted. "We'll be dealing here with some very bright people. We —"

"You're talking about the cops?"

He nodded. "And the FBI. Most of what really will have happened is going to come out. Right now, they can't prove — although I'm sure they suspect — that you've been holding the money for them. Maybe throwing the money in the river is the best thing to do with it. You would have to lie under oath — or at least claim the Fifth Amendment — that you never had it."

528

"I'm not a very good liar."

"You're better than you think you are," he said. "On the other hand, we could try this. . . ."

He stopped, and visibly considered what he was about to say until Susan's curiosity got the best of her.

"What, Matt?"

"It's closer to the truth. Hell, it is the truth. Our story is that I made you realize the error of your ways. I convinced you that holding the money for these people was the wrong thing to do, and that your only chance was to cooperate with the authorities — me — and you (a) turned the money you had been holding over to me, and (b) arranged for me to meet, and thus be able to arrest, Jennifer, in exchange for me offering you immunity from prosecution."

"Can you do that?"

"I wish I could. No, I can't. But cops have lied before, to get information they want, and if a lawyer can make the jury feel sorry for the accused, because she — you — were lied to, they might go a little easier on you. Maybe, knowing they were facing a damned good lawyer, the U.S. Attorney might decide to *nol pros* that one charge. It's unlikely, but possible. He's got other charges against you — meeting Chenowith in the Poconos, for one example — that he's not going to have any trouble proving."

"I am going to prison, aren't I?"

"It looks that way," Matt said almost idly. "But going with this repentant-sinner line, let me think out loud a little more. Are you *sure* you know where Chenowith is?"

"I know where they were living, if that's what you mean."

"You could lead someone there?"

"I'm not going to lead the FBI there, if that's what you're suggesting, not with Jennie and the baby in the house. He's not just going to give up, and you told me he's got a machine gun. I don't want Jennie or the baby shot."

"How do you feel about this?" Matt asked. "We meet Jennie. She has the baby. I arrest her. We take the money — hers and yours — and turn it over to the FBI. Who you then lead to Chenowith's house. It seems to me that a good lawyer just might be able to convince a jury that the repentant sinner was really trying to make things right, and was a nice person, to boot. She didn't want to tell the FBI where Chenowith was until she was sure the other misguided innocent, Jennifer, and her appealing babe-in-arms, were safe from danger from both the wicked Chenowith and the noble forces of law and order. But once she was sure the —"

"I don't like you very much when you sound so cynical," Susan said.

"Oh, Jesus!"

"Sorry."

"While we were talking about this — you being repentant and wanting to make amends — the situation was unexpectedly brought to a crisis when Jennifer called, announced she wanted to get away, in fear of her life, from the monster Chenowith, and we had to act."

Susan looked at him, her lips pursed, for a long moment.

"How did we act?" she asked finally.

"I call Jack Matthews, and tell him I have to talk to him. He meets us in the restaurant. In Doylestown. While we are explaining to Jack how you have decided to do the right thing, Jennifer shows up — so far as Matthews is concerned — much earlier than she is supposed to. There is no time for Matthews to summon the Anti-Terrorist Group, or, for that matter, the local cops. We arrest Jennifer. You tell her not to say a word to anybody about anything until she's talked to a lawyer."

"She might not listen to me. As far as she is concerned, I will have betrayed her. Which is what I would have done."

"Get it through your head, goddamn it, that neither of you is going to walk on this. All we can do is cut our losses. If Jennifer insists on being a revolutionary heroine, that's her choice. And once she does that, you shift into your save-my-own-ass mode. Otherwise, you're going down the toilet with her."

"Maybe that's what's going to happen anyway," Susan said.

"What about us? Does this nutty bitch mean more to you than I do?"

She met his eyes, then shook her head.

"You know better than that," she said.

"There's something I think I should tell you," Matt said. "I was thinking about this too, watching that stupid cowboys-and-indians movie. And my solution to this problem — and I had damned near made the decision, before you knocked at the door — was to go out to your house, get your father out of bed, tell him all about the fucking mess you're in, and tell him that as far as I'm concerned, the best thing he can do for you is to convince you that your only chance to keep from going to jail for a long, long time is to go to the FBI right now and not only show them where Chenowith is, but cooperate with everything they ask you to do."

"You mean, without considering Jennifer and the baby at all?"

"Who's more important, what's more important? Us, or Jennifer?"

She looked into his eyes but said nothing.

"Honey, I don't want you to go to jail," Matt said. "I want to spend my life with you." His voice broke. "I love you, goddamn it!"

She touched his face.

"Oh, Matt!"

"Honey, I've been in women's prisons. Jesus Christ, I don't even want to think of you being in one of them."

"I don't want to go to prison," she said. "But I can't just — cut Jennifer loose. I just can't!"

"Even if it fucks us up once and for all?"

"Can we at least try to help Jennie and her baby?" Susan asked.

"And if it doesn't work? And I have to tell you, I don't think it will."

"I would have tried," Susan said.

"Is it that important to you?"

She nodded.

"I wish it wasn't," she said.

"Okay," Matt said. "We'll give it a shot."

"Thank you."

"You're welcome."

Lieutenant Daniel Justice, Jr., reputedly the smallest, and without question the most delicate-looking White Shirt in the Philadelphia Police Department, was sitting at the lieutenant's desk in South Detectives when Detective Harry Cronin walked in.

"Danny the Judge," as he was universally known, was connected by blood and marriage to an astonishing number of police officers, ranging from a deputy commissioner to a police officer six months out of the Academy. It was said that his mother needed help to raise her left wrist, on which she wore a charm bracelet with a miniature badge for each of her relatives on the job, including her husband, Detective Daniel Justice, Sr., Retired, known of course as "Big Danny."

The only scandal ever to taint the name of the Justice family occurred when "Danny the Judge," in hot pursuit of a sixteen-year-old car thief he had detected trying to break into an automobile, slipped on the ice and broke his wrist.

"To what do we owe the honor of your presence, Cronin, at this hour of the morning?" Danny the Judge asked.

"I need a favor, Lieutenant," Harry Cronin asked.

Danny the Judge could see in Cronin's face that whatever it was, it was important.

"What?" he asked.

"Call my wife and tell her I'm working," Harry Cronin said.

"Are you?"

"Yes, sir."

"Doing what?"

"I'd appreciate it if you'd call my wife first, Lieutenant," Harry said.

Danny the Judge looked at him a moment, then consulted a typewritten list of the home phone numbers of all the detectives in South Detectives, found Cronin's number, and called it.

"Patty? Dan Justice. Harry asked me to call. He's on the job and can't tell right now when he'll get home."

There was a pause as Mrs. Cronin replied.

"Patty, I wouldn't do that. When I tell you Harry's on the job, he's on the job. As soon as he can find a minute, I'll have him call you himself."

Danny the Judge replaced the telephone in its cradle and looked at Detective Cronin.

"Okay, Harry. Tell me how you're really on the job."

"I think it would be best if you came with me, Lieutenant," Cronin said.

Danny the Judge rose from behind his desk — it was rumored that when he was seated behind the desk, his feet did not quite reach the floor — and followed Harry Cronin down to the parking lot and to Harry's Chevrolet.

In the backseat was a man wearing a too-small overcoat and handcuffs.

534

And what looked like nothing else.

Danny the Judge looked closer to confirm the nothing else.

"Who's this?"

"You have absolutely no reason to hold me against my will," the man wearing handcuffs and a too-small overcoat said without much conviction in his voice.

"His name is Ketcham, Ronald R."

"Really? Didn't you think that the Locate, Do Not Detain meant 'Do Not Detain'?"

"Sir?" Cronin asked. It was the first he'd heard of the Locate Do Not Detain.

"Where's Mr. Ketcham's clothes?"

"I left them back there," Harry said.

"Where's 'there,' Harry?" Danny the Judge asked, a tone of impatience entering his voice.

"In the NIKE site," Harry said. "I found this guy, wearing nothing but the overcoat, locked up in one room, and his clothes in another."

"In the NIKE site? What the hell were you doing in the NIKE site?"

"I had a gut feeling that there was something wrong in there," Harry said. "So I went and had a look, and there he was."

Danny the Judge looked at Mr. Ketcham.

"Mr. Ketcham, what were you doing in the NIKE site?"

"I'm not going to say a word until I have a chance to consult with my attorney."

"Yes, sir," Danny the Judge said and turned to Harry. "You left his clothes there?"

"Yes, sir. I went through them until I found his wallet. But I thought . . ."

"We'll be with you in just a minute, Mr. Ketcham," Danny the Judge said and closed the door of Harry's Chevrolet.

He signaled Harry to follow him back into the building.

"You know, Harry, right, that we have no authority inside that fence? It's federal property?"

"Yes, sir."

They entered the building, and Lieutenant Justice signaled to the trainee behind the glass window to open the door.

"Wait," he said to Harry, then went through the door, where he removed the clipboard from its peg and read the Locate, Do Not Detain on Ketcham, Ronald R. again.

He first thought he should call his brother-in-law the deputy commissioner. There was no question that what he had in his hands was shortly going to come to the attention of the upper echelons of the Philadelphia Police Department.

But the Locate, Do Not Detain — more than a little unusually — specifically ordered that ChInsp. Coughlin, Insp. Wohl and/or Sgt. Washington be notified immediately.

It had been Lieutenant Justice's experience that one got one's ass a little less deep in a crack if one followed one's orders to the letter, rather than doing what seemed like the logical thing to do.

He turned to the sergeant on duty.

"You know what kind of a car Cronin drives?"

"Yes, sir."

"There's a man in the backseat. Get him out of there. Put him, alone, in a detention cell. A clean detention cell. Take the cuffs off him and

536

get him a couple of blankets. Don't talk to him, and don't let him near a telephone."

"Yes, sir."

Taking the Locate, Do Not Detain with him, Danny the Judge left the office and motioned for Detective Cronin to follow him up the stairs.

He took a copy of the Philadelphia *Daily News* from the sergeant's desk, handed it to Cronin, and ushered him into the captain's office.

"Read the newspaper, Harry," he ordered. "And stay in here. And don't talk to anybody."

"Yes, sir," Detective Cronin said. By now he had come to deeply regret having taken a look around the NIKE site.

Danny the Judge went back to the lieutenant's office, consulted the Locate, Do Not Detain, and dialed a number.

"Dan Justice at South, Chief," he said. "I hope I didn't wake you up?"

"How are you, Danny? How's Margaret?" Chief Inspector Dennis V. Coughlin replied.

"Just fine, Chief. About that Locate, Do Not Detain on a man named Ketcham?"

"You found him?"

"Yes, sir. I just put him in a detention cell downstairs."

"It said 'do not detain,' Danny," Coughlin said.

"Chief, I think it might be a good idea if you came down here."

"What happened, Danny?"

"A detective — Harry Cronin — found him

537

wearing nothing but an overcoat in one of the NIKE sites."

"They're federal property," Coughlin said. "Wearing nothing but an overcoat, you said?"

"Yes, sir."

"You notify anybody? The feds?"

"No, sir. This is my first call."

"Don't call anybody else. No. Call Inspector Wohl and Sergeant Washington — you have their numbers — put the arm out for them, if necessary, and ask them to meet me there as soon as they can get there."

"Yes, sir."

"And I mean, don't call anybody else, Danny. And don't let Mr. Ketcham call anybody until I get there."

"Yes, sir."

"And don't let the detective — Cronin? —"

"Yes, sir."

"— talk to anybody, or get away."

"Yes, sir."

"Inspector Wohl," Peter said to the telephone, aware that despite his best intentions, he had not been able to answer the official telephone beside his bed soon enough to prevent Amelia A. Payne, M.D., who was sleeping with her head on his chest, from waking.

"Dan Justice, sir, at South Detectives."

"How are you, Danny?" Wohl replied. "What's up?"

Amy pushed herself off him, sat up, and looked down at him. Inspector Wohl was not sure whether it was in annoyance or simple female curiosity.

"We located Ketcham, Ronald R., sir," Danny the Judge said.

"Great! Where is he?"

"In the detention cell downstairs, Inspector."

"Danny, that was a Locate, Do Not Detain!"

"Yes, sir," Danny the Judge admitted, sounding a little sheepish. "Inspector, I just talked to Chief Coughlin. He told me to put the arm out for you and Sergeant Washington, and to tell you to meet him here."

"Okay. Where was Ketcham, Dan?"

"One of our detectives — Harry Cronin — found him in a deserted NIKE site. Wearing nothing but an overcoat."

"Let me have that again?"

"Harry Cronin found him in one of the NIKE sites. His clothing was in one room, and he was locked up in another."

"I'll be damned," Peter said. "You talk to Washington yet?"

"He's next, sir."

"Tell him I'll be in my car in three minutes, and to give me a call if he wants me to pick him up; it's on my way."

"Yes, sir."

Wohl replaced the telephone in its cradle and sat up.

"Tell me why you'll be damned, Peter," Amy said.

"Go back to sleep, honey. I've got to go to South Detectives."

"Who is Ronald . . . What was that? 'Ketcham'?"

"Oh, Jesus, honey!"

"The way you said that, I really want to know."

"The missing boyfriend," Peter said.

"Cynthia Longwood's boyfriend?"

Wohl nodded.

"He's been arrested? What for?"

"Honey, it's sort of complicated," Peter said as he swung his feet out of bed and stood up.

"I want to know, Peter. I have a right."

"The minute there's anything I can tell you, I will. I promise," Wohl said as he took linen from a chest of drawers and ripped open the paper wrapped around a stack of laundered shirts.

"You're going to see him?" Amy asked, and before he could reply, added: "I'm going with you."

"No, you're not," Wohl said firmly. "Honey, as soon as I have anything for you, I'll tell you."

One corner of her mind was impressed with the rapidity with which he was changing from a naked man — a naked lover — into a fully dressed police officer.

Is that what married life would be like with him? The phone rings in the middle of the night, he throws on his clothes like a quick-change artist, and he goes out to return who the hell knows when?

"Peter, I want to go with you. You wouldn't even know about him — how did you get his name, by the way? — if it wasn't for me."

"Amy, please don't push me on this," Peter said.

She didn't reply. She pushed herself up so that her back rested on the headboard, folded her arms under her breasts, and watched as he tied his necktie without using a mirror.

He went into his bedside table for his revolver, slipped it into a waist holster, and leaned down to kiss her.

"If I can't get back here, I'll call you," he said.

The kiss she gave him was considerably less enthusiastic than the previous kiss had been.

And then he was gone.

She didn't move for several minutes, during which time she heard the sound of his car door opening and closing, the sound of his engine starting, and then of the car driving away.

Then she reached for the telephone book on the shelf under the bedside table, started to thumb through it, and realized there was probably a quicker way to get the information she needed, plus directions on how to get there.

She dialed the telephone.

"Police radio."

"Could you give me the address of South Detectives, please?"

"Is there some way I can help you, ma'am?" the female voice countered.

"This is Dr. Payne, of University Hospital," Amy said. "I just got a call asking me to meet Chief Inspector Coughlin at South Detectives. I need to know where it is and the best way to get there?"

"You're at University Hospital, Doctor? Could you give me the number?"

"I'm at the residence of Inspector Wohl," Amy said. "The number here is . . ."

The police radio operator decided the call was legitimate. She had, within the past five minutes,

received calls from both Chief Inspector Coughlin and Inspector Wohl announcing they were en
route to South Detectives, and she knew the
number the caller had given was that of the official residence telephone of Inspector Wohl.

She gave Dr. Payne what was in her opinion
the quickest way to get from the 800 Block of
Norwood Street in Chestnut Hill to South Detectives at this hour of the morning.

"Do you want me to tell Chief Coughlin you're
on your way, Doctor?"

"That won't be necessary," Amy said. "He
knows I'll get there as soon as I can. Thank you
very much."

Amy hung up and got out of bed and started
to get dressed.

The police radio operator opened her microphone.

"Isaac Three."

"Go ahead."

"Chief, I just spoke with Dr. Payne. She's en
route to South Detectives."

"Give me that again?"

"Dr. Payne is en route to South Detectives."

"Okay. Thank you," Chief Coughlin said and
dropped the microphone on the seat of his car.
And added, "Oh, shit!"

Sergeant Leonard Moskowitz of South Detectives had figured that he owed Mickey O'Hara a
big one since the previous December, when
Mickey had arranged for a photograph of his
eldest son, Stanley, at his bar mitzvah at Temple
Israel to be prominently displayed in the society

section of the *Bulletin.*

This might not entirely repay Mickey for his kindness, but it would be at least a down payment.

"O'Hara," Mickey answered his telephone somewhat sleepily.

"Lenny Moskowitz. I didn't call you."

"What didn't you say when you didn't call me?"

"I don't know what the hell this is all about, Mickey, but I thought you might be interested."

"In what?"

"About an hour ago, Harry Cronin, who went off at midnight, brought a citizen in here wearing nothing but an overcoat. Danny the Judge put him in a detention cell, and Harry in the captain's office. Then he called Denny Coughlin, Inspector Wohl of Special Operations, and Jason Washington of Homicide."

Jason doesn't work in Homicide anymore. I'm surprised Moskowitz doesn't know that.

"And?"

"They're all here. Plus some guy, a heavy hitter, from the FBI. And a lady doctor."

"Has the guy in the overcoat got a name, Lenny?"

"Ketcham, Ronald."

"Nice not to talk to you, Lenny. I owe you a big one."

"I figure I still owe you," Sergeant Moskowitz said and hung up.

On being advised by Lieutenant Daniel Justice that Mr. Michael J. O'Hara of the *Bulletin* was in the building and desired a minute or two of his time, Chief Inspector Dennis V. Coughlin left the small room equipped with a one-way mirror adjacent to the interview room and went to speak to him.

"We're going to have to stop meeting this way, Mickey," he greeted him. "People will start to talk."

"Ah, Denny, you silver-tongued devil, you!"

"I'd love to know who tipped you to this. He would be on Last Out for the rest of his life, walking a beat in North Philly." Last Out was the midnight-to-eight shift.

"What do you mean, 'who tipped me'? I was on my way home, Denny, for some well deserved rest, when what do I hear on the radio? You're coming here. Peter Wohl is coming here. So I figured, what the hell, I'd come down here, we'd all have a cup of coffee, chew the rag a little —"

"Chew the rag a little about what, for example?"

"For example, why did you put the arm out for Mr. Ronald R. Ketcham?"

"Ronald R. Ketcham? I don't seem to recall the name."

"And why, if it was a Locate, Do Not Detain, did he wind up in a holding cell?"

"A holding cell?"

"Wearing nothing but an overcoat."

"Mickey, you have your choice between me throwing you out of here myself, or agreeing to really sit on this one. And that may mean permanently sitting on it. Now and forever."

"You got a deal, Denny."

"I'll fill you in later," Coughlin said. "I don't

544

want to miss any of this."

He waved O'Hara into the small room with the one-way mirror adjacent to the interview room. There Mr. O'Hara found Inspector Peter Wohl; Amelia Payne, M.D.; Mr. Walter Davis, Special Agent in Charge of the Philadelphia office of the Federal Bureau of Investigation; a well-dressed individual Mr. O'Hara correctly guessed was also in the employ of the FBI; and Lieutenant Daniel Justice.

Through the one-way mirror, he saw Sergeant Jason Washington and a distraught-looking man sitting in a chair wearing nothing but a blanket around his shoulders.

Mickey waved a cheerful hello.

The FBI agent Mickey didn't recognize looked confused.

Mr. Davis of the FBI looked very uncomfortable, as did Danny the Judge.

Dr. Payne smiled at him absently, her attention devoted to what was going on on the other side of the mirror.

Inspector Wohl smiled in recognition and resignation.

Mickey helped himself to a cup of coffee, then sat down, backward, in a wooden chair and watched Sergeant Washington interviewing Mr. Ketcham.

Twenty-One

"I could use another cup of coffee, Mr. Ketcham, how about you?" Sergeant Jason Washington inquired of Mr. Ronald R. Ketcham.

"What I want is my clothes," Ketcham replied.

"Well, I certainly understand that," Washington said. "And they should be here by now. I'll check. Cream and sugar?"

"Black, please," Ketcham said.

Washington left the interview room, and closed the door after him. Ketcham, who had seen enough cops-and-robbers movies to suspect that he might be under observation by persons on the other side of the mirror, tried very hard to look righteously indignant, rather than uncomfortable.

Washington stuck his head into the room on the other side of the mirror, and motioned for everyone to come into the main office.

As Michael J. O'Hara passed through the door, Washington draped his massive arm around Mickey's shoulders.

"You will understand, old friend," Washington said, "why my usual joy at seeing your smiling face is tempered by the circumstances."

"How goes it, Jason?" Mickey O'Hara replied.

"Mickey, sit in there for a minute, will you?"

546

Chief Inspector Coughlin said, indicating Captain Henry Quaire's office. "Amy, you keep him company."

Mr. O'Hara and Dr. Payne went into Quaire's office. Chief Coughlin closed the door after them.

"You didn't get much, did you, Sergeant Washington?" Mr. Walter Davis of the Federal Bureau of Investigation asked.

"If we are to believe Mr. Ketcham, which I find difficult to do," Jason replied, "he was abducted, in what he believes to be a case of mistaken identity, from the garage of his home by persons unknown."

Inspector Wohl chuckled.

"Letting your imagination soar, Jason, what do you think happened?"

"I would hazard a guess that Mr. Ketcham has no idea who transported him to the NIKE site, beyond a deep suspicion that it has something to do with his trafficking in controlled substances," Washington said. "About which, of course, he is understandably reluctant to talk. That position, I would think, is buttressed by his being aware that he was not in possession of any narcotics at the time of his abduction."

"Put it together for me, Jason," Chief Coughlin said.

"I have several tentative theories," Washington said. "We have these facts: Mr. Ketcham was involved with Miss Longwood. To what degree we do not know. There was a telephone call to Dr. Payne at the hospital — the language of which was not consistent with the vocabulary of the caller — which alleged . . ."

547

He consulted a pocket notebook:

". . . that 'Cynthia Longwood was stripped naked and orally raped by a policeman under circumstances that were themselves traumatic.' Dr. Payne believes this is consistent with Miss Longwood's physical condition. The question then becomes, Who made the telephone call to Dr. Payne, and how did he come into possession of the knowledge of the rape?"

"Vincenzo Savarese," Mr. Walter Davis said.

Sergeant Washington looked at Mr. Davis in such a manner as to make clear he did not like to be interrupted, then went on:

"I think it is reasonable to believe that Mr. Savarese, whose deep concern for his granddaughter has been made obvious, wondered if her gentleman acquaintance, Mr. Ketcham, might have information bearing on the situation. We must keep in mind here that Mr. Savarese had to move carefully. His relationship to Miss Longwood has been carefully concealed, and if Mr. Ketcham was not involved in the assault . . ."

Wohl and Coughlin grunted, accepting Washington's theory.

"I think it bears on the equation," Washington went on, "that Mr. Ketcham has not come to the attention of either Intelligence or the Drug Unit. Neither by name or by physical description. It is possible that Mr. Savarese's contacts on the street, or within the drug community, came up with his name, but I have the feeling that was not the case, and even if it was, his acquiring that knowledge would have been after Miss Longwood required medical attention."

"Okay," Coughlin agreed.

"But it is reasonable to assume that Mr. Savarese heard — probably from his daughter — that his granddaughter was involved with a man named Ketcham."

"Yeah," Wohl said.

"Mr. Savarese naturally wondered, I theorize," Washington went on, "if perhaps Mr. Ketcham had knowledge of the cause of Miss Longwood's mental stress. Even, perhaps, if Mr. Ketcham forced himself on his granddaughter. Dr. Payne told Peter that Mr. Ketcham had not been to see Miss Longwood. It seems reasonable that Mr. Savarese would have learned this, too, from the girl's mother."

"And had Joey Fiorello," Coughlin interjected, "hire Phil Chason to make discreet inquiries regarding Mr. Ketcham . . ."

"Which discreet inquiries," Peter Wohl chimed in, "revealed exactly what kind of an upstanding citizen Ketcham is. And Chason told Fiorello."

"Precisely," Washington said. "What I don't understand, since we may presume it did come to Mr. Savarese's attention that his granddaughter was keeping company with someone who uses controlled substances — and probably introduced her to the use of them — is why Mr. Ketcham is not, to use that lovely euphemism, 'swimming with the fishes.' "

Wohl grunted in agreement.

"Once Mr. Savarese had learned that — what shall I say? — Mr. Ketcham was not a really nice fellow," Washington continued, "I think it is reasonable to presume that he ordered his minions to find Mr. Ketcham and to transport him to a place where he could be interrogated — the NIKE site — both at length and, should it turn out that Mr. Ketcham had no knowledge of what had transpired, in such a manner that there would be no connection Mr. Ketcham could make with him. I mean, in the sense that he is Miss Longwood's loving grandfather, the Mafia don."

"That constitutes kidnapping," Mr. Walter Davis interjected, "and makes it a federal offense."

Washington ignored him.

"I further postulate," he went on, "that the interrogation revealed the exact circumstances — 'that were themselves traumatic' — of Miss Longwood's rape."

"The drug bust at the Howard Johnson motel," Coughlin said.

"Yes. Mr. Ketcham — who, incidentally, I don't think has any idea of the relationship between the girl and her grandfather — almost certainly told —"

"Told who, Sergeant?" Walter Davis interrupted.

"Excuse me?" Washington said in strained courtesy, making it again clear he did not like being interrupted, even by the Special Agent in Charge of the Philadelphia office of the Federal Bureau of Investigation.

"This interrogation you're talking about. Who conducted it?"

"I have no idea," Washington said.

"You think Vincenzo Savarese was there?" Davis pursued.

"Interesting question," Washington said. "Given Mr. Savarese's demonstrated ability to distance himself from criminal activity conducted for him by others, I am tempted to say no, of course not. But this is a different circumstance. And we know of his deep concern. So my answer is, I just don't have an opinion."

"Dennis, I'd really like to get Savarese on unlawful abduction," Davis said.

"May I continue?" Washington asked.

"Go on, Jason," Coughlin said.

"At the very least, I think we can reasonably presume that Mr. Ketcham told his interrogators that Narcotics officers were present at the Howard Johnson motel. Since Mr. Ketcham didn't have any names to give him . . ."

"Back to Joey Fiorello and Phil Chason," Wohl said.

"So goes my theory," Washington said. "The reason that Mr. Fiorello knew about the drug bust at the motel was that Savarese had learned about it from Ketcham."

"And to go by the message he left for Amy," Wohl said, "Ketcham must have convinced Savarese that one of the Five Squad raped the girl; in other words, that he didn't."

"Yes," Washington said. "And now Mr. Savarese wishes to discuss the incident with the officers involved. Hence, he needs their names."

"That doesn't explain why Ketcham is still alive," Danny the Judge said. "It seems to me that just getting his granddaughter in a situation like that would be enough for Savarese to — what did Jason say? — send Ketcham 'swimming with the fishes.' "

"After first cutting him in small pieces with a dull saw," Coughlin agreed.

"I read somewhere," Wohl said softly, "that death by starvation is one of the more painful ways to die."

"You mean Savarese was just going to leave him there?" Walter Davis asked, visibly shocked.

"Now that Peter has raised the point, I believe that is entirely possible," Washington announced. "Imaginative forms of retributive homicide are consistent with the Sicilian code of honor. Dishonoring the females of the tribe is really a no-no."

"That makes it attempted murder, too," Walter Davis said.

"That would not be easy to prove," Coughlin said. "I'm not even sure we have enough to get an indictment, much less a conviction."

No one said anything, and then Coughlin had another thought. "I got the impression, Jason, that Ketcham not only has no idea who grabbed him, but didn't even get a look at them?"

Washington nodded.

"I, for one, feel that nothing has been uncovered so far that should cause us to deviate from our original plan," Washington said.

He looked at Chief Coughlin for an answer.

Wohl spoke first.

"What do you think we should do, Jason?"

"I think we should show Mr. Ketcham the photographs," Washington said. "There will be a certain shock to them. So far we haven't even touched on the fringes of the rape. If we know about that, he will reason, what else do we know?"

"That's good enough for me," Coughlin said. "Go do it, Jason."

"Just a minute," Walter Davis said.

Everyone looked at him.

"We have a chance here to prosecute Vincenzo Savarese for kidnapping and attempted murder," he said. "I would hate to lose that opportunity."

"I would prefer to strike, to coin a phrase, while the iron is hot," Washington said.

"I really would like to bring the U.S. Attorney in on this now," Davis insisted.

"Walter, what we're talking about here is the prosecution of a police officer who committed a felony — the oral rape — while acting under the shield of his office," Coughlin said.

"Dennis, I'm wholly sympathetic to your desire to uncover corruption in the Five Squad, but an opportunity like this, vis à vis Savarese . . ."

"Walter, you don't really think that slime in there is going to get up in court and testify against Savarese, do you?" Wohl said.

"I think we should discuss the whole situation with the U.S. Attorney before we take any further action."

"Go do it, Jason," Coughlin ordered, then looked at Walter Davis. "Sorry, Walter."

Davis's face was white, but he said nothing.

Wohl handed Washington a large manila envelope.

He walked out of the room and into the interview room.

Wordlessly, he took a dozen eight-by-ten-inch photographs from it and spread them on the table before Mr. Ronald R. Ketcham.

Ketcham did his best to appear to be confused by the photographs.

"Where's my clothing?" he asked. "You said someone had gone for my clothing."

"Would you please examine the photographs, Mr. Ketcham, and identify the police officer who committed oral rape upon the person of Miss Cynthia Longwood?"

"I have absolutely no idea what you're talking about."

"The time has come, Mr. Ketcham, for you to disabuse yourself of the notion that you are intellectually equipped to parry with me, and that you will somehow be able to dig yourself out of the hole you dug for yourself."

"I want my lawyer."

"We know, Mr. Ketcham. All you are doing is wasting time."

"You know what?"

"Please examine the photographs, Mr. Ketcham, and identify the police officer who, following your detention in connection with illegal trafficking in controlled substances, committed oral rape upon the person of Miss Cynthia Longwood."

"I have never been arrested in my life, and neither has Cynthia. Where the hell are you coming from?"

"If you are willing to cooperate with us in the prosecution of this police officer, which would require your testimony in a court of law, on our part we will do whatever is necessary to protect you, and additionally will not bring narcotics charges against you."

"Protect me from what? Who?"

"The same persons who took you to the NIKE site and left you there to die of starvation."

"Oh, come on. I told you the whole thing is a case of mistaken identity."

"You don't believe that any more than I do," Washington said. "Mr. Savarese knew precisely whom he ordered be taken to — and left to die a painful death by starvation at — the NIKE site."

"Mr. who?"

"Mr. Vincenzo Savarese."

"The gangster?"

"It has been alleged that Miss Longwood's maternal grandfather has a connection with organized crime."

"You're not actually trying to tell me that gangster is Cynthia's grandfather?"

"You seem surprised. You really didn't know?"

"No. I didn't know, and I don't believe it now."

"In other words, you decline to identify the rapist and cooperate with us in his prosecution?"

"I don't know what the hell you're talking about."

"We all must make decisions in our lives," Washington said. "I must in all honesty tell you I think you have just made the wrong one. But I'm sure you have your reasons. If you will wait here, Mr. Ketcham, I'll inform the FBI agent that we're through with you. Perhaps they're finished with your clothing by now."

"What does the FBI want with me?"

555

"Your being taken to the NIKE site against your will constitutes kidnapping. That's a federal offense. They will ask your help in identifying the people who committed this crime against you."

"And I will tell them the same thing I told you. I have no idea. It was obviously a case of mistaken identity."

"You don't really believe that will make any difference to Vincenzo Savarese, do you?" Washington asked. "You are the man who not only introduced his beloved granddaughter to the use of cocaine, but put her in a dangerous situation where she was brutally raped."

Washington walked to the door, put his hand on the knob, and then turned to look at Ketcham.

"Shortly after the FBI releases you — Mickey O'Hara of the *Bulletin* is outside, convinced that his many readers will be fascinated to learn about the stockbroker who was found in a deserted NIKE site wearing nothing but an overcoat — Mr. Savarese will learn you are still alive. The next time he abducts you, it will be to a place where no one will find you."

Mr. Ronald R. Ketcham looked at Detective Jason Washington, licked his lips, and announced, "The bastard that did that to Cynthia is the one on the top."

Washington said nothing.

Ketcham picked up the photograph of Officer Herbert Prasko of the Five Squad of the Narcotics Unit of the Philadelphia Police Department and held it up for Washington to see.

"He was dressed like a bum when he did it, but that's the son of a bitch!"

"You're quite sure?"

"Goddamn it, of course I'm sure. He hand-cuffed me to the toilet, and then did that to Cynthia. The filthy bastard!" Ketcham said, and then self-righteous outrage overcame his discretion. "And he stole twenty thousand dollars from me!"

"Nice job, Jason," Chief Inspector Dennis V. Coughlin said to Sergeant Washington when Washington came back into the room adjacent to the interview room.

"The question, Chief," Washington said, not quite able to convincingly pretend he was not interested in the compliment, "is now that we know, what are we going to do?"

"Who did he pick out?" Inspector Wohl asked.

"Officer Prasko," Washington said as if he had something distasteful in his voice.

"What do we have on Prasko?" Wohl asked.

"The pertinent personnel documents are in my briefcase," Washington said. "If memory serves, there was nothing significant —"

He stopped in midsentence when the door opened.

"I've taken my walk," Mickey O'Hara said, "and am not in a receptive mood for a suggestion to take another one."

"Mickey, what would it take for you to go home and call me in the morning?" Chief Coughlin replied. "With the understanding that I would fill you in completely then?"

"A blare of celestial trumpets, and a voice even deeper than Jason's saying, 'Mickey, my son, do

557

what the nice old man asks you to do.' Failing that . . ."

Wohl and Washington chuckled, which earned them a dirty look from Chief Coughlin.

"You agree to sit on it, right?" Coughlin said.

O'Hara nodded.

"Where's Amy . . . Dr. Payne?" Coughlin asked.

"She has a rather touching faith in you to do the right thing," O'Hara said. "But she is showing signs of impatience."

Coughlin went to the door, located A. A. Payne, M.D., and waved her into the room.

"Amy, honey, you realize that you really have no business here —" Coughlin began.

"Uncle Denny, you know I love you," Amy interrupted. "But right now, I think it had better be 'Chief' and 'Doctor.' "

"*Uncle Denny,*" O'Hara said highly amused, "what the good doctor means is 'cut the crap.' "

"That man wouldn't be in there if it wasn't for me," Amy said gesturing through the one-way mirror at Ronald R. Ketcham. "I need the answer to two questions, and then you'll be rid of me."

"Fair enough," Coughlin said after a just-perceptible pause. "What are the questions?"

"Did that man tell you what happened to my patient?"

"Yes, he did," Coughlin said. "The information in your message is apparently the fact."

"Do you have the name of the animal who did that to her?"

"What animal?" O'Hara asked. "Did what to who?"

558

Coughlin held his hand out to indicate Mickey should wait.

"Yes, we do," Coughlin said.

"Can I tell my patient that he is about to be arrested?"

"No. Not yet."

"Why not?" Amy snapped. "And don't even think of telling me I've had my two questions."

"Honey," Peter Wohl began, and instantly realized that Coughlin and everybody else had instantly picked up on the term of endearment. He plunged ahead. "There are several investigations going on here . . ."

"You can call me 'Doctor,' too, Inspector Wohl," Amy said.

"Look at him blush," O'Hara said. "I will be damned. Cupid's finally managed to —"

"Shut up, Mickey," Coughlin said.

"And the doctor, too," O'Hara went on, unabashed. "It's not every day you see a *doctor* blush —"

"Goddamn it, Mickey," Coughlin flared. "For once in your goddamn life, put a lid on it."

O'Hara, recognizing genuine anger, fell silent.

"As you were saying, *Inspector?*" Amy said.

"Honey," Wohl replied, heard himself with disbelief and horror repeating the term of endearment, and then decided to hell with it. "Everybody in this room wants to see Officer Prasko in a cell. But what we've got right now is just one person who can testify in court against him."

"What exactly did Officer Prasko do?" O'Hara asked.

Wohl glowered at O'Hara, then looked to Coughlin for guidance.

Coughlin shook his head in resignation.

"Okay, Mickey," he said. "This is what you sit on. Prasko committed the act of oral rape upon a young woman during a drug bust. The boyfriend, the man in the interview room, just identified him from a selection of photographs. He said that Prasko first handcuffed him to a toilet and then attacked the girl."

"Nice fellow," O'Hara said. "Where does Officer Prasko work?"

"Narcotics. Five Squad," Coughlin said.

"If you know who he is, have a witness, and know where he works, why don't you arrest him?" Amy demanded.

"I'm coming to that," Wohl said somewhat impatiently. "And that witness, if we manage to keep him alive until we can get him into court, is not going to be a credible witness."

"Keep him alive?"

"We have every reason to believe . . . the girl's grandfather —"

"Who is?" O'Hara asked.

Wohl didn't reply.

"Somebody important," O'Hara went on. "Or you wouldn't have danced around using his name. Who is he, Peter?"

Wohl again looked at Coughlin for guidance, and again Coughlin chose to answer the question himself.

"Vincenzo Savarese," he said.

"Holy Christ! And Savarese knows the name of this dirty cop?"

"Not yet. Or at least we don't think so. You're getting the idea, Mickey, why this is sensitive?"

"I'm getting the idea," O'Hara said. "So where does that guy fit in?" he asked, gesturing toward Ketcham.

"He's the girl's boyfriend," Wohl explained. "Savarese — this is the theory we're working under — suspected he might know something about what had happened to his granddaughter, scooped him up from his apartment, and took him to a deserted NIKE site for a little talk. We think the story came out."

"And that guy's still alive?"

"We think Savarese left him there to starve to death," Coughlin said.

O'Hara considered that a moment, then said: "Yeah, that fits." He nodded, then went on: "But that guy didn't identify the cop to Savarese?"

"I don't think Mr. Ketcham knew Officer Prasko's name," Washington said. "When I go back in there, I will delve into that further."

"If Officer Prasko is still alive, Vincenzo Savarese doesn't have his name," O'Hara said flatly.

"I don't need that, for God's sake!" Amy exclaimed in horror.

"Need what?" Wohl said.

"Mickey means this gangster will take the law into his own hands, right?"

"Well, maybe not the *law*, Amy," O'Hara said. "An *ax* possibly, or maybe a chain saw, something to cut Officer Prasko slowly into small pieces. . . ."

"I have a sick girl — a very nice sick girl —

561

who has been subjected to an unspeakably brutal rape. She is on the edge of schizophrenia right now. If she hears now, or at some later time, that her grandfather brutally —"

"I get the picture," Wohl said. "And believe me, we're going to try very hard to keep Savarese from getting at Officer Prasko."

"Answer Amy's question, Peter," O'Hara said. "Why don't you arrest Prasko? If nothing else, that would it make it harder for Savarese to get at him when he gets his name. And he will get his name."

"We have reason to believe the whole Narcotics Five Squad is dirty," Coughlin answered for Wohl.

"*That's* interesting," O'Hara replied. "You are going to tell me about that, right?"

"Jesus!" Danny the Judge said. It was the first time he'd heard anything about that.

"I shouldn't have to tell you, Danny," Coughlin said "that that doesn't go any further than this room. And that includes your brother-in-law, the deputy commissioner."

"Yes, sir," Danny the Judge said.

"Afterward, I'll tell him I ordered you to keep him in the dark," Coughlin said. "He won't like it, but we're too close to getting these scum to take any chance of having it go down the drain because too many people know what we're doing."

"Thank you," Danny the Judge said.

"Now that Five Squad is on the table," Wohl said, "we theorize that the rape of Miss — the girl was raped during a Five Squad drug bust.

And that the bust itself was dirty."

"How?" O'Hara asked.

"This is all speculation, Mickey," Wohl said. "But I think what we're going to find is that when Five Squad makes a bust, and there are seized drugs — and/or cash — not all of it makes it to the evidence room."

O'Hara picked up on that immediately.

"And what drug dealer is going to complain to anybody that he had three kilos of shit when he was arrested, and only two was turned in as evidence?"

"That is the theory," Washington said. "Buttressed a few minutes ago when Mr. Ketcham indignantly announced that not only had Officer Prasko raped the girl, but that he had also stolen twenty thousand dollars from him."

"What's the girl's name?" O'Hara asked.

"You don't need to know that, Mickey!" Amy said.

O'Hara ignored her.

"I can find out," O'Hara said.

"Right now, Mickey," Wohl said, "we're friends. We have been friends for a long time. Don't do anything to change that."

"That sounds like a threat," O'Hara said.

"Not a threat, a statement of fact," Wohl said.

"From me, Mickey," Coughlin said "you can consider it a threat."

"I ally myself with Chief Coughlin," Washington announced. "We are not talking of soiling the girl's reputation, we are dealing, according to Dr. Payne, with shoving the girl over the precipice into schizophrenia. Your readers do not need to know the girl's name, if schizophrenia is to be the price."

"I'm missing something here," O'Hara said. "When they try this slimeball — you *are* going to prosecute the bastard, I presume? — her name will be a matter of public record."

"My God, I didn't think of that!" Amy said in almost a wail. "If that girl is subjected to the kind of humiliation she would get in a trial, the damage would be devastating. And irreparable."

"They will, of course, correct me if I err," Washington said "but what I think Chief Coughlin and Inspector Wohl have in mind is seeing that society is protected from this individual for a very long time by seeing that he is prosecuted — and incarcerated — for all of his criminal activity *except* the rape."

"Do you think a jury is going to get all worked up because a poor, underpaid cop has ripped off a drug dealer?" Mickey said. "A good lawyer — even one six months out of law school — would have the jury voting him cop of the year."

"What I have been thinking, Dr. Payne, listening to all of this . . ." Walter Davis of the FBI began. It was the first time he had opened his mouth since Chief Coughlin had ordered Washington to proceed, over Davis's objections, with his interrogation of Ketcham. ". . . is that if we can bring to the U.S. Attorney appropriate evidence, Officer Prasko — and the others — can be prosecuted under civil rights statutes."

"Run that by me again, Walter?" Coughlin asked.

"Maybe I'm wrong, Denny," Davis said, "but

it seems to me that you and Peter are thinking that what Officer Prasko — and the others — have done is — and it certainly is — a number of things: simple theft, theft of evidence, dereliction of duty, perhaps extortion, et cetera, et cetera."

"And?" Coughlin asked.

"I'm suggesting that perhaps you haven't considered that it is a violation of an individual's civil rights — a federal felony — to extort money — or anything of value — from him, or her, under color of office."

"I don't under—" Coughlin began.

"You're saying the U.S. Attorney would prosecute these clowns for violating the civil rights of drug dealers?" Wohl interrupted.

"Yes, I think that's entirely likely."

"The 'color of office' meaning that police officers are officials of the City of Philadelphia?" Wohl pursued.

Davis nodded.

"Wouldn't that then permit the drug dealers to sue the City of Philadelphia for damages, since their civil rights had been violated by officials of the city?"

Coughlin thought: *Peter's already starting to think like a police commissioner.*

"Possibly," Davis said.

"And in a civil suit," Coughlin interjected, "presuming that these dirty cops were found guilty of violating the civil rights of drug dealers, wouldn't that be all the proof needed to find the city liable for the actions of its officers?"

"I think it would," Davis said. "But it would

also have put Officer Prasko and the others into a federal prison."

"May I suggest, gentlemen," Washington said, "that while I find these arguments fascinating, none of us — with all due respect — know what we are talking about. I think Mr. Davis is right. The U.S. Attorney should be brought into this as soon as possible, and so should our beloved District Attorney Tony Callis."

There were nods of agreement, and then Washington looked at Coughlin and went on: "If I may be permitted to make a further suggestion, Chief . . ."

"Sure."

"Mr. Callis personally. Not one of his assistants, not even Harrison J. Hormel, Esquire."

"You have a reason for saying that?" Coughlin asked.

"The same reason you gave Danny Justice here when you suggested he delay informing the deputy commissioner of the situation — to reduce the risk that the wrong people might learn of our activity."

"And what, Jason, would you suggest we do about Mayor Carlucci?" Wohl asked. "When do we tell him?"

"I am but a lowly sergeant, Inspector," Washington said. "I don't have to make dangerous decisions like that."

Coughlin looked at Wohl.

"The minute we tell him what this Prasko did, he'll go ballistic," he said. "Unless we have a plan, a detailed plan, one that he can't find fault with, he'll tell us what to do. So let's come up with one

566

— a damned good one — before we call him."

Wohl grunted his agreement.

"Have we heard anything from Harrisburg?" Washington asked.

"The last I have is that Matt doesn't have anything except that Officer Calhoun went into a safe-deposit at the bank, and that the woman in charge says she has no record of his doing so."

"That's the last I had," Washington said. "But that suggests to me there's something there."

Wohl grunted his agreement again.

"When are we going to find out more?" Coughlin asked.

"Probably in the morning," Wohl replied. "Why are you asking?"

"Calhoun may be the key to this, is what I'm thinking," Coughlin said. "Presuming there is something in the safe-deposit box. We arrest him first —"

"We don't know if he's still in Harrisburg," Washington interjected. "If, presuming he did put something incriminating in the safe-deposit box, I think it's likely that he would immediately return to Philadelphia after having done so."

"This is hanging by a thread, isn't it?" Wohl said. "So let's see what we do have, and do this one slow step at a time."

He reached for the telephone.

"Operator, person-to-person, Matthew Payne, Penn-Harris Hotel, Harrisburg . . ."

He stopped when Washington held his hand out for the telephone, then gave it to him.

From memory, Washington gave the operator the number of the Penn-Harris Hotel, and then

567

the number of Matt's room.

"Make that station-to-station, please, Operator," he said, and handed the telephone back to Wohl.

Until the third ring, Matt Payne seriously considered not answering the telephone, and even specifically — by picking it up, immediately hanging up again, and then leaving it off the hook, so that if they called back there would be a busy signal — how not to answer it.

Susan was asleep in his arms, really out. She was exhausted, he had decided, both by the intensity of their coupling — *couplings* — and by her emotional state. They had screwed, he had somewhat ungallantly decided, as if it might be the last time, and when he thought that it was a genuine possibility, the ramifications of it had brought him back to wakefulness.

She stirred but did not waken when he moved to pick up the telephone.

I'm going to have to wake her and send her home soon.

"Payne," he said softly into the telephone.

"It's Peter, Matt."

"What's up?"

"There's been a couple of unexpected developments," Wohl said. "Things are going much more quickly than anyone expected."

"What developments?" Matt asked, and then had a second thought: "Vis-à-vis which bad guys?"

"Five Squad," Wohl said. "Calhoun may be the key. Bring me up-to-date on that."

At the least the sky is not about to fall in on Susan. Or at least Peter Wohl isn't about to drop it on her. On us.

"Not much to report, beyond what I already have. I saw him go into the safe-deposit vault."

"You're sure it was Calhoun?"

"Either him or his twin brother," Matt replied. "And then when I got my contact here to ask discreet questions, he reported that the safe-deposit vault lady — her name is Adelaide Worner — had no record of anybody going into any box. As far as I'm concerned, that eliminates the possibility that I thought I made the wrong guy; if I had, she would have had a name. She denied anyone had been into a box. Ergo sum, she's lying, and I saw Calhoun."

"And what happens next?"

"I went to Lieutenant Deitrich with it. He's going to see what he can turn up for me. He said he'd get back to me at eight."

"Where?"

Matt was looking down at Susan. He felt her body tense, and then she turned her face on his chest so that she could look at him. He put his finger in front of his lips. She nodded, then sat up and looked at him.

All I want to do is put my face between her breasts and have her hold me there and caress the back of my head.

"Here."

"What do you think he might have?"

"I think I know what he's looking for — a connection between Adelaide Worner and Timothy J. Calhoun — but I have no idea if he'll find

569

one. Or what else he might come up with."

"Best possible world, Matt. Your Lieutenant Deitrich comes up with a strong enough connection so that you — I mean *you, there* — can go to a judge and get a search warrant for the box. You serve the search warrant and find something — drugs would be best, but a large amount of cash would also work — in the box . . . Wait a second . . ."

Matt heard what he presumed was the sound of a hand covering the microphone.

He looked down at Susan again. His hand reached out and he touched, almost reverently, her right nipple with the balls of his fingers. She looked down to see what he was doing, and then looked into his eyes. Her hand covered his and pressed it against her breast.

"Walter Davis just said . . ."

Christ, the FBI guy. What's going on down there?

". . . that if you have anything at all, he'll call Chief Mueller, who probably knows the right judge to go to for the search warrant."

"Okay."

"Hold it again," Wohl said and went off the line for almost a minute.

Susan moved close to Matt and kissed him tenderly, then touched his face with her hand.

Wohl came back on the line: "Chief Coughlin just decided it would be better if you didn't go to Deitrich tonight. But Mr. Davis will call Chief Mueller, as soon as I get off the phone, and call in a favor about the warrant."

"Okay."

"So. Leave it this way. At eight o'clock, you

570

will learn from Deitrich if he's come up with a connection. Or something else. Either way, you call . . . wait a second. . . . Okay. You call *Washington* as soon as possible after eight, and tell him what's happened to that point. He'll tell you either to go get the warrant and serve it, or something else. Do you happen to know if Calhoun is still out there?"

"I have no idea."

"Maybe Walter can ask Chief Mueller to have an RPC discreetly check if his car is parked at one of his relatives' houses. If that happens, Washington will let you know when you speak with him. If you learn, for sure, that he's in Harrisburg, or has left, you call Washington."

"You mean in the morning?"

"I mean whenever you find out. We're going to arrest Calhoun in any event. The question is when, and whether you will do it up there, based on what you find in the safe-deposit box, or we do it here in Philadelphia."

"Are you going to tell me what these 'new developments' are?"

"There's no time for that now. If there's time in the morning, Washington will fill you in then."

"Okay."

"Hold on once more," Wohl said, went off the line for another forty seconds, and came back on. "Mr. Davis wants to know how you're doing with the Reynolds woman."

"Tell him she's naked in my bed right now."

"Goddamn it, that's not funny! Do you have anything or don't you?"

"No, sir."

"You going to see her anytime soon?"

"Tomorrow, probably."

"Calhoun is your priority, but the other remains in place. If you think she's going to meet with Chenowith, call Jack Matthews."

"Yes, sir."

"Washington will be waiting to hear from you around eight."

"Yes, sir."

"We'll be talking," Wohl said. "Good night, Matt."

The line went dead.

" 'She's naked in my bed right now'?" Susan quoted when he had hung up the phone.

"I don't think he believed me."

"I really think you have a screw loose," she said.

"Well, now that we're wide awake, *whatever* shall we do?"

"I should get dressed and go home," Susan said.

"It's only . . ."

"Quarter past three," Susan furnished. "My God!"

"*That* late? I had no idea! Say, I just had a *marvelous* idea! Why don't you just lie back down, we'll leave a call for, say, half past five, have a good breakfast . . ."

"Matt, I had to sneak out of the house to come here. The last thing I need now is for my mother to catch me sneaking back in. Sometimes she gets up early. . . . I have to go."

"Spoken like a true member of the next generation of a Bennington mommy."

"We have enough trouble without her finding out that I've been with you all night."

"You think Mommy doesn't already have deep suspicions — with more than a little reason — that you and I have been playing Hide the Salami?"

"Of course she doesn't! Why should she? And I really hate you when you're vulgar!"

"Princess, that model of the Bennington mommy — and God knows, I know them well; your mommy, Chad's mommy, Daffy's mommy, and Penny's mommy were all stamped out of the same mold — is not really as airheaded and naive as they would have their children believe."

"Meaning what?"

"They've figured it out that if the children think they're stupid, the children won't try so hard to put something over on them, and thus they get to know what's going on."

"You really think my mother knows about us?"

"Knows? No. Not unless she's climbed the fire escape to look in the window — which I suppose is possible. But does she have deep, and justifiable, suspicions? Hell, yes, she does."

"I don't believe that!"

"Susan, you told your mother you were out with me listening to jazz in Philadelphia until six in the morning. You don't really think she believes that, do you? That all we were doing was holding hands, snapping our fingers to the music, and having good clean fun?"

Susan's face showed that she had never considered this before.

"Do you really believe this, or are you just

saying it to get me to stay?"

"I really believe it; *and* I'm saying it because I don't want you to go. And what the hell difference does it make? In three days, maybe — probably — much sooner, the fact that we've been playing Hide the Salami won't seem at all important to your mother — or, for that matter, your father. When the problem has become how to keep their Presbyterian princess out of the slam, the fact that she has been —"

"Oh, God!" Susan said. "God, you can be cruel! Sometimes I hate you!"

He looked up at her and was as astonished by the wave of fury that suddenly swept through him as he was by what he heard himself say.

"Well, fuck you, too, Susan!"

"What did you say?" she asked, horrified.

"I said 'Fuck you.' Goddamn you, go home and play the goddamn game with your god-damned mommy!"

He jumped out of bed and marched angrily into the bathroom.

He half expected her to come knock at the bathroom door. Or throw something at it. Or scream at him.

There was no response from the bedroom at all.

He looked at the closed door and decided the gentlemanly thing to do would be to give her the time to get dressed and make a dignified with-drawal from the scene of battle.

That gentlemanly decision lasted approxi-mately ninety seconds.

Fuck it! Why should I wait in here? Screw her!

He pulled the door open.

Susan, still naked, was sitting on the bed, talking on the telephone.

"Be sure to give Mommy my best regards!" Matt said nastily.

"Thank you," Susan said into the telephone, and hung up.

She looked at Matt. He saw there were tears in her eyes.

"I was ordering our breakfast," she said.

Captain David Pekach was at the urinal mounted on the wall of the bathroom of the master suite of the Peebles mansion on Glengarry Lane when the telephone rang.

He had been examining his reflected image in the mirror that lined the upper half of the wall. He was wearing silk pajamas, because he had come to understand that Martha — although she had said nothing — thought that his pre-Martha sleeping attire — a T-shirt — was a little crude.

The pajamas bore the label of A. Sulka & Company, Rue de Castiglione, Paris. Pekach had never been to Paris, although Martha thought it would be a nice place to spend at least a few days of their upcoming honeymoon.

The pajamas had been purchased by Martha's late father in Paris, and then brought home and apparently forgotten. When Pekach found them in what was now his dresser (Martha called it a chest of drawers), they were still in their cellophane packaging.

The truth was, he had just concluded when the telephone began to buzz (not ring), that he really liked the pajamas, although the buttons had been a little hard to get used to at first, and woke him up when he rolled over onto his belly. And he also liked taking a leak in the urinal, the first he had ever seen in a private home.

And he thought again that it was a shame he'd never gotten to meet Martha's father. He had apparently been one hell of a man. A man's man, and not only because he had hunted and shot at least one each of the world's big game, but also because he did things like install a urinal in his bathroom, because that's what he wanted, and to hell with what people thought.

Martha had told him she was positive her father would have loved him. Pekach wasn't so sure about that. He thought it more likely that if he were Alexander F. Peebles he would have wondered long and hard about whether Captain David Pekach was in love with his daughter or her money.

As far as Dave Pekach was concerned, if Martha didn't have a goddamned dime, she would still be the best thing that had ever happened to him in his entire life. But right now, there were only two people who believed that: he and Martha. Well, maybe Matt Payne. And probably, too, Matt's father, the lawyer.

If Brewster Cortland Payne thought all he was after was Martha's money, he would have done something about it. He'd been Martha's father's lawyer — and friend — for a long time. He wasn't going to stand idly by and just watch her get screwed. *Get taken advantage of.* If he believed that, or even suspected it, Brewster C. Payne would not be going to give the bride away when they got married. More than that, he wouldn't have gone to so much trouble to fix their getting married by both a Roman Catholic monsignor (to satisfy Dave's mother) *and* an Episcopalian (to satisfy what Martha thought her father would want).

But everybody *else* figured that he was going to marry her for her money. Nobody was willing to believe that it had been love at first sight, any more than anyone would believe that he was the first man Martha had ever gone to bed with. And, of course, he couldn't say anything about that.

When the telephone began to buzz, Dave Pekach was nowhere close to finishing what he had risen from bed to accomplish.

He was, therefore, not surprised when he went back into the bedroom to find that the bedside lights were lit, and that Martha was sitting up against the massive carved headboard (her father had bought the bed in Borneo; the most prominent of the bas-relief carvings was of a snarling tiger with ivory teeth) holding the telephone out to him.

"It's Peter Wohl, precious," she said.

Martha had long hair, which she braided at night, and which Dave thought was really beautiful. He could also see her nipples through her thin nightgown. Just the sight of Martha's nipples made his heart jump, and he sometimes wondered if that was dirty of him, or whether it was just one more proof that he loved her.

"I'm sorry you woke up," he said as he sat down on the edge of the bed.

"I always wake up whenever you get up," she said.

"Yes, sir," Dave said into the telephone.

"Sorry to do this to you, Dave," Wohl said. "But I want you in my office, in uniform, and in a Highway Patrol car as soon as you can get there."

"What's up?"

Wohl did not respond to the question.

"If I'm not there — I'm calling from South Detectives — wait for me," Wohl said, and hung up.

"What is it?" Martha asked.

"He wants me in his office right away," he said. "What time is it?"

Martha glanced at the clock on her bedside table.

"Twenty after three," she said and started to get out of bed.

"What are you doing?"

"You're not going out at this hour without at least a cup of coffee," she said.

"Sweetheart, there's no time."

"By the time you've dressed, I'll have it ready."

"You don't have to, baby."

"Precious, I want to."

He returned his attention to the telephone and dialed a number from memory.

"Special Operations, Lieutenant Malone."

"Dave Pekach, Jack. Is anything going on around there?"

"No, sir. Quiet as a tomb."

"I'm on my way in," Pekach said.

"Is something going on?"

"Beats the shit out of me," Pekach said "Wohl just put the arm on me. I have no fucking idea what he wants."

He hung up, then looked at Martha, who had a somewhat pained look on her face. "Sorry, baby."

"I understand," she said. "You're upset."

"I'm really sorry. I really try to watch my language, but sometimes I just forget."

"I understand," she said. "And I know you're trying."

"Jesus Christ, I love you!"

" 'Jesus Christ' you love me?"

He threw his hands up helplessly.

"I love you, too, precious," she said.

Twenty-Two

Gertrude — Mrs. Thomas J. — Callis reached over the curled-up body of her husband and picked up the telephone, thinking as she did so, for perhaps the five hundredth time, that if he insisted on having the phone on his side of his bed so he wouldn't disturb her when the inevitable middle-of-the-night calls came, the least the son of a bitch could do was wake up when the damned thing did ring.

"Yes?"

"Gertrude? Dennis Coughlin. I'm sorry to bother you at this —"

"I'll see if I can wake him, Denny. He's sleeping like a log."

The district attorney for Philadelphia was brought from his slumber by a somewhat terrifying feeling that he was being asphyxiated. He swatted at whatever was blocking his nostrils and mouth, and fought his way to a sitting position.

"What the hell?"

"Denny Coughlin," Gertrude said, handed him the telephone, and lay back down with her back to him.

"Yeah, Denny."

"Sorry to wake you up, Tony."

"No problem, what's up?" Callis said. He picked up the clock on the bedside table and looked at it. "Christ, it's twenty-five after three!"

"I didn't think this should wait until morning," Coughlin said.

"What wouldn't wait until morning?"

"We have just found some very dirty cops," Coughlin said.

"That won't wait until morning? Nothing personal, Denny, but these are not the first dirty cops you've found this year."

That's not true. There have been dirty cops, but Denny Coughlin didn't find them. Peter Wohl did. What's going on here?

"This is sort of complicated, Tony. What I would like to do —"

"How complicated, Denny?"

"This is a real can of worms," Denny Coughlin said. "And it won't wait. I'd rather explain it to you in person, if that would be possible. The FBI is involved, and —"

"The FBI is involved?"

"— and Walter Davis just spoke with the U.S. Attorney. He's going to meet with us right now. I just sent a car for him, and I'd like to send one for you."

"Okay. If you think it's that important, I'll give you the benefit of the doubt."

"Thank you, Tony."

"What cops, Denny? Can you tell me who?"

"I don't think you'd know the names. The Narcotics Unit Five Squad."

"And what did some narc do to attract the interest of the FBI?"

"It's more than one narc, Tony. I'm afraid it's the whole Five Squad."

"Now I'm getting interested."

"I'll explain it all when I see you," Coughlin said. "By the time you walk out your front door, there will be a Highway Patrol car waiting for you."

"Okay."

"Thank you, Tony," Coughlin said, and hung up.

Callis swung his feet out of bed. Gertrude rolled onto her back.

"You're not going out?"

"Go back to sleep, honey."

"What's going on?"

"I don't really know," Callis replied, thinking aloud. "But Denny Coughlin doesn't do something like this —"

"Like what?"

"— like sending a Highway Patrol car for me at half past three in the morning unless it's important."

"But he didn't say what?"

"Only that the FBI is involved, and that the whole Five Squad is dirty."

"What's the Five Squad?"

"The Narcotics Unit has sort of a special squad, the Five Squad, that works the more serious drug cases."

"And you have to do whatever you're going to do at half past three in the morning?"

"According to Coughlin, there's some sort of time problem," Callis said.

He didn't say that. But that's obviously what it has to be.

Callis walked into his bathroom and plugged in his electric razor.

As he was slapping aftershave on his face, he heard the wail of a far-off siren. It seemed to be getting closer, and then the sound died.

He went back into his bedroom, dressed, and leaned over the bed to kiss Gertrude.

She rolled on her back again.

"You're getting too old for this, Tony," she said. "It's not good for you to have to get out of bed at half past three in the morning."

"I think I have a couple of good years left," he said.

He pulled down a couple of slats on the venetian blinds and looked out to the street.

A Highway Patrol sergeant, with his cartridge-studded Sam Browne belt and motorcycle boots, was leaning against the fender of an antenna-festooned car, waiting for him.

That was the siren I heard. They turned it — and the flashing lights — off when they got close. And as soon as we're half a block away from the house, I'll bet they turn them on again.

The truth of the matter is, I like this. I'd make a hell of a lot more money if I went into private practice, but divorce lawyers don't often get to ride through town in the middle of the night in a Highway Patrol car with the siren screaming.

And knowing that the cops need me makes me feel like a man.

Or a boy playing at cops and robbers? Is Gertrude right? Am I getting too old for this?

I wonder what the hell this is all about?

There was not much going on at 3:40 A.M. in Central Lockup in the Roundhouse. It had been a relatively slow night (the moon was not full, for one thing) and the usual ten-thirty-to-one-A.M. busy period was over.

Sergeant Keyes J. Michaels, on the desk, had been reading the Philadelphia *Daily News* when he heard the solenoid that controlled the door from the corridor between the lobby of the Roundhouse and the Lockup room buzz.

What looked to Michaels like one more ambulance-chaser — a rumpled-looking, plump little man wearing eyeglasses and needing a shave — came through the door and walked toward Michaels's desk.

Michaels wondered how come they had passed him into Lockup — the ambulance-chasers were ordinarily not allowed in Lockup — but really didn't give much of a damn. It was almost four o'clock, and he was sleepy.

The ambulance-chaser stood patiently in front of Sergeant Michaels until Michaels raised his eyes to him.

"Can I do something for you, sir?"

"Who's the supervisor on duty? I'd like to speak to him, please?"

The supervisor on duty, Lieutenant Mitchell Roberts, after making sure that nothing further required his attention, had retired to a small room in which there just happened to be a cot.

Michaels, who liked Roberts, was reluctant to have him woken up by an ambulance-chaser who almost certainly wanted special treatment for some scumbag.

"Can I help you, sir? The supervisor's not here at the moment."

"I'm afraid not, Sergeant. I need to speak to the supervisor on duty."

"I just told you, sir, he's not here at the moment."

"Where is he?"

"Just who the hell do you think you are?"

"My name is Weisbach," the ambulance-chaser said. "Staff Inspector Michael Weisbach. Does that change anything, Sergeant?"

"Sorry, sir. The lieutenant has stepped out for a moment. I'll let him know you're here, sir?"

"Where is he? In that little room with the cot?"

"I'll get him for you, sir."

"Keep your seat, Sergeant," Weisbach said. "I know where it is. I've crapped out there myself more than once."

"Yes, sir."

Weisbach went to the closet-size room, opened the door, and snapped on the lights. He knew the large, muscular man sleeping on his back, his mouth open, snoring lightly, but not well; they had never really worked together. Searching his memory, he couldn't come up with one thing, good or bad, about Lieutenant Mitchell Roberts, except what everybody thought about him. He was a good cop. Not an exceptional cop. It had taken him four shots at the lieutenants' examination before he scored high enough on it to make the promotion list.

Lieutenant Mitchell Roberts woke and pushed himself up on the cot, supporting himself on his elbows, squinting in the sudden light.

"Who are you?" he asked, half indignantly, half curiously.

"Mike Weisbach, Mitch. Sorry to wake you."

"Jesus, Inspector, I didn't recognize you right off. Sorry."

"Sorry to have to wake you."

"What can I do for you?"

"I need to look at some of your records," Weisbach said.

"Sure," he said, and then had a second thought: "Jesus, at this time of night? I thought you guys worked the day shift."

"At this time of night," Weisbach said, and then made a decision based on nothing more than intuition: Lieutenant Mitchell Roberts could be trusted.

"I'm really glad to see you here, Mitch."

"Asleep?" Roberts asked.

"I've taken a nap or two in here myself," Weisbach said. "What I meant was that I know I can trust you to keep your mouth shut."

"Yes, sir. Sure you can."

"Can you tell your sergeant he didn't see me in here? And expect him to keep his mouth shut?"

"Yes, sir," Roberts replied, after taking time to think it over. "Michaels is a good cop."

"Ordinarily, that would be good enough, but sometimes good cops change when it has to do with dirty cops. I don't pretend to understand that, but that's the way it is. They start thinking 'It's we cops, we brothers, against everybody else' even when — as in this case — the dirty cops are really slime."

"Is that what this is about? Dirty cops?"

" 'Dirty' — or 'slime' — doesn't do these scumbags justice," Weisbach said. "I really want these bastards, and I don't want your sergeant to keep me from getting them by running off at the mouth to anybody."

"Oh," Roberts said. "Okay. That's good enough, coming from you, for me. Don't worry about Michaels."

"I'll worry," Weisbach said. "Prove me wrong."

"What do you need?"

"I want you to get me the records of everybody the Narcotics Five Squad has brought in here in the last ten days."

"One of those Narcotics Five Squad hotshots is dirty? But you said 'these scumbags,' plural 'scumbags', didn't you?"

"I don't want you even to say 'Narcotics Five Squad' out loud, Mitch. And I don't want your sergeant, or anybody else, to know what records you took out of the files."

"What am I going to do with the records, once I get them out of the file?"

"I'm going to leave Lockup now, before you come out. I'm going upstairs to Chief Coughlin's office, where you will bring the records. After we Xerox them, you will bring them back here and put them back in the files."

"Chief Coughlin's office? He's up there?"

"No, but by the time I get there, Frank Hollaran is supposed to be there and have the Xerox machine warmed up," Weisbach said.

Sergeant Francis Hollaran was Chief Inspector Coughlin's driver, a somewhat inexact job description that really meant his function was to do whatever possible, whenever possible, to spare his chief from wasting his time.

But it was more than that. Most of the inspectors and chief inspectors of the Philadelphia Police Department had learned what was expected of very senior supervisors by serving as "driver" to a chief inspector earlier in their careers.

"It'll take me a couple of minutes, Inspector," Roberts said.

Captain David Pekach pulled into the space reserved for the commanding officer of the Highway Patrol in the parking lot of the Special Operations Division at Castor and Frankford avenues and got out of the car.

A handsome young Irishman in a Highway Patrol sergeant's uniform stepped out of the shadows and extended a mug of coffee to him.

"I thought you might need this," he said with a smile.

Sergeant Jerry O'Dowd was on the manning charts as the administrative assistant to the commanding officer, Highway Patrol. He performed essentially the same duties for Captain Pekach as Sergeant Hollaran performed for Chief Inspector Coughlin, and in fact, everybody thought of him as Pekach's driver. But, as a captain, Pekach, who really needed someone to run intelligent interference for him, was not authorized a driver, and to assign him one would have further antagonized a large number of inspectors and chief inspectors in the department who believed that Highway Patrol and Special Operations White Shirts were already enjoying far too many perquisites.

Naming O'Dowd as Pekach's administrative

assistant had been Wohl's idea.

Pekach took the coffee mug.

"The question, Jerry, is how did you know I would probably need a cup of coffee at" — he looked at his watch — "ten minutes to four in the morning?"

"Jack Malone called me," O'Dowd said. "He said he didn't know what was going on, but that Inspector Wohl had put out the arm for you, and that Inspector Weisbach called in saying he would be unavailable until further notice. I figured you might need me."

"I probably will, and I appreciate your coming, but until I find out what the hell is going on, I think you better wait in my office — out of sight. Malone meant well, but he really shouldn't have called you."

"Yes, sir."

"As soon as I find out what's going on, I'll let you know," Pekach said and, carrying the coffee mug, went into the schoolhouse.

There was no one in the former principal's office that now served as the office of the Special Operations commander and his deputy. Pekach even had to turn on the lights.

The first person to appear, five minutes later, was Sergeant Jason Washington.

"What the hell is going on, Jason?" Pekach greeted him. When Washington didn't immediately reply, Pekach added: "The inspector told me to meet him here."

"I have something delicate to say," Washington said. "Under the circumstances — which I will explain if Peter Wohl doesn't arrive in the next few minutes to explain himself — I believe that while Wohl certainly would like to have Captain Sabara here, he may have forgotten —"

"And Mike would be pissed not to be here, right?"

Washington nodded.

Pekach reached for one of the telephones on the desk of Officer Paul T. O'Mara, Wohl's administrative assistant.

He was not quite through dialing when Wohl walked in the office. He stopped dialing.

"Weisbach here yet?" Wohl asked.

"No, sir," Washington and Pekach said in chorus.

"Who are you calling?" Wohl asked.

"Mike," Pekach said.

"Whose idea was that?"

"Mine," Pekach said, as Washington held up his hand like a guilty child.

Wohl, smiling, shook his head.

"Whichever of you two is really to blame, thank you very much," he said. "As I was coming up Frankford Avenue, I thought of him, and of Tony Harris, McFadden, Martinez —"

He stopped when Washington held up his hand again.

"Be advised, sir, that my entire command, save, of course, the absent Detective Payne, is at this very moment rushing to the sound of the guns."

"Thank you, again," Wohl said.

"And Jerry O'Dowd got here before I did," Pekach said. "What's going on?"

"Just as soon as you get Mike out of bed, I'll tell you," Wohl said.

A very large, very black woman, attired in a flowered housecoat, opened her front door and examined her caller with mingled annoyance and curiosity.

"This better be something important, Dennis," the Hon. Harriet M. "Hanging Harriet" McCandless, judge of the Superior Court, announced. "I'm an old woman and need my sleep."

"Thank you for seeing me, Your Honor," Chief Inspector Dennis V. Coughlin said. "I think you'll agree with me that this is important."

"It had better be," Judge McCandless announced. "Come in. I made a pot of coffee."

"Tony Callis is in my car, Your Honor," Coughlin said.

"Are you hinting that you would like to have him come in?"

"Yes, Your Honor."

Judge McCandless considered that for a full thirty seconds.

"Well, we can't have our distinguished district attorney sitting outside in the dark, can we?" she said finally. "You may fetch him, Dennis."

"Thank you, Your Honor."

"Now, just to make sure I have everything straight in my mind," Judge McCandless said, leaning back in her armchair as if she expected the back to move as her judge's chair did. "You, Tony, are going to come to me to appeal the decision of the magistrate to permit these people bail."

"Yes, Your Honor," District Attorney Callis said.

"Then, their bail having been revoked, you are going to return them to custody. Once in custody, in exchange for their testimony against the police officers in question, you are going to drop the charges on which they were arrested."

"If it gets to that, Your Honor. Only as a last resort will we agree to drop the charges."

"Come on, Tony," Judge McCandless said. "These people aren't stupid. They're going to want a deal, and you're going to give it to them. Your priority is to get the Five Squad."

"Jason Washington, Your Honor," Coughlin said, coming to Callis's assistance, "can often work miracles."

"I am second to no one in my appreciation of the Black Buddha's skill as an interrogator," Judge McCandless said. "But I repeat, these people aren't stupid. They are going to want to do a deal, and Tony is going to have to make one."

"We'll try, Your Honor," Tony Callis replied, "if it comes to that, to make the best deal possible."

"Several things occur to me," she replied flatly. "The second being that you'll make whatever deal you have to."

"And the first?" Tony Callis asked, as ingratiatingly as he could manage.

"If you get away with this," she said, "I will have to disqualify myself."

There was no reply.

"And while neither one of you is a nuclear

scientist, I feel sure you considered that before you decided to wake me up at four o'clock in the morning."

And again there was no reply.

"Which suggests to me that this is very important to you," she finished. "So important that you are willing to take the risk that when these vermin are brought to trial, it might very well be before a brother or sister of mine on the bench who will desperately search the law for an excuse to let them walk."

Coughlin and Callis looked uncomfortable.

"But that's moot," Judge McCandless went on. "You in effect disqualified me by simply coming here and asking me about what you want me to do. If these vermin walk, it will be on your shoulders, not mine."

"I don't think they'll walk, Your Honor," Callis said.

She ignored the reply.

"Finally, on what grounds are you asking me to reverse the magistrate's decision to grant bail?"

"That these people pose a threat to society," Callis replied. "That there is a strong possibility they will jump bail, that they are continuing to engage in criminal activity . . ."

"How can you possibly know these things, Mr. District Attorney, if you can't even give me the names of the people we're talking about?"

"By now, Your Honor," Coughlin said, "Mike Weisbach should have the names."

"You don't *know* that, Dennis," she said.

"May I use your phone, Your Honor?"

She waved at the telephone on an end table.

Coughlin went to it and dialed a number from memory.

"Malone, have we got a location on Inspector Weisbach?" he asked.

There was a reply.

Coughlin smiled and hung up.

"Well?" Judge McCandless asked.

"Your Honor, I was just informed that Staff Inspector Weisbach has for the past ten minutes been parked outside."

Judge McCandless nodded.

"Well, Dennis, why don't you go out and ask him to come in?" she said. "The more the merrier, so to speak."

"Thank you, Your Honor."

Weisbach came into the comfortably furnished living room two minutes later, carrying a large manila envelope stuffed with Xerox copies of the records from Central Lockup.

"Good morning, Your Honor," he said.

"If I knew you were coming, Inspector Weisbach, I would have baked a cake," Judge McCandless replied. "What have you got?"

"The names of all prisoners transported to Central Lockup after their arrest by the Narcotics Five Squad in the last ten days, Your Honor."

Judge McCandless put out her hand for the envelope. Weisbach gave it to her.

She went through each record carefully. From time to time, her eyebrow rose, or her mouth pursed, or she shook her head from side to side in what could have been contempt or resignation.

Then she handed the stack of paper back to Weisbach.

"You've got twenty-two — give or take a couple — names in there —"

"Twenty-two, Your Honor," Weisbach said.

"In my opinion, the magistrates erred in granting bail in eleven cases, on various grounds, such as the individual has in the past violated the bail privilege; and/or in my judgment poses a threat to society; and/or based on past criminal behavior with which I am personally familiar is probably continuing to engage in criminal activity."

"Just eleven of them, Your Honor?"

She ignored the question. "If presented by an appeal to override the magistrates' decision to grant bail by competent authority — such as the district attorney — I would be inclined to override."

"Just half of them, Your Honor?" Coughlin pursued.

"How clever of you, Dennis. Despite allegations to the contrary, you *can* divide by two, can't you? Don't push your luck. Just pick your eleven."

"I'll have the appeals in your chambers by ten o'clock," Callis said. "I presume we may act now on Your Honor's verbal authority?"

"You may not," Judge McCandless said. "You put a duly executed appeal in my hands, and I'll sign it. You don't move until then."

"That'll take hours!" Coughlin thought aloud.

"Unless you type them yourself," the judge said. "I have a typewriter. Can anybody type?"

"I can, Your Honor," Weisbach said.

"And I wouldn't be at all surprised if Tony remembers what to say in an appeal," she said.

"May I suggest you pick your eleven and get started?"

Detective Kenneth J. Summers, a portly forty-year-old, looked around the Homicide Unit and saw there was no one else immediately available to answer the telephone, muttered an obscenity, and punched the flashing button on his telephone.

"Homicide, Detective Summers."

"This is Chief Coughlin," his caller announced. "Who's the lieutenant?"

"Lieutenant Natali, sir."

"No one answers that phone."

"The lieutenant must have stepped out for a minute, sir."

What the hell does Coughlin want this time of the morning?

"Who's the sergeant?"

"Sergeant Hobbs, sir."

"Get him on the horn, will you?"

"He's with Lieutenant Natali, sir. Is there anything I can do?"

"What I'm trying to do, Summers, is avoid having to wake up Captain Quaire. Or, for that matter, Chief Lowenstein."

Captain Henry C. Quaire was the commanding officer of the Homicide Unit. Chief Inspector Matt Lowenstein was commanding officer of the detective division, which includes the Homicide Unit.

"What do you need, Chief?"

"I need — specifically, Sergeant Washington needs — the use of your interview room."

"I'm sure there'll be no problem about that, sir."

"I don't want anybody asking questions about it, or talking about it."

"No problem there, either, sir. When does Jason want to use it?"

"Right now. As soon as he can get there."

"It's his, sir."

"Highway is about to bring you the man he wants to interview. What I want you to do, Summers, is handcuff him to the chair and leave him there until Washington shows up."

"Yes, sir."

"When Lieutenant Natali returns, you tell him I'll explain this to him later, and in the meantime, I want him to sit on it. Same thing if Captain Quaire shows up there. If Chief Lowenstein does, ask him to call me."

"Yes, sir."

The line went dead in Detective Summers's ear.

Five minutes later, a Highway Patrol sergeant and a Highway Patrol officer appeared in the anteroom of the Homicide Unit, which is on the second floor of the Roundhouse. With them they had a very large, angry-appearing black man wearing a gray sweatshirt, baggy blue athletic trousers, bedroom slippers, a golden chain with a three-inch gold medallion, and handcuffs.

"What the fuck am I doing in here?" Mr. Marcus C. (aka Baby) Brownlee inquired.

"Put him in there," Detective Summers said, pointing to the interview room.

"I want my fucking lawyer!" Brownlee announced.

The Highway Patrol sergeant, a slight, very intense black man, guided Mr. Brownlee into the interview room, indicated that he should take a seat in a metal captain's chair bolted to the floor, and turned to Detective Summers.

"One wrist, or both?"

"Did you hear what I said?" Brownlee indignantly demanded.

The Highway Patrol sergeant put his index finger before his mouth and said, "Sssshhh!"

"He's big, but one should hold him," Detective Summers decided and announced.

Brownlee's right wrist was placed in a handcuff, the other end of which passed through a hole in the seat of the steel captain's chair.

The Highway Patrol sergeant left the interview room and closed the door after him.

"I don't suppose you can tell me what the hell this is all about?" Detective Summers said.

"I can, if I want to go back to Traffic on the Last Out," the Highway Patrol sergeant said. "The Black Buddha's on his way. Maybe he'll tell you."

"You just going to take off?"

"We got three more to pick up," the Highway Patrol sergeant announced, gestured to his partner — a Highway patrolman of Polish extraction even larger than Brownlee — to follow him, and walked out of the Homicide Unit.

Detective Summers went into the room adjacent to the interview room and looked through the one-way mirror at Brownlee.

Brownlee was testing the security of the handcuffs restraining him to the chair. Detective Summers wondered if he should have suggested to the Highway sergeant that both Brownlee's wrists be manacled.

Five minutes later, Sergeant Jason Washington walked into the Homicide Unit. Despite the hour, he was the picture of sartorial elegance. He was wearing a double-breasted dark blue silk suit, a crisp white shirt with a flower-pattern silk necktie that matched the handkerchief in his breast pocket, and a gleaming pair of black Amos Archer wing-tip shoes.

"Welcome home, Jason," Summers said.

"You would be ill-advised, Kenneth, to rub salt in my open wound at this hour of the morning."

The open wound to which Washington referred was his involuntary transfer from Homicide to Special Operations.

"He's in there," Summers said, chuckling. "You want to tell me what's going on?"

Washington considered that a full thirty seconds.

"Solely because a witness might be useful, you have my permission to watch me interview Brownlee. With the clear caveat that I am not furnishing you with something interesting with which to amuse, or edify, others. Do you understand?"

Washington was dead serious, Summers saw.

He nodded his acceptance.

"If anyone else comes in, you will pass on to them Chief Coughlin's admonition that if anyone lets this cat out of the bag, they may look forward to spending a good deal of time on Last Out."

"You got it, Jason," Summers said.

"The question, Kenneth, is whether or not you do."

"*I've* got it, Jason," Summers said.

"In that case, into the breach," Washington said, and walked into the interview room.

Summers went into the room adjacent to the interview room and took a chair.

"Who the fuck are you?" Brownlee inquired of Sergeant Washington.

"My name is Washington, Mr. Brownlee. I'm a police officer."

"You're not going to get away with this bullshit. I know my rights!"

"Get away with what, Mr. Brownlee?"

"Coming to my place in the middle of the fucking night and hauling me off."

"If you are suggesting that something illegal has transpired —"

"I want to call my fucking lawyer!"

"— you err. Would you like me to explain your situation to you?"

"I got my rights, motherfucker. I got the right to see my lawyer."

"Your attorney is free to visit you during the prescribed visiting hours at the Detention Center," Washington said.

"What's with this Detention Center bullshit? I made bail!"

"You *were* out on bail," Washington said. "As I am sure the officers who returned you to custody informed you at the time of your rearrest,

600

the magistrate's decision to grant you freedom pending trial has, on appeal, been overridden."

"What the fuck does that mean?"

"The Honorable Harriet M. McCandless, *Judge* McCandless, on reviewing your case, decided there was a real possibility that you would fail to appear for your trial. And/or, based on your criminal record, that there was a real possibility that you would engage in further criminal activity while free on bail. And/or, that you posed a real danger to society. She therefore overturned the magistrate's decision and ordered you remanded."

"Ordered me what?"

"Returned to custody. Which is your status now."

"How long am I going to be in here for?"

"If you mean 'in custody,' I devoutly hope for a very long time."

"I want to make bail."

"You don't seem to be able to grasp your situation, Mr. Brownlee. Let me go over it again for you. You were arrested, charged with the possession of a quantity of controlled substances — which was later determined to be cocaine. At the time of your arrest, you were brought before a magistrate in the police administration building. He decided that, upon posting a bail of twenty-five thousand dollars, or having a bail bondsman post it for you, you could be released until your trial. The bail was posted, and you were released from custody. The decision of the magistrate was appealed by the district attorney to Judge McCandless — are you familiar with Judge

601

McCandless, Mr. Brownlee? I understand she is known within the criminal community as 'Hanging Harriet.' "

"I know who the bitch is."

"I believe that somewhat rude nickname is based on Her Honor's reputation for sentencing those found guilty in her court to the most severe penalties provided for in the law."

"I told you, I know who she is."

"Well, as I said before, when the district attorney appealed the magistrate's decision to grant you a conditional release, she granted the appeal and ordered you remanded."

"So what happens now?"

"When we have finished our little talk, you will be transported to the Detention Center and held there until your trial. I understand, with the load placed on the criminal justice system, that it will be at least ninety days, and very possibly longer, before you will be brought to trial."

"You can't do that!" Brownlee said indignantly, but without very much conviction.

"I think you would be astonished at what a judge can do, Mr. Brownlee."

"So what am I doing here?"

"We are going to have a little chat," Washington said.

"About what?"

"If there is anything lower than a drug dealer, Mr. Brownlee, anyone deserving to be punished to the full extent of the law, it is a police officer involved in drug trafficking. That, unfortunately, may work to your advantage."

"I don't know what the fuck you're talking about."

"According to the record of your arrest, which took place at the Howard Johnson motel on Roosevelt Boulevard last Thursday evening, you were found in possession of a package of cocaine weighing approximately one kilo, or a little more than two pounds."

"I never saw that shit before in my life," Brownlee said. "What that was was a frame."

"And in possession of a loaded, snub-nosed Smith and Wesson .38 Special–caliber revolver, serial number J-384401."

"I never saw that gun before, either."

"Possession of which, since you are a convicted felon, violates not only the Philadelphia ordinances proscribing possession of a pistol without a license, but also federal law, which proscribes possession of *any* firearm by a convicted felon, or by someone under indictment for a felony. Both conditions apply to you. You are a convicted felon, and you are under indictment for several instances of drug dealing, in addition to what happened last Thursday evening. I think you should be prepared to see yourself arrested on firearms charges by both Philadelphia and federal authorities."

"We'll see what happens. I don't know nothing about no gun."

"Finally, your arrest record shows that you had on your person one thousand four hundred and thirty dollars and fifty-two cents."

"So what? Is that against the law?"

"Now, Mr. Brownlee, what we find interesting

is that Mr. Ronald R. Ketcham, to whom you apparently intended to sell the cocaine —"

"Never heard of him," Baby Brownlee interjected.

"As I was saying," Washington went on, "Mr. Ketcham, to whom you and Mr. Amos J. Williams planned to sell the cocaine, had in his possession twenty thousand dollars. Twenty thousand dollars ordinarily buys two kilos of cocaine."

"So what?"

"Mr. Ketcham has given us a sworn statement that he went to the Howard Johnson motel with twenty thousand dollars in cash to meet Mr. Williams — who is again in custody, by the way — and exchange it for two kilos of cocaine."

"I told you I never heard of him."

"Tell me, Mr. Brownlee, did you ever wonder why Mr. Ketcham was not arrested at the time you were?"

That caught Baby Brownlee's attention, Washington saw, although he said nothing.

"Let me tell you what happened, Mr. Brownlee. You went into Mr. Ketcham's room at the motel. He showed you that he did in fact have the twenty thousand dollars, the agreed-upon price. You then left his room —"

"Bullshit."

"— went to Mr. Williams's blue Oldsmobile, went into the trunk, and took from it a beach bag. At that time the narcotics officers, who were watching the entire transaction, arrested you, and Mr. Williams, and the others."

Baby Brownlee shrugged.

"What Mr. Ketcham has said, in a sworn statement, is that at that point — immediately after your arrest — a narcotics officer came to his room, and in exchange for the twenty thousand dollars, did not arrest him."

Baby Brownlee's eyes showed interest in that.

"If what you say happened, how come he would have told you? How did you even know that he was there, if the cops let him buy his way out?"

"Mr. Ketcham is in some other difficulty with the law — the nature of that being none of your business — and this is his way of trying to strike a deal with us."

"What kind a deal?"

"That brings us back to what I said a moment ago," Washington said. "Specifically, that if there is anything lower than a drug dealer, it is a police officer involved in drug trafficking."

"So you want the dirty cop?"

Washington nodded.

"Corrupt police officer. Officers, plural. That, unfortunately, may work to your advantage."

"Keep talking."

"It's a question of priority. It has been decided that our priority is to see that corrupt police officers are removed from the Philadelphia Police Department and brought to trial. To that end, the district attorney has informed Mr. Ketcham that, in exchange for his cooperation — in other words, giving us a sworn statement and later testifying in court against the corrupt police officers in question — the charges against him, conspiring to traffic in controlled substances, will be dropped."

"And that's the deal you're offering me?"

Washington did not reply.

"If you have Ketcham, why do you need me?" Brownlee thought aloud.

"Because we wish to make sure the corrupt police officers are convicted," Washington said.

"And maybe you're a little afraid that a jury would believe the cops instead of this guy they ripped off?"

"You are very perceptive."

"He's a fucking drug dealer, right, and maybe out to get the cops? That's what the jury would think, right?"

"We have to consider that possibility."

"And so two witnesses would be better than one, right?"

"As three witnesses would be better than two."

"And I get to walk. That's the deal?"

"That would depend on what you have to tell me."

"No fucking problem, brother. You tell me what to say, and I'll say it."

"I am not your brother, Mr. Brownlee. Nor am I your friend. I am a police officer, an honest police officer, investigating allegations of corruption. What I want from you is the truth. Nothing but the truth."

"I think I better talk to a lawyer," Brownlee said. "Let him make the deal."

"Mr. Brownlee, I'm going to say this just once, so pay attention. There is no question in my mind that you went to the Howard Johnson motel last Thursday with the criminal intent of trafficking in cocaine. The idea of seeing you escape prose-

606

cution deeply offends me."

"But you're sort of stuck with me, right? If you want to get these cops, you need me."

"No. I don't need you. Judge McCandless remanded to custody eleven individuals such as yourself. We need only two of them to cooperate. You do not have to be one of the two. The only reason I spoke with you now is because you were one of the first to be rearrested."

"Meaning what?"

"You are in no position to bargain, Mr. Brownlee. You can either cooperate or not cooperate. The choice is yours. What's it going to be?"

Baby Brownlee considered that for a moment.

"I think I want to talk to my lawyer," he said.

"Thank you for your time, Mr. Brownlee," Washington said, and walked out of the interview room, closing the door behind him.

There were four Highway patrolmen in the office, and sitting in a row of wooden armchairs along one wall, five prisoners, among them Mr. Amos J. Williams.

Detective Summers came out of the room adjacent to the interview room.

"Didn't work, huh, Jason?"

"Oh, ye of little faith!" Washington replied.

He motioned to a Highway Patrol sergeant.

"This is the script," he said softly. "Each detail is important, and please try not to overact. First, you, Sergeant, will go to Mr. Williams and inquire if he is 'Williams, Amos.' When he replies in the affirmative, you will unshackle him from his chair, ask him to stand, handcuff him *behind* his back, and then move him to one of the chairs against the opposite wall, to which you will handcuff him."

"Okay."

"Then you will bring . . ." he paused as he looked carefully at each of the remanded prisoners ". . . the beady-eyed specimen second from the right, handcuffed in *front*, and stand him near the door to the interview room."

"Okay."

"I will then announce that I am about to answer nature's inevitable summons, and exit stage left — in other words, in the direction of Captain Quaire's office," Washington went on. "You will then enter the interview room, free Mr. Brownlee from the chair, handcuff him, again *behind* his back, and lead him out of the room, carefully holding his chained wrists. You will stop at a position from which Mr. Brownlee can clearly see the specimen whom you have moved to the position indicated. At that point, you will turn to Detective Summers and inquire, 'Where does the boss want this one to go?' or words to that effect, whereupon Detective Summers will say, 'He said put the ones going to the Detention Center over there,' or words to that effect, as you point at Mr. Williams. You will then take Mr. Brownlee to the chair beside Mr. Williams and handcuff him to the chair, *and* to Mr. Williams. You will then lead the previously positioned specimen with the watery eyes into the interview room and cuff him to the chair."

"Okay," the sergeant and Detective Summers said, smiling.

"I will then reappear, enter the interview room,

and chat with the specimen for no more than three minutes. I will then open the door and order that he be taken to a stenographer — tangentially, I presume that the good ladies have answered the call to duty despite the obscene hour?"

"One of the ladies is a him," Summers said. "Guy named Forbes. But he's good."

"Washington, you really think you can get that scumbag to talk in three minutes?" the Highway sergeant asked.

"I'm not even going to try," Washington said. "Just *look* at him. He would make a terrible witness. What I *will* do is ensure he will come out of the interview room looking enormously relieved, or pleased, and possibly both."

"Which, Sergeant," Summers said, "will not be lost on the two who think they're going directly to the slam, do not pass Go, do not collect two hundred bucks. They will wonder what they're missing out on."

"I think three minutes will be sufficient time for Mr. Brownlee to inform Mr. Williams of the deal he was offered and rejected, and for Mr. Williams to conclude that Mr. Brownlee made a gross error in judgment in not accepting it."

"You really think that will work?" the sergeant asked, smiling.

"Are you a betting man, Sergeant?" Detective Summers asked. "I'll give you three-to-one that it will. I've seen this guy at work before."

Twenty-Three

"Thank you, Jason," Peter Wohl said, his voice very serious, even disappointed. "It was worth a try."

Wohl dropped the telephone handset into its cradle and looked, not smiling, at Dennis Coughlin.

He shook his head sadly, but said nothing.

"You might as well tell me, Peter," Coughlin said.

"Mr. Amos J. Williams and Mr. Marcus C. — also known as 'Baby' — Brownlee," Wohl began, and smiled broadly before going on, "either having recognized the error of their sinful ways, or perhaps in the misguided belief that the charges against them will be dropped, have given statements to Sergeant Washington indicating that the amount of narcotics seized as evidence from them at the motel was approximately twice the amount Officer Grider and the rest of Five Squad turned in to the evidence room."

"You bastard!" Coughlin said. "You had me going."

"I'm not finished," Wohl said. "Additionally, Mr. Williams has given a sworn statement that he had approximately three thousand dollars in his possession at the time of his arrest, which is fifteen hundred more than was turned in, and Baby Brownlee is about to sign his statement, in which he says he had approximately two thousand dollars more in his possession than Five Squad turned in, *and* was wearing a Rolex wristwatch which seems to have disappeared between the time it was taken from his person at the place of arrest and Central Lockup. He actually *bought* the watch, and is sure Bailey, Banks and Biddle has a record of the transaction, including the serial number. Do you suppose we'll get really lucky and find one of these —"

"Forget it, Peter. These characters didn't get this far by being stupid."

"I suppose . . ."

"And Washington didn't have to make a deal?"

"He assured both of them he would personally go to the judge and tell him, or her — it's a shame that won't be Hanging Harriet — how cooperative they have been."

"They didn't give him anything that can tie Prasko to what he did to the Longwood girl?"

Wohl shook his head, "no."

"When do we lock them up, Peter?"

"The statements will be enough to get warrants for their arrest, which I think we should do as soon as we can, but I'd rather wait and see what happens in Harrisburg before we actually bring them in," Wohl said.

"And what if there's nothing in Harrisburg?"

"If Matt says he saw Calhoun go into the bank, I think he did."

"And what if Savarese is two steps ahead of us and already knows it was Prasko who raped the girl?"

"As angry as he is, I don't think he'll get reckless," Peter said.

"This is his granddaughter. All bets are off."

Wohl shrugged.

"Let's talk about Harrisburg," Coughlin said.

"Okay," Wohl said, "what are you thinking?"

"I always look for the black cloud inside the silver lining," Coughlin said. "For the sake of discussion, Matt was wrong. The guy he saw go into the safe-deposit box was really a shoe salesman from Shamokin."

"Chief, I don't think Matt would make that kind of mis—"

"Indulge me," Coughlin shut him off.

Wohl nodded.

"Sorry."

"But we have enough to arrest Officer Calhoun anyway."

"And we know he's there," Wohl said. "Or at least his car is parked at his uncle's house. "

"I wonder what kind of favor Chief Mueller owes Walter Davis?" Coughlin said. "That didn't take us long to find out, did it?"

"No. Maybe there is a role for the FBI in law enforcement, after all."

"Don't get carried away," Coughlin said. "And say something you'll regret later."

"Maybe I'm just carried away with the Jason Washington style of psychological interrogation — but I was thinking this before he called just now."

Wohl waited for him to go on.

"Let's say I'm right. For whatever reasons, we can't tie Calhoun to the safe-deposit box, but we arrest him anyway. *Matt* would arrest him anyway, on the warrant here. This guy is not stupid. He's not going to say a word until he talks to a lawyer, and he'll figure out that if we had something on him about the safe-deposit box, we would have used it."

"I don't see where you're going, Chief," Wohl said.

"And Matt has no idea what's happened here," Coughlin said.

"So?"

"McFadden and Martinez go to Harrisburg now, with the warrant. They're with Matt when Lieutenant Deitrich tells Matt what, if anything, he's come up with. If zilch, finding the black cloud, Deitrich has the Harrisburg police pick up Calhoun. After he's been in the holding pen an hour or so, here come McFadden and Martinez — who used to be undercover narcs themselves, and who Calhoun knows. That should upset Calhoun a little. McFadden and Martinez transport Calhoun here, and en route, they convince him how much trouble he's in. I would like to have Officer Calhoun in a very disturbed state of mind when Washington talks to him."

"That makes sense," Wohl said.

"And it leaves Matt in Harrisburg," Coughlin said. "I figure we owe Davis that."

"Martinez and McFadden will be curious about that," Wohl said. "If Matt doesn't come back with them."

"Yeah. Let me think about that," Coughlin said. "But let's suppose we get lucky again, and Deitrich can tie Calhoun to the safe-deposit box, *and* there's something in it. Same scenario, in

613

spades. Calhoun will know we have him, and then spending two hours, handcuffed, in the back of McFadden's car on the way to Philadelphia, while those two inform him of all the nice things that are going to happen to him in the slam, and Calhoun will beg Jason for a chance to tell him everything he knows."

"That makes sense, Chief," Wohl said.

"So why will Matt stay in Harrisburg? To tie up loose ends? It's none of their business?"

"When all else fails, tell as little of the truth as possible," Wohl said. "Matt is working on another case. Not specified. None of their business."

"I'm a little afraid of that," Coughlin said. "You ever hear 'a little knowledge is a dangerous thing'?"

"You mean, tell them everything?"

Coughlin nodded.

"Yeah. I think that would be safer in the long run. And have them bring Matt up-to-date on what's happened here."

"Including the rape? The connection to Savarese?"

"I don't like that, frankly. But I'm at the stage where I don't know who knows what. That's a bad situation, Peter. I can't see where these three knowing everything is going to cause any trouble, and I can see something going wrong if they don't. You agree?"

"Yes, sir."

"Because you agree, or because you're afraid to disagree?"

"A little of both," Wohl said.

"Okay. Decision's made. Get them in here, tell them everything, and send them to Harrisburg."

Wohl reached for one of the telephones on his desk, punched a button, and told Officer Tiny Lewis, who answered the Investigations Section telephone, to send Detectives McFadden and Martinez to his office right away.

It was five minutes to seven when Detective Charles McFadden pulled his unmarked Plymouth up in front of the Penn-Harris Hotel.

He looked at Detective Jesus Martinez.

"I think we just broke the Philadelphia–Harrisburg speed record," he said.

"Oh, shit!" Detective Martinez replied.

"I mean it, Jesus," Charley said. "I mean, think about it. Who else has a chance to come *all the way* from Philly out here to the sticks like we did and fuck the speed limit?"

"Grow up, for Christ's sake, Charley. You almost got us killed, the way you was driving!"

Martinez got out of the car and walked toward the revolving door.

They had been stopped twice for speeding on their way to Harrisburg. The first time, on the Pennsylvania Turnpike, Detective McFadden had been at the wheel. In the rather pleasant conversation he had had with the state trooper, the state trooper told him, before waving a friendly farewell, that he had clocked him at eighty-seven miles per hour.

The second time, shortly after they had turned off the turnpike onto 222 and made a piss stop at a diner, Detective Martinez had been at the wheel. In the rather unpleasant conversation he had had with the local cop, Detective Martinez had been told that he had been clocked at sixty-four miles per hour in a fifty-five-mile per hour zone, and that the local cop personally didn't give a damn for professional courtesy, and that unless he could come up with a better reason for Martinez having exceeded the posted limit than having to get to Harrisburg in a hurry, he was going to write him a ticket.

Charley asked the local cop if he could talk to him a minute, took him behind the car, and managed to talk him out of writing Jesus a ticket, but only on condition that he get back behind the wheel.

Detective Jesus Martinez had thereafter been in a rather nasty mood.

A doorman came out and told Charley he couldn't leave the car where he'd stopped, and directed him to a parking garage.

Jesus was waiting, impatiently, slumped in an armchair, when, maybe five minutes later, Charley finally walked into the hotel lobby.

He got to his feet when he saw Charley, and motioned toward the bank of elevators.

"Where the hell have you been?" he demanded when Charley had joined him there.

"I stopped to get laid, okay? Where the fuck do you think?"

"He's 'not taking calls.' Can you believe that shit?"

"I don't know what you're talking about."

"I tried to call him," Martinez said, and then, in falsetto, quoted the hotel operator: " 'I'm sorry, Mister Payne is not taking calls until seven forty-five. May I ask you to call back then?' "

Charley was amused — by Jesus's indignation, his accurate mimicry of the telephone operator's voice, and by Matt "not taking calls."

He smiled, which was the wrong thing to do.

"Who the fuck does he think he is?" Jesus demanded indignantly.

"What's the big deal, Jesus? He wants his sleep."

"Fuck him and his sleep."

They rode to the sixth floor and got off.

McFadden consulted a well-battered pocket notebook and came up with the room number Inspector Wohl had given him.

"Six twelve," he said. "To the right."

There was a room-service cart with breakfast remnants in the corridor outside Suite 612.

"What the fuck is that?" Jesus asked. "He's too good to eat breakfast in the fucking dining room, right?"

"If it feels good, Jesus, do it," Charley said. "He can afford it, okay?"

"Knowing your buddy, he's probably figured some scam to get the department to pay for it."

There was a brass knocker on the door. Jesus thumped it, several times, and much harder than Charley thought was necessary to attract the attention of someone inside.

When there was no immediate response, Jesus put his hand to the knocker again.

McFadden, who was nearly a foot taller and seventy pounds heavier than Martinez, shouldered him aside.

617

"Cool it, Jesus, okay? Give him a second!"

At the moment the door opened, Detective Payne looked out the crack, saw Detectives McFadden and Martinez, said, "Oh, shit!" and started to close the door.

Detective McFadden, in what was a Pavlovian response — he was accustomed to having people attempt to shut doors in his face — shoved his foot into the doorjamb and pushed against the door with his shoulder.

He didn't get it open, but neither did Detective Payne manage to close it.

They looked at each other through the crack.

"Can I come in or what?"

"Open the fucking door, Payne!" Jesus said.

Detective Payne shrugged, and opened the door.

"Surprise, surprise!" he said.

McFadden and Martinez walked through the door.

"What was that all about?" Charley asked, making reference to Matt's attempt to close the door in his face. And then he looked across the sitting room to the bedroom, and saw a damned good-looking female getting dressed. She was fastening her brassiere; apparently she had not yet had time to put on her underpants.

"You son of a bitch!" Charley said, somewhat admiringly.

Matt went to the door to the bedroom and pulled it closed.

"I don't believe this. I honest to Christ don't believe this!" Jesus said.

"Sorry, Matt," Charley said. "What do you

want us to do? Wait in the hall?"

"Why?" Matt said. "The cat, so to speak, is out of the bag. Just tell your friend there if he says something out of line, I'll tear his leg off and shove it up his ass."

"Try it, hotshot!" Martinez said.

"Shut up, Jesus," Charley said firmly. "And keep it shut!"

"What's going on? What are you doing here?"

"Wohl sent us. Or maybe Chief Coughlin did. We got a warrant for Calhoun. . . . How long is — your friend — going to be in there?"

"She's about to leave," Matt said.

"Why don't we wait until she does?" McFadden said.

Matt nodded and went into the bedroom.

Susan was zipping up her skirt. She looked frightened, on the edge of tears.

"They're two guys I work with . . ." Matt began.

"You could have closed the goddamn door!" Susan said, almost sobbed.

"Honey! I didn't know. . . ."

"What do they want?"

"They've got a warrant for a guy, the dirty cop, I've been watching."

"I thought they'd come for me!"

"They don't even know who you are," Matt said reassuringly.

"Just some bimbo you spent the night with, right?" she said, trying to make a joke of it.

"Well, I could introduce you to them as my fiancé, I suppose," Matt said, and then had a sobering thought. "What I am going to do is introduce you as somebody else. How about 'Patricia Walsh'? How does that sound?"

She looked at him with a blank expression.

"Just trying to cover all the bases," Matt said.

She went into the bathroom. He followed her and watched as she combed her hair and put on her lipstick.

"I'll call you at the office when I find out what's going on," Matt said.

"They have a recorder on my telephone at the office," Susan said.

"Shit," Matt said, furious with himself for not remembering that. "Okay. Unless something happens, meet me downstairs at noon. We'll have lunch."

"Not at the bank?"

"Downstairs," he said. "Honey, I didn't have any idea those two were going to show up here!"

She walked out of the bathroom past him and stopped by the side of the bed to slip her feet into her shoes.

Matt thought there was something delightfully graceful and feminine in the way she did that, standing on one leg at a time, and then he saw the briefcase half full of the money Bryan Chenowith had stolen from banks and had given Susan to hold for him where he'd put it, between the bedside table and the bed.

Shit!

Susan finished putting on her shoes, smiled uneasily at him, walked to the door to the sitting room, and waited for him.

He walked to her.

"I love you," Matt said.

"Oh, God!" Susan said, and put her hand up to touch his cheek.

Matt opened the door and motioned for her to precede him through it.

"Pat," he said. "This is Detective McFadden and Detective Martinez. This is Patricia Walsh."

"I'm happy to meet you, Pat," McFadden said, and smiled.

"How do you do?" Susan said.

Martinez said nothing.

Matt led Susan to the door to the corridor and opened it.

She looked up at him and then kissed him, rather chastely, on the lips.

"I'll see you later," Matt said.

Susan nodded and went out into the corridor. Matt closed the door after her.

"Very nice, Matt," McFadden said. "Sorry we walked —"

"Shit," Martinez said.

"What's with you?" McFadden snapped.

"I'm not sure if you're trying to cover for your buddy, or just stupid."

"What are you talking about?" McFadden asked, genuinely confused.

"Patricia Walsh, my ass! That was Susan Reynolds!"

"Jesus, Mary, and Joseph!" McFadden exclaimed in an exhale.

"What do you know about Susan Reynolds?" Matt asked Martinez.

"Wohl briefed us just before he sent us up here," McFadden said. "We know all about her."

"You're supposed to be surveilling her, not

fucking her!" Martinez said. "I can't believe this. Not even from you, hotshot!"

Matt looked at Charley McFadden.

"Charley, it's not like that. I'm not just . . . fucking her!"

"What were you doing in there, then?" Martinez said. "Making another fucking bomb?"

Matt, his fist balled, took two quick steps toward Martinez.

McFadden, moving with surprising speed, stepped between them and put his hands on Matt's shoulders.

"Cool it, Matt!" he ordered.

He maintained the pressure of his massive hands on Matt's shoulders until he felt him relax, then let him go and turned to Martinez.

"What Wohl told us, Jesus, was that we have nothing to do with what Matt's doing for the FBI. He said he was only telling us about that, those people, so that we wouldn't fuck it up by saying something, doing something, that might fuck up what *he's* doing."

"What he's doing is —"

"Whatever he's doing is none of our fucking business, okay?" McFadden interrupted him.

Martinez shrugged.

"We're here to do what Wohl told us to do, and nothing more. You got that?"

"I hear what you're saying, Charley."

McFadden looked at his watch.

"It's ten minutes after seven. You're meeting this Lieutenant . . . whatsisname?"

"Deitrich," Matt furnished.

"At eight, right? Where?"

"Here."

"That gives us fifty minutes," McFadden said. "That ought to be enough time for us to tell you what's been going down. And to have breakfast. I'm starved."

"I think it would be better if we ate up here," Matt said. "What do you feel like eating?"

"I've been up all night. I could eat a fucking horse," Charley said.

"I don't think they have any horse," Matt said. "But they do a nice breakfast steak."

"Sounds good."

"Martinez?" Matt asked.

Martinez shrugged.

Matt picked up the telephone and ordered the Penn-Harris steak and eggs breakfast for two, and an extra-large pot of coffee.

"Good morning, Mr. Savarese. This is Chief Inspector Dennis V. Coughlin of the Philadelphia Police Department. I hope I didn't call too early."

"What's on your mind, Mr. Coughlin?"

"I think it's quite important that we have a talk, Mr. Savarese, at your earliest convenience."

"I'm sure that you do, inasmuch as you are calling me at my home — and on my unlisted number — at seven forty-five in the morning."

"Believe me, it is."

"You wouldn't care to tell me what it is that's so important?"

"I would rather do that when we meet."

"And where, and when, Mr. Coughlin, do you suggest that we meet?"

623

"If this would be agreeable to you, I was thinking of the restaurant in the Hotel Warwick. I thought we could talk over breakfast."

"You mean, right now?"

"I believe that it would be in our mutual interest, Mr. Savarese, if we met as soon as possible."

"But you're not willing to tell me why you think it would be so?"

"I think it would be better if we talked privately."

"And would you be alone, Mr. Coughlin?"

"I will have Inspector Wohl with me, but the conversation I hope we can have will be just between us. It's a rather delicate matter."

"Inspector Wohl is a splendid police officer, as, indeed, was his father. What I think would be possible, Mr. Coughlin, is that I would come to the Warwick accompanied by my chauffeur, Mr. Pietro Cassandro. He and Inspector Wohl could have their breakfast together, and see that you and I are not disturbed while we are enjoying ours."

"That would be perfectly satisfactory to me, Mr. Savarese."

"Perhaps this might be a good omen, Mr. Coughlin," Savarese said. "But Pietro just walked in the door. Shall we say in thirty minutes? Would that be convenient for you?"

"Yes, it would. Thirty minutes it is. I look forward to seeing you, Mr. Savarese."

"Good-bye, Mr. Coughlin."

Coughlin hung the phone up and turned to look at the other people in his office. In addition to Inspector Peter Wohl, they were Jerry Carlucci, mayor of the City of Philadelphia; Chief Inspector Matt Lowenstein; Lieutenant Jack Fellows, the mayor's bodyguard; and Frank F. Young, Assistant Special Agent in Charge (Criminal Affairs) of the Philadelphia office of the Federal Bureau of Investigation.

Young had absolutely nothing to do with what was going on, but when Walter Davis had announced, at six-thirty — to everybody's initial relief — that he had things pending in the office that just could not be put off, and would have to leave, he finished the announcement by saying not to worry, he would call Frank Young and have him come to Special Operations to see what help he could be.

Coughlin could not think of any credible reason to suggest that all Young would do would be in the way. There was no question in his mind that Young's presence would be primarily to make sure the FBI didn't get left out of anything that would accrue to the interest of the FBI.

"Thirty minutes," Coughlin announced. "Peter gets to have breakfast with Pietro."

"I can hardly wait," Wohl said.

"You really think this is necessary, Denny?" the mayor asked.

"I don't want Prasko killed before we get the Five Squad to trial," Coughlin said.

"We'd really look bad, Jerry," Lowenstein said, coming to his aid, "if somebody stuck a knife in Prasko in the Detention Center."

The mayor threw up his hands, admitting he could not counter that argument.

"Frank," Coughlin said, turning to the FBI

official, "we don't want to spook Savarese. Could you, without making many waves, see if you could keep the FBI — or, for that matter, any other feds — away from the Warwick from now until, say, nine-thirty?"

"FBI. No problem. I'll get right on that. Have you got any idea what other agency might be interested in Savarese?"

Coughlin saw Wohl's eyes roll before he answered for Coughlin.

"Frank, if Savarese sees anybody who looks like a cop, or a fed, doing anything at the Warwick, he will think they're interested in him. Whether or not they are. The safest thing to do is keep everybody with any kind of a badge away from the Warwick for an hour or so."

"Well, I understand that, certainly," Young said, a little lamely. "I'll call around."

"I'll put the word out that nobody is to go near the Warwick," Matt Lowenstein said. "Which will probably have the result that every cop in Philadelphia will show up to see what's going on."

"What are we waiting for now?" Mayor Carlucci asked.

"To hear from Matt Payne in Harrisburg," Wohl said. "To see if he's got anything on Calhoun or not."

"I've been thinking about that," the mayor said.

"We should hear something in fifteen or twenty minutes, Mr. Mayor," Peter said.

"A lot can happen in fifteen or twenty minutes," Carlucci said. "Why don't you do it now, Peter?"

"Mr. Mayor, we gave that a lot of thought. And we decided —"

"You're a good cop, Peter. And I love you. But the last time I looked, I was mayor of Philadelphia. Arrest the bastards!"

"Yes, sir," Wohl said.

Detective Matt Payne looked at his watch when there was a knock at the door. It was 7:59.

He opened the door. Lieutenant Paul Deitrich was standing there.

"Good morning, sir," Matt said. "Please come in."

Deitrich nodded but didn't say anything.

"Lieutenant, these are Detectives McFadden and Martinez," Matt said, making the introductions. "Charley, Jesus, this is Lieutenant Deitrich."

Deitrich nodded, just perceptibly, then looked at Matt for an explanation for the two detectives.

"They've got a warrant for Calhoun," Matt said.

"We got lucky," McFadden said. "Somebody dumped the answer in our lap."

"I got lucky here, too," Deitrich said. "I remembered that if you really want to find something out, ask the cop on the beat."

"Our guy was a retired detective, who smelled something rotten."

Deitrich looked at Matt.

"I know one of the guys who work that area pretty well," Deitrich said. "I went to see him. He told me — without me having to tell him why I was asking — that Mrs. Worner lives at 218

Maple. Her yard backs up against 223 Elm, which is where —"

"Vincent T. Holmes, Calhoun's uncle, lives," Matt furnished.

Deitrich nodded.

"You're talking about the lady who works in the bank, right?" Martinez asked.

Deitrich nodded again.

"Holmes's wife died two years ago, of cancer," Deitrich went on. "About the time Mrs. Worner finally gave up and put her husband away."

"Excuse me?" Matt asked.

"He got hurt bad in Korea," Deitrich said. "Lost one leg above the knee and the foot on the other leg. She married him anyway. He got a one-hundred percent disability pension. They weren't hurting for money. But he couldn't work, and he got into the sauce pretty bad. I guess he was in pain a lot, and he just sort of went downhill until she couldn't handle him anymore. The last time he got arrested for drunken driving, the judge gave him the choice of going into the VA hospital or two years in jail. He went to the VA hospital."

"And enter the friendly neighbor, right?" McFadden said.

Deitrich nodded again.

"She's Catholic, so she won't divorce her husband. Maybe she wouldn't marry Holmes anyway. He's not a real catch. He works for Pennsylvania Power and Light as a lineman, and he doesn't look much like Paul Newman. But anyway, she sneaks over to his house at night, or he over to hers, fooling nobody in the neighborhood, of course, but everybody feels sorry for them — mostly for her — and nobody says anything."

"Shit!" McFadden said.

"So there's your connection, Payne," Deitrich said. "What do you want to do about it?"

"The question is, what did she do?" Matt asked.

"You know fucking well what she did, Payne," Martinez said. "She conspired with Calhoun to hide whatever those Five Squad scumbags wanted to hide in a safe-deposit box. That makes her an accessory after the fact."

"First of all, we don't know if anything connected to Five Squad is in that safe-deposit box —"

"We will, the minute we go into the box."

"Which box, Jesus?" Matt said, patiently. "When we go to the judge for a search warrant, he's going to want to know what box we have cause to believe there is something in. He's not going to give us a warrant to go in every box in the bank."

"Maybe Calhoun will have the key on him when we arrest him, Matt," McFadden said.

"And maybe he won't," Matt said. "Maybe the uncle keeps the key for him."

"And maybe," Deitrich chimed in, "the key never leaves the bank."

"Excuse me?" Matt said again.

"You're working on the idea that there is a box in there rented under a phony name," Deitrich said. "What I'm thinking is maybe Mrs. Worner, who is in charge of the whole operation, is just letting your man use a box that's *not* rented. Who would know? He goes in, she gives him the key, and that's the end of it. No record, of course."

"That makes a lot of sense," Matt said.

"Have we got enough to arrest the uncle on?" McFadden asked.

"After we get in the box, presuming we find something in the box, then maybe. Right now, no."

"It's eight o'clock," Martinez said. "Wohl is waiting to hear from you whether or not we can tie Calhoun to anything in the box."

"I have an idea," Matt said. "Let's scare everybody."

"What the fuck does that mean?" Martinez asked.

"We go along, right now, when the Harrisburg cops go to Uncle Vincent's house to arrest Calhoun. We don't do it quietly. We make sure Mrs. Worner sees the police cars at Uncle Vincent's house. Following good police procedure, the Harrisburg cops send a couple of uniforms to make sure Calhoun doesn't get out the back door. Looking out her kitchen window, she'll see that. Charley and I will also be at the back door. She'll see us. Calhoun is taken off."

"So?" Martinez asked.

"Nothing else happens. Except that a police car stays at the curb in front of Uncle Vincent's. So Uncle Vincent, already worried about Calhoun getting hauled off, has two options. He can either pretend he has no idea what's going on — which I don't think he'll want to do — or he can go to work as usual. In which case the police car follows him. The last thing I think he'll do is try to get in touch with Mrs. Worner, which he can't do in person, with the cops watching. And I don't think he'd try to use the telephone, because he'd be afraid it was tapped. So he goes to work. And sees that he's being followed by the cops."

"What is this shit, Payne?" Martinez asked.

"Then Mrs. Worner has one of two options. Well, maybe three. She could run, but I don't think that's going to happen. She either goes to work as usual, or she stays home. If she stays home, we go to see her. If she goes to work, she is called into her boss's office, where there are two policemen, the same two she saw standing outside Uncle Vincent's place. We then tell her we know all about the safe-deposit box, and if she cooperates with us, it will go easier on her — you know that routine."

"That's pure bullshit!" Martinez said. "Hotshot here has been watching too much TV."

"I don't know, Matt," McFadden said. "It might work, but there's a lot of ifs."

"What I'm going to do," Martinez announced angrily, "is go down to police headquarters here, get a couple of local uniforms to back me up, go arrest Calhoun, and then call Wohl and tell him we have Calhoun and probably don't have anything with the safe-deposit box."

"No, you're not," Matt said. "We're going to do it my way."

"Who the fuck do you think you are, hotshot?"

"I was assigned to this case first," Matt said. "That makes it mine."

"Oh, fuck you, hotshot," Martinez said, and

walked to the telephone.

"Who are you calling?" Matt asked.

"Who the fuck do you think? Wohl. We'll settle this shit right now!"

"Put the phone down, Jesus," Charley said, choosing sides.

"Let him go, Charley," Matt said.

"Put the phone down, Jesus," McFadden repeated, walking up to Martinez.

Literally quivering with rage, Detective Martinez looked up at Detective McFadden.

"For the last time, Jesus, put it down."

"Well, fuck you, too, McFadden!" Martinez said, and slammed the telephone down in its cradle.

"I'm sorry you had to see all this, Lieutenant," Matt said.

"Why do I have the feeling you two don't like each other much?" Deitrich said.

"They love each other, Lieutenant," McFadden said. "They just have a strange way of showing it."

"So what have you decided to do?" Deitrich said.

"Unless somebody can show me what's wrong with my idea . . ." Matt said.

"It's your ass, hotshot," Martinez said.

"How long would it take to get two — better even, three — patrol cars out to Maple Avenue?"

"Five minutes after I get on the radio."

"How about one car to meet us on Maple Avenue?" Matt asked. "And two cars to Elm Street, to go noisily through Mrs. Worner's backyard to make sure nobody gets out Uncle Vincent's back door?"

"No problem."

"Screaming sirens and flashing lights would be nice," Matt said.

"No problem."

"Martinez, are you going with McFadden, or would you rather stay here and sulk?" Matt asked.

"You son of a bitch!" Martinez spluttered.

"Jesus Christ, Matt," McFadden said. "You never know when to quit."

"This gentleman," Vincenzo Savarese said softly to the waiter, "is my guest, and so are those two."

He pointed to a table near the door of the Hotel Warwick's small, elegant dining room, where Pietro Cassandro and Peter Wohl were holding large, ornate menus.

"That's very kind," Chief Inspector Dennis V. Coughlin said, "but why don't we go Dutch?"

"I am Italian, and you are Irish. How can we go Dutch?" Savarese asked. "Besides, it'd give me pleasure. Please indulge me."

"Thank you," Coughlin said, giving in.

He ordered freshly squeezed orange juice, scrapple, two soft-scrambled eggs, biscuits, and coffee. Savarese — surprising him, for Savarese was slight, almost delicate — ordered a much larger breakfast of freshly squeezed orange juice, eggs Benedict, a side order of corned beef hash, biscuits, and coffee, and asked that his coffee be served now, with fresh cream only — if they had only milk, then black.

"Looking at Inspector Wohl reminds me how quickly the years pass," Savarese said. "I remember him, in short pants, at baseball games with his father."

"I think he'll be police commissioner one day," Coughlin said. "He's a fine man."

"And when are they going to make you police commissioner?"

"The day after Miami gets twelve inches of snow," Coughlin said.

"I think you are much too modest," Savarese said. "You are universally recognized as one of the best policemen in Philadelphia."

"Thank you, but police commissioner is not in the cards for me."

The waiter appeared with their coffee and a small pitcher of fresh cream.

"One never knows what the future will bring," Savarese said.

Coughlin waited until they had put cream and sugar in their coffee.

"Let me begin, Mr. Savarese, by telling you how sorry I am, both professionally and personally, about what happened to your granddaughter."

Savarese's expression didn't change at all. After a moment, he said: "Thank you. We can only pray for her full recovery. We have tried to get the best possible medical attention."

"I think you have found the best," Coughlin said.

Savarese nodded.

"As I was just saying, one never knows what

the future will bring."

"I thought you would like to know that at seven fifty-eight this morning, the animal responsible for your granddaughter's difficulty was stripped of his police officer's badge and arrested. The entire Philadelphia Police Department is deeply ashamed that he once wore our uniform. He has brought shame on us all."

Savarese looked directly at Coughlin, but said nothing.

The waiter appeared with their orange juice, a wicker basket full of assorted biscuits, rolls and croissants, two tubs of butter, and a selection of marmalades.

Savarese absently selected a croissant, broke it in two, and buttered the half he kept in his hand.

"You're sure you have the right man?" he asked finally.

"We're sure."

"He has confessed to this outrage?"

"At this very moment, he is being interviewed by the man I believe to be the best interrogator in the department."

"But he has not confessed?"

"There was a witness, Mr. Savarese. He has positively identified him."

"But he has not confessed," Savarese insisted.

"That's one of the things I wanted to talk to you about," Coughlin said. "Under the circumstances —"

"What circumstances?"

"To bring this animal to trial, Mr. Savarese, it would be necessary to identify the victim of his unspeakable behavior to the court and his defense counsel —"

"We are speaking, aren't we, as man-to-man?" Savarese interrupted.

"Yes, we are."

"I'm sure you'll understand that I cannot permit my granddaughter to suffer any more than she has already suffered."

"I understand that," Coughlin said. "More important, Mr. Callis, the district attorney, understands that."

"There is only one situation that I can imagine that would guarantee that what happened to my granddaughter would not become public knowledge . . . ," Savarese said.

"That's what I wanted to speak to you about, Mr. Savarese," Coughlin said.

". . . and that would be the unavailability of this animal to stand trial," Savarese finished.

"That sounds to me, Mr. Savarese, as if you are suggesting this animal be killed."

"What I said, Mr. Coughlin, is that the only way I can see that my granddaughter's name will not be dragged through the sewer, as it would be if there was to be a trial, would be if there was no trial. And there can be no trial if there is no accused."

"The man we're talking about was not arrested on a rape charge, Mr. Savarese, but on a wide array of other charges that should see him sent away for a very long time."

"What you have this man on, Mr. Coughlin," Savarese said patiently, as if explaining something to a backward child, "is nothing more than allegations that he stole from drug dealers. He will not spend much time — if, indeed, any — in prison."

The waiter appeared with Savarese's eggs Benedict and Coughlin's scrapple and scrambled eggs.

Coughlin had not seen him coming, and when he looked up at him in surprise, he knew from the look on the waiter's face that he had heard at least the end — the "time in prison" — of Savarese's last sentence.

He laid the food before the two of them and fled.

"I'm surprised you know about the charges," Coughlin said.

"And I'm surprised that you got to this animal before I did," Savarese said. "Perhaps we have both underestimated the other."

"I've never underestimated you, Mr. Savarese, but I think you may have underestimated me. Or at least the Philadelphia Police Department."

"Why would you say that?" Savarese said.

"Mr. Ronald R. Ketcham is now under the protection of the U.S. Marshals' Service . . ."

"I don't believe I know the name, Mr. Coughlin."

". . . as a material witness to an unlawful abduction on federal property."

"As I said, I don't believe I know the name, Mr. Coughlin."

"Oh, I think you know the name, Mr. Savarese," Coughlin said. "And a good deal about Mr. Ketcham. I'm sure Joey Fiorello told you everything Phil Chason found out about him."

"I don't know either of those names, either, I'm afraid."

"I thought we were speaking man-to-man," Coughlin said.

Savarese took a bite of his eggs Benedict, chewed them, and then dabbed delicately at his mouth with his napkin.

"Has it occurred to you, Inspector," Savarese said, "that if you — the police department — had not been so efficient — more efficient, frankly, than I would have believed — the problem would have been solved?"

"Mr. Savarese, I know that you take pride in your reputation as a man of honor," Coughlin said.

Savarese raised his eyebrows questioningly.

"I also like to think of myself as an honorable man," Coughlin said.

"And you are so regarded by me."

"I have taken an oath — a vow before God — to uphold and defend the law."

"Someone once said, 'The law is an ass.' "

"I think that's often true," Coughlin said. "But when that is true, what we should do is change the law, not ignore it."

"Man-to-man, you said," Savarese said. "Man-to-man, taking into account what it says in the Bible about an eye for an eye and a tooth for a tooth, what do you think should happen to an animal who did what this animal did to my grand-daughter? Who took from her her innocence, her dignity, her sanity . . ."

638

"When I consider that question I have to remind myself that in the Bible it also says, 'Vengeance is mine, saith the Lord.' "

"That's avoiding the question," Savarese said.

"I can't let myself think about things like that," Coughlin said.

"Is there justice, would you say," Savarese asked, "in permitting an animal like this one to escape any punishment at all for the terrible things he did, because to punish him according to the law would mean bringing even greater pain and humiliation to the innocent person he violated?"

"Man-to-man, no, Mr. Savarese," Coughlin said.

Savarese held up both hands, palms upward.

"Thank you for your honesty," he said.

"I was hoping, Mr. Savarese, that you would decide, perhaps to save your granddaughter the risk of any further pain, that my assurance that this animal will be behind bars for a very long time would be enough punishment."

He looked into Savarese's eyes and was surprised at the cold hate he saw in them, and even more that he felt frightened by it.

And then the hate in Savarese's eyes seemed to diminish.

"Forgive me," Savarese said.

"Pardon me?"

"For a moment, I thought I heard a threat," Savarese said. "And for a moment, I forgot that you are an honorable man, incapable of even thinking of using my granddaughter as a pawn."

"One of my concerns, as a man, and a police

officer, is to spare your granddaughter any further pain," Coughlin said.

"Yes, I believe that, and you have my gratitude," Savarese said. "It seems to me that what this amounts to is the dichotomy between your belief that 'Vengeance is mine, saith the Commonwealth of Pennsylvania,' and my belief that that vengeance, as limited as we both know it will be, is not nearly enough."

Coughlin shrugged.

"I will do, Mr. Coughlin, what I believe is both my right and my duty to do, and I'm sure you will do the same."

"Mr. Savar—"

Savarese held up his hand to shut him off.

"I don't think, on this subject, that we have anything else to say to each other," Savarese said. "Why don't we just finish our breakfast?"

Twenty-Four

Officer Timothy J. Calhoun was sitting with his wife on the couch in the living room watching the *Today* show on the tube when he heard the siren.

Police sirens were a part of life in Philadelphia. Out here in the sticks, you seldom heard one.

And this was more than one siren. Two. Maybe even three.

He took his sock-clad feet off the coffee table, then put his coffee cup on the table and stood up, slipping his feet into loafers.

"What is it?" Monica Calhoun asked.

"Probably a fire," Tim said. "Right around here someplace. Them sirens is getting closer."

He walked to the front door and opened it and looked up and down the street. He could see neither a fire nor police nor fire vehicles, and pulled the door closed.

Just as he did, he heard one siren abruptly die. He knew that meant that whoever was running the siren had gotten where he was going.

There was still the sound of two sirens.

Monica joined him at the door.

"You didn't see anything?"

He shook his head, "no."

The sound of the sirens grew very loud, and then, one at a time, died suddenly.

Monica opened the door.

"Jesus, they're right here!" she said.

There was a Harrisburg black-and-white in the driveway, and what looked like an unmarked car with two guys in it at the curb, and as Tim watched two uniforms jump out of the car in the driveway, a second Harrisburg black-and-white came screeching around the corner and pulled its nose in behind the black-and-white in the driveway.

"What the fuck?"

The first uniform reached the door.

"Timothy J. Calhoun?"

"What the hell is going on?"

"Timothy J. Calhoun?"

"Yeah, I'm Calhoun."

"Timothy J. Calhoun, I have a warrant for your arrest for misprision in office," the first cop said. "You are under arrest!"

"Timmy!" Monica wailed. "What's going on?"

"Turn around, please, and put your hands behind your back," the first uniform said, as the second uniform put his hands on his shoulders and spun him around.

"Timmy!" Monica wailed again.

"You have the right to remain silent . . ." The first cop began very rapidly to give him his rights under the Miranda decision.

"It's some kind of mistake, baby," Tim said.

What did the uniform say? Misprision? What the fuck is misprision?

"Do you understand your rights as I have outlined them to you?" the first cop asked.

"Yeah, yeah, yeah," Timmy said. "Look, I'm

a cop, I don't know what the hell is going on here."

"You're being arrested for being a dirty cop, Calhoun," a voice — somehow familiar — said.

The uniform who had spun him around to cuff him now spun him around again.

Jesus Martinez, onetime plainclothes narc, was standing there looking at him with contempt.

"What the hell is going on here, Jesus?"

"You're on your way to the slam, big time," Martinez said. "I'll need your badge and your gun."

"Timmy, for Christ's sake," Monica wailed. "Why are they doing this to you?"

One more uniform and two guys in civilian clothing came around the side of the house. Tim recognized the big guy first. Charley McFadden, who had also been a plainclothes narc — the other half of Mutt & Jeff, which is what everybody had called the two of them.

The other wasn't nearly as familiar, and it took a moment for Tim to recognize him.

It's that hotshot from Special Operations, Payne. The guy who shot the serial rapist. The last time I saw him was in the Roundhouse parking lot.

"I'm really sorry about this, Timmy," McFadden said. "Jesus, how could you be so stupid?"

"I don't know what the hell you're talking about," Tim said.

"He didn't do anything!" Monica wailed. "Charley, he's a good cop! You know that!"

"I know he's not a good cop, Monica," Charley said. "He's dirty, and he got caught."

"Charley, what are they talking about?" Monica asked.

"Call the FOP in Philly and tell them I was just arrested," Tim said.

"Where are they taking you?"

"He'll be in the detention cell in Harrisburg police headquarters for a while, Mrs. Calhoun," Matt Payne said. "They can contact him there."

"Who the hell are you?" Monica snapped.

"My name is Payne. I'm a detective assigned to the Special Operations Division. I'm sorry about this, Mrs. Calhoun."

"Yeah, you look like you're sorry!"

"I'm going to be at the bank," Matt said to Charley McFadden. "As soon as I have the safe-deposit box, I'll meet you at police headquarters."

"Right," McFadden said.

"Have you got his gun and his badge?"

"Not yet," Martinez said.

"If you would give me the key to the safe-deposit box, Calhoun, you'd save everybody a lot of time and inconvenience."

"I don't know nothing about no safe-deposit box."

"Why am I not surprised?" Matt said.

He looked at the Harrisburg uniforms.

"Take him away, please," he said.

Mrs. Timothy J. Calhoun, holding her balled fists to her mouth, watched with horror and disbelief as her husband was led down the path and loaded into the backseat of the Harrisburg black-and-white.

Then she watched until it drove out of sight.

"I'll need the gun and the badge, Mrs. Calhoun," Detective Martinez said.

"And if you know where the key to the box is, Monica," Charley McFadden added.

"You're supposed to be his friend, Charley!" Monica said. "How could you do this to him?"

"He done it to himself, Monica," Charley said. "Let's go get his gun and badge."

"You stay here! I'll go get it."

"I can't let you do that, Monica," Charley said. "I'll have to go with you."

When Harrison J. Hormel, Esq., first among equals of the assistant district attorneys of Philadelphia, arrived at work, he heard the sound of an electric razor coming from the office of the Hon. Thomas J. "Tony" Callis, the district attorney of Philadelphia.

He looked at his watch. It was 8:35, a good hour or hour and a half earlier than Callis's usual appearance.

He turned and knocked at the unmarked private door to Callis's office. When there was no answer, he tried the knob, and it turned, and he was able to push the door slightly open.

Callis, in a sleeveless undershirt, his suspenders hanging loose, was standing at the washbasin in his small private bath.

Hormel walked to the door. Callis saw his reflection in the mirror and took the electric razor from his face.

"What's up, Harry?" he asked.

"I was about to ask you the same thing."

"It's a long story," Callis said. "One I'm not really ready to pass on right at this moment."

"What's the big secret?"

"I'll give you a thumbnail, but no questions, okay?"

"You're the boss."

"Dirty cops. Lots of them."

"Doing what?"

"I said no questions. The arrests are not finished yet. There's an incredible amount of ifs in this one, Harry. If this happens, then that will. If that doesn't happen, then this will. You follow?"

Hormel shook his head, "no."

"I've been up since half past three," Callis said. "Coughlin sent a Highway Patrol car for me. What I need now is to finish my shave, put on a clean shirt, have a couple of cups of coffee and thirty minutes to settle my thoughts."

"Since when is Denny Coughlin investigating dirty cops?"

"Since Carlucci — who they got out of bed at six thirty, by the way — told him to."

"And he's found some, I gather?"

"There's going to be a meeting in Carlucci's office at half past nine. There's a couple of things supposed to happen before then."

"What kind of things?"

"Jesus, Harry, don't you understand 'no questions'?"

"Sorry, I'm just trying to be useful. You say Coughlin sent a Highway car after you?"

"Nice try," Callis said. "Yeah, Coughlin sent a Highway car for me. Period, that's all I can give you now. When the meeting is over, I'll probably be able to tell you what's going on."

"Okay."

"Now let me finish my shave and get a fresh shirt."

"Nothing I can do right now?"

"Not a thing," Callis said.

Harry had almost made it to the door when Callis had another thought, tangentially connected with the Five Squad.

"Harry?" he called.

"Yes, sir?"

"Tell Phebus I'll want to see him sometime this morning. I don't give a damn what else he's got on his plate, I want him around here this morning where I can lay my hands on him in ten seconds. *Capisce?*"

"Yes, sir."

"If he asks why, tell him I want to know what's going on with the Leslie case."

"Yes, sir."

Assistant District Attorney Hormel went immediately to the office of Assistant District Attorney Anton C. Phebus. He had not yet come to work.

He walked back down the corridor thirty minutes later and found that Mr. Phebus had come to work, and to judge by the briefcase in his hand was about to leave it.

"Where are you headed?"

"For a conference with the Goddamned Nun."

"What does she want?"

"Haven't the faintest. Some deal, certainly. She's determined to see that Leslie gets no more than a slap on the wrist."

"Well, you're going to have to postpone it."

"Why?"

647

"Because Tony said he wants you around here all morning where he can lay his hands on you in ten seconds."

"Did he say why?"

"He said he wants to talk to you about the Leslie case. He's in his Mr. Super-DA-Man role. Coughlin, he announced like a happy child, had sent a Highway car for him in the middle of the night, and he's on his way to a meeting in the mayor's office."

"What's that all about?"

"He said something about dirty cops, but what I think it is, is that he thinks Carlucci is liable to ask him about the Leslie case."

Anton C. Phebus, who was not a stupid man, felt a sudden pain in the pit of his stomach.

"Okay," he said. "I hear and obey."

As soon as Hormel had left his office, he called the Goddamned Nun's office and left a message for her to the effect that an emergency situation had arisen that would preclude his meeting with her as scheduled. He would call her later in the day and attempt to schedule another meeting at a mutually convenient time.

Then he dialed the home telephone number of Officer Joe Grider. Mrs. Grider informed him that Joe hadn't come home yet.

He dialed the home number of Officer Herbert Prasko, and there was no answer. He remembered that Prasko's wife had a job, which would explain why nobody answered the phone, particularly if Prasko, like Grider, had worked until the wee hours and then had a couple of belts afterward. There wasn't much sense — unless all you wanted to do was sleep — in going home if the old lady was out working.

There was one way of finding out for sure, of course. Call the Narcotics Unit and talk to somebody and find out what had happened the previous night. He dialed the number of the Narcotics Unit, but changed his mind and hung up before it was answered.

He was letting his imagination run away with him. He had thought this whole thing through very carefully. Nothing had gone wrong because nothing could go wrong.

"Well, good morning!" Vice President James C. Chase of the First Harrisburg Bank & Trust Company cried cheerfully when he saw Lieutenant Paul Deitrich and Detective Matt Payne walk into his outer office. "You wanted to see me?"

"We'd appreciate a few minutes of your time, Mr. Chase," Deitrich said.

"Anytime, Paul, you know that," Chase said. "Come on in."

They went into the inner office.

"Actually, Matt," Chase said, "I was hoping to catch you before you went across the floor. Our Mr. Hausmann is back from Boston, and we're going to have to find you another desk somewhere."

"I won't be needing a desk anymore, Mr. Chase," Matt said.

Chase picked up on something in Matt's voice, or perhaps his demeanor.

"That sounds, forgive me, a little ominous, Matt. Is something wrong?"

"I'm afraid so, sir," Matt said. "I'm afraid I was right when I thought I saw someone I recognized going into the safe-deposit area yesterday, Mr. Chase."

"But Adelaide, Mrs. Worner, had no record —"

"We just arrested him, Mr. Chase," Matt said. "On charges of misprision of office as a Philadelphia police officer. We have reason to believe that Mrs. Worner has been making a safe-deposit box available to him off the records."

"That's hard to accept," Chase said, somewhat coldly. "Paul?"

"We could, of course, be wrong, Mr. Chase," Deitrich said. "But I don't think so."

"To what end? You're not trying to tell me Adelaide could possibly have any involvement with a call girl ring in Philadelphia?"

"We believe the box is being used to hold money — and maybe drugs — acquired illegally by Philadelphia police officers," Matt said.

"And maybe *drugs?*" Chase quoted, horrified. "And you've come equipped with a search warrant, is that what you're telling me?"

"No, sir," Deitrich said. "We don't have a search warrant, Mr. Chase. We can get one, but we're hoping that won't be necessary."

"Well, certainly — as I'm sure you understand, Lieutenant — I can't permit you access to a safe-deposit box without one."

"We're hoping that we can get Mrs. Worner to show us which box it is, and give us the key to it, without our having to get a search warrant," Matt said.

"If she has been up to what you're suggesting, Matt, why would she do that? I must tell you, I find this entire —"

"I don't think Mrs. Worner really knew what she was doing, Mr. Chase," Deitrich said. "I don't know how familiar you are with her personal situation . . ."

"I know that she has had a very difficult time with her husband, if that's what you mean. And that he is a highly decorated, grievously wounded —"

"We think she has been used, Mr. Chase," Matt said. "I can't really believe there will be much interest in putting her in prison. Providing, of course, she comes to understand the mess she's in, and cooperates."

"Used by whom?" Chase asked coldly.

"Her across-the-backyard neighbor," Deitrich said. "Who is the uncle of the police officer now under arrest."

"You're suggesting that she's . . . that they're involved? Personally, I mean?"

"It looks that way, Mr. Chase," Deitrich said.

Chase considered that a moment.

"The poor woman," he said, and then shifted into his banker's role: "Exactly what is it you want from me? How is the bank involved in this?"

"We just learned — we left a car watching her house; they got on the radio — that she is in her car, and apparently on her way here, to work," Deitrich said.

"You mean she's not here now?"

"I suppose she's come in late today," Matt said.

Chase gave him a dirty look. This tragic situation was obviously not the place for levity.

"When she comes in, Mr. Chase," Matt said, "we'd like to talk to her here, in your office."

"To what end?" Chase demanded coldly.

"Detective Payne thinks," Deitrich picked up on Chase's annoyance with Matt and answered for him, "and I agree, that when she sees us here, and knows that we know, she'll give us what we want."

"I just can't believe this of Adelaide."

"Frankly, I feel sorry for her," Deitrich said. "I hope that she sees that the only thing for her to do is admit that she's done something really foolish, and tries to help us straighten it out."

"And the alternative?"

"We're prepared to arrest her on suspicion of receiving stolen property," Matt said. "Other charges are possible."

"You're going to arrest her, here, now, right in the bank?"

"If that becomes necessary, yes, sir," Matt said.

"And once you arrest her, then what?"

"We'll interview her. Ask for her cooperation. If she's unwilling to cooperate, then we'll get a search warrant for the safe-deposit box."

"No judge will give you — no judge should give you, it wouldn't be fair to our customers — a warrant to go into every safe-deposit box in the bank."

"No, sir," Matt said. "But I'm sure I can get a judge to give me one requiring the bank to give me access to every unrented safe-deposit box. I think that's what Mrs. Worner has done, permit Calhoun to use an unrented box. Or maybe she's got a box, and she's letting him use hers. But I think we'll find we're talking about an unrented box."

Chase looked at him coldly, then at Deitrich, and then back at Matt.

"And what you hope I'll do — this is it, isn't it? — is that I'll talk to her."

"That would be in everybody's best interests, Mr. Chase," Dietrich said.

"Yes, I suppose it would," Chase said thoughtfully, and sighed audibly. "We'll have to let her go, of course. The bank simply cannot tolerate —"

"There she is," Deitrich said softly, gesturing through the glass wall to the wide lobby.

Mrs. Adelaide Worner was pulling at the knob of a door marked "Employees Only" to make sure that she had closed it well. Then she started to walk across the polished marble floor of the bank lobby toward the safe-deposit-box vault.

She was plain, gray-haired, and a little plump. But there were vestiges of what probably had been above-average youthful beauty.

She looks, Matt thought, *like somebody who sings in a church choir.*

Chase stepped to his door and opened it, and leaned over his secretary's desk to say something very quietly to her.

"I don't like this part of the job very much," Lieutenant Deitrich said softly.

Chase's secretary got up from her desk and walked across the lobby after Mrs. Worner. A moment later, they both came out of the safe-deposit-vault entrance and started across the lobby.

Chase stood in the door between his desk and his outer office and waited for them.

"Good morning, Adelaide," he said.

"Good morning, Mr. Chase."

"Would you step into my office, please? These gentlemen want to have a word with you."

"Mr. Chase," Mrs. Worner said. "I can't tell you how sorry, how ashamed, I am to have involved the bank in this."

Chase put his arm around her shoulders.

"Come in, and sit down, and we'll see if we can't try to straighten things out," he said.

He looked at Matt with what Matt recognized was more than distaste. It was closer to hate.

"Do you remember me, Adelaide?" Deitrich asked.

"Yes, sir," Mrs. Worner said. "Before we had to send Al to the hospital, we used to see you down at the VFW."

"That's right," Deitrich said. "Adelaide, this is Detective Payne of the Philadelphia Police Department."

Mrs. Worner looked at Matt with terror in her eyes.

"Good morning, Mrs. Worner," Matt said.

"Good morning," she said.

"I'd like you to tell me about the safe-deposit box you've been letting Timmy Calhoun use. Are you willing to talk to me about that?"

"I really don't have much choice, do I?" Mrs. Worner said.

"Are we all ready for this?" Matt asked, and

654

looked around the safe-deposit vault. There were nods.

"Okay," Matt said. "Here we go. I am Detective Matthew M. Payne, Badge 701, of the Philadelphia Police Department."

"A little slower, please, if you can, Detective," the stenographer said.

"I'll try," Matt said.

"This is an interview of Mrs. Adelaide Worner being conducted in the First Harrisburg Bank and Trust Building, Harrisburg, Pennsylvania. In addition to myself and Mrs. Worner, present are Lieutenant Paul Deitrich of the Harrisburg Police Department and Mr. James C. Chase, Vice President of the First Harrisburg Bank and Trust. The interview is being recorded and transcribed by Mrs. . . . . I'm sorry, I forgot your name."

"Grace Placker, Mrs. Grace Placker," the stenographer furnished.

"Mrs. Grace Placker, of the Harrisburg Police Department," Matt went on. He looked at Adelaide Worner.

"Mrs. Worner, you have already been advised of your rights under the Miranda decision. . . ."

"Yes, I have."

"But to make sure that we have crossed all the *t*'s and dotted all the *i*'s, I'm going to go over your rights again. All right?"

"Yes, sir."

"I'm going to ask you questions about Officer Timothy Calhoun of the Philadelphia Police Department having access to a safe-deposit box in the Harrisburg Bank and Trust vault."

"Yes, sir."

Matt took his leather credentials folder from his pocket, took out a small cardboard card, and read from it:

"I have a duty to explain to you and to warn you that you have the following legal rights: You have the right to remain silent and do not have to say anything at all. Anything you say can and will be used against you in court. You have a right to talk to a lawyer of your own choice before I ask you any questions, and also to have a lawyer here with you while I ask questions. If you cannot afford to hire a lawyer, and you want one, I will see that you have a lawyer provided to you, free of charge, before I ask you any questions. If you are willing to give me a statement, you have a right to stop anytime you wish."

He stopped reading and looked at her.

"Do you understand your rights, Mrs. Worner?"

"Yes, sir, I do. Lieutenant Deitrich went over all that with me before in Mr. Chase's office."

"And, Adelaide, I told you then that I'll get you a lawyer if you want one," Chase said.

"If I'm going to tell the truth, why do I need a lawyer? I've caused you enough trouble as it is."

"We just want to be sure you understand your rights, Mrs. Worner," Matt said.

"I do."

"Then you are," Matt dropped his eyes to his Miranda card and read, "willing to answer questions of your own free will, without force or fear, and without any threats and promises having been made to you?"

"Yes, sir."

"Mrs. Worner, are you acquainted with Officer Timothy J. Calhoun of the Philadelphia Police Department?"

"Yes, I am."

"How did you come to meet Officer Calhoun?"

"He's the nephew of my neighbor."

"Is your neighbor's name Vincent T. Holmes?"

"Yes, it is."

"At any time, did you make available to Officer Calhoun a safe-deposit box in the vault of the First Harrisburg Bank and Trust Company?"

"Yes, I did. I told you that."

"Did Officer Calhoun follow the usual procedures to get a safe-deposit box? I mean, did he identify himself, fill out an application, and pay a rental fee?"

"No, he didn't."

"In other words, you let him have the use of a safe-deposit box for free, and without making any records for the bank?"

"That's right."

"Why did you do this?"

"Because he asked me to."

"Did he tell you why he didn't want to give his name, fill out the application, and pay rent?"

"Oh, I didn't understand what you were asking," Adelaide Worner said. "He said, or maybe it was Vincent who said . . . One or the other of them, anyway, said that Monica had gotten in an automobile accident in Philadelphia, and that they were going to be sued, and were probably going to lose, and if they lost, they were going to take everything they owned, because they hadn't been able to afford insurance, you see, unless they could put a little bit away somewhere where the lawyers couldn't find it."

"Money, you mean?"

"Money and some jewelry Monica inherited from her grandmother."

"Let me see if I have that straight, Mrs. Worner. You were told that Mrs. Calhoun was about to be sued because she had been involved in an automobile accident; that the Calhouns did not have insurance; and that if they lost the lawsuit, the lawyers were going to take everything they owned?"

"That's what they told me. Vincent first, and then Timmy and Monica, later."

"So you helped them hide money, and jewelry, by making a safe-deposit box available to Officer Calhoun?"

"Yes, sir."

"Just Officer Calhoun? Did Mrs. Calhoun ever use the box?"

"Yes, she did."

"And Mr. Holmes? Did he ever go into the box?"

"Yes, he did. Both of them did."

"Did you ever see what Officer Calhoun, Mrs. Calhoun, or Mr. Holmes put into the safe-deposit box, or took out of it? Did you ever see any of the money, or the jewelry Mrs. Calhoun inherited from her grandmother?"

"No, sir."

"Can you explain that to me, please? Why not?"

"Because, except for not making a record that

they had rented a box, I treated them like any other customer. They came to my desk, I went with them to the box with my — the bank's — key and unlocked the bank's lock. They unlocked their lock — you understand there's two locks on every box?"

"Yes, ma'am."

"And then they took the box into one of the little rooms, closed the door for privacy, and then either put things into it, or took things out of it."

"So you have no personal knowledge of what went into the box we're talking about?"

"No, sir."

"Did it occur to you, Mrs. Worner, that what you were doing might be illegal?"

"Yes, sir, it did. I realized I was cheating the bank."

"Out of the box rent, you mean."

"Yes, sir, that's what I mean. That bothered me."

"Mrs. Worner, did you have any idea that Officer Calhoun might be engaged in an illegal activity besides concealing his assets?"

"I knew he was a policeman. I didn't even think of anything like that. I knew his wife had stubbed her toe."

"Excuse me?"

"That she'd had a couple of drinks in her when she'd had the accident. That was why — even though the accident wasn't really her fault — they were going to lose in court."

"But aside from Mrs. Calhoun's drunken driving, and the Calhouns' desire to conceal their assets from the court, you had no knowledge or suspicion of any other criminal activity on the part of Officer Calhoun?"

"Not until this morning," Adelaide said.

"What happened this morning?"

"After the police went to Vincent's house and arrested Timmy, Vincent went over there —"

"Excuse me. Vincent — Mr. Holmes — 'went over there'? By over there, you mean to his house?"

Mrs. Worner lowered her head and blushed.

"He . . . Vincent had spent the night at my house," she said.

"Okay. And after the police arrested Officer Calhoun, he went to his house to see what was going on?"

"Yes. And Monica told him what had happened, and Vincent came back and told me he didn't know what, but Timmy was in some kind of trouble with the police, and that if I didn't want bad trouble myself, I should never tell anybody, ever, about the safe-deposit box."

"But you're talking to me now?"

"I am not a criminal-type person, Mr. Detective. As soon as I could work up the courage, I was going to see Mr. Chase and tell him what I had done."

"Mrs. Worner, let's talk about the safe-deposit box," Matt said.

"Yes, sir. Four twenty-one. It's a C-size box," she said, and pointed.

"A 'C-size box'?"

"There are six sizes, A through F, A being the largest, F the smallest."

"I see. Now, I want to be very careful about

660

this. Do you know who the last person to go into that box was?"

"Yes, sir. Timmy."

"By Timmy, you mean Officer Timothy J. Calhoun?"

"Yes, sir."

"Is there any possibility at all that anyone else has had access to that box since Officer Calhoun went into it?"

"Absolutely not."

"How can you be sure?"

"Because I am in charge of the safe-deposit boxes. No one gets into one of them unless they come by my desk and sign themselves in."

Matt turned to Chase.

"Mr. Chase, as an officer of this bank, do you have the authority to grant Lieutenant Deitrich and myself access to safe-deposit box number 421?"

"Yes, I do."

"I ask you now, Mr. Chase, for permission to examine box 421, which has been identified to me as the box to which Mrs. Worner arranged . . . irregular access. Do I have your permission?"

Chase nodded.

"Would you verbalize your answer, please, sir?"

"You have my permission to go into the box," Chase said.

"You're going to need Timmy's key," Mrs. Worner said. "It takes two keys to get into a box."

"The bank doesn't have a master key?" Matt asked, surprised.

Chase shook his head.

"We'll have to call a locksmith," Matt said. "Or break into it."

"Now, wait a minute," Chase said. "Who will pay for repairing that damage?"

"I will," Adelaide Worner said. "This is my fault."

"Give me the bank's key, Adelaide, please," Lieutenant Deitrich said.

"It's in my desk outside," she said. "I'll have to get it."

"Please," Deitrich said.

"Why don't we send for a locksmith?" Chase asked. "I'll pay for it."

"We may not have to, Mr. Chase," Deitrich said. "Let me see what I can do with that lock."

He took a leather case, about the size of Matt's credentials folder, from his jacket pocket. It contained an array of small stainless-steel picks.

Twenty seconds after Mrs. Worner had given him the bank's key to box 421, Deitrich pulled the stainless-steel door to it open.

"There it is," he said to Matt.

"Let's see what's in it," Matt said.

The box was nearly full of stacks of currency, neatly held together with rubber bands.

"My God! Look at all that money!" Mrs. Worner exclaimed.

There was something else. Matt took a ballpoint pen from his pocket and fished a large gold-cased wristwatch with a matching band out of the box. The bezel of the watch was diamond-studded, and there was a diamond chip on the dial where each of the hour numbers would normally be.

"Does anyone really think Mrs. Calhoun inherited this from her grandmother?"

"What is it?" Deitrich asked.

"It's a Rolex, of course. What else?"

Matt held it out for Deitrich to see, and then let the gold-cased watch slip back off the ballpoint pen into the box.

"I think we should have pictures of this," he said. "And I'd like to fingerprint the watch and the box. Maybe they can even get something off the currency. How much trouble would that cause you, Lieutenant?"

"No more than dialing a telephone," Deitrich said. "I can have a forensic-evidence team here in five minutes."

"There's a telephone on my desk," Adelaide Worner said. "You first dial nine, that gets you an outside line, and then you dial your number."

"Thank you, Adelaide," Deitrich said.

"When you come back — we don't want some shyster lawyer accusing us of breaking the chain of evidence — so one of us is going to have to stay here until we get pictures and fingerprints. I need to call Philadelphia."

"I'll be back in thirty seconds," Deitrich said, and walked out of the room.

"What happens to me now, Mr. Chase?" Adelaide Worner asked.

"We'll have to think about that, Adelaide," Chase said. "We'll try to work something out."

"Inspector Wohl," Wohl said.

"Matt, boss."

"What have you got?"

"A forensic-evidence team is on its way here — here being the safe-deposit vault of the First Harrisburg Bank and Trust — to see if they can lift some prints from, and in any case, photograph box 421 and its contents."

"In other words, you served the search warrant?"

"We didn't need to; it was an unauthorized box, still under the control of the bank. The defense can't claim that the accused had a right to privacy by keeping something in a box that wasn't under his control. The lady let us into it. And a Harrisburg police stenographer is about to type up her statement, which ties Calhoun to it with a big red bow."

"Good job!"

"The difficult takes a little time, the impossible a little longer."

"What's in the box?"

"What looks like thirty, forty thousand dollars. Maybe more. I'm going to wait until they take pictures and maybe lift some prints before I count it. But a whole great big bunch of money! And a wristwatch that looks like something a drug dealer, or a pimp, would have on his wrist."

"A Rolex, maybe?"

"Uh-huh."

"Have you got the serial number? It's on the back of the case."

"No, but I can get it in thirty seconds."

"Get it," Wohl ordered.

A minute later, Matt had read the serial number to him over the phone.

"Mr. Marcus Brownlee," Wohl said, "has given

us a sworn statement that his Rolex watch was taken from him at the time of his arrest, but never made it from the place of his arrest to either the evidence room or personal property at Central Lockup. Tiny just got the serial number of said timepiece from Bailey, Banks and Biddle —"

"And it matches?"

"It matches."

"Who is Marcus Brownlee?" Matt asked.

"Didn't McFadden fill you in?"

"I didn't hear that name."

"One of the drug guys the Five Squad busted at the Howard Johnson motel," Wohl explained.

"Then we have them."

"It's not quite that simple," Wohl said. "I'll fill you in later. What I want you to do now, once you work the box, is get Calhoun and the watch — the money would be nice, too, but that can wait — back to Philadelphia."

"Yes, sir."

"Be damned careful with the chain of evidence on this one, Matt, if I have to tell you that. And make sure Mutt and Jeff do."

"Yes, sir."

"Where's Calhoun now?"

"McFadden and Martinez have him at Harrisburg Police Headquarters."

"Have them bring him to South Detectives at Twenty-fourth and Wolf," Wohl ordered. "We're using the First District detention cells downstairs as our own Central Lockup."

"I don't understand," Matt said.

"I'm not trying to shoot you down, Matt — right now you're at the head of my good-guy list for tying Calhoun to the box — but right now you don't have to understand. Just do what I told you. I'll fill you in later."

"Yes, sir, " Matt said. "One question: Do we let Calhoun know we got into the box? Or about the watch?"

Wohl thought that over for fifteen seconds, which seemed longer.

"Yeah, let him know. I'd rather he spend the time riding back here wondering what's going to happen to him knowing we have his ass than trying to convince himself he shouldn't be worried, we don't have anything."

"Yes, sir."

"You stay there and keep your eye on the Reynolds woman."

The phone went dead in Matt's ear when he was halfway through saying, "Yes, sir."

"Okay," the Hon. Jerome H. Carlucci said, looking around his conference table. "Where are we? Who wants to start?"

Present were Thomas J. Callis, Philadelphia's district attorney; Taddeus Czernich, police commissioner; Chief Inspector of Detectives Matthew Lowenstein; Chief Inspector Dennis V. Coughlin; Inspector Peter Wohl; Staff Inspector Michael Weisbach; and Lieutenant J. K. Fellows.

In the wings, so to speak, in case they were needed, were Captain Michael Sabara and Detective Tony Harris (physically in the mayor's outer office); Captain David Pekach and Lieutenant John J. Malone of the Highway Patrol (sitting in their cars in the courtyard of City Hall);

and Lieutenant Daniel Justice, Jr., and Sergeant Jason Washington (within two rings of a telephone at the 1st District/South Detectives).

Inspector Wohl motioned with his hand to indicate that he thought Staff Inspector Weisbach was the man to bring the mayor — and for that matter, everybody else — up-to-date. Mike Weisbach first shook his head, then inclined it toward the head of the table. Peter Wohl followed his eyes and saw that the mayor was looking at him impatiently.

He started to stand up. The mayor waved him back into his seat.

"Yes, sir," Wohl said. "The entire Five Squad has been arrested, and are presently being held in the detention cell of the First District."

"What are we charging them with?"

"Right now, with misprision in office, specifically the theft, under cover of office, of evidence," Wohl said. "Mr. Callis will, of course, add other charges later when we decide who's going to be charged with what."

"Does he mean the rape, Tony?" Carlucci asked.

"What Denny and Matt and I have been thinking, Jerry," Callis said, pointing vaguely at Coughlin and Lowenstein, "is that once Prasko understands we have them for the theft of evidence — and simple grand larceny — once, in other words, he understands that they're going down on that, we can let Prasko know we know about the rape, and get him to testify against the others, in exchange for his being allowed to plead guilty to violating the civil rights of Williams and

667

Brownlee — and probably half a dozen others."

"He plea-bargains to a federal rap and gets what?" Carlucci said.

"I talked to the U.S. Attorney just before I came over here, Jerry. Nothing's set in cement, but he thinks he can find a judge willing to go along with five years on each charge, sentences to be served consecutively, so figure at least four charges, so twenty years."

"Which means he'd really do what?" Carlucci asked coldly.

"He'd probably be out in six, seven years," Callis said.

"You and Denny and Matt decided that between you?" Carlucci asked. "What about him?" He pointed at Police Commissioner Czernich. "Was he involved in your discussion? The last I heard was that he's the police commissioner. You didn't think you had to discuss that with him?"

The translation of that was that Jerry Carlucci did not like what he had heard, and because he did not like it, neither would Commissioner Czernich.

"I'm not sure," Czernich began, understanding his role and taking his cue, "that I could —"

"Well, Tony?" Carlucci interrupted him.

"Would I be wasting my breath to tell you why we think that's the way to go?" Callis asked.

"Try me. Find out."

"The priority here is to put the Five Squad away. Do we agree on at least that much?"

The mayor shrugged.

"Unless we can have somebody on the Five Squad turn state's witness, all we have on them is the testimony of drug dealers in the one case we really know about, what happened at the Howard Johnson motel last Thursday. Juries are funny, Jerry. If the defense brings in weeping cops' wives and scared-looking kids in the courtroom, what a lot of jurors might decide is that 'fuck the drug dealers, they got what was coming to them.' "

Carlucci's face tightened, but he didn't say anything.

"They're going to look like good cops to the jury, Jerry," Lowenstein said. "I went over their arrest records last night. Lots of good busts, lots of convictions. A couple of them got hurt. All that will have to be made available to the defense, and it can't help but impress a jury."

"On that subject," Mike Weisbach said. "The defense —"

"The goddamn FOP!" the mayor exploded. "I am unable to believe that one cop in five hundred wants his FOP dues used to defend scumbags like these!"

"They call that, Jerry, 'innocent until proven guilty,' " Callis said.

Carlucci glowered at him.

"In this case, it's moot," Weisbach said. " 'Armando C. Giacomo for the defense, your honor.' Manny does it *pro bono;* it won't cost the FOP a dime."

"Jesus!" the mayor said.

"When did you find that out?" Coughlin asked.

"About thirty minutes ago," Weisbach said. "He called Sabara — I guess he heard they were picked up by Special Operations — and Mike passed him on to me. He wants to know where he can speak with them at half past ten."

"How the hell did Giacomo get involved so quickly?"

"I think he calls the FOP and makes himself available when he has some free time," Callis said. "All that does is reinforce my argument that unless we can get at least one of the Five Squad to roll over, the testimony of a couple of drug guys like Williams and Brownlee probably isn't going to be enough."

"If Manny Giacomo talks to any of these guys at half past ten, at ten forty-five, Vincenzo Savarese will have their names," Lowenstein said.

"He'd get the names eventually anyway," Coughlin said. "But I'd much prefer later than sooner. Maybe I can talk to him."

"Don't hold your breath, Denny," the mayor said.

"I think it's worth the effort. When I spoke to Savarese this morning, he made it pretty clear he intends to whack the guy who raped his granddaughter."

"It would be nice, wouldn't it, if we caught him doing that?" Carlucci said. "This scumbag would get what he deserves, and we'd have Savarese on premeditated murder."

"The philosophy of that aside, Jerry," Lowenstein said, "Savarese wouldn't whack Prasko. And he would be in church with the archbishop when one of his thugs did."

Wohl saw that Carlucci was going to angrily respond to that, and jumped into the conversation:

"There was some good news from Harrisburg," Wohl said. "Matt Payne got into the safe-deposit box they were using. Got a statement that Calhoun, Timothy J., was the only one with access to the box, in which there was probably forty thousand dollars — maybe more — and a gold Rolex that Baby Brownlee says was stolen from him last Thursday night."

"And?" the mayor asked.

"That may be enough to convince Calhoun that the thing for him to do is roll over," Wohl said. "I told Payne to get Calhoun back here as soon as he can, and to take him directly to Jason Washington."

"Who is where right now? Washington, I mean?" Carlucci asked.

"South Detectives," Coughlin said.

"Doing what?"

"Trying to pick the right moment to let Prasko know what he did to the girl, and what Savarese is going to do to him unless he can hide out in some nice safe federal prison."

"I thought we had the guy he locked up in the NIKE site? An eyewitness to the rape? What happened to him?"

"I told Washington to wait until we saw what happened in Harrisburg," Wohl said. "Then we let Prasko know we have the money, maybe a rolled-over Calhoun *and* Ronald R. Ketcham, who saw him rape the girl."

"You made that decision? By yourself, Inspector?"

"Yes, sir," Wohl said. "By myself."

"When I was a policeman, I respected the chain

of command," Carlucci said. "You should have discussed that with Coughlin and Lowenstein. And then they should have discussed it with the commissioner."

"Yes, sir," Peter said.

"Just for the record, Mr. Mayor," Coughlin said, "if Inspector Wohl had come to me — and I wouldn't have expected him to — I would have told him I thought it was the way to go."

Carlucci visibly debated whether to respond to Coughlin and then changed the subject.

"When is the Harrisburg scumbag due here?"

"An hour, I'd say," Wohl replied. "I told Matt to send him back with McFadden and Martinez, and to worry about sending the evidence later."

"Send the evidence? Or bring it?"

"Payne's still working on the terrorist thing for the FBI," Coughlin said. "I don't know when he's coming back to Philadelphia."

"But the bottom line here is that what we're hoping for is that you can get a couple of these scumbags to roll over, right?"

"That's right," Callis said. "In my judgment, that's the way to put these dirty cops away."

"And you're the district attorney, right?"

"Yes, I am, Mr. Mayor."

"And since all the decisions have already been made, what that boils down to is that the commissioner and I are about as useful as teats on a boar hog, right?"

"Let me think about that," Lowenstein said.

Carlucci glowered at him.

" 'Teats on a boar hog'? Is that what you said, Mr. Mayor? God, I wish I had your colorful command of the language, Mr. Mayor!"

Carlucci's scowl changed into a smile.

"Screw you, Matt," he said. "Get out of here. All of you get out of here."

They all started to get to their feet.

"It's a good thing we're all friends," the mayor said. "And that you know me well enough to know what I'm pissed at is not you. You've done a good job, all of you, and I'm grateful. The commissioner and I are grateful, isn't that so, Tad?"

"Absolutely, Mr. Mayor," Commissioner Czernich said.

"Peter, as soon as you hear something, let me know, will you?"

"Yes, sir. Of course."

"And pass my 'well done' down the line, will you?"

"Yes, sir."

They shuffled out of his office.

"I'm going to try to see Manny," Coughlin said. "Before he sees the Five Squad."

"And ask him what?" Lowenstein asked.

"To hold off on giving Savarese the names of the Five Squad."

"Good luck," Lowenstein said.

"At least hold off for a while. Until we get somebody to roll over. Or know nobody is," Coughlin said.

"You know, I got a guy in my office, Phebus," Tony Callis said. "He used to be a sergeant in Narcotics. Do you think he'd be useful? I mean, they see one of their own. . . . They just might listen to him."

"I don't see how it could hurt," Wohl said. "But . . . could you send him out to South Detectives and tell him Washington's in charge?"

"Sure," Callis said. "I know he's in the office. I left word that I wanted to see him about the guy who shot Officer Kellog. That can wait. I'll have Phebus at South Detectives in thirty minutes."

Twenty-Five

"My arm is going to sleep," Officer Timothy J. Calhoun said to Detective Charles McFadden. He moved his right arm, which was held by handcuffs to the strap on the rear of the front seat of the unmarked Plymouth.

McFadden was sitting beside him. Martinez was driving. They were on U.S. 222, five miles out of Harrisburg, headed for the Pennsylvania Turnpike.

"What do you want me to do?" McFadden asked. "I can't take the risk of you doing something stupid, Timmy."

"He already did a lot stupid," Jesus said from the front seat.

"Like what?" Calhoun asked, trying to ignore Martinez.

McFadden went along with him. He felt a little sorry for him, and Jesus could be a real prick. Timmy had enough on his back without Jesus digging at him.

"Like jumping out of the car, for example," Charley said.

"I wouldn't do that, Charley," Calhoun said.

"I can't take that chance," McFadden said.

"Cuff me behind my back," Calhoun said.

"Fuck you, Calhoun," Martinez said. "Just sit there and shut up."

"Ease off, Jesus," Charley said.

675

"When they get you in the slam, Calhoun," Martinez said, "and some sweaty two-hundred-fifty-pound lifer starts shoving his schlong up your ass, you'll look back on your fucking arm going to sleep as the good old days."

"Just drive the car, will you, Jesus?" Charley said.

"I could be wrong," Martinez said. "Maybe he'll like getting fucked in the ass."

"Put your left hand behind your back, Timmy," Charley said. "Jesus, let me have your cuffs."

"Why?"

"Because I'm going to cuff Calhoun behind his back."

"Fuck him, let his arm go to sleep. Let his arm turn black and fall off."

"Give me your goddamn cuffs, goddamn it!"

Martinez grunted as he shifted around on the seat trying to get his handcuffs out from where he carried them, in the small of his back. He finally succeeded and laid them on the back of the seat.

McFadden placed one of them on Calhoun's left wrist, and then freed his right wrist from the handcuff shackling him to the front seat. Then he put Calhoun's right wrist behind his back and clipped the handcuff to it.

Calhoun slumped back against the seat.

"Thanks, Charley."

"Okay," McFadden said.

Ninety seconds later, Calhoun announced: "Charley, I got to go to the toilet."

"Fuck you!" Martinez said. "Crap in your

676

pants, you dirty cocksucker!"

"What the hell is the matter with you, Martinez?" Calhoun asked. "What did I ever do to you?"

"You were born, is what you did to me," Martinez said, and then seemed to warm to the subject. "I don't like dirty cops, is what's the matter with me," Martinez said. "And you know — you're a goddamn narc — what that shit does to people, and you were selling it. Stealing it from drug people, and then selling it! Probably to kids! You are the lowest of the fucking low, Calhoun!"

"Ease off, Jesus," Charley said.

"Fuck you, ease off! What I would like to do to this miserable shitheel is shoot him with a .22 in both knees, and make him crawl to jail."

"I'm telling you to ease off, goddamn it!"

"With that damned Rolex watch shoved up his ass!" Martinez went on, undaunted.

"Charley, unless I get to go to the toilet, I'm going to crap in my pants!" Calhoun said plaintively.

"I don't give a shit!"

Two minutes later, Martinez turned off 222 into a Cities Service complex, a large service station with two rows of pumps, a store offering tires and other automotive accessories, and a restaurant.

He pulled the unmarked Plymouth up in front of the restaurant and jumped out of the driver's seat. He took his identification folder from his pocket and opened it so the shield was visible, then pushed his jacket aside so that his holstered pistol was visible. He waved his badge around at shoulder height.

"Nothing to worry about, folks. We are police officers!"

That, of course, caught the attention of everyone within fifty feet, including several people seated at tables inside the restaurant.

"Let him out, McFadden!" Martinez ordered.

Charley reached over Calhoun and opened the door.

Calhoun made his way awkwardly out of the backseat.

Charley slid across the seat and got out after him.

"You go set things up in the restaurant," Martinez ordered.

"I'm not going to leave you alone with him," McFadden said.

"You don't think I'd shoot him right here, do you?"

"I'm not going to leave him alone with you, Martinez," Charley repeated.

"Suit yourself," Martinez said, and walked into the restaurant, where, from the door, he repeated the "Nothing to worry about folks, we're police officers" routine.

By the time Charley marched the handcuffed former police officer Timothy J. Calhoun through the door of the restaurant, the eyes of everyone in the restaurant were on them, and Calhoun was so humiliated Charley thought he might actually cry.

Charley marched Calhoun past the fascinated restaurant customers to the men's room.

Martinez preceded them, and ran a frightened-looking civilian out of the place before he would permit Charley to lead Calhoun inside.

Charley marched him up to a stall and turned him around.

"Aren't you going to take the cuffs off?" Calhoun asked.

"Timmy, I just can't take the chance," Charley said, sounding genuinely sorry.

He unfastened Calhoun's belt, unbuttoned the flap, pulled down his zipper, and pulled first his trousers and then his shorts down over his hips.

"Back in there," he ordered.

Calhoun, his trousers at his ankles, backed into the stall and finally managed to lower himself onto the toilet.

"How am I supposed to wipe myself?" Calhoun asked.

"When you're finished, I'll uncuff you to do that," Charley said.

It became evident to Officer Calhoun that Detective McFadden had no intention of closing the door, but instead was leaning on the frame, obviously intending to watch him.

"You're not even going to close the door?"

"Timmy, I just can't take the chance," Charley said. "If I was in your shoes, I think I'd eat my gun."

"Maybe that's what I should have done when I saw the cars outside."

"Too late for that, now, Timmy. You're going down."

"Shit!"

In Detective McFadden's professional judgment, Officer Calhoun was about to cry. Which meant that he had swallowed the good cop–bad cop routine hook, line, and sinker. He hadn't thought it would be this easy, but on the other hand, Calhoun had never had a reputation for being very smart, just a good guy.

"What are you going to do, Timmy?" Charley asked sympathetically.

Calhoun looked up at McFadden. There were tears in his eyes.

"What the hell can I do?"

"Timmy, how the hell did you ever get into this mess?" Charley asked. "Didn't you even think what would happen to Monica when you were caught?"

"We weren't supposed to get caught!" Calhoun said indignantly. "That fucking Phebus said there was no way in the fucking world we were going to get caught!"

Bingo! Former Sergeant Anton C. Phebus! I'll be damned!

"You're going to have to give them Phebus, Timmy. Before somebody else does. It's not like you'd be ratting on another cop. He's not a cop anymore, he's a lawyer, an assistant D.A., for Christ's sake! And he got you into this."

"We weren't supposed to get caught," Calhoun said. "Shit!"

"What we're going to do now, Timmy, is get on the phone to Sergeant Washington, who is my boss, and a good guy. You're going to tell him that as soon as we get to Philadelphia you're going to give him Phebus. He already knows about Phebus, of course, but with a little luck, you'll be

680

giving him Phebus before anybody else on the Five Squad does. That should help you."

Calhoun nodded.

"I'll be right back, Timmy," Charley said.

"Where are you going?"

Charley didn't reply.

Detective Martinez was leaning on the wall just outside the men's room.

"Anything?"

"You remember good old Sergeant Anton C. Phebus?"

"Yeah. What about him?"

"He's the brains behind the whole thing."

"No shit?"

"No shit," Charley said. "See if you can borrow an office with a phone. I want to get Calhoun on the phone, talking to Washington, before he changes his mind."

Although he scanned the lobby for her carefully, Matt Payne did not see Susan Reynolds when he returned to the Penn-Harris Hotel a few minutes after twelve.

As he got on the elevator, he decided he would call her at the Department of Social Services. Even with her line tapped, it would raise no suspicions on the FBI's part if he telephoned and asked her if she was free for lunch.

As he put the key in the door of Suite 612, he sensed movement, and glanced down the corridor. Susan was trotting toward him, obviously distraught.

"Hi!" he said. "I was just about to call you."

"Where have you been?" she asked.

Calm down," he said, opened the door, and waved her inside ahead of him.

He closed the door and put his arms around her.

"Where the hell were you?" she asked, her voice muffled against her chest.

"I was out arresting a dirty cop," he said. "My boss just told me I was at the head of his good-guy list."

She pushed away from him and looked up into his face.

"Say what you're thinking," she said.

"I'm not thinking anything," he said.

"Yes, you are."

"There was a certain irony in that, wouldn't you think?"

"In other words, what you're going to do for Jennie makes you feel dirty?"

"Whatever I wind up doing, honey, it's not going to be for your pal Jennie."

"I could meet her by myself, Matt, and try to reason with her. I really hate what this is going to do to you."

"That's very tempting, but for several reasons, it wouldn't work," Matt said. "And I'm a big boy. I know what I'm doing."

"Why wouldn't it work?"

"Well, I think it's entirely possible that the FBI has got somebody on you — besides that woman in your office, I mean. If they see you leaving town, they'll follow you — keeping track of a Porsche isn't hard. And the minute you meet Poor Jennie, surprise, surprise! Go directly to jail, do not pass Go, do not collect two hundred bucks. I don't want you to go to jail, honey."

"You don't *know* the FBI is watching me. Watching me that close, I mean."

"They're tapping your phones twenty-four hours a day. Your pal keeps calling — it doesn't matter what name she gives, I told you that, they know who it is. They're under pressure to put the arm on Chenowith and Company. They may not have the manpower to do it twenty-four hours a day, seven days a week, but whenever they can find the people, they're on you, Susan. Believe me."

"Jennie called," Susan said. "This morning."

"And?"

"I told her I would meet her."

"She called you at your office?" Matt asked. Susan nodded. "And you went to some pay phone and called her back? Or she called you at a pay-phone number you gave her?"

"At a number I gave her."

"Okay. So the minute you left your office, we can count on your friendly coworker listening to what you and Jennie had to say to each other. We can also count on her reporting that, right then, to the Terrorist Unit. If they had somebody available, you might have been followed to the phone booth. Hell, they might have followed you here."

"And there's a microphone in the light fixture?" Susan said, pointing at the ceiling. "And they are listening to everything we're saying now?"

"I don't think so. They think I'm on their side. But there's no telling, really. I should have thought of that. I'm used to planting mikes, not

683

having them planted on me."

"I was kidding," Susan said. "You really think they could have a microphone in here?"

"Well, if they do, we're all going to jail," Matt said.

"I never know when you're serious," Susan said.

"Tell me about Poor Jennie," Matt said. "Softly. The FBI may be listening."

"She really wants to give me whatever it is she wants me to keep for her."

"The translation of that is that, to cover his ass, Chenowith wants to get rid of the bank loot," Matt said. "And what did you tell her?"

"That I would meet her the same place I met her last time," Susan said.

"The restaurant in Doylestown?" Matt asked. Susan nodded. "When?"

"I told her I couldn't take off from work without questions being asked," Susan said. "I told her I'd try to get there by seven."

"Speaking of work, you're on your lunch hour, right?"

She shook her head, "no."

"After I talked to Jennie, I didn't go back to work."

"Why not?"

"I was afraid to," Susan said.

"Did something happen? What were you afraid of?"

"I didn't like the way Veronica was looking at me."

"So, what did you do?"

"I came here, looking for you, and you weren't

here, so I walked around the block, and came back, and walked around the block. . . . The last time I came in the hotel, I saw you getting on the elevator."

"By now, Veronica is wondering where the hell you are. You didn't call up and say you were sick or anything?"

Susan shook her head, "no."

"Do it now. Tell her you felt dizzy and got sick to your stomach."

"I don't work for Veronica. I'd have to call my supervisor."

"Whoever. Tell whoever that you got sick and felt dizzy, and are going to see your doctor at half past three, and that you'll probably be in after that."

"You want me to go back to work?"

"No. But that may stall them a little. They may — just may — decide to wait until after you don't show up at four, or four thirty, before deciding that you've taken off."

"What are we going to do about Jennie?"

"What is she going to do, just wait for you in the restaurant?"

"There's an outside pay phone — actually, there's three of them — and she's going to start calling them at seven. When I answer, she'll know I'm there."

"Which one? You said three?"

"Whichever one rings," Susan said, and smiled. "I guess she has the numbers of all of them. If one of them is busy, she'll try another. She's good at this sort of thing."

"Call your supervisor," Matt said.

"And then what?"

"And then we go."

"Go where?"

"Ultimately to Doylestown. But right now, just out of here."

"I'm not due in Doylestown until seven."

"So we'll stop at Hershey and shoot a quick eighteen holes," Matt said.

"That would be nice, wouldn't it, if we could do things like that? Play some golf? Are you any good?"

"I'm very good, thank you for asking," Matt said. "Call your supervisor, Susan."

Armando C. Giacomo, Esq., had more than a little difficulty finding a place to park his Jaguar sedan in the parking lot shared by the 1st District and South Detectives. The three spots reserved for visitors outside the ancient, run-down building were occupied, which was not really surprising. But so were the two spots reserved for inspectors; and the two spots set aside for the two captains of the 1st District and South Detectives.

He finally figured to hell with it, and parked in an "Absolutely No Parking at Any Time" slot near the rear door of the old, shabby building. His car was subject to being towed away there, but he suspected that before his shiny new Jaguar was hauled off, inquiries would be made to establish its ownership, and he could then explain to whoever came asking, how hard he had looked for a place to park and how reluctant he was to leave it on the street, where some happy adolescent would write his initials in the shiny green

686

lacquer with a key.

Most cops, he knew, bore him little ill will for defending individuals alleged to have a connection with organized crime. For one thing — which explained to Manny Giacomo why the cops didn't climb the walls and pull their hair out when a genuine bad guy walked on a legal technicality — most cops drew a line between what they did and the criminal justice system did.

They arrested the bad guys. That was their job. What happened with the lawyers and the district attorneys and juries wasn't their concern.

There were even a few cops who really believed — as Manny Giacomo did — that even the worst scumbag was entitled to the best defense he could get, that it was on this that Justice with a capital *J* was really based.

And just about every cop knew that if they were hauled before the bar of justice, lowercase *J,* on an excessive-brutality rap or the like, they could expect to hear, "Armando C. Giacomo for the defense, your honor" when they stood up to face the judge.

Just before he pushed open the door to the building, Manny Giacomo saw a new Buick coupe, bristling with an array of antennas, parked where no civilian vehicle was ever allowed to park, in one of the spots reserved for district radio patrol cars.

Mr. Michael J. O'Hara of the Bulletin *is obviously up and about practicing his profession,* Giacomo thought, and wondered if he could somehow put the power of the press to work defending the officers he had come to protect from the unjustified accusations of the police establishment.

Just inside the door, Lieutenant Daniel Justice of South Detectives, who had probably been waiting for him, stuck out his hand.

"Good morning, counselor."

"Danny the Judge!" Giacomo said, shaking his hand.

Danny needed a shave, and looked as if he had been up all night. Giacomo remembered the last time he'd seen him, he'd told him he was working Last Out. He therefore should now be home asleep.

"I thought you were working Last Out," Giacomo said.

"You know what they say, 'no rest for the virtuous,'" Danny said. "Chief Inspector Coughlin would be most grateful if you could spare him a moment of your time."

"Before I talk to the unjustly accused police officers, you mean?"

"Now, is what I mean," Danny said. "I'll pass on agreeing that they're unjustly accused."

Danny the Judge guided Giacomo across the room to the office of the district captain and pushed open the door.

Dennis Coughlin and Michael O'Hara had apparently evicted the district captain from his office. O'Hara was sitting behind his desk. Coughlin was sitting in the one, somewhat battered, chrome-and-leather armchair.

"Mr. Giacomo, Chief," Danny announced. "Should I have his illegally parked car hauled away now, or wait awhile?"

"Declare it abandoned, have it hauled to the Academy, and tell them I said they should use it for target practice," Coughlin replied. "Good morning, Counselor."

"You heard him, Mickey," Giacomo said. "Blatantly and shamelessly threatening the desecration of a work of art."

O'Hara got up from behind the desk and walked toward the door.

"Somehow, I get the feeling that Denny would rather talk to you alone, Manny," he said, touching his shoulder as he walked past him.

Danny the Judge pulled the door closed.

"There's coffee, Manny," Coughlin said, indicating a coffee machine.

Giacomo walked to it and helped himself.

"Being a suspicious character," he said as he looked with distaste at a bowl full of packets of nondairy creamer and decided he was not going to put that terrifying collection of chemicals into his coffee, "I suspect that there may be more here than meets the eye. Or, more specifically, what I was led to believe by the vice president of the FOP."

"What did he lead you to believe?" Coughlin asked.

"For one thing," Giacomo said, taking a sip from his coffee mug — which bore the insignia of the Emerald Society, the association of police officers of Irish extraction — and deciding the coffee was going to be just as bad as he was afraid it would be, "the last I heard, Chief Inspector Coughlin was not running Internal Affairs."

"What did they tell you at the FOP?" Coughlin repeated.

"That several all-around scumbags engaged in the controlled-substances distribution industry had made several outrageous allegations against a number of pure-as-freshly-fallen-snow police officers."

"Well, they got the 'scumbags' part right, at least," Coughlin said.

"I am now prepared to listen to — if you are inclined to tell me — the opposing view."

He sat down at the district captain's desk and looked at Coughlin.

"Off the record, if you'd rather, Denny," he added.

"Thank you for off-the-record, Manny," Coughlin said. "Okay. We have the entire Five Squad of the Narcotics Unit under arrest. The charge right now is misprision in office."

"The entire Five Squad? That's interesting. And so is 'misprision.' And what inference, if any, should I draw from 'right now'?"

"One of the charges that may be placed against one of these officers is rape," Coughlin said.

" 'May be placed'? Was there a rape? Can you prove it?"

"There was a rape. An oral rape. We have a witness to the rape."

" '*May* be placed'? I don't understand that."

"I understand, Manny, that you took Vincenzo Savarese to Brewster Payne's office, where Savarese begged Brewster to lean on his daughter to treat Savarese's granddaughter?"

"What we're talking about here, Denny, is the

690

Narcotics Five Squad," Giacomo said. "Not Vincenzo Savarese."

"Shortly after Dr. Payne took Cynthia Longwood under her care," Coughlin went on, "a message was left for her at University Hospital —"

"I'm really disappointed in Dr. Payne. And/or Brewster Payne. If what you say is true, then either Payne told his son — which is the same thing as telling the police — or Dr. Payne clearly violated patient-physician —"

"Let me finish, Manny," Coughlin said.

"I'm about to say, Chief Coughlin, that we are back on the record."

"Give me another ninety seconds on that, Manny, please."

Giacomo considered that.

"Ninety seconds, no. We're still off the record. We go back on at my option."

"Thank you," Coughlin said.

Coughlin reached in his pocket and took out a sheet of paper and read from it, slowly:

" 'Miss Cynthia Longwood was stripped naked and orally raped, by a policeman under circumstances that were themselves traumatic.' "

"Jesus!" Manny Giacomo said, and was immediately furious with himself for letting his surprise show.

"Dr. Payne believes that having suffered a traumatic experience like that is consistent with Miss Longwood's condition, which is, in Dr. Payne's opinion, very close to serious schizophrenia. I'm not too good with medical terms, Manny, but what Amy means is that if the girl gets that far,

691

she won't come back soon, or at all."

"You're saying that one of the Five Squad narcs did this to her?"

"Yes, I am. And does Savarese know? He knows. He doesn't have the name of the cop yet."

"Aren't you presuming a lot, Denny? How do you know Savarese knows?"

"We know that Joey Fiorello hired a private investigator — a retired detective — to see who the girl's boyfriend was. His name is Ronald R. Ketcham. The retired detective told Fiorello that Ketcham wasn't quite the respectable stockbroker he's supposed to be; that he's into selling drugs. He also told Fiorello that it was logical to presume that Ketcham's girlfriend was also into 'recreational' drugs.

"Shortly after that happened, Ketcham was snatched from the garage of his apartment. They took him to a deserted NIKE site in South Philadelphia, took his clothes away from him, and left him there in the dark overnight. The next day, they came back and asked him questions. He had no idea he was keeping company with Savarese's granddaughter. He thought that the people who had snatched him were in the drug business."

"I don't understand what you're telling me."

"Last Thursday night, Ketcham went to the Howard Johnson motel on Roosevelt Boulevard to do a drug deal with a guy named Amos Williams. He had Savarese's daughter with him. The Five Squad was apparently onto both of them. They busted Williams, and the people he had with him. One of the cops went into Ketcham's room, stole twenty thousand dollars from him, handcuffed him to the toilet, and raped Savarese's granddaughter."

"You can prove all that, I suppose?"

Coughlin ignored the question.

"Ketcham told Savarese's thugs what happened. His assumption was that Williams thought he had given Williams to the Five Squad, and that Williams had sent the people to snatch him. You with me?"

"I don't know, keep talking."

"So Savarese left Ketcham in the NIKE site . . ."

That I don't believe. If Savarese thought this guy was responsible for his granddaughter getting raped — or just for getting her on "recreational" drugs — he just wouldn't walk away and leave it at that.

But the rest of this is probably true. Savarese wanted me to get an investigator for him. Jesus Christ, I'm glad I didn't do that!

". . . and told Joey Fiorello to have the private investigator find out what cops were at the Howard Johnson motel when they busted Amos Williams. They gave the guy a bullshit story why they wanted to know, and the guy went to Mike Sabara and told him he smelled something fishy."

"How did you know that person or persons unknown had left the boyfriend in the NIKE site?"

"We're still off the record, right, Manny?"

"I'll tell you when we go back on."

"Amy Payne called Peter Wohl and told him about the message at the hospital. Peter brought it to me. I put out a Locate, Do Not Detain on Ketcham. Danny the Judge read it. When a South detective went to Justice and told him he had found a guy named Ketcham wearing only an overcoat locked up in the NIKE site, Danny called me."

"That's why everything is going on here?"

Coughlin nodded.

"You don't have any authority in one of those sites, you know. They're federal property."

Coughlin ignored that.

"Ketcham positively identified one of the Five Squad as the guy who raped the granddaughter, and gave us a sworn statement to the effect. Plus, that the same guy had stolen twenty thousand dollars from him."

"I wonder how convincing a witness Mr. Ketcham would be," Giacomo said.

"I went to Hanging Harriet McCandless — Tony Callis did — and got her to overturn the magistrate's decision to grant bail to Amos Williams and one of his thugs, a scumbag named Baby Brownlee. Jason Washington got them to give statements saying they had more cocaine at the time of their arrest than Five Squad turned in as evidence, and more cash, and in the case of Brownlee, a gold Rolex that until a couple of hours ago seemed to have disappeared."

"Same question, Denny. I wonder what sort of witnesses Mr. Williams and Mr. Brownlee would make against fine police officers? Frankly, I would be prone to ask them, several times, so the jury would be sure to hear their answer, whether the police or the district attorney had offered them anything — like immunity from prosecution — in exchange for their agreeing to say these terrible

694

things about these fine police officers."

"Baby Brownlee's gold Rolex showed up this morning in a safe-deposit box in Harrisburg, the only key to which was in the hands of another fine pure-as-the-driven-snow police officer assigned to the Narcotics Unit's Five Squad. And there was some fifty thousand–plus in cash in the same box."

"I presume you think you can prove the watch in question is actually Mr. Brownlee's?"

"He bought it at Bailey, Banks and Biddle. They made a record of the serial number."

"Very interesting story, Denny. Is that all of it?"

"Not quite," Coughlin said. "I had breakfast with Savarese this morning."

"Did you really?"

"I told him that we didn't want to subject his granddaughter to the humiliation of having to testify against her rapist, and that what we proposed to do was have him plead guilty to enough charges of violating the civil rights —"

"Violating somebody's civil rights? Whose civil rights?" Giacomo interrupted.

"Williams's and Brownlee's, for sure. Probably some others. We picked up everybody they arrested within the last ten days when their bail was revoked, and reinterviewed them. We're prepared to go further back, if necessary."

"Why would you believe that an attorney would recommend that this guy cop a plea like that? It seems to me that, in this case, there is very little chance that the victim would ever testify against him."

"Savarese put it another way," Coughlin said. "He said he didn't think there could be a trial if there was no one around alive to try."

"He has a point," Giacomo said. "You didn't think that simple observation about life in general could in any way be construed as a threat against anyone, did you?"

"Manny, he as much as told me he's going to kill this guy just as soon as he finds out who he is."

"Not in so many words, right?"

"Not in so many words."

"If Mr. Savarese is, in your opinion, so prepared to cause the unlawful deaths of others, in particular those who have in some way caused harm to members of his family, why do you suppose he didn't do something dreadful to Mr. — Ketcham, you said? —"

"Ronald R. Ketcham," Coughlin furnished.

"— when he had the opportunity?"

"Peter Wohl thinks Savarese wanted him to starve to death," Coughlin said.

My God, that's probably exactly what Savarese intended to do.

"What do you want from me, Denny?"

"I want — what the hell, you'd have his name in a couple of minutes anyway — Officer Herbert Prasko to roll over on the Five Squad. In exchange for which, he'll get a twenty-year plea bargain, which means probably seven years in a federal prison."

"Why should I encourage him to do that?"

"Because otherwise you know that Savarese will have him killed."

"I know nothing of the kind!"

Who do I think I'm fooling?

"Come on, Manny!" Coughlin said.

"You've got the deal lined up?"

"The U.S. Attorney has been very helpful."

"Why?"

"Because — I'm guessing — he thinks he'd have a hard time convicting Savarese on an unlawful-abduction charge. And maybe because he thinks he'll look good in Washington if he put a local cop away on a civil rights charge. And the FBI will get the credit for uncovering that travesty of justice."

"Very interesting," Giacomo said.

"That's it, Manny," Coughlin said.

The two men looked at each other. First Coughlin shrugged, and then Giacomo.

"Let's go back on the record, Counselor," Coughlin said.

Giacomo shrugged again.

"I presume, Mr. Giacomo," Coughlin said, "that you are here to represent one or more of the police officers we arrested last night and this morning on charges of misprision in office?"

"That's right, Chief Coughlin."

"I advise you herewith that I am about to arrest one of those officers, specifically Officer Herbert J. Prasko, Badge Number 5292, on additional charges."

"What would those charges be?"

"That Officer Prasko, at gunpoint, stole twenty thousand dollars, more or less, from Mr. Ronald R. Ketcham, of Philadelphia, who then occupied Room 138 at the Howard Johnson motel on

Roosevelt Boulevard in this city, such acts constituting armed robbery in the first degree."

"Anything else, Chief Coughlin?"

"That Officer Prasko, in Room 138 of the Howard Johnson motel on Roosevelt Boulevard in this city, forced Miss Cynthia Longwood, of Bala Cynwyd, Pennsylvania, by threatening her life, to disrobe, and thereafter did force Miss Longwood to take his penis into her mouth, where he therein ejaculated, such acts constituting Involuntary Deviate Sexual Intercourse."

They looked at each other.

"Do I understand, Mr. Giacomo, that you are representing Officer Prasko?"

"I am willing to represent Officer Prasko if that is his desire. I have not yet had the chance to confer with Officer Prasko."

"I will take you to him now, Counselor," Coughlin said.

He pushed himself out of the armchair, walked to the door, and opened it.

"Where's Prasko, Danny?"

"In the interview room, upstairs," Danny said.

Coughlin waved Giacomo ahead of him toward the stairs that led up to South Detectives.

Officer Prasko, who was handcuffed to the metal chair in the interview room, smiled when he saw Armando Giacomo come into the room.

"Boy, am I glad to see you, Mr. Giacomo," he said.

"Officer Prasko, I am Chief Inspector Coughlin," Coughlin said. "I am placing you under arrest for armed robbery and rape."

"What?"

698

"Before we go any further, Officer Prasko, this is Mr. Armando C. Giacomo, who is an attorney, and who has been sent by the Fraternal Order of Police to render such assistance to you as may be mutually agreeable."

"I know Mr. Giacomo," Officer Prasko said.

"Chief, may I have a minute alone with Officer Prasko?" Giacomo asked.

"Certainly," Coughlin said.

He walked to the door.

"Chief Coughlin!" Giacomo called. Coughlin turned.

Very discreetly, Manny Giacomo indicated the one-way mirror on the wall, and shook his head, "no."

"When we're through, I'll knock at the door," Giacomo said.

Denny Coughlin, very discreetly, signaled — by holding his balled fist, thumb extended upward, at waist level — that he understood Mr. Giacomo did not wish anyone looking into the room through the one-way mirror, and that he agreed to grant the wish.

Coughlin closed the door to the interview room and walked into the adjacent room. Captain David Pekach, Sergeant Jason Washington, and Detective Tony Harris were sitting on chairs looking through the mirror.

"Out," Coughlin ordered.

Captains, sergeants, and detectives do not question the orders of chief inspectors.

They left the room.

"I'm a little disappointed to see Giacomo," Captain Pekach said. "I thought even he drew a line someplace."

"Would you like me to represent you on the charges that have been laid against you, Officer Prasko?" Giacomo asked.

"Yes, sir. Very much. Thank you."

"You understand that we now have an attorney-client privilege? Everything that you tell me in confidence will not go any further than me?"

"Yes, sir."

"Very well. Just a quick answer. We can get into details later. What about the original charge? Essentially that you diverted evidence to your personal use?"

"That's bullshit, Mr. Giacomo. What that is is a couple of nigger drug dealers trying to take me down, take the whole Five Squad down."

"And the second charge, that you robbed a man of twenty thousand dollars at gunpoint?"

"I don't know what the hell that's all about."

"And the rape?"

"Jesus, I'm a married man, Mr. Giacomo."

"Now, listen to me carefully, Officer Prasko," Giacomo said. "I'm a pretty good attorney, and with just a little luck, I could probably convince a jury that what you are is an honest cop with a good record."

"Thank you."

"And that the allegations made by the drug dealers — who would believe a drug dealer against someone like yourself? — were simply an attempt by them to get back at you for arresting them."

"That's what it is, Mr. Giacomo."

"Even though the police have in their possession the gold Rolex one of your crooked pals stole from Baby Brownlee."

"Excuse me?"

"Let me talk," Giacomo said reasonably. "Please don't interrupt my chain of thought."

"Yes, sir. Sorry."

"I could probably even manage to convince a jury — especially after we marched all your character witnesses to the stand — your parish priest would stand up for you, wouldn't he, Officer Prasko?"

"Absolutely. I'm sure Father —"

Giacomo held up his hand to silence him.

"I could probably convince a jury that Mr. Ketcham was doing the same thing the drug dealers were doing. I mean, after all, what's the difference between them except the color of their skin, right?"

"Ketcham is the man they say I stole money from?"

"Yes, he is. They say you stole twenty thousand dollars from him. So does he. He also says you handcuffed him to the toilet in his motel room and then raped his girlfriend."

"That's absolute bullshit!"

"Well, you don't have to worry about that. I'm sure I could convince a jury that an outstanding police officer such as yourself isn't capable of committing the crimes the police say you did."

"That's a weight off my shoulders to hear you say that, Mr. Giacomo."

"What you have to worry about, you despicable

asshole, is what Vincenzo Savarese is going to do to you."

"Huh?"

"The girl you made suck your cock, you contemptible pervert, is Vincenzo Savarese's granddaughter. The only reason you're alive at this moment is that the cops got lucky and got to you before Savarese did."

"I don't know what you're talking about, Mr. Giacomo."

"You stupid piece of shit!" Giacomo, his face red with fury and disgust, shouted. "You're not even smart enough to know when to stop lying, are you?"

Armando C. Giacomo stormed out of the interview room, slamming the door behind him.

He walked directly to the Coke machine against the wall and fed it some money.

Coughlin walked over to him.

"That was quick," Coughlin said.

"I'm very good, Denny. You know that. I presume you have a stenographer on call?"

"Over there, reading the *Daily News*," Coughlin said, nodding toward a middle-aged Latin woman sitting in a chair.

"I'm going to give that piece of slime a couple of minutes to ruminate on what his alternatives are, and then I will go in and offer him your deal. I would be very surprised if he declined it."

"Thank you, Manny."

"Between you, me, and the Coke machine, Denny, it posed a problem of personal morality for me."

"How's that?"

"My personal inclination was to get him off —
and I really think I could have — and then let
Vincenzo . . . what would almost certainly have
transpired, transpire. Six years in a federal country club doesn't strike me as a fair payback for
what he did to that girl. I know her."

"Do me one more favor, Manny. Reason with
. . . the grandfather. Convince him that this is
the way, that this is enough."

"I'll try," Giacomo said. "But don't, as they
say, hold your breath."

Susan Reynolds and Matt Payne had a very late
lunch in Trainer's Restaurant outside Allentown.

Neither of them had had any appetite in the
Penn-Harris, and they had ridden most of the
way down U.S. 222 to Allentown in silence. In
his mind, Matt was going over all of the things
that could go wrong with the scheme, all the
things that had to be done, and trying very hard
to ignore a feeling of impending doom. He wondered, idly, once or twice, what Susan was thinking about, but didn't ask.

By the time they got to Allentown, however,
they were both hungry, and Susan directed them
to Trainer's, which she said was on the way to
Doylestown.

"What are we going to do now?" Susan asked
when they had finished their coffee and were
waiting for the check.

"First thing, you're going to show me where
your friend Chenowith lives," Matt said.

He knew that she wasn't going to like this announcement at all, and waited for what he was

sure would be an angry reaction. He didn't get it.

"He's not my friend, Matt. I've told you that and told you that."

"I still want to see where he lives."

"Why?"

"So, when this is over, I can take the cops there," Matt said. "You may be in jail."

The waitress appeared with the check in time to hear the last part of the sentence.

Matt smiled at her in what he hoped was a disarming way.

"Or married, or have entered a convent," he added.

The waitress smiled. Susan shook her head at Matt.

When they got back in the car, Matt asked, "How do I get to Chenowith's house?" again expecting a negative response, and being surprised when he didn't get one.

"Go into Doylestown, turn right at the Crossroads Diner," Susan said.

"Is that where you're going to meet her?"

"That's where I met her the last time," Susan said. "She may change her mind this time."

"But she is going to call you there, right?"

"Yes."

"I'm going to cut over through Quakertown and go down Route 611," he said.

"Any special reason?"

"No."

"I'm a little afraid of showing you the house," Susan said a minute or two later.

"Don't start now," Matt said. "I want to be in

a position where I can truthfully tell the FBI that you led me to the place."

"What if she leaves the baby in the house when she comes to meet me?" Susan asked.

"The FBI is not going to go after him with guns blazing if they know there's a baby around," Matt said.

"He's crazy, Matt, you know that. What's the FBI going to do if he starts shooting his machine gun?"

"The way that happens is that they will surround the place. Then somebody will get on a bullhorn and tell him — hell, you've seen the movies — 'This is the FBI. We have you surrounded. Come out with your hands on your head, and no harm will come to you.'"

"And what if he starts shooting his machine gun? The both of them start to shoot their machine guns?"

"They'll look out the window and they won't see anything to shoot at. The FBI's not going to stand there in the open where they can get shot. They're not stupid."

"And if Bryan doesn't come out with his hands on his head?"

"Probably nothing. They don't want to start shooting unless they have to. With or without knowing there's a baby inside. After a long time — a long, long time — they might shoot some tear gas into the place. But that's it. Once they have the place surrounded, that's it. They can wait; time is on their side."

She didn't reply.

"And with that thought in mind, probably the

smartest thing we could do right now would be to call Jack Matthews, have him meet us, you show him where Chenowith is, and let the FBI do their thing."

"If I show you where the house is, you'll have to promise you won't tell the FBI until after we meet with Jennie."

"Jesus!"

"Promise!"

"Okay, okay."

Several minutes later, moving down a narrow, winding road, Matt said:

"You know what worries me the most? That your friend Jennie, once I put the arm on her, is not going to listen to one goddamn word you say to her about keeping her mouth shut until she sees a lawyer. You're not going to be the friend trying to save her ass, trying to keep her baby from getting hurt, but the traitorous bitch who turned her in to the cops."

"And?"

"She starts screaming that you were in on this whole thing from the beginning. If she and Chenowith are going down, I think it's entirely likely they'll want to take you down with them."

"I was, more or less," Susan said. "I'll just have to take that risk."

"Another option, of course, is for me to stop the car and start slapping you around until you tell me where the bastard is."

"Oh, stop it!"

"That's the best idea I've had all day," he said. "I really have no idea at all why I'm going along with this bullshit idea just to try to save your friend, who, I am growing more and more convinced, is just as dangerous as her boyfriend."

"You could slap me around all day, and I'd never tell you where the house is," Susan said.

She believes that. She's probably never been slapped in her life

Could I slap her?

Yes, I could.

And get her to tell me where this goddamn house is?

Yes, I could.

And the FBI takes the house, and the asshole shoots off his homemade terrorist machine gun, and the FBI blows him, his girlfriend, and the baby away.

And whose fault would that be?

For the rest of her life, for the rest of our life, I would be the son of a bitch responsible for Poor Jennie and/or her precious child getting blown away.

Not Jennie herself. Not even Chenowith. He's crazy, so it's not even his fault, no matter what the son of a bitch does.

Me. I would be the son of a bitch.

He looked over at Susan.

Moot point. No, I never could slap the information out of her. Not for any gentlemanly reasons, but because I could not stand the way she would look at me for having betrayed her.

Susan seemed to be able to read his mind.

She looked at him.

"Could you really slap me around?"

"Absolutely," he said.

"You are really terrible," she said, but she took his hand.

He saw a sign reading "Doylestown 8 Miles."

707

He freed his hand and reached across and punched the button opening the glove compartment. Then he reached in and took out the microphone.

"Radio check, please," he said into it.

There was no answer.

"I keep forgetting this is a police car," she said.

"Well, if we had come in your red Porsche, we would have been a lot easier to spot, wouldn't we, especially if someone — for example, the FBI — was trying to keep tabs on the owner of a red Porsche?"

He reached across her again and changed frequencies. He again asked for a radio check, and again there was no answer.

He tried it on every frequency he had available. There was a reply on the last one.

"Who wants a radio check?" a female voice responded.

"I'm a Philadelphia unmarked passing through Doylestown. I wanted to see if there was anyone I could talk to."

"You got the Bucks County sheriff's administrative channel, Philadelphia."

"Well, thank you very much," Matt said. "Nice to talk to you."

He reached across Susan a final time, turned off the radio, put the microphone in the glove compartment, and slammed the door.

"Satisfied?" Susan asked.

"Now I know I can call the cops — or at least the sheriff — if I need to."

"What's the administrative channel?"

"Beats the hell out of me," Matt confessed.

"But whatever it is, that operator can talk to other people."

Two or three minutes later, he saw what he thought must be the Crossroads Diner up ahead on the left.

"That it?"

"That's it."

"I've been in there," he said. "I once took Penny to a gambling hell in the Poconos and we stopped in there on the way back."

"A gambling hell?"

"A mob-run joint outside Stroudsburg."

"What for?"

He didn't reply as he turned into the parking lot of the Crossroads Diner. He drove slowly through the complex. Susan showed him where the telephones were. He stopped the car, told Susan to wait, and went inside the restaurant. He took a good look around, found three places from which he could see the bank of telephones, and then left. He got back in the car and started up.

"Okay, show me the house," he said.

She gave him directions.

Twenty minutes later, they were almost there.

"About a hundred yards ahead is the driveway," she said. "The house is a couple of hundred yards down the drive. If you go in, they're liable to see you."

He drove past the driveway, around the next curve in the road, and then stopped.

"What I want you to do," he said, "is slide over and drive. When we're fifty yards from that driveway, stop. I'll get out. Then you drive down the road, turn around again, go back where I turned around, wait until" — he stopped and looked at his watch — "quarter after five, and then come back to where you dropped me off. I'll get in the back, and you head down the road."

"What are you going to do?"

"I'm going to walk through the woods and take a look at the house."

"If Bryan sees you sneaking through the woods, he'll shoot you."

"I don't intend to let him see me," Matt said, and got from behind the wheel and walked around the front of the car.

Susan had not moved.

"Slide over," he said. "I have to do this."

"Oh, God!" she said, but she moved.

"Not to worry, fair maiden, I am a graduate — *summa cum laude* — of the U.S. Marine Corps how-to-sneak-through-the-woods course offered by the Camp LeJeune School for Boys."

"I don't want you to get hurt," she said.

"Neither do I," Matt said. "And I don't intend to. Drive, please, Susan."

She started up.

He opened the glove compartment again and turned on the radio.

"However," he said as they neared the drop-off point, "to cover every possible eventuality, if you hear gunshots, or I do not come out of the woods by twenty after five, you pick up the microphone and push the thing on the side, and say — pay attention: 'Officer needs assistance. 4.4 miles East on Bucks County 19 from intersection of Bucks County 24.' If you hear shots, say: 'Shots fired.' If they come on and ask you who you are, say you are a civilian in Philadelphia Special Operations, car William Eleven."

"Matt, I can't remember all that," Susan wailed. "Please don't do this!"

"Do your best," he said. "If you have to. I don't think you will."

"Don't do this!"

"Stop the goddamned car!" he said.

She looked at him, then slammed on the brakes.

"Start back down the road to pick me up at quarter after five," Matt said, and got out of the car.

He ran across the street into the woods.

Susan didn't move the car for a long time. He was on the verge of running back toward it when she finally started off. He could see that there were tears on her cheeks.

What's going to happen now is that this asshole Chenowith is going to spot me out here, fill me full of holes, then take off for parts unknown. And I will have seen the love of my life for the last time, without even thinking to kiss her good-bye!

It didn't happen that way.

Aside from tearing the pocket of his suit jacket on a protruding limb, he made it through the woods to the house, got a good look at it — it was an ancient, run-down, fieldstone farmhouse with diapers and underwear drying on a line on the narrow front porch; and an old Ford station wagon and a battered Volkswagen parked next to it — saw that it would not only be fairly easy to surround without being detected but that the woods would offer all the cover the FBI would need, and made it back to the road with plenty of time to spare before Susan, on schedule, came down the road.

He jumped in the car and she drove off.

"I think I hate you," Susan said. "God, that was stupid!"

"Nothing happened. I saw what I had to see, and everything's all right."

"You're as bad as Bryan," she said, on the edge of hysterics. "He's playing revolutionary, and you're playing heroic policeman."

"There's a difference, Susan," he said, and he fought back the wave of anger he felt growing inside him. "I am a policeman, not a heroic one, but a policeman. I don't know if your fucking friend is a revolutionary or not, but he kills people, and my job is to put the son of a bitch away."

"I don't want you to die!" she said.

"Look for a telephone," he said. "It's time to call Jack Matthews."

Twenty-Six

At six-thirty — fifteen minutes earlier than Matt had told him to be there — Special Agent John J. Matthews of the FBI walked into the paneled bar of the Doylestown Inn, across the street from the Bucks County courthouse, and saw Detective Matthew Payne sitting at the bar nursing what was probably a scotch and water. Beside him, looking better in the flesh than in the photographs he had seen of her, was Miss Susan Reynolds, a known associate of the Chenowith Group.

He walked to them and tapped Detective Payne on the back.

"Hello, Matt," he said. "What's going on?"

Matt turned on the swiveled bar stool, smiled, and touched Matthews on the shoulder.

"You're early, buddy. I thought you might be. Tell me right now if you're alone."

"You said come alone, I came alone."

"Good boy! Susan, this is Jack. Jack, Susan."

"Hello," Susan said, torn between curiosity and not wanting to look at the FBI agent.

"How do you do, Miss Reynolds?" Matthews said stiffly.

"I think your reputation has preceded you, honey," Matt said. "Jack knows who you are."

"Matt, what the hell is going on?" Matthews asked.

"What are you drinking, Jack?" Matt said.

"Nothing, thank you. What I want, Matt, is to know what's going on."

"Have a drink, Jack," Matt said, and waved for the bartender. "Another of these, please, for this gentleman," he said.

"Goddamn it, I don't want a drink!"

The bartender shrugged and walked away.

"Okay," Matt said. "Let me pay for these, and we'll go someplace where we can talk."

He looked at the cash register tab on the bar, then reached in his pocket and peeled two bills from a wad of currency and laid them on the bar. He picked up his drink and drained it.

Matthews saw that Reynolds's glass was still full.

"Where's your car, Jack?" Matt asked.

"Out in back."

"Good. So's mine," Matt said.

He politely gestured for Susan to precede him out of the bar.

When they were in the parking lot, Matthews pointed at his car. Matt nodded.

Matt led Matthews to his unmarked Plymouth, unlocked the trunk, opened it, handed the keys to Susan, and then reached inside and came out with a briefcase.

"What's that?" Matthews asked.

"It's a briefcase full of money, Jack," Matt said. "Let's go sit in your car."

Matthews's eyebrows rose high in exasperation.

They walked to his car, a new Chevrolet four-door sedan with Maryland license plates.

"What's with the Maryland plates?" Matt asked.

"My car collapsed," Matthews said. "I borrowed this one."

He unlocked the car, Matt got in the front seat and Susan in back.

"Okay, Matt, now what the hell is going on?"

"To answer the question I am sure is foremost in your mind, Jack: Yes, Miss Reynolds and I are emotionally involved."

"Oh, my God!"

"Keep that in mind. It bears very heavily on all of this."

"Matt, I'm going to have to report that," Matthews said. "Jesus Christ! I can't believe this, even of you!"

"You're going to have a lot to report," Matt said, then pushed the briefcase across the seat to him. "I transfer to your custody, Agent Matthews, preserving the chain of evidence, one leather briefcase."

"What's in that?" Matthews asked, not touching it.

"Said briefcase was given to me by Miss Susan Reynolds," Matt said. "It contains a sum of money given into Miss Reynolds's custody by one Jennifer Ollwood."

Matthews looked over the seat back at Susan.

"On several occasions, Miss Ollwood has told Miss Reynolds that she fears for her life, and for that of her infant son —"

"What infant son?"

"Miss Ollwood has borne a son to Mr. Bryan Chenowith," Matt said. "Mr. Chenowith, of

715

course, is a fleeing felon wanted on charges of murder, so Miss Ollwood takes his threats to her and her child quite seriously."

"What the hell are you up to, Matt? What's going on?"

"Miss Ollwood has told Miss Reynolds that the monies she placed in Miss Reynolds's care came into her hands from Mr. Chenowith. Naturally fearing for her own life, Miss Reynolds did nothing about the money until questioned by the authorities — me — whereupon she immediately and unhesitatingly turned the evidence over to me."

"That's not going to get her off, Matt," Matthews said. "If that's what you're thinking. They're going after your girlfriend as an accessory after the fact. The fact that she received what she knew to be stolen property —"

"She didn't know it was," Matt said. "All she knew was that it came from Bryan Chenowith. It was not until I suggested to her that it might be the loot —"

" 'Might be the loot'? Jesus!"

"— from the banks Chenowith has been knocking off that this occurred to her. She was naturally — being a respectable citizen from a somewhat sheltered background — very distressed to consider that she had been used."

"Matt, that's not going to work. Christ, they've got film of her — you saw it — of her meeting with Chenowith in the Poconos!"

"We're going to give it a shot, Jack," Matt said.

"What I'm going to do right now — Christ, do

716

you realize what a spot you've put me in with Davis?"

"What we're going to do right now, Jack, is go arrest Jennifer Ollwood," Matt interrupted.

"And what is that supposed to mean?"

"It means we're going to arrest Jennifer Oll-wood."

"You know where she is?"

"I know where she's going to be," Matt said. "And once we have her in custody, I will lead the FBI to where Miss Reynolds has shown me we can find Mr. Chenowith and his pimply-faced sidekick."

"If you think I'm going off with you, alone, to arrest that woman, you're out of your mind."

"Okay, then you stay here in your car and wait for me to bring her to you."

Matt reached up and snatched the keys from the ignition switch.

"Don't be childish!" Matthews said, as much in disgust as anger. "Give me the keys back!"

"I figure it will take you five minutes to find the police station, and another ten before you can find someone who will both believe the wild story you're going to tell him and has enough authority to act on it, and another ten minutes — minimum — before they can locate an unmarked Plymouth. By that time, I'll have the Ollwood woman in the back of my car."

"And then what do you think is going to happen to you?"

"Then I will lead the FBI to Chenowith."

"That's not what I meant. And you know it. You're going to go to jail, Matt."

Susan inhaled audibly in the backseat.

"For what? For arresting somebody wanted on a murder rap? For stealing your car keys?"

"They call it obstructing justice," Matthews said. "And interfering with a federal officer in the execution of his office, and —"

"On the other hand, you could go with me," Matt said. "We grab Ollwood, take her to the locals, tell them who she is, and ask them do they want to grab Chenowith?"

"You mean not even call the Anti-Terrorist Group?"

"It would take them at least an hour, probably much longer, to get up here. No telling where Chenowith would be by then, particularly if Ollwood doesn't come back when she's supposed to."

"That's insane."

"Ollwood has got another 'package' she wants Susan to keep for her," Matt said.

"More bank loot."

"What else? And you could grab that, too. Which do you think Walter Davis would prefer? That — presuming Chenowith and whatsisname, acne face? —"

"Edgar L. Cole," Matthews furnished.

"— Cole aren't long gone by the time they get up here — that those Anti-Terrorist clowns grab them, in his area of responsibility? Or that one of his own agents, seizing the moment, did?"

"Goddamn you, Matt!" Matthews said.

"Is that a yes or a no?"

"Give me the damned keys," Matthews said, putting his hand out for them.

"After you tell me where we're going."

"We're going to go and play supercop, what did you think?"

"In three minutes," Matt said.

"What?"

"Go on, Susan," Matt said.

" 'Go on, Susan'?" Matthews parrotted.

"You don't have to go, either of you," Susan said. "Let me try to reason with her, Matt."

"We've been all over that," Matt said angrily. "It's damned near seven. Get going!"

"Oh, God," Susan said, but she got out of the car and trotted over to Matt's Plymouth.

"What makes you think she's going to do what you want her to do?" Matthews asked.

"She will," Matt said as he watched Susan get in the car.

"Are you really *involved* with her, Matt?"

"I'm in love with her."

"You poor son of a bitch!"

Susan started the car and drove out of the parking lot.

Matt handed the ignition keys to Matthews.

"Give it a minute, and then head up Route 611," he said. "I didn't want it to look, if Ollwood is already there, as if somebody was tailing Susan."

Matthews nodded.

"How far is Chenowith?" he asked.

"About fifteen miles out of town," Matt said. "I checked the place out. You'll have no trouble surrounding it. And there's no other houses near."

Matthews grunted, and started the engine.

"Jack, Susan got into this because she felt sorry for the Ollwood girl. She's not part of that bunch of lunatics."

"Oh, you poor son of a bitch! You really believe that, don't you?"

"Yeah, I believe it," Matt said. "Okay. Here's what's going down. We're going to the Crossroads Diner."

"I know it."

"Behind it is a bank of pay phones. At seven o'clock, Ollwood is going to call Susan on one of them, to see if she's there. One of two things will happen then. Ollwood will either come to the restaurant, or she will tell Susan to meet her someplace else."

"Maybe at Chenowith's?"

"I don't think so. I don't think Chenowith wants Susan to come to his house; otherwise, he would have just told her to. But someplace else, that's possible. If that happens, we'll have to play that by ear."

Matthews put his Chevrolet in reverse, backed out of his parking slot, and drove slowly out of the parking lot.

"What if Ollwood is already at the restaurant, gives your girlfriend the package, and takes off?"

"That's possible. When we get there, cruise the parking lot. We're looking for an old Ford station wagon and/or a battered Volkswagen."

"If Ollwood has taken off, then what, Matt?"

"This is as far as I'm going, Jack. We go to the locals and ask for their help."

Susan was talking on one of the pay phones

when Matthews drove around to the back of the Crossroads Diner.

So was a young, grossly obese young woman in overalls with a small child perched on her hip.

Susan gave no indication that she had seen Matthews's car as they drove by her.

Matthews turned the corner of the building and stopped.

"I didn't see a Bug or a station wagon," Matthews said. "Did you?"

"No. What's likely to happen is that Ollwood will come here and just give her the package. We don't want her to get out of the parking lot."

"Okay. You get out, see what Susan has to say, and I'll start looking for Ollwood's car. I'll try to block it. If necessary, I'll ram it."

Matt jumped out of the Chevrolet, and Matthews began to turn his car around.

Matt entered the front of the restaurant, then looked out a window to see that Susan, now off the phone, was still at the bank of pay phones.

Then he went out the back door of the restaurant and made his way through the parked cars until he was across the lane from Susan.

He had to call "honey" twice before she saw him crouched low between the fenders of a Dodge and a Ford.

"She's coming, right away, to pick me up," Susan said.

The grossly obese young woman, in the act of counting change, looked at Susan curiously, and then even more curiously when she saw Matt.

Matt backed up and retraced his path through the restaurant.

Jack's car was nowhere in sight, but a row of garbage cans had been placed across the road to block it.

Matt could see curious faces on people wearing cook's whites looking out from the restaurant's kitchen; Jack Matthews had obviously shown them his badge and explained what he was doing with the garbage cans.

And, as obviously, he planned to block the lane from the other end.

Matt walked quickly down the front of the restaurant, looking for Matthews's Chevrolet. He found it and started to walk toward it, when he saw the battered Volkswagen turning into the parking lot.

He walked, as quickly as he could — without appearing to be running, just some guy going to his car — forcing himself not to look again at the Volkswagen, until he was parallel to where Susan stood at the bank of pay phones.

He got there just as the Volkswagen stopped.

Susan went to it and pulled the door open.

Matt ran to the Volkswagen and tried to pull the driver's door open. He had decided the best way to restrain Jenny Ollwood was to jerk her out of the car and throw her on the ground.

He had solved the problem of having no handcuffs by "forgetting" to return the pair he had borrowed from Lieutenant Deitrich when they had arrested Calhoun. He would put the borrowed set on Jennifer Ollwood.

The Volkswagen driver's-side door was locked. "You are under arrest!" he shouted.

Jennifer Ollwood looked up at him, not in fear but fury.

"Motherfucking pig!" she screamed.

The Volkswagen raced off.

Matt dropped to his knees to take his pistol from his ankle holster.

There was a burst of carbine fire, seven, eight, ten rounds. Matt looked down the lane.

Chenowith was standing in the center of it, trying to clear a jam.

"Drop the gun!" Jack Matthews shouted.

Chenowith turned to look at him.

Matthews, his issue .357 revolver held in the position prescribed, shot him twice, calmly and deliberately.

Matt, his pistol now in hand, ran after Jennifer's Volkswagen.

She had apparently decided to ram her way past the garbage cans Matthews had placed in the lane. The one she had hit had wound up under the nose of the Volkswagen. Unsteerable, the Volkswagen had crashed into another parked car. Jennifer Ollwood now had the Volkswagen in reverse, trying to free herself. The Volkswagen's tires were smoking, but the car was just barely moving.

Matt ran to the Volkswagen, smashed the window with the butt of his pistol, and then aimed it right at Jennifer Ollwood's face.

She took her hands off the steering wheel, and the sound of the racing engine died.

Matt opened the door and then grabbed Jennifer's sweater front and jerked her out of the car, tripped her, and threw her on her face on the lane.

She kicked and fought, and he hit her on the side of her head with the butt of his pistol. It didn't knock her out, but it made her groggy enough so that he could pin her left arm behind her and, with his knee in her back, start to put the handcuffs on.

He heard a female voice say, indignantly, "He didn't have to do that to her!"

And then he heard a baby start to howl.

He jerked Jennifer to her feet, looked in the back of the Volkswagen, and saw the baby.

Susan can handle the baby.

"My baby!" Jennifer screamed. "Somebody help my baby!"

Matt turned to look at the growing crowd of spectators.

"Nobody go near that car!" he ordered. "I'm a police officer, and I'm going to get someone to take care of the baby!"

"Goddamn cops!" the same indignant female voice muttered.

Matt propelled Jennifer around the corner of the building, back toward the bank of pay phones.

Jack Matthews saw him coming, and stepped into the lane. He held both hands up, as if stopping traffic, and there was a pained look on his face.

Matt saw the obese young woman sitting on the ground, screaming, and after a moment, saw that she was holding her bloody right leg.

"Matt, don't come down here!" Jack called.

Matt had just enough time to wonder what the hell was wrong with Matthews, when he understood.

Susan was on the ground, too. Matt put his foot in front of Jennifer Ollwood and pushed her hard. She fell again to the pavement, and started to scream obscenities.

He ran to Susan. Jack tried to stop him, but he wouldn't be stopped.

Susan was on her back, her mouth and her sightless eyes open. There was a small, neat hole just below her left eye. Her blond hair was in a spreading pool of blood.

"Oh, God!" Matt howled, and dropped to his knees and cradled her limp body in his arms.

"You wanted to see me, Mr. Mayor?" Inspector Peter Wohl asked, standing in the open door to the mayor's private office in City Hall.

"You took your sweet goddamn time getting here, Peter," Jerry Carlucci snapped.

"I didn't think you wanted me to turn on the lights and siren, sir."

"Don't smart-mouth me, Peter!"

"No, sir."

"Have you seen this?" Carlucci said, sliding the *Philadelphia Bulletin* across his massive desk toward Wohl.

Wohl glanced at it.

"I haven't had a chance to read it, sir. I heard about it."

"Read it. Improve your mind," Carlucci said.

"Yes, sir."

Wohl picked up the newspaper, and read the lead story:

'COLD-BLOODED TERRORIST' MURDERS FBI INFORMANT MOMENTS BEFORE HE FALLS TO FBI'S BULLETS IN BLOODY DOYLESTOWN GUN BATTLE; SPECTATOR WOUNDED IN HAIL OF GUNFIRE

by Michael J. O'Hara
Bulletin Staff Writer

Doylestown, Bucks County — Bryan C. Chenowith, described by the FBI as a 'cold blooded terrorist,' was shot to death shortly after 7:00 P.M. last night by FBI Agent John D. Matthews in the parking lot of the Crossroads Diner here moments after Chenowith machine-gunned to death Susan Reynolds, 27, of Camp Hill, Pa., who FBI officials described as a 'public-spirited citizen' who had been assisting the authorities in their years-long, nationwide search for Chenowith and his associates.

Mrs. Deborah G. Dannmeir, 24, of Upper Black Eddy, who was using an outdoor pay telephone when the shooting erupted, was struck by one of the bullets fired from Chenowith's fully automatic .30-caliber military carbine. She is reported in 'satisfactory' condition at Bucks County Hospital.

Chenowith; his common-law wife, Jennifer Ollwood, who was apprehended by Philadelphia Detective Matthew M. Payne at the scene of the gun battle; Edgar L. Cole; and Eloise Anne Fitzgerald were indicted for murder following the bombing of the Biological Sciences building at the University of Pittsburgh, in which eleven people lost their lives. "The Chenowith Group" has been the target of an intense nationwide FBI search ever since.

Cole and Fitzgerald were arrested without incident at approximately 9:00 P.M. last evening at a remote Bucks County farmhouse to which Miss Reynolds, shortly before her death, had directed Detective Payne. Miss Reynolds, according to the FBI, had known the women at Bennington College, Vermont. She was an appeals officer with the Pennsylvania Department of Social Services in Harrisburg.

According to Walter Davis, Special Agent in Charge of the Philadelphia Office of the FBI, the Chenowith Group had turned to bank robbery, and said 'there is incontrovertible evidence' that Chenowith, masquerading as a woman, had in the past few weeks robbed banks in Riegelsville, Pa., Clinton, N.J., and elsewhere.

"The Chenowith Group was armed with fully automatic weapons," Davis said, "stolen from the National Guard at Indiantown Gap, and was clearly prepared to use them. Both Special Agent Matthews and Detective

Payne knew this. It is clear proof of their courage and devotion to the public's safety that they attempted to apprehend a criminal like Mr. Chenowith, disregarding the risk to their own lives."

Davis went on to explain that there had been no way, given the circumstances, that either Matthews or Payne could have requested assistance.

"I can't, of course, go into the details leading up to this incident," Davis said, "except that it was one more example of the close cooperation between the FBI and the Philadelphia Police Department."

Peter Wohl, commanding officer of the Special Operations Division of the Philadelphia Police Department, to which Detective Payne is assigned, declined to comment on the shooting, or on Detective Payne's performance, stating that the case was under review.

"Yes, sir?" Peter asked, looking at the mayor when he had finished.

"What's the matter with you, Inspector, cat got your goddamn tongue?"

"Sir?"

" 'Inspector Peter Wohl declined to comment,' " Carlucci quoted in a high falsetto.

"What was I supposed to say?"

"Use your fertile imagination! Do you like the FBI grabbing all the credit for what was clearly our bust?"

"No, sir."

"Payne got that dame to roll over on Chenowith, not that FBI agent," Carlucci said. "You wouldn't know that to read Mickey's story."

"No, sir," Peter said. "You wouldn't."

"You're not going to ask me how I know that?"

"Sir, how do you know that?"

"Detective Payne told me," Carlucci said.

"You've seen Payne?"

"Did you see that thing on TV — goddamn, they shouldn't put things like that on TV — I mean, Payne standing there soaked in that girl's blood, watching them carry her body off?"

"Yes, sir, I saw it. It was pretty rough."

"So I called up and asked what happened to him, and where he was, and then he told me he went from the restaurant to arrest the rest of those slime. And then, when I called Special Operations, Mike Sabara told me you had sent him home."

"Actually, I placed him on administrative leave," Wohl said.

"Yeah, that's what Mike said, while it was decided whether or not charges would be brought against him."

"Yes, sir."

"I told Mike Sabara you made a mistake. He could take it from me that no charges were going to be brought against Detective Payne. Detective Payne is on compensatory time. He's put in a lot of overtime lately, what with bagging Officer Calhoun and this cooperation with the FBI. Are we clear on that, Inspector? That Payne is on compensatory time?"

"Yes, sir. Sir, he disobeyed a direct order!"

Carlucci ignored what was for Peter Wohl a somewhat emotional outburst.

"So I went by his apartment on Rittenhouse Square. I figured it was the least I could do. And he wasn't there, so Jack and I went out to Wallingford to his father's house. First time I'd ever been there. It wasn't as big as I thought it would be. I really felt sorry for him. He was all broke up that the girl got killed. I mean, really broke up. And then, on top of that, he's worried about you and Coughlin . . . because he disobeyed some bullshit order you gave him."

"I didn't think it was a bullshit order, sir."

"We talking about the same order? The one Payne told me he got was he was not supposed to try to arrest this Chenowith character by himself under any circumstances. Is that the order we're talking about?"

"Yes, sir."

"Just between you and me, Peter, who issued Payne that stupid order? You or Denny Coughlin?"

"I did, sir."

"That's what Denny said when I asked him just a couple of minutes ago. He said he did. That's nice, the two of you being loyal to each other. Both of you trying to take responsibility for doing something stupid. I appreciate that. They call that loyalty up and loyalty down."

"Yes, sir."

"Do we understand each other, Inspector?"

"Yes, sir. I get the message."

"That will be all, Inspector. Thank you for

coming in to see me."

"Yes, sir."

Wohl had just reached the door when Carlucci called after him.

"Peter!"

"Yes, sir?"

"Two things, Peter. Be sure to give your father my warmest regards."

"Yes, sir, I will. Thank you."

"And why don't you take the rest of the day off. You've been working very hard lately; you deserve a little time off. Take a ride. Go out to Wallingford, maybe. Take Denny with you. See Payne. He thinks you two walk on water."

"Yes, sir," Inspector Peter Wohl said.

Assistant District Attorney Anton C. Phebus, Esq., disappeared shortly after having been informed by District Attorney Thomas J. Callis that all the police officers assigned to the Five Squad of the Narcotics Unit had been arrested on a variety of charges, and that "Wohl, Washington, and Weisbach have got at least two of them singing like the Vatican Choir."

Later the same day, District Attorney Callis issued a warrant for Mr. Phebus's arrest on charges of complicity in the charges laid against members of the Five Squad.

He was arrested on charges of unlawful flight to escape prosecution by the Federal Bureau of Investigation six weeks later in Fort Lauderdale, Florida, where he was working as a security guard at a Kmart. He was subsequently extradited to Philadelphia and brought to trial before the Hon.

Harriet M. McCandless. On a finding of guilty, Judge McCandless sentenced Mr. Phebus to fifteen to twenty-five years' imprisonment.

Mr. Ronald R. Ketcham was found dead in his apartment of an overdose of heroin two weeks after he was released from the NIKE site.

Although defended by Armando C. Giacomo, Esq., all members of the Narcotics Unit Five Squad were found guilty of various charges placed against them for criminal activity, and received sentences ranging from eighteen months to five years in prison.

It was generally believed that not even Armando C. Giacomo could have gotten acquittals given the devastating state's witness testimony of former officers Herbert J. Prasko and Timothy J. Calhoun.

In a separate action, former officer Timothy J. Calhoun pleaded guilty before a United States court to one charge of violating the civil rights of Mr. Amos Williams. He was sentenced to one year in federal prison. After seven months he was released on parole, and he is now a truck driver in Philadelphia.

In a separate action, former officer Herbert J. Prasko pleaded guilty before a United States court to seven violations of the civil rights of Mr. Amos G. Williams and Mr. Marcus C. Brownlee, and was sentenced to four years on each charge, the sentences to be served consecutively. He was

confined to the Federal Penal Facility at Eglin
Air Force Base, Florida, where he was assigned
duties in the mess-hall kitchen. Two months after
his arrival, he failed to meet roll call and was
declared an escapee.

Three weeks later, his remains were found tied
to a log in the swamp surrounding the air base.
Who tied him to the log is not known, but he is
believed to have met his death by being eaten
alive, by feral hogs, herds of which roam the Eglin
Reservation.

The employees of G.K. Hall hope you have enjoyed this Large Print book. All our Large Print titles are designed for easy reading, and all our books are made to last. Other G.K. Hall books are available at your library, through selected bookstores, or directly from us.

For information about titles, please call:

(800) 257-5157

To share your comments, please write:

Publisher
G.K. Hall & Co.
P.O. Box 159
Thorndike, ME 04986